The Chronicles of Valonia

The Battle of the Underworld

Katie Paterson

due for publication in 2011

'The Quest for the Immortal Walker' the fourth book
in 'The Chronicles of Valonia'

Titles by Katie Paterson

'The Jewels of Valonia'
'The Golden Casket and the Spectres of Light'
'The Battle of the Underworld'

The Chronicles of Valonia

The Battle of the Underworld

Katie Paterson

HandE Publishers Ltd

Published by HandE Publishers Ltd
Epping Film Studios, Brickfield Business Centre,
Thornwood High Road, Epping, CM16 6TH
www.handepublishers.co.uk

First published in the United Kingdom 2010
First Edition

ISBN 978-1-906873-24-0

A CIP catalogue record for this book is available from
The British Library

Illustration design concept by Katie Paterson
Illustrations by Trevor Reavesly
Cover design by Ruth Mahoney and Trevor Reavesly
Typeset by Ruth Mahoney
Edited by Natalie-Jane Revell, Kayleigh Hart and Sarah Cheeseman

Printed and bound in England
by CPI Bookmarque, Croydon, Surrey

To
Thomas Crockett
A very special man.
My father.

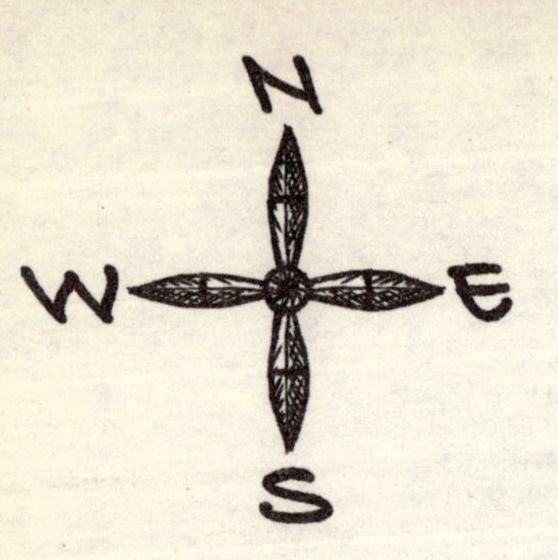

N
W
E
S
ENTRANCE TO
RATHYEN'S CAVERNS
MOUNTAIN TRACK

RATHYEN'S
CAVERNS
WATERFALL
STREAM
Morgana Le Fey

Chapter One
Two Knights Too Many

Gareth rushed up the long path to Warwick Castle, aware that he was late and that he only just about had time to change before his tournament. He entered through the gateway and pushed his way past the queue of tourists waiting to buy tickets to view the medieval castle. He arrived at the locker room by the stables out of breath, to find that his friend Mark was already there, half dressed in his costume.

"You're cutting it a bit fine aren't you? Late night, last night?" Mark enquired.

"Yeah, just a bit!" Gareth answered. "Oh no, I'd forgotten it's my turn for the heavy armour this week, that's all I need!"

"Well, I had it last week!" his friend answered, "and it nearly killed me! Every time you aimed at me, it was as much as I could do to stop myself from toppling off the horse! I really don't know why they have to give us that suit, it weighs a ton! They must have a lighter one somewhere we could use."

Mark was referring to the mock jousting tournament they had acted out the week before for the castle visitors. This had been

Gareth's weekend job since he had started at Warwick University and apart from the alternation of the suits of armour, one he enjoyed enormously. Once he and his sister Rachel had finished their A-levels at their old school, they had both decided to go to university. Rachel had chosen one close to Chesterton so that she could still live with Bronwyn and Mr Moore and Gareth had enrolled at Warwick, finding for the first time that he was living away from home and parted from his family and twin sister. The part-time jousting job at the castle was an opportunity just too good to refuse. It reminded him of the knights and their visits to Tintagel, even though the armour at Warwick Castle was medieval and very different.

"I'll see you out there, and good luck with the armour… you'll need it!" said Mark.

"Thanks a bundle!" Gareth replied, hastily struggling to get ready.

"If you can beat me with that suit on, it'll be my shout at the 'Hungry Man' later! Deal?"

"Well, if you want to pay for lunch, I'm up for that! It's a deal, but I don't suppose your keenness to go there has anything to do with the new waitress, of course?" Gareth shouted after him.

"I don't know what you're talking about!" said his friend, putting his head back round the door, with an expression of mock innocence.

"No, course you don't," laughed Gareth. "I did notice that last time, you spent all night trying to attract her attention!"

"Me?" questioned his dark-haired friend, with a wide-eyed, blameless look. "As if I would do that!"

"Yeah, right, you need look like that! You're dreadful, and no doubt there will be a different one next week! Are any girls in Warwick safe from you?" Gareth asked with a chuckle.

"No, not really, I like them all!" Mark answered. "If you're ready, we'll go down together to get the armour."

"Yeah, I'm done now, let's go," replied Gareth, banging his locker door shut. "I hope they've got a crane to lift me onto the horse once they've suited me up!"

It took three of them to help Gareth into the heavy metal armour and finally lever him up onto his chestnut horse. His visor snapped down firmly, leaving with him with six thin slits to look through, as he urged the large horse forwards.

The horse walked sedately, following their usual procedure, and halted on the mound beside the drawbridge for the tourists to take their photographs. Once the cameras had finished snapping they walked the horses through the high stone archway into the castle compound, their hooves clattering noisily on the cobbled stones.

The stately medieval castle sat majestically on a small hill surrounded by a deep indentation that once held its moat. A wide sweeping pathway led up to its drawbridge and gatehouse, where its towers and battlements all rose imposingly, surrounding the main castle buildings. The horses walked slowly and carefully through the main square, waiting for the odd straggling tourists to finally notice the large horses and armoured riders and move out of their way. Behind the main compound there was a purpose built jousting set already lined with tourists. There were two lanes divided by a heavy, wooden fence-like structure in the middle and two conical tents at the end for authenticity. The edges were lined with red and white striped tapes strung from poles to separate them from the spectators on the bank.

Gareth and Mark waited for the girls in their period costumes to give them a coloured scarf, which they held up for the crowd to see before tying them to their lances, as part of the usual staged drama. They turned to go and to take up their positions, at each end of their opposite lanes.

"Ok, let's get this over with. One more at two o'clock and you'll be buying lunch afterwards," said Gareth, his voice muffled by his heavy visor.

"In your dreams!" Mark replied. "I hope you've brought your wallet, 'cos there's no way you can beat me in that suit! You'll be lucky if you stay on the horse!"

"We'll see, best of two then?"

"You're on!" Mark replied with a laugh. "Hang on a minute, who the hell is that?"

Gareth turned and squinted through the narrow slits in his visor to see a horse and armoured rider already in his friend's position. The horse was jet black and heavy set; it pawed the ground and snorted, shaking its head. The rider's black armour was solid and heavy looking and covered him completely. His lance was adorned with a small red flag bearing a black crest. He faced them, not moving, in Mark's position at the end of the set.

"What's going on, have they changed the routine without telling us?" asked Mark.

"No idea mate. You'd better go and talk to him," answered Gareth. "Maybe there's some mistake - I was late so maybe they've put another rider on."

"They can't have, they only use these two suits," answered Mark, "and that's not even one of our horses - it's huge!"

"Don't know, you'd better go and see what he's doing here," said Gareth.

"Damn right I will! I'm not having some agency bloke stealing my thunder!" said his friend, as he rode down towards the unknown rider.

Gareth waited patiently, already in position at his end, confident that Mark would send away the unwanted person with a few choice words. Instead he was amazed to see the stranger charge towards Mark, his lance striking him firmly, catching him off guard. He followed this with a hefty swipe from his heavy shield, knocking Mark straight off his horse and sending him through the tapes where he landed heavily amongst the crowd.

"What is he doing?" thought Gareth, shocked by the man's actions. Once the crowd had recovered from their surprise, they let out a cheer and clapped, assuming it all to be part of the show.

Mark didn't appear to be getting up and Gareth wasn't sure what to do next. Their routine was quite strict, they played it out every week and this was not part of it. 'Have they altered it and not told us?' thought Gareth, racking his brains, trying to remember if he'd missed a meeting.

The black armoured rider paused at the end, still in Mark's position and lifted his visor. He looked steadily at Gareth and slowly pointed his lance at him. Suddenly he snapped the visor down and galloped down the marked lane, his lance directed towards Gareth in a full charge.

"Well he's obviously carrying on with the show, even if he is a bit too enthusiastic about it," muttered Gareth, and he urged his own horse forwards to do the same. As they passed each other in the middle, the rider's lance hit him heavily and Gareth toppled sideways, the weight of his armour dragging him down, forcing him to hang on to the horse's neck to stop himself falling off completely.

At the end, the well-trained horse turned automatically to face the lane again, and Gareth finally managed to drag his unyielding, heavy suit of armour back up into a sitting position, only to see his opponent charging towards him again.

"What the hell is he doing now?" grumbled Gareth in exasperation, as he saw the rider galloping down the other lane towards him. 'Hasn't anyone told him it's meant to be entertaining?' he thought wryly, as he urged his own horse forwards.

The new rider hit him so hard this time that Gareth toppled backwards and if he hadn't let go of his shield to hang on to the saddle he would most certainly have disappeared over the back of the horse. It took every bit of strength he had to haul himself back up again in the weighty, stiff metal suit. The crowd apparently loved it and cheered even louder.

'This is now beyond a joke! This idiot is a danger!' thought Gareth crossly. The jousting was normally played out safely and any injuries were only mock ones. They deliberately made the strikes look real but they were by no means as heavy as the ones that this man was inflicting.

By the time Gareth had turned his horse, the black suited rider was already thundering down the set again and Gareth reluctantly galloped off, determined to get in first this time. He struck the new rider with his lance much harder than he would ever have struck Mark. The solid man hardly flinched and he roared as they clashed and parted, and rode back to the end.

There was something familiar about the fierce bellow that the man emitted and Gareth's blood ran cold at the sound. He was sharply reminded of his swordfight with Mordred, and the last time he had ever heard a deep angry roar like that. Gareth turned his horse at the end of the lane and thought how ridiculous he was being. After all, that was years ago and in another time, quite apart from the fact that Mordred was dead. He was temporarily distracted as he saw a cluster of people around Mark, who was still lying on his back behind the tapes. The crowds parted to allow the first aid car through and Gareth saw the manager, Mr Bryant, heading onto the set with a face like thunder.

The manager strode out into the taped lane and waved both of his arms in the air, signalling for them to stop just as the large black horse began to gallop down the lane again. The unknown rider made no attempt to halt, even though the manager was directly in front of his horse. He would have trampled him down if the small grey-haired man hadn't quickly leapt through the tapes into the crowd, landing on a large lady eating an equally large ice-cream.

This time the rider headed straight for Gareth down his own lane, his lance pointed at him, and with a shock Gareth suddenly realised that this person wasn't acting. He really meant it!

Gareth quickly turned his horse and headed away from the jousting set, swerving in between the two conical tents, just missing them in his haste to get away. Several of the costumed girls screamed and ran, thinking his horse must have bolted, as nothing this dramatic ever happened on their routine performance.

The castle grounds were full of visitors and Gareth knew he had to ride out onto the more deserted grounds slightly further away. 'If the safety of the manager hadn't bothered this new rider, then he probably wouldn't be worried about his large horse trampling over a few tourists either,' Gareth thought, swiftly riding away from the castle. He could hear the huge hooves of the other horse thundering behind him and he stopped, turning his horse to face his challenger. The long, shiny lance was coming for him again, so he chose to meet it. He galloped fast towards it and they clashed. He was satisfied to see that his strike almost unseated the other rider, but struggled for balance himself after the impact. They turned again, racing towards each other, their lances poised.

This time the blow hit Gareth so hard that he lost his balance completely. He slid sideways and the weight of his armour did the rest, sending him crashing to the floor. He struggled to sit up, but only managed to prop himself up with one arm, before seeing the rider turn and pull up his horse. The black knight's lance came down again, and the big horse's hooves churned up the grass as he headed straight for him.

Gareth struggled to pull himself up again, but the armour was so heavy, stiff and inflexible, that he knew he would never be able to get back on his feet without help. Panic set in as he realised that the rider was intending to finish what he had started. For a second there was a bright flash of light over by the castle and Gareth was surprised to see his dark opponent draw up his horse sharply. Something in the distance had obviously caught the rider's attention, and his horse skidded to an abrupt halt.

Half lying on his side on the ground, Gareth tried to manoeuvre the weighty armour to allow him to turn towards the castle. One final heave sent him rolling over and as he pushed himself up again by digging his elbow into the ground, he was astounded to see another knight slowly riding out by the wall. His armour shone like silver in the light and he rode a white horse with black markings. He carried a long, silver lance with no flag and a silver shield.

Gareth twisted again to look back at the other black knight, but he'd gone. He managed to pry open his heavy visor and scan the area, but the black knight was nowhere to be seen. The new knight paused as though looking at Gareth. He lifted his visor and gave him one long slow nod, as though in acknowledgement, turned his horse, and walked slowly away.

Gareth managed to pull off his helmet to see better, as the silver armoured knight disappeared at the end of the wall.

There was a crowd running towards Gareth now and they reached him just as he'd forced the heavy suit upwards into a sitting position. The first aiders fussed around him, and once he had declared that there was nothing wrong with him, his armour was removed and they hauled him up. He was driven back to the staff quarters in the first aid car, his armour creaking and groaning with every bump.

Once Gareth was back in the castle, the rest of his suit of arms was removed and he returned to the locker room to get dressed, agreeing to be checked over by the first aiders once he was clothed. He was greeted there by the manager, who, in his temper forgot to even enquire if Gareth was all right.

"What in blue blazes did you think you were doing out there?" Mr Bryant demanded. "Horses galloping all around the castle! Jousters chasing each other with lances! If health and safety ever got wind of this we'd be closed down tomorrow! Can you imagine if one of the visitors had been knocked down by the horses? Oh, it doesn't bear thinking about! And who in the name of thunder was that maniac on the black horse?"

"Well, I was just about to ask you that!" replied Gareth, indignantly. "And yes thanks, I am okay, but what about Mark - is he hurt?"

"Oh, oh, well, yes he is, they think he may have a broken arm, he's gone to hospital to have it x-rayed," the manager replied furiously. "No less than he deserves really, pulling a stupid stunt like that. This is what I keep telling you boys, health and safety, health and safety. That's why we have rules; this is exactly why we insist that things are done in the correct way..."

"Hold on a minute, we've always done things correctly! I didn't employ that lunatic on the black horse - you did!" interrupted Gareth, "and what do you mean Mark deserved it? What stunt?"

"The other horse! The other rider! That's the stunt I'm talking about!" Mr Bryant shouted. "I certainly didn't employ him! I employed you and Mark and I expect you both to act within our rules!"

"Well if you didn't bring him in, who did?" asked Gareth.

"I think we both know the answer to that, don't we?" Mr Bryant replied, caustically. "No doubt this was one of those stupid university pranks that you students are so well known for! Well it won't wash here! Do you understand?"

"I don't believe I'm hearing this," said Gareth, angrily. "That was no prank! I've no idea who he was and we could have been killed by him. As it is Mark's been hurt - you've just said he may have a broken arm. Do you think we planned that as well?"

"Well, I am suspending the jousting show temporarily," Mr Bryant replied, haughtily. "And I am suspending you until we get to the bottom of this!"

"Oh great, thanks!" replied Gareth, as the small man left.

"Oh and by the way," the manager continued, putting his head back round the door, "do make sure there is a full report in the accident book won't you."

'Accident book,' thought Gareth crossly as he left. 'He's lucky there isn't another one to report! His own!'

Muttering to himself, he pulled on his clothes, incensed by the injustice of it all. He slammed his locker door shut and went back to the first aiders who warned him that, at worst, he may have some bad bruises coming up. They told him the name of the hospital that Mark had been taken to and Gareth decided to go straight there to see how his friend was.

He eventually found Mark in a curtained cubical, where he was waiting to have his arm put in plaster.

"Are you all right?" Gareth asked him, as he pulled the blue curtain back.

"Yes, I've got a fractured arm though," he answered. "I landed with it underneath me. It hurts like hell!"

"I'm so sorry," said Gareth.

"Why? It's not your fault," his friend answered, good-humouredly. "I'm just glad you're okay. I was watching from the bank, and whoever that guy was on the black horse, he wasn't interested in me, it was you he was after! Who on earth was he?"

"I don't know, it's all a bit of a mystery," replied Gareth. "I've just had old Bryant screaming at me about it. He's saying that they didn't bring him in. In fact, he's blaming me! He's saying that we staged it all!"

"What?" replied Mark. "How does he think we managed that?"

"No idea, but he's suspended the jousting and he's suspended me, pending an investigation!" he replied.

"I don't believe this, how can he blame us?"

"Haven't a clue! Even if we had staged it, we would have had to bring in two horses. I think someone might have noticed that!" said Gareth, pulling up a chair next to him.

"Two horses?" questioned Mark. "Don't you mean one, that black monster he was riding?"

"No, I meant two, there was another one as well, a white one with black markings and a black mane, complete with another knight sat on its back!"

"Another one?" said Mark, looking astounded. "I missed what happened, after they carted me away."

"Oh you missed the best bit then. Old Bryant walked out onto the set, waving for us to stop and the black suited rider nearly mowed him down!"

"Oh, wow, now I would've loved to have seen that!" remarked Mark, wincing with pain as he sat up.

"Yeah, that bit was quite good really," laughed Gareth. "Bryant leapt out of the way, through the tapes and fell into the lap of a woman in the crowd with the biggest ice-cream you've ever seen! He still had big pink and white splodges all down his jacket when he was telling me off."

"Oh brilliant!" breathed Mark. "But what about this other knight, when did he turn up?"

"This is where it gets really strange," said Gareth, relaying the story of the chase and the second knight's appearance.

"We don't have any black and white horses in the stables! So who was he then?" Mark asked, referring to the second unknown knight.

"I have no idea!" replied Gareth, interrupted by the appearance of a young, dark-haired nurse with a wheelchair to take Mark to have his arm plastered.

"I'll wait for you and drive you home," said Gareth, as she wheeled him away.

Gareth sat in the waiting room with plenty of time of think about the day's unusual events and the more he thought about it, the more he was becoming convinced that this must be something to do with his past or his inheritance. For a moment the thought crossed his mind that he may have somehow inadvertently caused it himself.

Unknown to his family Gareth had travelled back through time to Tyntagel on many occasions. He had already spent a long time there when Bronwyn and Rachel had returned to Valonia without him, and he had never told his sister or mother exactly how long he had stayed. His other visits at half term and several weekends had been equally long, enabling him to become an accomplished rider and swordsman. With time standing still for him whilst he was there, it had been easy to stay there unnoticed by his family. 'Had he upset the balance of things by doing it?' he wondered. But even if he had, the two knights here were in medieval attire, a time much further forward than the one in Tyntagel. 'No, it couldn't possibly be anything to do with that surely?' he reasoned.

Eventually his friend was wheeled back, donning a large plaster cast on his arm, and Gareth went to fetch his car. They drove back towards Warwick discussing the mystery of the unknown knights. Unfortunately neither of them could come up with a rational explanation, which worried Gareth even more.

"Where are you going?" asked Mark, as Gareth turned left towards the university halls.

"I'm taking you home," replied Gareth.

"So what happened to the 'Hungry Man' then?"

"You are joking aren't you? You've got a broken arm; surely you don't still want to go there?" said Gareth.

"Well it seems a shame..."

"Look mate, I'm really not in the mood for it. To be honest I'm a bit shaken up by all this myself..."

"Yeah, you're probably right," answered Mark. "Still every cloud has a silver lining as they say."

"Have I missed something?" asked Gareth, as they turned into the car park. "Do please tell me where the good bits were!"

"Well, I've got a date with Jane the nurse, and the phone number of a very nice blonde girl who was looking after me when I was waiting for the first aiders," he replied. "So, it wasn't all bad."

"I don't believe you sometimes!" retorted Gareth, shaking his head as he helped him out of the car. "You must be the only person I know who could get a date out of all that!"

"Err, maybe even two," Mark answered. "I'll get loads of sympathy."

"Two? Well, that's even worse then," laughed Gareth, as he helped Mark out of the car and they made their way towards the halls of residence.

Chapter Two
An Episode in the Library

Gareth woke on Monday morning and went to his lectures as usual, but the strange events at the castle were still playing on his mind. He found it difficult to concentrate and, on returning back to his room in the evening, he decided to phone home. The phone rang several times in the neat house in Chesterton before Rachel rushed down to answer it.

"Hi, stranger," she said, on hearing her brother's voice. "How's it going in Warwick then?"

"Yeah, it's okay," he replied. "I was beginning to think you were all out though."

"Sorry, I thought Bronwyn was going to answer the phone, but I think she's too preoccupied with her suitcase. She's packed it six times already, and I just can't get it across to her that it's going to be hot in Spain. I've taken her sweaters out more times now than I can remember!"

"Oh, yes, when do they go?" asked Gareth, having quite forgotten that his father and Bronwyn were going on holiday.

"Tomorrow, the flights are quite early," answered Rachel. "She is so excited! She's never been anywhere abroad before, bless her! But between you and me, I'll almost be glad when they've gone. I've got so much work to do. I've only got a couple of weeks to do a really big assignment and I just can't concentrate here at the moment!"

"Yeah, right, you just want the house to yourself for a bit!"

"Well, that as well!" she laughed. "Dad's just come in, do you want to talk to him?" she asked, assuming that Gareth had phoned to speak to their father before he went away.

"Yeah, yeah I will do, but before you go, has anything strange happened to you lately?"

"No, why?" she answered, puzzled.

"No reason, I just wondered that's all," he answered, having second thoughts about mentioning his encounter with the knights. He had wanted to talk to her about it, but to do that he would have to come clean about his visits back in time, and decided against it.

"That's an odd question, why did you ask that?"

"Well, you know... it's been a long time, but it's still always there, hovering in the background isn't it? I... well, I just wanted to make sure you're all right I suppose," Gareth mumbled, wishing that he hadn't said anything at all. He didn't even need to explain what he meant, as Rachel knew instantly that he was referring to their strange heritage and Valonia.

"Oh, that's really nice, thanks, but I'm fine, nothing strange to report apart from Bronwyn behaving like a sixteen year old going away for the first time!"

"Well, that's all right then," he replied.

"Hang on, I'll get Dad for you. Look after yourself," his twin said, and called Mr Moore.

She left them to their conversation and went into the lounge.

Her father joined her shortly afterwards.

"Nice of Gareth to call up," he remarked. "I'm surprised he even remembered we were going on holiday tomorrow."

"Of course he would," Rachel replied firmly. "Did he sound okay to you? I thought he sounded a bit down."

"Oh, I'm sure he's just getting a pang of home sickness," said Mr Moore. "It happens when you're away from home for the first time, not that he would admit to it! His mates are probably busy tonight and he's found himself on his own. He'll be fine by tomorrow," he replied reassuringly.

"Yes, I'm sure you're right. I'm glad he called though," she said, planting a kiss on her father's forehead as she went up to her room and back to the dreaded assignment.

Rachel waved her parents off in the morning, Bronwyn's case finally packed with suitable clothing for Spain, and Rachel breathed a big sigh of relief as their taxi left for the airport.

"Yes!" she said out loud. "Two weeks, with the house all to myself!"

Just over a week later, and no further forward with her assignment, she was regretting the late nights that she and her friends had enjoyed, thanks to the absence of her parents. She dragged herself into the early lecture with Mr Pinfold, who had a reputation at the best of times for sending his students to sleep with his monotonous droning voice, and struggled to concentrate.

She looked out of the window in her efforts to keep awake and saw a strange sight. A student wearing fancy dress was making his way across the car park. She looked harder, in disbelief, taking in his ridiculous outfit. He wore a short leather skirt, long boots, a strange waistcoat edged with shaggy fur and a leather helmet. His hair was long and he carried an enormous axe. She nudged her friend Silvia with a smile, indicating silently towards the car park.

Silvia looked out of the window and back at Rachel with a shake of her head and a shrug of her shoulders, before returning her attention back to Mr Pinfold's lengthy explanations.

The lecture finally finished and there was a quick exodus of students, most thankful that they were still awake and relieved that it was over.

"Did you see that guy in the costume?" asked Rachel, as they went through the door.

"No, what guy?" asked Silvia.

"Oh, you missed a treat. There was a student dressed as a Viking or something like that, and he was just walking across the car park as though it was quite normal," she replied, laughing. "I have to say; whoever he is, he's got some guts doing that on his own!"

"I didn't see anyone," answered her friend, as they tried to push their way through the crowd in the busy corridor.

"You must have just missed him. When I looked back again he was walking into the woods," Rachel replied.

"Woods? What woods? There aren't any woods here, there's a very high brick wall all around the campus, in case you've forgotten," answered Silvia, looking strangely at her.

She was right - there *was* a wall, thought Rachel with a shock. In fact, there wasn't a tree in sight in their purpose-built university grounds!

"You must have dozed off," laughed Silvia. "Listen, late nights and Pinfold don't mix. If aliens landed and he gave a lecture on it, he could still make it sound boring! I was finding it very hard to stay with it, especially when he started on the evaluations. I have to admit that I was thinking about what to wear tonight, at that point! Come on, let's get you a coffee before the next one."

"I can't believe I did that," said Rachel, sipping her coffee in the student's restaurant. "I've never gone to sleep and started dreaming in a lecture before!"

"I'm sure you won't be the last one to nod off in one of Pinfold's," laughed her friend. "Are you coming tonight? It should be a good party!"

"No, I really can't, I'm so behind with this assignment. I'm going to go to the library to do as much as I can until it closes, and then I'm going to carry on at home. I've only got a few days before I have to hand it in, and I'm nowhere near even half way through yet!"

"Shame, it would've been really good if you were coming."

"Oh well, I'm sure there'll be more!" Rachel answered, before they parted company.

She attended her afternoon lecture, and then made her way to the library. She was disappointed to find the Head Librarian Miss Smyth-Jones at the desk as she went in, and had to wait while the sour-faced woman told off the girl in front of her, whose books were late. She fined her and the poor girl spent ages rummaging for loose coins in the bottom of her large, striped canvas bag. She finally counted out a small pile of pennies and five-pence pieces, only to find that she was still twenty-pence short. Miss Smyth-Jones refused the coins almost gleefully and told her sternly to come back tomorrow with the correct money, warning her that she would incur another day's fine.

"Here, have this," said Rachel, handing the girl a twenty-pence piece, as she was anxious to start work. The girl accepted it gratefully and the middle-aged, grey-haired librarian looked down her long, sharp nose at Rachel as she put the girl's books to one side. Miss Smyth-Jones inspected the dates on Rachel's books very carefully before scanning them in and Rachel was sure the librarian looked disappointed when the she saw that they were on time.

Rachel found the reference books she needed and piled them

up on a desk at the back of the room, settling herself down to work. The time passed quickly and she made good headway. She was concentrating so hard that she hadn't even noticed that she was the only one left, until Miss Smyth-Jones came over.

"Were you intending to be much longer?" she enquired, with a disapproving sniff. "I will be closing the doors at five thirty, on the dot!"

"No, no, I should be finished by then," said Rachel.

"You *will* be finished by then," Miss Smyth-Jones corrected. "Make sure you leave enough time to put the books back." Her flat rubber-soled shoes squeaked on the polished floor as she walked back to her desk, obviously put out that Rachel wasn't immediately rushing to pack up.

Rachel submerged herself again in the heavy books, intending to do as much as possible in the time she had left.

The library suddenly seemed almost strangely quiet and Rachel glanced up. Miss Smyth-Jones was arranging some books on the shelves at the far end of the room and for a moment Rachel felt inexplicably uneasy. For a second she ignored the feeling, after all, libraries were always quiet so why should she even think it odd? But she did.

She looked around the quiet, empty room and felt a feeling of dread come over her. Her heart started to race and she looked around again. Her gaze turned to the long shelves of books, and to her amazement she saw the man in costume that she had seen earlier in the car park. He walked purposely between the rows of shelves, swinging his axe. Several rows of books scattered behind him and he carried on, undeterred, towards her. As he drew nearer, Rachel realised that he was far too old to be a student. He had long matted hair and a bushy beard and moustache. Rachel was temporarily rooted to her chair in shock. The man looked directly at her and smiled: a wide, evil smile with several teeth missing that was not one of acknowledgement or friendship.

He stepped forwards again and raised his axe, this time Rachel screamed and jumped up. Her chair crashed backwards and the pile of books she had been using slipped off the table and clattered to the floor.

"For heaven's sake, what on earth do you think you are doing?" came the disapproving voice of Miss Smyth-Jones from across the room, and her flat shoes squeaked quickly towards her. Rachel looked back again and the man had gone.

"What on earth are you doing, girl? These books cost a lot of money. You students just don't seem to have any respect for them at all!" admonished Miss Smyth-Jones, clearly annoyed to see the books on the floor.

"Didn't you see him? Didn't you see that man with the axe?" asked Rachel almost hysterically, clutching the librarian's arm.

"No, I did not!" said Miss Smyth-Jones, removing Rachel's hand from her arm. "I can assure you that you and I are the only people here. I purposely locked the door twenty minutes ago so that no-one else could come in," she finished, looking at Rachel suspiciously. In all her years as librarian there, she had dealt with all kinds of student behaviour, and this girl was clearly one of the problem ones, imagining things or probably just making them up. Well, it was only to be expected of the youth of today, she sniffed disdainfully as she picked up the books. "I suggest that you pack up your things and go home," she added.

"I need those," said Rachel, as she saw the books about to disappear with the librarian. "I need to finish my assignment."

"Then I will stamp them out, while you collect your things together," the librarian replied haughtily, squeaking back to her desk again.

Rachel hurriedly stuffed everything into her bag, still looking around her nervously. She looked back at the two rows of shelves where the man had been, expecting Miss Smyth-Jones to blame her for all the books he had knocked down. But there were no books on the floor. All the shelves were neatly stacked as before. She went to the desk, still shaking, and Miss Smyth-Jones handed her the books, with an even more disapproving look.

"Make sure they're not late back!" she said, as she escorted Rachel to the door and locked it behind her as she left.

Rachel ran to her car and locked the doors as soon as she was in it. She started the engine and left quickly, still shaken by her experience. She calmed down on the journey home, eventually deciding that she must have dozed off again and dreamt it. She opened her window, worrying now that, despite not feeling tired, she might go to sleep again at the wheel, which would be even worse!

She was relieved when she arrived home safely, and locked all the doors as soon as she was in. She switched on the television and went into the kitchen to find something to eat. For the first time she wished that her father and Bronwyn were there so that she didn't have to spend the night on her own. She left the dishes and decided to have a really early night and finish her assignment the next day. This had to be the problem, she decided as she ran a bath, she must have just had too many late nights and she wasn't used to them.

She woke in the morning after a fitful sleep. She knew that she had been dreaming, as she had woken up with a start several times, but she couldn't remember what she had dreamt on waking.

She went down to the kitchen and made some tea and toast, surprised that having had so much sleep, she still felt tired.

She worked all day on her assignment and at teatime it was

finished.

"Hallelujah!" she said, putting it into her bag ready to hand in the next day, relieved that she had finally finished it. She spent the evening watching a DVD she had been meaning to see and had a long hot bath before bed.

She handed in her assignment in the morning, attended a couple of lectures and met her friends afterwards in the student restaurant. She left at about half past six and returned home, pleased that she wasn't going to have to cook.

Her friend Susie called in to see her and they listened to music in her room. It was quite dark when Susie left and Rachel realised that she hadn't pulled the curtains downstairs. She put the kettle on and pulled down the blind, checking that the back door was locked. She made a cup of coffee and went into the lounge, switched on the television and, half-watching the end of the news, she went to close the long curtains.

As she glanced into the darkness outside, she suddenly noticed something really strange; there was an orange glow to the left as though someone had lit a large bonfire. She switched off the light to have a better look and to her amazement their neatly fenced garden had gone! It had been replaced by an open grassy space with a wood in the distance and a camp of conical tents where a fire glowed brightly. She was so shocked and astounded that for a moment she just stared. She peered over towards the right and was almost certain that she was looking at the castle of Tintagel.

She looked harder and seeing two figures approaching, she hastily jumped back behind the curtain. She nervously peeped out and to her horror she saw the man she had seen in the library talking to another figure who was swathed in a long cloak. She pulled the curtains as fast as she could and dashed, shaking, into the kitchen. 'Phone the police' she told herself sensibly, and she crept into the hall towards the phone. But as she picked up the receiver, she realised that she couldn't.

What on earth was she going to say? 'The garden's gone and there's a strange man dressed as a Viking?' Reality dawned on her that this was not normal - gardens don't disappear, and it had to be a vision of some sort that only she was seeing. After all, neither her friend nor the librarian had seen the man earlier.

It took all the courage she could muster to go back into the lounge and peep through the curtains again. To her relief the garden was back to normal again, there was no castle, no wood and no fire! She turned the television up, but was far too nervous to concentrate on it. She decided to ring Gareth, she had to tell someone about it and he was the only person who would understand.

Gareth's phone immediately went on to voicemail and she left a message asking him to call her. An hour later he still hadn't called and she left another message. After several more attempts she gave up, thinking that since it was quite late, he must be asleep. She decided to go to bed herself and try again in the morning.

Rachel went up to bed after checking all the doors and windows again and leaving all the lights on downstairs to reassure her. After a long time listening to every noise outside, she eventually went to sleep. However in the early hours of the morning, she woke with a start from a dreadful nightmare, and sat up in panic, her heart thumping in her chest.

The dream had been awful: she saw the same view that she had seen from the lounge window earlier and the two men. They stood talking briefly before parting, but she didn't hear what they were saying. The man in the costume went to the tunnel entrance, which she recognised instantly, and more men dressed the same as him filed out silently, carrying axes. They crept along the edge of the wood, towards the camp of conical tents. The fire had burned low now and the camp seemed deserted. The men waited under cover of the trees and then suddenly she saw more dark figures surrounding the camp and the men moved forwards.

There appeared to be hundreds of them and they made no sound at all as they made their way into the camp. It was as though she had moved closer herself, and as soon as she had a better view of the camp, she recognised the flags perched on top of the tents. This was Galahad's camp, she thought with horror, as the men surrounded each tent.

A large man waved his axe in the air and they attacked the tents. There was a frenzy of activity and screams were heard from inside the tents, followed by a silence, as though they had been cut short. Rachel knew with a sickening horror that they had been killed. Some of the remaining inhabitants from the tents tried to leave but the Saxons were in wait for them outside and finished them off quickly with their axes. A hush fell over the camp for a second and then the Saxons let out a cheer. They picked up torches and lit them from the fire, throwing them into the tents, until every last one was ablaze, before they disappeared into the woods.

Rachel switched on her light, and looked at her clock - it was five thirty. Shocked to the core, she knew that in her dreadful nightmare she had just witnessed Galahad and his men being slaughtered. She also knew now that the strange man in the costume that she had seen before wasn't a Viking. He was a Saxon!

Chapter Three
Gareth's Confession

Rachel couldn't go back to sleep, in fact she didn't even want to, in case she started dreaming again. Or was it a dream? She asked herself, thinking about the two appearances of the Saxon man that no-one else had seen. It would be understandable to have a nightmare after that, she reasoned, as she went downstairs in her dressing gown. But three strange things in one day, given her heritage was just far too much of a coincidence. She decided that it had to be a warning, and left yet another message for Gareth to ring her, while waiting for the kettle to boil.

As she had her shower Rachel made a decision, that if Gareth hadn't contacted her by lunchtime, she would go to Warwick to see him. Besides, she had no desire to stay in the house another night on her own, in case anything else happened.

She packed an overnight bag before leaving for university and just about to shut the front door behind her, remembered the old, black Keepers book at the bottom of her wardrobe. She ran back upstairs, unearthed it and zipped it into her bag, just as a precaution, hoping that it wouldn't be needed.

Lunchtime came and went and there was still no word from her brother, so she stuck with her decision and looked at her map book. Her route memorized, she headed for the motorway in her small green car. She stopped once at the services briefly and arrived at Warwick University several hours later, very tired after her early start to the day. She parked outside the Halls of Residence and a helpful student pointed her in the direction of Gareth's block.

She knocked on the door several times and could hear music coming from inside Gareth's shared flat. After her fourth knock the door was opened by an untidy-looking youth in an open striped dressing gown that revealed a pair of greying underpants underneath.

"Woah, sorry!" he said, hastily pulling his dressing gown firmly around him. "I was expecting someone else!"

"Evidently!" replied Rachel, trying hard to imagine who he could possibly be expecting in that state. "Is Gareth there?" she enquired sharply.

"Yeah, yeah come in," he said, opening the door wider, still hanging on tightly to the front of his dressing gown which was obviously minus its belt. "He's in the room at the end - go down. Is he expecting you? I didn't know he had a girlfriend!"

"I'm his sister!" she replied frostily.

"Oh no, look I'm really sorry," he said, sheepishly, clutching his dressing gown securely.

"The door at the end you said?" she asked, anxious to be rid of the scruffy youth. He nodded and she swept past him, wrinkling her nose as she passed the shared kitchen, with its draining board full of dirty plates.

There was a strong, stale smell of curry in the air and she noticed that the carpet hadn't seen a vacuum cleaner in a long while.

She knocked loudly on Gareth's door and received no answer.

Extremely irritated now, she banged again and, when there was still no reply, she went in anyway.

Gareth's room was in a complete mess. The room was small and the bed was unmade. There was a large desk in the corner for his computer, which could hardly be seen amongst the mountain of books and papers. The floor was adorned with what looked like a month's washing and more papers and clutter. Rachel stepped over the clothing and heard the watery warbling of a chart song, coming from a closed door on the left. Realising that her brother was in the shower, she automatically straightened up his duvet and sat down on the bed to wait for him.

The door opened and Gareth appeared in a towel amidst the steam escaping from his bathroom.

"Finally!" she said, impatiently.

"Rachel!" he exclaimed, almost dropping his towel with shock. "What in the name of Zeus are you doing here?"

"Well, since you don't bother to answer your phone, however many messages people leave you, I've had to drive up here!" Rachel answered crossly.

"Oh, sorry have you been calling me?" he asked. "I haven't checked my mobile for a while, and I haven't got any credit anyway so I couldn't have called you back. How did you get in?"

"One of your flat mates let me in," she answered, "in his underpants!"

"Oh, right, that'd be Westy then," laughed Gareth, "And it's no good you looking all indignant, if we'd known you were coming, he'd have put some clothes on. We don't get many female visitors!"

"I'm not surprised, given the state of this place!" she retorted. "Even if they came once, I shouldn't think they'd ever want to come again!" Demonstrating her point, she lifted a pair of underpants off the floor with the toe of her shoe and Gareth hastily grabbed them. "So when did you start to become such a slob?" she asked.

"Probably as soon as I got here and didn't have anyone to nag me," he chuckled. "Like I said, if we'd known you were coming… anyway let me put some clothes on and I can talk to you then." He grabbed a pair of jeans and a sweatshirt off the floor, ignoring another look of disgust from his sister.

Rachel waited while Gareth dressed in his bathroom and finally came out, combing his hair.

"Something must be pretty important for you to drive all the way up here, you don't even like motorways!" he said seriously. "What's up then?"

Rachel told him about her strange experiences and the dream.

"I don't like the sound of this," he said, his face solemn.

"You don't think I'm being stupid then?" she asked. "Do you think this is some kind of warning?"

"I have no idea," Gareth replied, "but one thing I do know, is that you only ever see something when there's a reason for it."

Rachel smiled for a second. Long gone were the days when Gareth called her weird and ridiculed her strange premonitions. Now he automatically listened to her. "I haven't had anything happen for years, and this was very extreme," she continued. "It frightened me to death at the time, but now it's worrying me. Do you think it's something that's happened already? Do you think that Galahad and all of his men have been killed?"

"I hope not, but if it is a warning, then maybe we're meant to stop it happening. Either way, I think we ought to go back and find out!"

"Are you serious?" she asked, horrified. "We can't just go back in time again!"

"Well, we've done it before, what's different now?" he replied.

"I've got to work tomorrow morning, but I'll be finished by one o'clock, we could go straight down there then."

"I really don't want to go back there," said Rachel, thinking about the awful scene in her dream. "But if we are meant to warn them, I suppose I'll have to," she said, knowing that she couldn't live with the thought that by not going, she could be allowing the atrocity to happen.

So they agreed on their plan for the next day and at Rachel's insistence, Gareth reluctantly cleared his room up. Later they went to the student cafe, where they sat with some of his friends to eat. It was quite late when they went back to his room and Gareth produced a sleeping bag and pillow for her.

"I'm still confused about this Saxon attack though," Rachel said, her thoughts returning back to their problem. "I thought that all of the Saxons had been driven out of Cornwall when Arthur was alive."

"They were," said her brother, "but later on there were some leaders that were stupid enough to actually invite the Saxons back, thinking that they would protect them as the Romans had, in exchange for land. Needless to say it didn't work because as soon as the Saxons arrived they resorted to their usual way of taking whatever they wanted."

"You're very knowledgeable about all of this!" said Rachel impressed.

"Yeah well, it's in the history books," he mumbled, still not telling her that most of his information had been gained from his frequent visits there.

"So have you been reading many history books then?" she asked, still surprised.

"Actually, I have," he replied. "In fact, I've got some here if you want to have a look." He rummaged around in an untidy pile in the corner of his room and produced three very large books.

Rachel flicked through the pages and shivered as she saw a picture of a Saxon warrior.

"Is that what he looked like?" asked her brother and she nodded silently.

In the morning Gareth made them tea and toast and got ready for work.

"I'll have to go soon," he said. "You can stay here for now, and then come up to the castle at about one o'clock. I'll meet you by the main entrance. If I'm not there, my friend Mark's on the gatehouse today, he'll look after you. You can't miss him, his arm's in plaster!"

"Hang on, what am I going to do here all morning?" she asked.

"Whatever you girls normally do for a couple of hours, I don't know, paint your nails or something!" he laughed. "And if all else fails, you could always read the history books!"

By eleven o'clock she was bored. She'd had a shower, tidied his room and flicked through the books. She'd heard about Warwick Castle and decided that rather than sit in the small room any longer, she might as well go and have a look at it. The castle was only a few minutes away; she parked her car and walked along the wooded pathways towards the entrance.

It was easy to spot Mark by the large white plaster cast on his arm and she introduced herself to him.

"I'm really early," she said apologetically. "I had no idea the entrance was so far away from the castle. I thought I could have a quick look round outside while I was waiting for him."

"No problem," replied the good-looking, dark-haired, Mark. "You can't see much from outside, and the castle's fantastic you ought to see it while you're here! I'm due a break now, and I can take you up into the main area."

Rachel thanked him, and he let her through the barrier. They walked up the sweeping pathway towards the castle, which she had to agree was really impressive.

"In fact," Mark said looking at his watch, "you're just in time to watch Gareth. I'll take you straight through to the lanes at the back."

"Watch him?" asked Rachel.

"Yeah, the jousting starts at half past."

"Jousting!" shrieked Rachel. "Gareth's jousting?"

"Yes, hasn't he told you?"

"No he hasn't," she replied, still stunned. "He told me he helped out with the tourists, but he didn't actually say what he did!"

"Well, I suppose he does in a way," laughed Mark. "He helps to entertain them! I can't believe he hasn't told you though. I normally ride against him, but obviously I can't with this," he finished, indicating the heavy plaster.

"Oh dear, how did you do it?" asked Rachel, feeling rather guilty that she hadn't already asked.

"Oh, I suppose he didn't tell you about that either?" he replied. "We had a bit of a strange incident here a little while ago, and I came off my horse and broke my arm."

"What sort of a strange incident?" asked Rachel suspiciously.

"I'll let Gareth tell you about it, it's a bit complicated," Mark returned cautiously, wondering if he should have mentioned it, since Gareth hadn't even told his sister about the tournaments.

"Why doesn't that surprise me!" she answered. "How long has he been doing this?"

"Ever since his first week at uni," Mark replied. "But it's been cancelled since I broke my arm. They didn't put it on last week because..." he saw Rachel's eyebrows disappearing upwards and realised he had said too much. "Listen I'm going to have to leave you now, if you stand in the middle over there you'll get a good view," he added hastily.

"Oh, my goodness!" said Rachel as the horses came out onto the set. She stared in shock at the heavy armour and long silver lances, as the riders took their tokens from the maidens. "Which one's Gareth?"

"He's on the chestnut horse - don't look so worried," Mark laughed. "Gareth's the best rider here. The guy on the grey is my replacement and he doesn't stand a chance against your brother!"

"That armour must weigh a ton, how can they even ride with all that metal?"

"Yes it's heavy all right, but you get used to it," said Mark, sensing her concern for her brother. "I'll tell you something though, all of the rest of us took weeks of training to get used to holding a lance and a shield, never mind the armour. Gareth just picked up the lance on his first training session and looked as though he'd been doing it for years! Anyway, better dash, I'll see you later."

Rachel thanked him and turned her attention to the tournament that had just started. If she hadn't been so stunned, and if one of the knights hadn't been her brother, she might have actually enjoyed it.

She was amazed at how easy Gareth made it look, and his friend had been right, he was by far the better rider of the two. The other rider looked tentative and a bit clumsy compared to Gareth as they charged back and forth down the lanes, lances clashing now and again.

The tournament over, won by her brother, they completed their pageant by riding out with the maidens to a loud round of applause from the crowd. The horses disappeared through an archway into the castle grounds, and Rachel hurriedly pushed her way through the crowd to follow. She walked into the stable area in time to see them dismounting. Gareth pulled off the heavy metal visor and saw her watching him.

"Ah, Rachel!" he said, looking guilty. "You're early!"

"And when were you going to tell me about all this then?" she asked crossly.

"Funnily enough, this afternoon," he replied. "Well, since you've seen it, what did you think?"

"You were very good," Rachel admitted begrudgingly. "But I'd love to know where you learnt to do it!"

"Ah, yes, well, that's something else I was intending to tell you about later," Gareth returned sheepishly. "Look, let me go and get this armour off and I promise I'll tell you everything."

She waited for him and he arrived back dressed in his own clothes again.

"How long did you stay at Tintagel with Johnny after we came back?" she asked immediately, having guessed that his skills were learnt with the knights.

"A long time," he answered. "Look, we'll go and get a quick bite to eat before we start on the journey."

"Don't avoid the issue, I want some answers!" she said crossly. "How long is a long time?"

"I'm not avoiding anything, I've just given you an answer - I was there a long time!" he replied, leading her down some steps into the back of the castle. "We've got a long drive this afternoon and I can tell you all about it then."

She was about to protest but they had entered a large room, full of the castle staff on their breaks. So again she had to wait, knowing that at least he couldn't get away with it in the car.

They didn't stay long, and left after a sandwich and a cup of coffee. They met up with Mark again at the gatehouse, who asked

Rachel if she would like to go to a party that night, with Gareth of course, he added quickly.

"Leave it out, mate," said Gareth. "Haven't you got enough girlfriends without chatting up my sister as well?"

"Well, you know me, never one to miss an opportunity," Mark laughed, as they left him. "Besides, your sister's better looking than the others!" he called after them.

"Ignore him," said Gareth good-humouredly. "Do you want to drive or shall I?"

"I thought he was quite nice," Rachel replied, waving to Mark.

"Yeah, you and every other female here!" Gareth grumbled. "Come on, let's get going."

They took Rachel's car but Gareth drove and Rachel managed to wait until they were doing a good speed down the motorway before she tackled him again about his jousting.

"So why didn't you tell me then?" she asked, "and how long was a 'long time' in Tintagel?"

"It's difficult to say really, it could have been as long as a year," he answered.

"A year!" shrieked Rachel. "What about Johnny, did he stay that long as well?"

"Johnny's still there," Gareth informed her. "He stayed."

"Did he? Hang on, how do you know he's still there?" she questioned. "He could have gone home since then, that was a long time ago!" Gareth didn't answer, making her even more suspicious.

"You've been back there since, haven't you?" she demanded. "How many times?"

"Quite a few," he replied. "Half term, weekends."

"Oh no, Gareth, you're not meant to do that!"

"I know, but at least I've done what I said I would do, which was to learn to use a sword properly," he answered, referring to the promise he had made to Arthur. "I can hold my own on a horse with most of the knights now, and with a sword! Well, except with Galahad, he's still got the edge on everyone."

"How is Galahad?" asked Rachel.

"He was fine last time I saw him. He always asks about you as well, funnily enough," he remarked. "In fact, I always thought you had a bit of a 'thing' about him."

"I did not have a 'thing' for him at all," retorted Rachel indignantly, "and there's nothing funny about him asking about me. Galahad's very polite; he would ask you how your sister was!"

"I'm only winding you up," he laughed. "Don't you want to hear about the others?"

"Of course I do. How's Johnny and what about Bran and Sarah? Did they stay at the castle after all?"

"Bran and Sarah are married. Bran's a knight now and they live at the castle. Johnny's a knight as well and you should see him, he's absolutely brilliant. I don't think you'd even recognise him now and he has a lot of admirers, I can tell you!"

"Oh I'm so glad, good old Johnny!" she said. "I'm really pleased that everything worked out for him!"

"Look, I'm going to come clean about everything," Gareth stated seriously. "I've spent a long time there, every time I've been. With time standing still here, it was so easy, but I'm a bit concerned that I might have somehow triggered something off."

"What do you mean?" she asked, and he told her all about the strange events that had happened with the two unknown knights at the castle.

"This is unbelievable! Mark said something had happened, but he didn't say what. Why didn't you tell me?"

"I was going to the other week, that's why I rang you, but I'd have had to tell you about all my visits there, so I decided not to," he admitted.

"So, no-one has any idea who these knights were?" asked Rachel.

"No, I was suspended for a week, because the manager blamed me, but everyone saw me come through the gate on my own and go straight to get changed, so they reinstated me today."

"Do you think that all of this is connected then? I mean, it's a bit strange that I'm seeing Saxons and you're seeing knights."

"I don't see how they can be related, the knights here were in medieval armour, and I've checked in the history books! The time is all wrong - they would be too far ahead in history to be connected! The Saxons I can half understand. Not that I can imagine anyone stupid enough in Tintagel to invite them there, but it would at least be in the correct period."

"It's all sounding a bit far-fetched really, if you think about it," remarked Rachel.

"When has anything to do with our past ever *not* sounded far-fetched," responded Gareth. "But it gets worse. When I hit the knight with my lance, he roared, and for a moment I thought it was Mordred!"

"Mordred? But he's dead!" she answered, horrified. "We saw him in the quicksand!"

"I know, and it sounds really stupid, but even Mark said that he looked as though he was out to get me! If the other knight hadn't come when he did, I'm fairly sure he would have killed me!"

"But you said the other knight didn't do anything. Who was he?"

"I have no idea, and no, he didn't do anything, but as soon as the black knight saw him he stopped immediately, and the next time I looked he'd disappeared! The knight in the silver armour nodded to me as though he knew me, and then he disappeared - it was all just too strange!"

"Do you think that maybe you travelling back and forth in time somehow attracted this black knight, and maybe the silver knight was sent by the Power to protect you?" asked Rachel.

"Yes, I've been thinking along the same lines," he answered, "but it doesn't explain your Saxon though does it?"

Chapter Four
Deliberations and Premonitions

Eventually Gareth and Rachel arrived at the country village in Cornwall and parked the car near the small station where they normally got off the train to go to the pass. They collected a few things from their bags and continued on foot up the hill and along the overgrown pathway. The walk took them longer than usual as there was no horse and buggy waiting for them by the pass. As they reached the sleepy innocent-looking village, they decided to go to the farm first to borrow Rufus, the big, black horse that Rachel was so used to riding.

Betsy was pleased to see them and even more delighted when they told her that they were going to visit Johnny, (their excuse for being there.) They were quite grateful for the cup of tea and the large scones that Betsy insisted they had, whilst Abigail saddled up the large, gentle horse for them.

"You will give Johnny our love won't you," Betsy said, looking tearful. "We do miss him, but if he's well and strong, living there, then it can only be a blessing."

"He's fantastic there, Betsy, you'd be really proud of him," said

Gareth as they left.

Rufus recognised Rachel as usual and she stroked his big, silky, black nose. They climbed onto his back and waved goodbye to Betsy and Abigail.

"Doesn't Johnny ever come back?" Rachel asked Gareth, as they started up towards the pass.

"He came back once to visit and he started having really bad headaches as soon as he got here," Gareth answered. "When he returned back to Tintagel through time, Bors found him collapsed at the tunnel entrance and took him to Merlin. He recovered, but Merlin said it's too dangerous for Johnny to use the tunnel again, so he hasn't been back here since."

"Oh, poor Betsy, no wonder she looked upset," she replied.

They dismounted by the big stones that covered the tunnel entrance and Rachel got out the Keepers book. They both held it, closed their eyes and imagined the cavern entrance. When they opened them, the stones had moved and they led Rufus inside. The tunnel was the same as ever and Rufus's hooves clopped loudly, echoing all around them.

Once they had negotiated the tunnel of time they found themselves looking across the open plain towards Tintagel, just as they had done before. Rufus set off at a good pace and they were soon picking their way across the causeway to the castle. The sentry on duty recognised Gareth straight away and opened the heavy gate.

"Hi there, Eric, how are you?" said Gareth as they rode in.

"I am well, sir," Eric replied as he closed it behind them. They rode through to the inner courtyard, with many men speaking to Gareth as they passed.

"You're really one of the fixtures here now, aren't you?" Rachel said, rather sarcastically.

Before he could answer, a knight riding past gave a shout. "Gareth!" he yelled excitedly.

"Hey, Johnny, it's good to see you!" said Gareth jumping down.

"Wow, Rachel, you've come to visit us!" shouted the knight, and Rachel was amazed to see that it was Johnny, who was so transformed that she hardly recognised him.

"Oh, Johnny, look at you! I can't believe it!" Rachel exclaimed, as she dismounted. She looked at the now, handsome young man and was entirely surprised by the difference in his appearance. Johnny had filled out, put weight on, and looked much more muscular than she had remembered. He now wore his hair long like all of the other young men at Tintagel, but the big grin he greeted her with was exactly the same. "Aren't you the dashing knight now!" she laughed, pleased to see him.

Johnny jumped down and gave Rachel a hug, looking embarrassed at her compliments.

"Yeah, Johnny's very popular with the ladies these days, aren't you mate?" laughed Gareth, slapping him on the back.

"You're back soon," stated Johnny, ignoring his remarks. "Is there anything wrong?"

"Don't know, could be, we're going to run it past Merlin," replied Gareth.

"Well, if it's anything I can help with, let me know," said Johnny sincerely.

"Don't worry, mate, you'll be the first one I'll come to," answered Gareth. "See you later."

They went into the turret entrance and up to Merlin's door. The old man was delighted to see them, although once he got over his excitement at seeing Rachel, he looked sternly at Gareth.

"I thought you weren't coming back again, Gareth," he

reprimanded.

"I know, but this is different. We've had to come and see you," Gareth replied.

"Well, I am assuming that since your sister is with you, your reason must be a good one," said the old wizard. "Come, sit down and tell me all," he finished, patting the settle next to him.   They joined him on his big wooden chairs, pushing the cushions around them comfortably. They both told Merlin their stories and the ancient sorcerer stroked his beard thoughtfully.

"What does it all mean, Merlin?" asked Rachel. "Galahad and his men are all right, aren't they?"

"Yes, my dear, they are fine. But as to the meaning of all this, well, I'm not sure," he replied slowly. "I am almost convinced that these strange experiences are not related. They are both serious in their own right but it may very well be a coincidence that they have happened at the same time." He got up and paced for a few minutes, stroking his beard again. "Yes, I think we must look at them separately. Firstly, Rachel, your story worries me, and you were quite right to seek me out. I do believe that this is a warning; I think you have intercepted a plot to do exactly what you have seen. You said the Saxon was talking to someone, do you know who he was?"

"No, he had his back to me and he was wearing a long black cloak," she answered.

"If he wasn't Saxon, then could he have been from here?" asked Merlin.

"He definitely wasn't a Saxon, and I almost feel as though I should know who he is, but I just can't place him!" Rachel replied.

"Could he be a knight, or someone you have seen at the castle?" inquired Merlin.

"No, that just doesn't feel right," she said convincingly.

"Then he is not from here, or you would know," said Merlin. "Your vision, do you think it could it possibly happen somewhere else? The reason I ask this is, that there has been trouble with the Saxons much further north. Galahad, Kay and Percivale have been there with their men to stop them taking the villages and terrorising the people."

"No, it will definitely happen here, I saw the castle, and the Saxons all poured out of the tunnel - I recognised it straight away," she replied adamantly. "It was Galahad's camp they attacked, I recognised the flags."

"Well then, all we need to find out is when it will happen, so that we may stop it!" declared Merlin.

"But Merlin, no one here would invite the Saxons to help them. I know they have in other places, but not here surely?" said Gareth.

"I would agree with you, my boy," said the old man wisely. "But greed, power, or the thought of wealth can turn the head of many, and often has, as we already know. We must watch those around us carefully until we know who it is."

"So if Gareth's strange knights aren't connected, what on earth was all that about?" asked Rachel.

"Gareth's experience disturbs me as much as yours, Rachel, but for very different reasons," responded Merlin gravely.

"Do you think that Mordred could be the knight that tried to kill me?" asked Gareth.

"No, no, I do not. Mordred is dead, and even if his ghost were following you, it would not be able to inflict an injury or knock a man off his horse. You said your friend sustained a broken arm, this does not sound right!"

"Well believe me, it happened!" said Gareth.

"I am not disputing that," said Merlin. "I am merely exploring the possibilities."

"Is there any way that Mordred could still be alive?" asked Rachel. "After all, Gareth has travelled back and forth to Valonia for years. Is there any possibility that he has found a way to follow Gareth into our time?"

"No," said Merlin resolutely. "Mordred only ever had enough power to flit from this time into Valonia by using the tunnel. He most certainly could not travel into your time. He would have no way of getting there."

"Well if it wasn't him, who was it?" quizzed Gareth. "And aside from that, who was the other knight in the silver armour who rescued me from him? We thought the Power must have sent him to protect me."

"No, the Power would have given you Excalibur to defeat him yourself, as you have the skills to do that. It would not conjure up a second knight to do it for you."

"So who was he then, and where did he come from?" asked Gareth.

"At the moment, my dear boy, I am as mystified as you," replied Merlin. "But this problem lies in your time and we shall deal with it later. Rachel's vision is the most pressing problem that we need to solve, before lives are lost. We need to find out more, and the Orb of Resolution might show you something that will tell us when this Saxon attack will occur. Would you mind, Rachel?"

'Here we go again,' Rachel thought to herself, nodding reluctantly. She watched the old man unlock his cabinet and take out the strange Orb. He placed it on his desk and Rachel tried to prepare herself, knowing what would be in store for her once she started looking at it. She tried to think only of the questions they needed answers to, as she put her hands on the frame and gazed into the milky fluid depths of the mystical ball.

Colours floated and drifted around it until two shapes slowly began to appear. Rachel realised, as soon as they became clear, that this was the Saxon and the man in the cloak that she had seen before. She listened hard to try and hear their voices, and the Orb, realising this, took her closer.

"My men will come on the night of the full moon," growled a low guttural voice with a heavy accent.

"They must not come until after the feast, I have someone in the castle who will put a sleeping draught in their ale."

"My men will kill them awake or asleep," snarled the Saxon.

"No matter, it will help, besides the moon will be bright and they might be seen as they pull their boats ashore. After their ale every man at the castle will be asleep, it will make it easier," came the high-pitched, nasal voice of the man in the cloak.

"My men would kill them anyway," insisted the Saxon. "Why do you want this castle? Is it so much better than your own?"

"Oh no, you will be more than happy with my castle," replied the cloaked man, whom Rachel still felt she ought to recognise. "There are two villages close by: there are serfs you can take as servants and plenty of women for your men. This is a matter of honour; this castle should have been my father's."

"So why did he not take it himself?" asked the Saxon scornfully.

Rachel didn't hear his answer as the picture changed and it went dark. She could see a small beach lit up by a silvery light, where dark, pointed boats came silently in. The sea was full of them and they came in one after another on to the beach. The men jumped out and crept soundlessly into the trees - a black mass of hatchet-bearing Saxons.

The picture changed again and she saw Galahad's camp, a

circle of conical tents around a dying fire. The Saxon men crept up silently, half crouching and Rachel knew that what she was about to see, would be the same as her dream. Hastily she let go of the Orbs frame, and emerged from her vision with a shudder.

She told Merlin what she had seen and heard and he exchanged a worried glance with Gareth.

"I didn't recognise him, but I feel so sure I ought to! I don't think that was much help was it?" she asked. "This is so frustrating, I know that I should know who it is, his voice was almost familiar, but I just can't place it!"

"It will come in time, do not fear," replied Merlin. "At least we know it will be a night with a full moon and there is to be a feast. That tells me enough to know that we have two days," Merlin mused. "I shall check my charts to make sure, but there is a full moon two nights from now, the day after Galahad, Kay and Percivale return."

"Yes, and the return of the knights will bring a feast," said Gareth. "But I thought you said the men came out of the tunnel in your dream, Rachel?"

"They did," said Rachel, "but this is what I saw in the Orb."

"No matter," replied Merlin, poring over some ancient charts. "The tide will be good that night to bring in their boats. If they are intent on killing Galahad's men and taking the castle, whoever this person is, he has offered his own castle in return for this one. Who could this be?"

"That's it! I've got it!" exclaimed Rachel, "I knew I'd heard his voice before, although it's deeper now. It's Theodorus! It's Mordred's dreadful son! That's what puzzled me when he said the castle should have been his father's."

"Well, that would explain a lot then," said Gareth. "He would probably be the only person stupid enough to ask the Saxons to help him!"

"Theodorus knows this castle well, he has been here with his father, and if he has someone in the castle to help him, oh this is bad news indeed!" said Merlin, shaking his head. "It will not be easy to stop the men of the castle enjoying a flagon or two of ale!"

"Can we stop this happening altogether?" asked Rachel.

"Alas, no," said Merlin. "If the Saxons are already on their way, expecting great rewards, they will not leave without a fight. I'm afraid that a battle cannot be avoided."

"I'll stay and help," declared Gareth, "but I'm taking you back to the tunnel tomorrow, Rachel. You can go to back to Valonia and stay with Catherine, you'll be safe there."

"I'm not leaving you here on your own!" she replied indignantly.

"I agree with Gareth," said Merlin. "A battle against the Saxons is no place for a woman, seer or not. You have played your part and it is not safe for you to remain here. We will move all the other women from the castle to a place of safety. I will go down now to tell Bors what we have learnt."

"I'll come with you," said Gareth. "I'll go and tell Johnny and Bran."

Rachel suddenly found herself alone, as Merlin and her brother rushed away to warn everyone, and although she was relieved that she wasn't going to have to be there for the battle, she also felt rather left out. Their last encounters there with magic and the Chalice had put her in the centre of it all. It was strange for her to see her brother dashing off as though he belonged there and she was to be sent back.

Her thoughts were interrupted by a knock at the door and she opened it to find Isolde holding a pile of clothes for her. She smiled at the shy girl and let her in, quite grateful of her company.

"I've brought you several dresses' Miss," she said, "although Sir Gareth said that you would not be staying long."

Well, that was a surprise! Gareth had sent her, and Isolde didn't appear to have any male clothes for him either, Rachel noticed.

"Oh thank you, Isolde. How are you?" she asked, in an attempt at conversation.

"I am well, Miss and thank you for asking, Miss," Isolde said with a curtsy. "I will put these on your bed, Miss." She disappeared quickly up the narrow staircase and as she returned asked, "Will that be all, Miss?"

"Yes, thanks," said Rachel with a sigh, as the girl scuttled away. How was it that her brother seemed so comfortable here, and more to the point, why was everyone so at ease with him and not her? she wondered.

She decided to go upstairs to the small bedchamber and change, thinking that at least it would give her something to do for a while. She looked at the selection of garments that Isolde had carefully placed out for her. A dark green gown reminded her immediately of Guinevere's dress that she had worn last time. She shivered as memories of the Chalice and all of the dreadful events that had happened on their last visit, flooded back to her.

She chose a midnight blue one instead with a pleated, beaded bodice. She tried it on and it fitted beautifully. The skirt draped into soft folds and its long sleeves studded with small dark blue beads, gathered around her elbows and then again by her wrists. She brushed her hair and plaited the top section in an attempt to blend in with the other girls there.

The room below was still empty when Rachel returned, and she was cross with Gareth for leaving her on her own for so long. She suddenly noticed a black cat sitting on the back of the settle. It stood up haughtily, stretching its back as she drew nearer. It must have come in with Isolde, she thought.

"Here puss, come on then," she said softly, in a voice that is always reserved for pets. "Puss, puss... "

The cat arched its back, hissed, and drew its claws and Rachel stepped back quickly in surprise. A sudden inexplicable feeling of evil washed over her, which surprised her even more, and she felt the cat's eyes looking at her disdainfully. It padded across the settle, never taking its eyes off her. Black, hard eyes that, for a moment, made her shudder.

The door opened and Gareth walked in, laughing with Johnny. The cat shot between them and disappeared as they closed the door.

"You look lovely, Rachel," said Johnny admiringly.

She was surprised to see that Gareth had already changed into a tunic and loose-fitting trousers that he had tucked into a flat pair of boots. His attire was similar to Johnny's and he seemed quite comfortable with it.

"Where did you get those?" inquired Rachel, pointing to his clothes.

"Oh these, they're mine, I've got a room downstairs with Johnny, and I leave some clothes there," he replied casually. "Are you all right? You look as though you've seen a ghost."

"I haven't seen one, but I think I've just felt one," she replied with another quiver.

"How does that work then?" her brother laughed.

"I don't know, but there was a cat here - it just ran past you when you opened the door. I went to make a fuss of it, and I just had this black feeling come over me," she explained, as Gareth stopped laughing and looked puzzled instead. "It was only a cat but it felt for a moment... this sounds daft, but it felt like something else!"

"Something else?" repeated Gareth. "What else? It was a cat, I saw it shoot out."

"I don't know... it felt... evil," she replied, aware of how stupid it sounded and to add to her humiliation, she saw Gareth and Johnny exchange a glance.

"I think you're starting to worry too much about everything. In fact, I think it's a good job you're going back," reponded Gareth.

"There's loads of cats here, they keep the mice down," chipped in Johnny, in a much kindlier tone than her brother's. "They aren't really pets here; they're not used to being fussed."

"There's lots of them. There's nothing evil about them," insisted Gareth.

"Rachel, don't worry, what's happening now has nothing to do with magic," said Johnny. "This is just Theodorus - selfish, obnoxious and cowardly. He's invited the Saxons here to take Tintagel in return for his father's lands. We'll fight them and that will be an end to it."

"Johnny's right, it's not good for you to be here," agreed Gareth. "This is just another battle; they do it all the time here. You're just getting caught up with the memories of everything that happened last time!"

"I know what I felt," snapped Rachel. "I felt evil!"

Johnny and Gareth looked at each other in despair.

"Right, come on, we're taking you downstairs," said Gareth. "Don't look so worried, it's nothing grand, we'll get some food from the kitchen and have dinner together. Sarah's going to join us, she's on her own as Bran has already left to warn the villages, and Merlin's coming too," he finished, propelling her towards the door.

"It's really good to have you back with us," said Johnny as they left, and for a moment Rachel could see why he had so many admirers. He was gentle, earnest and trustworthy, and had been so brave when they had been there before. Her heart went out to him. No longer was he the bumbling farm boy, so eager to please them. He had become a man!

"I'm so pleased that you're happy here," she said, as they followed Gareth down the narrow stone steps. "Look at you! You're a new person, you're a knight!"

"I am!" he said proudly. "But if it hadn't been for you and Gareth, I would never have had this life. I'll never forget that, and you need never worry while you're here, because I'll always make sure you're safe!"

"Oh, thank you, Johnny, that's so nice!" she said, feeling a lump come to her throat.

"Not just me," he continued modestly. "Galahad, Bran, and Gareth - none of us would ever let anything happen to you!"

"I know that, Johnny and it's not the Saxons that are worrying me. I know that we've been warned about them and you'll defeat them."

"So what is it then?" Johnny asked.

"I've just got this awful feeling that I just can't get rid of, that this is not what it seems!" she said, as they walked towards the kitchens. "I don't know what it is, but ever since I saw that cat, I can feel that there is something coming that's much worse than anything the Saxons will bring!"

"You ought to tell Gareth about this?" Johnny replied in concern.

"I don't think he'll listen," she answered. "He thinks I'm being over sensitive because I'm here again, and maybe I am, I don't know. I just have a really bad feeling about all of this!"

"Well, I hope you're wrong then," replied Johnny. "But if ever Gareth won't listen to you and you need to talk to someone, I'll always be here for you."

"I know that, thanks!" she replied, and hugged him, leaving him red-faced with embarrassment.

Chapter Five
Drudwas

Johnny's kindness had made Rachel feel better, and she joined them all in a small room next to the kitchen. They sat around a rough wooden table and the food was hot and plentiful. Sarah joined them; she sat down comfortably laughing with the others until she saw Rachel. A look of uncertainty crossed her face and she sat rigidly in her seat, staring at Rachel. Rachel smiled at her, but instead of returning the friendly gesture, a look of fear crossed Sarah's face.

Rachel suddenly realised that Sarah must recognise her from their last visit, even though no-one else apart from Galahad remembered anything. Rachel had visited Sarah through the Orb of Resolution, to ask her to help them, and this would explain why the girl was looking so strangely at her. She felt that she ought to say something to put Sarah's mind at ease, but she had absolutely no idea what to say. Instead Rachel just wished that she had stayed up in Merlin's room.

The boys carried on a lively banter and Rachel inwardly fumed at their insensitivity. Eventually it was Sarah who approached her. "You are Gareth's sister I know, but I think I have seen you somewhere before," she said cautiously.

"Yes, you have," answered Rachel, slightly relieved. "You saw me by the stream at Mordred's castle when I came to ask you to unlock the castle door. You helped Bran and my brother escape and I'm so grateful that you did."

Sarah's look of confusion, told Rachel that she had just said the wrong thing. She had assumed that Sarah must have remembered what had happened at Mordred's castle, but she obviously didn't. When time had been corrected, the events that followed were different and Sarah had been branded as a witch because of it. No wonder she looks worried, thought Rachel, feeling even worse, and tried to offer her an explanation by saying, "Sarah, I know you don't remember exactly what happened and that's because of the magic that surrounded everything at the time. I heard that you had been blamed and I'm really sorry that you got caught up in everything afterwards."

Sarah's eyes lit up briefly with excitement that this strange girl understood and knew what she had been through, but this was followed quickly by fear, as she decided that Rachel must have been the sorceress that had caused it all. She retreated hastily back to her side of the table, too frightened to look at Rachel again.

Rachel sighed, feeling alienated again, and her mood was only lifted by the appearance of Merlin in his elaborate robes. The rest of the evening passed quite comfortably, and they talked until late. Gareth left with Johnny to retire to their rooms and Rachel found herself alone with Merlin as they went back to his rooms.

"You are finding this difficult, my dear," observed the old wizard, sensing her despondency.

"Yes, I suppose I am," she replied. "It's just that whenever we've been here before, it's always been so important that we stayed together, as the Keepers. Gareth has been here so many times without me it just feels really different now."

"You are still here together, your bond still binds you tightly, even though you may not realise it," said Merlin wisely. "You may not be constantly in the same room with Gareth, but you are both young adults and this is not such a necessity now."

"I know that Johnny and Bran are probably as much my friends as his," she replied, "but I don't feel as though I fit in the same as Gareth, if that makes sense."

"It makes perfect sense," sympathised Merlin. "As a seer, you are set aside from others. The people here lead a simple life, and they are mistrustful of anything that is unusual. In their ignorance or fear, they may shun you, or keep their distance because they do not understand your gift."

"You mean like Sarah. She loves Gareth, but she's terrified of me," Rachel answered.

"Yes possibly," the old wizard replied, lighting the lamps in his room. "The path of a seer or a sorceress can be a lonely one. Gareth is seen as a knight here, he has proved himself and is respected because of that. You, my dear, can prove yourself as a seer over and over, but you will still meet fear and suspicion. You will never have the same acceptance as your brother."

"I'm glad I'm going tomorrow then," Rachel replied.

"I am sorry, I have painted a very black picture," Merlin said, his hand resting on her arm. "There will also be those who will trust every word that you say, and take direction from it. These are the people closest to your heart and they will never let you down!"

"Johnny said something very similar earlier on," recalled Rachel.

"Then he is a good example of what I have just been saying.

The quest of a seer is not an easy one," he said sadly. "A sorceress, a wizard, a seer, call them what you may, we all stand alone because of our differences to others. This is our burden!"

"You're including yourself, Merlin," she answered in surprise.

"I am indeed. I am no different to you. I wandered lost for many a year. I had no one to guide me, and it was a long time before I found my place: a place where I am respected and trusted."

"I'm sorry; I suppose I'm quite lucky compared to that."

"You are indeed, my dear," he smiled. "I am old and now I need my bed, so I will bid you goodnight. Sleep well, my dear, and do not worry, you too will find your place," he said as he closed the door behind him.

Her answer, as he shut the door, probably would have been 'I don't think I want to,' but with a swirl of his gown, her words would have been lost, so she didn't utter them. Instead, she made her way up to the small bedchamber with the familiar, lumpy bed, where it took her a long while to go to sleep.

The light streaming through the window woke her quite early, and she washed with the cold water from the pitcher on the table and dressed in one of Isolde's selection of garments. A long, dark, wine-coloured dress, with the usual pointed sleeves and tight bodice. She went downstairs and looked out of the windows, the castle was starting to bustle with its usual morning activities and she watched distractedly. It was a long time before Merlin arrived with Isolde and their breakfast, announcing that Gareth had ridden out at first light with Johnny and Bors to warn the neighbouring villages of the Saxons return.

"Gareth will be back by lunchtime, and he and Johnny will accompany you to the tunnel," Merlin finished.

"That's nice of him," Rachel answered sarcastically, peeved that Gareth hadn't even bothered to tell her where he was going.

"Oh, Rachel," said the old wizard, taking her hand. "You must understand that Gareth is a knight now and he takes his duties seriously. He knows that you are safe here with me, and his efforts lie in warning those whose safety depends on it. Do not judge him too harshly; he is doing what is expected of him."

She had no reply to this, as she knew that Merlin was probably right, even though it didn't make her feel any less disgruntled.

It was early afternoon before she saw Johnny and Gareth return from Merlin's window. She saw Gareth jump down from Rufus, in one graceful leap, as she had seen all the other experienced horsemen do. She watched him enter the castle, but again it was a long time before he came to Merlin's room, with an apologetic look on his face.

"Look, I'm really sorry but I had to go and…"

"Merlin's already told me, I know where you've been," she answered curtly.

"Oh, well that's all right then," he answered, noticing her displeasure immediately. "Look, I'm famished; I'm just going to get something to eat. I'll come straight back and we'll take you to the tunnel," he said, leaving quickly before she could say anything.

Again, Rachel had a long wait, and was really quite cross by the time Gareth appeared with Johnny to take her back. By the time they set off it was well into the middle of the afternoon. Merlin walked with them to the main gate and briefly held both of her hands.

"Remember who you are, and never forget what you can do," the old wizard reminded her.

Rachel smiled and said goodbye, slightly puzzled by his statement, and mounted Rufus next to Gareth. They rode out across the causeway and over the open plain towards the tunnel. She could see an encampment of conical tents half erected in the distance to the right of them.

"Is that Galahad's camp?" she asked.

"Yeah," Gareth said over his shoulder. "They've only just arrived, so as soon as we've got you back, we'll ride over to warn them."

They reached the tunnel entrance and dismounted, leading the horses inside. The two young men walked with Rachel until they reached the point where they knew she would be transported back through time to Valonia.

"I'm sorry, Rachel, but you'll be much safer at Catherine's," said Gareth, "and I'll be back before you know it."

"Aren't you going with her?" asked Johnny, before Rachel could say anything.

"We haven't got time, mate, we've got to get back and warn Galahad," said Gareth. "You'll be all right from here won't you, Rachel?"

"Well, yes I suppose so," she answered, slightly hesitantly.

"Do you want one of us to come with you?" asked Johnny, aware that Gareth had no intention of accompanying her. "Will you be all right on your own?"

"Err… yes, I'll be fine from here," she answered rather uncertainly. "Anyway, there's no way I'd let *you* come with me, you're not supposed to use the tunnel, Johnny. Gareth told me it had a bad effect on you last time."

"Look, I'd come with you myself Rachel," said Gareth, "but we've got to go and see Galahad, and you'll be safe once you go through to Valonia. I know it's a bit of a trek back to the cottage, but you won't mind that will you?" he asked, making it sound more like a statement than a question.

"No," she answered resolutely. It was fairly obvious that Gareth couldn't wait to get rid of her and she had no desire to stay there when she felt so useless. So she waved them on and entered the time zone, where the strange feeling of walking and spinning at the same time took over.

She waited for the strange sensation to whisk her quickly into the next time. She felt herself lifted and the whirling started, but it seemed much slower than usual. The tunnel of time normally happened in a flash but this felt like a struggle. She spun slowly until she began to feel sick. Eventually the strange feeling passed and she staggered dizzily on finding her feet again. She looked down expecting to see her usual clothes, only to find that she was still wearing the same long dress.

Maybe Merlin had to arrange for their clothes to change and he hadn't done it this time, she thought as she continued down the tunnel towards Valonia. After all, they were all more preoccupied with the impending arrival of the Saxons. However, there was a nagging doubt in her mind that, for some reason, the tunnel hadn't worked and she was still in the same time.

Suddenly she heard a strange echoing noise, and voices. She ducked quickly into a passageway on her right, and hid behind a large boulder. The noises grew nearer, and she recognised them as horses' hooves, clopping noisily on the stone floor, echoing around the passageway. The horses stopped near the entrance to her passageway, and she held her breath as she instantly recognised the low guttural voice of the Saxon.

"No," she heard him say sharply. "My men come tonight."

"But that is not what we agreed," she heard the high-pitched, arrogant voice of Theodorus reply. "I have arranged it all. A sleeping potion will be put into the men's ale. You cannot do this a day early, besides there is only one encampment here, there are more knights to follow, with many men!"

Rachel put her hand over her mouth hastily to stifle a large involuntary gasp at the mention of the Saxon men coming tonight.

"Then we shall kill them when they arrive," the Saxon growled at Theodorus. "My men are warriors; they have no need of your potions. They will kill those that are camped tonight and take this great castle that you are so intent on. I have heeded your warning of the bright moonlight on the morrow, and so my men will move tonight!"

"Well, I suppose that I will at least get Tyntagel earlier than I expected," replied Theodorus haughtily.

"The boats will be on the beaches several hours before daybreak, and your knights will be dead long before the sun rises," the Saxon replied curtly, and she could hear his heavy footsteps as he walked away.

"Then we shall be ready as well!" shouted Theodorus after him. "Damn heathens," he muttered to his handful of men. "They had better keep their word, or they will have me to answer to!"

Behind her rock, Rachel could imagine Theodorus puffing out his chest in self-importance as he spoke to them, although what he thought he would be able to do against the Saxons if they didn't keep their word was beyond Rachel! She shook her head in exasperation at his sheer bombastic stupidity and was relieved to hear them moving on down the tunnel.

She waited in the darkness a long time until the hooves became faint, the full horror of their conversation gripping her. The Saxon boats weren't coming in two days time; they were going to attack Galahad's camp tonight. No one would be ready for them, because of what she had said! They had all trusted her and she had been completely wrong! Waves of guilt and fear consumed her in the darkness and she knew that she would have to warn them. She knew that she couldn't go back to Valonia now, and maybe the tunnel of time hadn't even allowed her to pass because of this.

How could I have been so wrong? she thought. Why had the Orb let her assume things that were incorrect when so many lives depended on it? Or was it just that she had blocked anything to do with magic out of her mind for so long, that she couldn't do it anymore? Her thoughts turned to her brother, who she had chastised for returning to learn to fight like the others, and almost wished that she had done the same.

The tunnel was quiet now and she ventured out, running back down the passageway the way she had come. A noise made her stop, and she realised it was men's voices again, several of them this time. Rachel rushed into the next small tunnel entrance, as the voices were getting louder. She hid in a narrow alcove in the rock, pulling her dark cloak tightly round her to blend in.

Fortunately the men stayed in the main tunnel and she realised that the voices belonged to many Saxons. Theodorus didn't seem to be with them this time and she couldn't understand what they were saying until the man she had heard earlier mimicked Theodorus in English, trying to copy his arrogant, whining voice.

"I shall haf my castle a day eear-ley," he squeaked as high as his gruff voice would allow, and there was loud, raucous laughter from his men. "No, no, you Ee-nglee-sh fool," he continued, his heavy accent making it sound even more ridiculous. "For wee shall haf both castles, and the Ee-nglee-sh fool wee-ll haf none!" His bellow of deep laughter startled Rachel as the men all joined in with cheers and shouts in their native tongue.

Rachel shivered as their strange language sounded sinister. She jumped with fright again as the man barked an order at his men and the noise stopped instantly. His growling voice with its short, guttural words were the only sounds in the tunnel and Rachel desperately wished that she could understand him as she was sure he was giving them instructions.

Shortly afterwards she heard them moving away but she waited for a long time before she moved. The last thing she wanted was to be captured by the Saxons, and she had to make sure that they were gone before she could leave. She waited in the dark recess until she was satisfied that she couldn't hear anything at all. She knew that she couldn't risk trying to get back to the castle; she would have to go straight to Galahad to warn him and decided that she might have to wait until it was dark before crossing the open space to his camp. She could follow the edge of the wood for a while but at some point she would have to go out into the open. She had no idea where the Saxons were, but she suspected that they were hiding in the cave network somewhere.

The thought crossed her mind that maybe this was why she had seen two visions of the Saxons, one of the men flooding out of the tunnel entrance and the other of them arriving in their boats. She also wondered if the brainless Theodorus even knew that they were already there. He had talked about the Saxon men arriving, but there was already a substantial amount of them in the tunnels if her vision was correct. Enough to do what they were planning, she thought with a shudder, especially with surprise on their side. It was also fairly obvious from what little she had understood of the last conversation that they had no intention of keeping whatever bargain they had made with Theodorus. Serves him right, she thought angrily.

Eventually she decided it might be safe to creep out. There had been no sound in the tunnel for a long time and she thought that it must be getting quite late. She fumbled her way out, feeling along the cold, damp cave walls to help her, until she entered the main tunnel. Here, a glimmer of light from the entrance lit the passage enough for her to move more quickly, and she went as fast as she could towards it, grateful that the soft, impractical slippers she was wearing made no sound on the stone floor.

She reached the entrance, where the light was beginning to fade, and ducked behind one of the huge rocks. She peeped over the top, and when satisfied that there was no one in sight, she carried on. She headed for the edge of the wood, grateful of its cover, as it was now pouring with rain and she was already saturated. She dragged her wet cloak and dress through the brambles and thicket as far as she could until there was no way through, around its perimeter.

It was dark enough now to continue in the open at the edge of the woods, although she lost any shelter from the rain that had previously protected her. On horseback, the tents had looked fairly near, on foot they looked miles away. The rain came down heavily. It poured as though the heavens had opened and she had to lift up her dress now as it hampered her steps with its soggy weight. Her soft slippers squelched and slopped, completely waterlogged, and her long, thick hair was plastered down her back. The rain dripped off it, running on to her already wet cloak as she continued in the deluge.

Uncomfortable though it was ploughing on through the heavy downpour, it did at least give her some comfort in the thought that everyone else would be sheltering from it and might not notice her. She arrived eventually at the conical tents, their flags hanging limp and wet, just as the rain began to ease up and turn into a damp drizzle.

She rushed into the camp, wet, muddy and bedraggled, as several men were venturing out of their tents. She recognised Galahad immediately and shouted to him.

"Galahad, oh thank God, I have to talk to you!" she said out of breath, as he turned and stared at her.

"What? Good Lord, Rachel, is that you?" Galahad stopped and turned, immediately recognising her voice. "What on earth are you doing here?" he asked, looking shocked. "Get a blanket, the girl is drenched!" he shouted to one of his men as soon as he realised the state she was in. "What are you doing? You are wet through. Here take off your cloak."

He took the sodden cloak from her and wrapped the blanket around her shoulders as she started to shiver.

"I have to warn you about the Saxons... the Saxons are coming, there are hundreds of them..." she said breathlessly.

"I know about them, Gareth has already told me," Galahad answered.

"No, no, you don't understand," she shouted almost hysterically. "They aren't coming in two days, they're coming tonight! I've just heard them in the tunnel, they had a deal with Mordred's son and they're going back on it. They've already got men hiding in the tunnels; the rest will come later in their boats. They're planning to kill you all tonight, in your beds!"

She was suddenly aware that every man in the camp had gathered around them, listening intently. There was a brief silence and they looked at her suspiciously until Galahad spoke to them. "The girl is a seer, she comes to warn us. You can trust what she says; the Saxons will be attacking tonight! Send riders to the villages and to the others!"

There was an instant, obedient flurry of activity as his men rushed off to do his bidding and Galahad led her into one of the tents, her teeth chattering noisily as she shivered with cold.

"You are soaked right through, you must take off that wet dress and wrap yourself in the blanket. I will get you some dry clothes," he said, before disappearing out of the tent.

She did as he said, rather quickly in case he came back while she was half undressed.

He put some clothes discreetly through the tent flap but did not enter. "I am sorry they are men's clothing but at least they are dry," he said, through the tent. "The rain has stopped and the men are building up the fire. Come and sit by it when you are ready."

Rachel dressed in the rough clothes, a long thick tunic and some baggy trousers that hung so loosely, she had to tie the rope belt around her small waist twice. She began to feel warmer as soon as she put them on, and wrapped the blanket around herself for warmth before venturing out. Galahad was instructing his men and came over to join her.

"Come, sit close to the fire, it will warm you," Galahad said, pulling a bale of hay nearer for her.

She sat down, grateful for the heat coming off the blazing wood that the men had banked up high. It sparked and crackled with flames dancing in-between the logs.

"Thanks, I feel better now I'm dry," she answered, quite surprised that she wasn't feeling the acute embarrassment that she normally felt around Galahad.

"What are you doing here?" the knight asked as he sat down next to her. "Gareth said you had left!"

"I did leave, but I didn't get very far," she answered, and told him what had happened to her.

"Gareth let you go on your own? That was very wrong of him!" Galahad said, sharply. "He should have made sure you were safe first."

"They were coming to warn you, and they did leave me where I should have been safe," she answered in her brother's defence.

"But you weren't safe; he should have gone with you. Johnny could have warned me!" he said. "With the threat of the Saxons upon us, no woman should be wandering around alone."

"Maybe it's just as well that they did, or I wouldn't have heard the men in the tunnel," Rachel answered. "I'm just so sorry that I got it wrong the first time!”

“No matter, we will be prepared for them. There will be no one in their beds tonight. The Saxons will find naught but piles of blankets. It will be us that take them by surprise when we attack them from the woods!” he answered. “Were it not for you, we would not have been expecting the Saxons any day! Gareth told me of your vision and the reason that you came back.”

“Talking of Gareth, I must get back to the castle, I need to know that he and the others are ready for the Saxons as well!” she said starting to rise.

“You will not,” Galahad said to her surprise, pulling her back firmly. “You will dry out properly, eat and rest before you go any further. I will send a rider to the castle.”

A large man handed them both a bowl of food and she accepted it gratefully, the aroma making her realise that she was quite hungry.

“Besides, I am concerned about you,” Galahad continued. “I would prefer that you stayed here, where I can protect you. I cannot return to the castle with you, I must stay with my men.”

“I wouldn’t expect you to. If you could give me a horse, it’s not far and I know the way,” Rachel started.

“I will most certainly not allow you to go on your own!” said Galahad, looking quite shocked at the idea. “’Tis not safe for any woman if the Saxons are already here! If you insist on going, I would at least give you one of my toughest men to ride with you, although I would still prefer to protect you myself!”

She smiled at him; he was just as she remembered, protective, honest and plain speaking. There was no teasing in his manner this time, and she felt more comfortable with him because of it. She knew how difficult it had been for him to accept the magic she had been involved with the last time, and yet now he treated her the same, as he would treat any woman. His immediate trust of her warning, and the way he had sent his men off to act on it, more than made up for all of the suspicious glances she had felt at the castle. For the first time since she had been there she felt accepted and comfortable.

The food and the warmth from the fire and the relief that Galahad had been warned made her feel drowsy and her eyes began to close. She was only asleep for about half an hour and as she stirred, in the zone of contentment between sleep and waking, she felt warm, and safe. She had the comforting feeling of being held tightly and her eyes flickered open to find she had her head on Galahad's shoulder and that he had wrapped his own cloak around her, holding her firmly.

"Oh, I'm sorry, I can't believe I went to sleep," she said, frantically trying to release herself from his cloak.

"You were tired, you needed to rest," he stated simply. "You will feel better for it."

"I know but..." she stuttered with embarrassment as she struggled to unwrap herself from the tight cocoon of cloak and blanket. "It's getting late, won't the Saxons be here soon?" she asked.

"No, it will be several hours before the tide will be high enough to allow them to bring their boats in," Galahad answered.

"I must go to the castle," she said jumping up. "I must make sure that Gareth and Merlin are ready for this."

"I had hoped that you were not going to pursue this notion," he said softly.

"I have to go back to the others at the castle!" she insisted.

"If you were to stay, I would make sure you were safe," he answered, rising, "but you may be right, the castle walls may serve you better than I can. I will get you a horse and an escort."

She watched him stride across the camp and almost felt tempted to stay. Galahad had played such a large part in helping them to regain the Chalice and put everything right on their last visit and Rachel felt that she knew him so well. The young knight's warmth was the same as always, along with his sense of duty.

As he walked back with a large man and two horses she noticed the moonlight flooding across the grass, making it shine like silver. She realised that this was what she had seen in her vision. It hadn't been a full moon at all! It was the light reflecting on the rainwater still clinging to the blades of grass.

Her escort was a huge man with a bushy beard and thick moustache. He smiled grimly at her as he mounted his horse. She saw a long, thick sword at his side and a large axe hanging from his saddle and decided that he looked ferocious enough to take on all the Saxons himself.

Galahad put a dry cloak around her shoulders. "Drudwas may not say much but he will get you there safely."

"I don't doubt it!" she agreed, looking at the formidable figure of Drudwas sitting on the biggest horse she had ever seen.

Galahad moved forwards to help her onto another large horse and stopped for a moment. "You look so different," he said.

"Well, I have been soaked," said Rachel, embarrassed for the first time as his deep brown eyes looked at her. "I probably look like a drowned rat!"

"A rat?" laughed Galahad. "A mermaid maybe, but never a rat!"

"Take care Galahad," she answered, as he helped her up onto the horse.

"I will see you at the castle when this is all over," he said, and she followed the bulky frame of Drudwas, both of them urging their horses into the darkness.

Rachel was surprised at the speed of the horses, they were obviously used to long miles at a fast pace, and made light work of the short distance to the castle. Soon she could see the causeway and they slowed down slightly. As they came towards it she was aware of a strange whirring noise and something flew past her shoulder, followed by another similar sound. She heard a groan next to her and she turned to see Drudwas clutch his chest and fall back in his saddle. For a moment she didn't understand what had happened until she saw the arrow sticking out of his chest as he keeled over and fell from his horse.

Chapter Six
The Bird and the Bones

Rachel stared in horror as Drudwas's large frame hit the ground and a second wave of arrows hurtled past her. She froze for a moment, not knowing whether to try and help him or to carry on. She heard shouts and saw men coming out of the undergrowth on both sides of the causeway as they fired their arrows at her again, so she urged her horse into a full gallop. Leaning forwards, she clung to its neck for protection and ducked to avoid the arrows.

It was too dangerous to turn back, so she rode towards the cliffs and, as she approached, she prepared herself to jump from the horse's back in the hope that the men might follow it in the dark, thinking that she was still on it. As the cliff top came nearer she slid her leg over the horses back and let go.

The horse carried on and Rachel landed hard, rolling dangerously close to the edge of the rocky height, where she could see the drop to the beach below. She grabbed on to a large clump of long wiry grass, which halted her before she plummeted right over the top.

Scrambling up quickly Rachel ran back to the pathway down the cliff that she and her brother had been down so long ago with

Merlin. The moonlight gave her just about enough light to see where she was going and this time she gave no thought to the drop on the other side of her as she made her way down the cliff path as fast as she could go.

She ran across the small patch of shingle beach to the entrance of Merlin's cave and dashed inside, winded and bruised. She could still hear shouts but at least she was hidden and, although she had no idea of how she was going to get to the castle, she hoped that at least they wouldn't look for her down here!

Finally Rachel got her breath back, still shaking with fear, and glanced back at the cliffs to see if she had been followed. It was quiet and still and she breathed a sigh of relief, until she saw a procession of torches going along the top. They were obviously looking for her and it was only going to be a matter of time before they found the pathway and made their way down to the beach. Panicking, she fumbled around the rocky walls trying to remember where Merlin had taken the torch from. Eventually her hand touched a conical object and she tugged it upwards to release it. She tried to stay calm as she passed her hand over it, asking it to light, and she was rewarded with a small orange flame.

Torch in hand, Rachel made her way through the rocky caves, hoping that she could find the right tunnels. Finally, she saw the narrow opening to Argante's grotto and bent low to pass through it. She entered the cavern and her torch immediately dimmed, almost in reverence, as though it realised it was no longer a necessity. The subterranean chamber's eerie green glow was exactly as she had remembered it and she stood nervously, looking at the misty vapours hovering over the green underground lake and wondered why she had come here. Would Argante help her?

She stood at the edge of the water and for a second, summoning the haughty green goddess was almost as frightening as the Saxons!

In her haste to turn to someone for help, Rachel had forgotten how unearthly and formidable this cave was.

"Argante," she called apprehensively. "Argante! It's Rachel. Please, I must talk to you, I need your help!"

For a moment, nothing happened and Rachel stared at the opaque cloudiness above the waters, willing it to do something.

"Argante, please help me!" she said louder. The mist began to move and a voice echoed around her.

"Who dares to call me?"

Rachel didn't know whether to be relieved or terrified at the answer to her plea.

"It's Rachel; I'm a Keeper of the Power. Merlin brought me to you with Gareth, my brother, a long time ago," she answered, and the mist swirled. She stepped back as the vision of Argante began to materialise floating up out of its depths.

"Please say you remember me," Rachel said, timidly.

"Of course I remember you," Argante replied scornfully. "Why would I not remember the day I was shown two Keepers who had no idea of their duties. You are the girl who was given a gift and chose to deny it?"

"I know and I'm sorry," Rachel humbly returned.

"Where is your twin brother? Is he not with you as your fellow Keeper, or is he still ignoring his duties?" Argante asked, her voice tinged with unmistakable anger.

"No, he isn't, he's been back many times to learn how to use the sword and become a knight. Gareth's done everything that he could, but he's at the castle with Merlin and I have to get back there to warn them about the Saxons."

"And what have you done, pray tell, to develop your powers as a seer, as a Keeper?" asked Argante.

"I, well... I haven't done anything, I haven't needed to until now," Rachel answered.

"And so now you come to ask for my help," Argante remarked coldly. "And why should I give it?"

"Argante, please, you must help me. I had a vision, we came back to warn Merlin that the Saxons were intending to kill all the knights and their men, but I was wrong. They thought they had longer to prepare, but the Saxons are here already. I have to get to the castle to warn them! The Saxons have killed my escort and they're coming down the cliff after me. I don't know what to do!" she finished. "Argante, please help me - I need to know how to use the Power."

"Stupid girl," retorted Argante, turning away from her and preparing to disappear into her lake again. "I have no desire to help those who have not wished to learn!"

"Please, Argante, if you won't do it for me, at least do it for Merlin. He's at the castle and I need to warn him!" pleaded Rachel.

"You would dare to tell me what I should do?" said Argante, pausing before her protective green vapours swallowed her up again. "You hold the Power, but you have not bothered to learn how to use it!" the cold, beautiful woman answered. "Why should I instruct you now, 'twas your duty not mine," she finished as she turned away and the mist started to envelope her again.

Rachel's temper began to flare in disbelief at this disdainful woman's attitude, Goddess or not! "Fine, go! Ignore my request! You might be very important, Lady of the Lake," Rachel shouted after her, "but you really aren't a very nice person are you?"

She felt Argante's anger immediately, as the temperature dropped dramatically.

"How dare you speak to me in this way!" Argante said, her voice accompanied by an icy blast. Rachel began to feel the same mind –

numbing, chilling sensation that she had experienced before with Gareth when he had annoyed the Goddess. But she was so angry with Argante that she faced the ethereal being squarely, defying her powers to work on her.

"I dare, because it's the truth!" Rachel answered, still fighting the chill that was trying to spread through her. "I can understand that you don't want to help me, but why won't you help Merlin? He's your friend isn't he? Well, where I come from we help our friends. You don't seem to care that a lot of people will be killed, including Merlin!"

The haze around the Goddess quivered as her emerald eyes searched Rachel's. The chill became stronger and Rachel had to fight to get her words out as her muscles became numb.

"I've offended you, so no doubt you'll turn me into a lump of stone. Well, you'll probably be doing me a favour because the Saxons will do much worse than that!" Rachel ploughed on, determinedly. "Merlin asked if we could come to you, and you agreed to that. So your promise to a friend obviously doesn't mean anything either! The people I know and respect all keep their promises, so do whatever you think is right, Argante!"

For a moment the mist became still and suddenly Argante laughed. Her laughter tinkled around the underground chamber and the chill disappeared immediately as the cavern lit up with her change of mood.

"Maybe I have misjudged you, maybe you have learnt something after all," said Argante. "You have strength and passion, and you hold me to task. I am not used to this, but maybe on this occasion you are right to do so. I did make a pledge to Merlin and I did say I would help you and I do not break my word!"

"I'm really sorry if I've been completely disrespectful," apologised Rachel, as the chill miraculously left her. "I have to get past the Saxons and get to the castle to warn the others, but there is more, I know that there is something else coming. I don't know what it is, but I can feel a dreadful darkness come over me when I think of it and I know that I have to be with them to help against whatever it is. I will need the knowledge that you quite rightly say that I have denied."

Argante searched Rachel's eyes again before she spoke. "Maybe you are deserving of your position after all," she replied. "I see a strong person in you, one that is more concerned with the fate of others than your own; because of this I will help you."

"Thank you so much," said Rachel in relief.

"Your perceptions are true," Argante continued, pausing for a second to stare up at the cavern ceiling, as though drawing from her own divinations. "The darkness that you have felt will come, and it will be the worst kind of evil that is known to mankind."

"What can I do?" asked Rachel.

"You will use your heritage, the one you have denied," answered Argante, with a hint of scorn in her voice. "The key to using the Power is in your mind. Ask and ye shall receive!"

Rachel recognised the biblical quotation but she still really didn't understand. Argante noticed her blank look and continued. "You hold the Power, acknowledge and accept that it is a part of you and within you. Imagine what you need to be, or what you need to do. See it firmly in your mind and ask for it. The Power will provide what you need. Your mind is strong, and you seek to help others, even with your lack of knowledge you will be able to do this."

"I still don't understand how," said Rachel.

"Do what I have just instructed you to do," answered Argante impatiently. "The Power will not fail you." With that she turned and the mist quivered around her again as though she was about to disappear into its mystical depths, but instead she looked back at Rachel.

"You were only ever meant to be a seer," she said, in a slightly more kindly tone. "The darkness that will come is beyond anything expected of you, or those around you."

Rachel stared at Argante, speechless, as the beautiful, ethereal woman took a large ring off her finger and handed it to her.

"Take this, it may help you," she said, her voice quite soft.

"Thank you, I'll return it as soon as I can," answered Rachel, placing the ring on her middle finger.

"There is no need, the ring is one of a pair," Argante replied. "This one is mine and the second is far away, with its true owner. There is no necessity for this one to remain with me any longer."

"Thank you," said Rachel again, still not entirely clear of what she was to do.

"I wish you good fortune in your quest, as you will have need of it," answered Argante, retreating into the mist. "We will meet again, for there will come a time when I may ask you for assistance."

"Thanks for your help," said Rachel as Argante disappeared into her mystical waters and she found herself alone again.

Rachel found herself alone in the cavern again, and breathed a sigh of relief that she had survived her encounter with the Green Goddess. Her relief was short lived when she realised that the Saxon men would be even closer to finding her, and even though she had spoken to Argante, she still had no idea what to do!

She retraced her steps through the caves with the torch, going over Argante's words in her head. *The Power was within her. Ask and ye shall receive. Use your mind, tell it what you need. Accept and acknowledge,'* Rachel thought frantically, trying to remember Argante's words as she made her way back, valiantly trying to work out how she was supposed to implement them.

Eventually Rachel reached the cave entrance, and she saw torches heading across the beach towards her. She immediately shrank back inside, hearing the guttural foreign language that she had heard in the tunnels, and she shivered as the men came towards the entrance, their feet scrunching heavily on the shingle.

'What am I going to do?' she thought, as she hid behind a rock. It was only a matter of time before their torches would illuminate her and she would be caught.

A squawk came from beside her as she disturbed a seagull nesting on the rock. It took flight and soared into the air, its wings spreading out to catch the sea breeze that lifted it across the sea on a current of air. She watched it enviously, wishing that she could do the same and fly up to the castle unhindered.

The Saxons were in the cave entrance now and their flaming torches spread an orange glow around them. Their strange language was louder, but Rachel couldn't understand what they were saying. She wished again that she were a seagull that could fly away so easily, as the orange lights headed towards her. As she stepped back to hide from them, her foot knocked a large stone and it rolled noisily away from her.

Rachel froze as a shout went out and a torch was lifted high, blinding her with its brightness and illuminating her to her enemies. She held her breath, expecting them to pounce on her and drag her out but instead they laughed. A stone was thrown at her and she moved out of its way, confused. She looked down as her clawed feet hopped away quickly onto another rock.

'Claws!' She didn't have claws! Where were her feet? She looked down to see that her strange, new feet were attached to a pair of thin, spindly legs that went up into a soft, plump downy body, covered in soft feathers. She stretched her arms out and found she had beautiful white, feathered wings. She moved them incredulously, realising that she was a bird, a seagull! She had wished for it and the Power had answered her! If she was a bird, then she could fly, she thought, still marvelling at it, as another large stone hit the wall behind, just missing her.

A large Saxon man lunged at her and, frightened, she leapt from the rocks and took flight. She flapped her arms frantically at first, then gently, as her feathered wings found a surge of air that lifted her quickly up and away from the cave.

Rachel flew out over the sea, and the beach and cave became distant, far below her as the night breeze took her away. She stretched out her wings, moving them gently as though she had been a bird all of her life. The feeling of the air in her wings, rushing against her face as she soared away from her pursuers was invigorating and yet so natural. She opened her wings wider and rode with the current of air into safety, peace and silence, apart from the gentle rush of the wind.

She was so distracted by the wonderful feeling that Rachel suddenly realised she was heading out to sea, and the shoreline and castle were becoming distant. She tilted her wings, rather like a plane circling before landing, and was transported swiftly and effortlessly towards the castle.

Rachel flapped her wings gracefully as she drew nearer to the tower, and landed neatly on the battlements, her long, bony feet gripping the stone beneath them. She closed her wings and a feeling of relief washed over her, until she saw the large black cat heading quickly towards her. It ran across the battlement edge and lashed out with its paw, catching the edge of her wing, almost knocking her off the ledge.

The thought passed quickly through her mind that she needed to be herself again, before the cat launched another attack. Rachel jumped quickly off the battlement and as she landed, she felt her feet make heavy contact with the stone floor. Her feathers were gone, replaced by the rough clothing that Galahad had given her, and she breathed another sigh of relief.

As quickly as she had changed back, the cat leapt off the battlements after her and, to her horror, it distorted and transformed into the black slender shape of Morgana, who now stood facing her. The dark sorceress's face looked even paler than before in the moonlight, and her long hair looked blacker than ever.

"Morgana?" Rachel breathed in shock, stepping back away from her, "but you're... you're..."

"Dead?" laughed the sorceress. "Oh, I almost was, since I was left bleeding to death on a cave floor! But then someone very kindly altered the time back to normal and suddenly the events had never happened, leaving me very much alive again!"

"So... so... what about...?"

"My mother? Morgause!" Morgana finished for her and Rachel nodded speechlessly.

"Oh, she is very much alive too!" she laughed coldly. "So nice of you to be so concerned, and I see that you have been developing your own skills. The little seer has become a fully fledged shape shifter."

"I'm not a shape shifter," replied Rachel indignantly.

"Did I not just see you transform back from the guise of a bird?"

"Yes, but that was nothing to do with being a shape shifter," she answered.

"Even if 'twas not, it would need powerful sorcery," answered Morgana, unconvinced. "And what would make you fly around the castle in the darkness of night, dressed as a boy?" she mused.

"I was escaping from the Saxons that your stupid nephew

invited here!" said Rachel angrily.

"What?" hissed Morgana, stepping towards her. "Your visions must be powerful for you to know this."

"Oh they are, we came a long way to warn everyone about Theodorus's plan," answered Rachel, unable to resist the temptation of not telling Morgana that, although she dreamt about the Saxons. The rest of her knowledge had been from overhearing Theodorus and the Saxons in the tunnels.

"You lie, you said you escaped from the Saxons, but they are not yet here. The Saxon boats will not come until tomorrow night, and I will not have you interfering with our plans," Morgana hissed menacingly.

"Wrong, Morgana!" retaliated Rachel with a certain amount of satisfaction. "Maybe your visions aren't as powerful as you think they are, because the Saxons are already here! There are hundreds of them in the tunnels and the boats are arriving tonight with more. Theodorus has been double-crossed by them, he doesn't know about the Saxons men that are already here and they won't be handing over this castle to him. If they win it, they'll keep it!"

"You are trying to deceive me," said Morgana, her dark eyes flashing with fury.

"No, I'm not, it's the truth," answered Rachel, realising that Morgana was between her and the doorway to the tower. She would have to get past her somehow to go and warn the others. "I heard the Saxons talking in the tunnels, I was chased by them and when I tried to come back to the castle, they were already here, hiding by the causeway. In any case, Galahad sent a rider to the castle to warn Merlin."

Morgana looked uncertain for a moment and glanced over the battlements, although the causeway was not in view from where they were.

"Maybe you should warn Theodorus!" said Rachel, in an attempt to appeal to Morgana's better nature, even though she actually doubted that the sorceress had one! It was at least worth a try though, as Morgana might, at least, be concerned about her nephew and leave her alone.

"You lie! No rider has entered the castle tonight!" declared Morgana. "Even Theodorus could not get it that wrong. He will become master of this castle in honour of his father!"

"In honour?" questioned Rachel. "So Mordred isn't alive then?"

"No, you killed Mordred in Avalon after time had been corrected. It would seem that your visions do not show you everything after all!" Morgana said angrily, sweeping towards her. Before Rachel could do anything Morgana grabbed her arms firmly and pinned her up against the wall. "I will show you a vision, a very powerful vision!" she continued. "I will show you what happened to my brother!"

Morgana's pale face was right next to Rachel's and the sorceress's black eyes bored into hers. Unable to move, Rachel could feel Morgana's anger as she gripped her wrists tightly. Then gradually the pale face in front of her started to grow distant, as a strange scene began to emerge.

Morgana's vision depicted a wild, windy night where the waves crashed unmercifully onto a beach. A lone, dark figure in long, ragged, black clothing danced in a circle, lit only by the moonlight. The wind tore at her clothing, and she danced wildly, holding up two bones, chanting furiously in a strange language. Her gyrating became more and more frenzied and there was a streak of lightening that hit the beach. The black swathed figure held the bones up to the moon, and the light bathed them. She screeched manically and resumed her frantic ritual. Rachel realised to her horror that this was Morgause and the place was where they had seen Mordred disappear into the quicksand.

Morgause stopped her fevered cavorting and raised the bones into the air again. There was a second streak of lightening, another crash of thunder and she threw the bones onto the sand, reaching into her tattered clothing to reveal a long dagger. She went over to a rock where she picked something up, and with a deranged scream she held up the limp, lifeless form of a large black bird. She cut it open and held it over the bones; its blood trickled down over them, spilling onto the sand. She threw the bird down next to the bones and raised her arms towards the heavens, chanting again in her pagan language.

Rachel found herself watching the macabre scene with a horrified fascination as the sand began to part, a hole started to appear and the bones and the bird disappeared into it. The sand didn't close around them, instead the hole appeared to get bigger and something began to push its way upwards. Rachel watched in horror, as slowly out of the sand appeared the dead, grey, soulless form of Mordred, propelled lifelessly upwards until the sand rushed around his feet, solidifying underneath his hideous form!

Chapter Seven
The Cat and the Conflict

Rachel knew that it was a vision and not real, but she still couldn't stop herself screaming at the dreadful sight of the grey, immobile shape of Mordred, the man they had watched die in the quicksand. Morgause chanted and shrieked abuse at her dead son's gruesome form until slowly his eyes opened, staring unseeing in front of him as she continued her frenzied tirade.

Suddenly the vision was gone and Rachel was aware of Morgana laughing with malicious satisfaction at her reaction.

"That was Morgause," Rachel said, shocked by the hideous scene she had just witnessed. "What on earth was she doing? That was Mordred!"

"Doing? I will tell you what she was doing," answered Morgana, nastily. "My dear mother was cursing her own son. She brought Mordred back from the dead and sentenced him to walk the earth until he destroys your brother, at whose hand he fell!"

"So Mordred is alive then?" asked Rachel, confused and still horrified by what she had seen.

"No, he is not alive and he is not even dead any more. Morgause has brought him back with her evil magic into the twilight realm of the undead!" said Morgana. "Mordred will walk as a creature with no soul and no mind forever, through every time and every passing year until he kills your twin! He will have no rest until he has done so!"

"That's disgraceful!" said Rachel, repulsed by the awful abomination she had seen. "What sort of dreadful mother would do that?"

"Mine!" spat Morgana venomously, and for a moment Rachel thought that maybe the beautiful, dark woman shared her own feelings on her mother's atrocious behaviour. The impact of Morgana's words and vision took shape in Rachel's mind and she realised that maybe Mordred had been the Knight at Warwick Castle that had tried to kill Gareth. Her blood ran cold at the thought of it.

"But the dead can't hurt anyone," she said, her words unconvincingly sounding more like a question than a statement.

"No they cannot," agreed Morgana, with a sinister smile. "But the undead can, their strength is immeasurable. In fact, they have an advantage, for they can kill the living if cursed to do so, but they cannot be killed, for they are already dead!"

This news was even worse and Rachel glanced past Morgana at the tower doorway and wondered if she could make a run for it. She had even more need to warn them now, especially if an undead Mordred could make an appearance at any time to kill Gareth!

"You will not escape me," said Morgana, as though she had intercepted Rachel's thoughts. "You will not spoil Theodorus's plans. You are coming with me!"

"Oh, no I'm not!" shouted Rachel, as the cold, black-haired sorceress muttered some strange words and pointed a long pale finger at her.

Suddenly, Rachel was hit by a force that took her breath away: she tried to cry out, but her mouth remained still. Morgana grabbed her again and pushed her along the battlements to the second tower. Although she tried to resist, Rachel's feet had a will of their own, and walked without protest, however hard she tried to stop them.

This must be one of her spells, thought Rachel, as she obligingly went against her will into the tower and down the stairs with Morgana, despite inwardly trying to fight against it.

Morgana took her through a small doorway underneath the stairs. It led to a long narrow tunnel that sloped downwards and Rachel felt as though it was going on forever until they came to a door. Morgana opened it and to her silent distress Rachel found that it led to yet another dark corridor. She wondered if these were the passages where her brother had lost his way, escaping from Gwelliant and Alfrick. Eventually they came to another opening, revealing a stone passageway with several small doorways. Morgana took her to the second heavy wooden door, opened it, and pushed her inside.

"Sit!" she said, pulling a chair into the middle of the spartanly furnished room and Rachel found her body again obligingly doing as the sorceress requested.

"You will stay here, where you can do no damage. I have used an obedience spell that even Merlin could not break. Your powers will be of no use to you!" Morgana informed her, as she went to the door.

Rachel struggled inwardly, willing her body to move or her mouth to speak, until finally, as Morgana was about to close the door behind her, she managed to shout. "No! You must listen to me! The Saxons are already here! They will turn against Theodorus and kill him as well! You must warn everyone!"

Morgana stopped in surprise. She looked at Rachel curiously for a moment before pointing at her again, delivering the same spell, which almost knocked her off her seat. The room went black and Rachel was silenced again.

Morgana closed the door behind her and pulled down a heavy latch, barring it completely. Just in case, she thought, now unsure of exactly how much magic Rachel could perform. Just in case the girl managed to defeat a spell again that should be impenetrable! The sorceress quickly transformed back into the form of a sleek, black cat and ran swiftly down the corridor, her soft paws making no sound.

Meanwhile, oblivious to his sister's predicament, or the death of Galahad's rider that had been sent to warn them, Gareth sat at the big table in the room next to the kitchen with Johnny and Bran. Completely unaware of the Saxons' new plans, they were all laughing over a jug of ale, the rest of the castle having retired long ago. Several of the other young knights had joined them and their mood was quite relaxed, thinking it would be another day before they would have to worry about a small Saxon invasion, one that the castle had already prepared for.

A black cat strolled lazily around their feet, and Gareth felt a curious shudder pass through him as it brushed past his leg. The cat padded over to the fireplace and curled up on its huge stone hearth, its dark eyes still watching him.

Gareth suddenly found himself rather guiltily, thinking about his sister.

"You've gone quiet, what's the matter?" asked Johnny.

"I was just wondering if Rachel was all right," Gareth answered.

"Well you did pack her off rather quickly!" said Johnny, reproachfully.

"I know I did, but I've just got used to doing things here on my own," agreed Gareth. "Anyway, I didn't want Rachel here if there was going to be a battle, but I'm just hoping that she got back okay."

"Yeah, of course she did, she'd be fine once she got to Valonia!" said Johnny. "There's no one that would hurt her there. I bet she's tucked up in bed at Catherine's, fast asleep after a mug of cocoa! Do you know, that's something I really miss here, a good cup of cocoa before bed!"

"That's sad!" joked Gareth.

"No, I miss my family even more, but I would still love a big mug of cocoa, all the same," said Johnny. "In fact, I'd even swap a jug of ale right now for a mug of cocoa!"

"Now, that's *really* sad!" laughed Gareth. "All this talk of cocoa's making me sleepy, it's really late, I'm going to have a walk and then go to bed."

"I'll come with you," said Johnny, and after saying goodnight to the others, they both picked up their swords and cloaks.

They walked through the castle and up the steps onto the battlements, unaware that the cat followed them silently. The wind hit them sharply as they walked, and Gareth still had a nagging feeling that something was wrong. He kept thinking about his sister, even though he knew that she was safe in Valonia.

"You've gone quiet again," stated Johnny. "Are you still worrying about Rachel?"

"I suppose so, I just can't shake off this really bad feeling that something isn't right!" he answered, "I can't explain it, but I keep thinking it's got something to do with Rachel!"

"You're just feeling guilty because you didn't go back with her. As I said before..."

"What the hell is that? It looks like a massive fire?" interrupted

Gareth, as they rounded the parapet overlooking the front of the castle. "Listen, there's a lot of noise over there, what's going on?" he said, pointing to the glow behind the trees in the distance.

"I don't know, but that's where Galahad's camp is," remarked Johnny. "You don't think the Saxons have attacked tonight do you?"

"I hope not, because they wouldn't be prepared for it. We'd better raise the alarm just in case. As long as there are sufficient men here to guard the castle, I think we ought to take as many as we can, to see if they need help."

"Yeah, hang on though; I'm sure I just saw some movement by the causeway. Look!"

"I can't see anything," said Gareth, scrutinising the area. "But, that definitely sounds like some sort of skirmish going on in the distance!"

"If that glow is from Galahad's camp, the Saxons may have already done their worst there, and they could be in place to start here."

"Right come on, we can't waste any more time," said Gareth. "You go down and send Bran and the knights to get everyone up and I'll go and tell Bors and Merlin."

They both ran off, Johnny along the battlements to the second tower and Gareth into the first to alert his mentors. The cat waited until they had gone and changed back into her human sorceress form.

Morgana leant against the battlements looking out in the same direction that the boys had done. Surely the girl hadn't been telling the truth, she wondered. Then she saw some movement in the undergrowth by the causeway and a thin glint of light as though the moonlight had caught a blade of steel. If the girl was right, and the Saxons were already here, could she also be correct that

Theodorus had been duped as a fool? Probably! Morgana thought. He was deserving of it, except that it now made her look as stupid as him, for going along with his ridiculous plans and agreeing to help him!

"Another failure!" Morgana said venomously, out loud. "Why did I ever believe that it would be any different with such an imbecile in charge?" Still, what did she care? If the Saxons won, she would creep off unnoticed, as a cat, or perhaps an owl, she mused. If the knights won, she could persuade them to take Theodorus's castle back; she had the girl to bargain with after all.

She heard the alarm go up and watched with indifference as the castle men ran out from every doorway to take up their positions. She heard footsteps running up the stairs to the battlements and quickly changed back into her feline form again, padding daintily along the parapet to take up a vantage point against the wall. After all, she thought, if the castle were to be finally taken, she might at least watch it! In the main courtyard, Merlin forbade Gareth and Johnny to ride out to Galahad. They both protested along with Bran, but were silenced.

"Merlin is right," said Bors. "There is naught that you can do for them. You cannot cross the causeway, if 'tis already surrounded. The Saxons would pick you off like ducks on the water! Do not worry, Galahad and his men are resourceful, they will be all right. There is plenty to do here: we might not be expecting many of them, but the Saxons are fierce in battle."

Reluctantly, they joined the others on the rampart looking out, waiting for any sign of movement and finding it unnaturally quiet and still.

"The noise from the camp has stopped," said Johnny. "I don't like this; I'm worried about Galahad and the others."

"We all are," replied Bran, putting his hand on Johnny's

shoulder. Gareth nodded sombrely in agreement as they waited silently with the rest of the castle for something to happen.

Rows of archers lined the walls of the battlements below them, tense and alert, waiting to fire the minute anyone approached the main entrance. Every man in Tintagel was armed with swords, bows or axes ready to defend it.

"Riders!" came a shout from below, and everyone's eyes looked to the causeway, where their approach could be seen. The lead rider was carrying Galahad's banner high. Gareth and the others recognised his colours straight away and breathed a sigh of relief that they were all right, until suddenly, the Saxons came out of hiding and swarmed up out of the bushes. The horses stopped and a fight broke out on the narrow strip of land as Galahad's men defended themselves.

"'Tis Galahad, the Saxons attack them on the approach! Make ready the Archers!" came a voice of authority, which they recognised as Bors. "Fire!" he commanded and arrows rained from the battlements.

"That's it! Get the others, we're riding out to help them!" shouted Gareth, and they all dashed for the stairway.

In the courtyard Gareth and Johnny ran for the horses, joined by Percivale and the young, newer knights that had become their friends. They mounted quickly and a party of twenty of them headed straight for the main gates. The men in charge were reluctant to open it, until Percivale instructed them, and they all rode through, armed to the hilt.

"Shut the gate behind us and tell the archers to keep firing on both sides of the causeway as they break their cover," Percivale commanded. "We will clear the approach for Galahad."

As they rode through the stone archway, they were immediately besieged by the Saxons. They had the advantage of being on horseback and their swords swept left and right as their enemies quickly converged on them from both sides. Johnny's axe made contact heavily with several men that leapt out at him, but as they fell back they were instantly replaced by more.

None of the horses could go any further as Percivale and the knights resisted their Saxon opponents on the causeway. One Saxon after another leapt at them fearlessly, only to met by a sword or an axe. The young knights fought with an equal ferocity and the archers above showered an experienced torrent of arrows on the Saxon men as soon as they came out into the open.

Eventually the party of young knights began to make slow progress forwards, still slashing their blades from one side to the other, as the blood thirsty Saxons attacked relentlessly. They managed to push their way to the middle of the causeway, where Galahad's men were still fighting, surrounded by the enemy.

Here, they banded together in a furious conflict against the Saxons. The knights turned their horses, and together they all fought their way back towards the gate with Galahad and his men joining them. A never-ending stream of arrows from the skilled archers flew down, hitting only their Saxon targets. Swords and axes swiped and hit, again and again, as the knights wrestled their way back to the safety of the castle.

The great gate opened again to allow them into the compound, where the knights and Galahad's men streamed in, all with blood on their swords. The last horse and rider rode through to safety, and the wooden gate closed behind them. The Saxons turned their assault to the castle walls, intent on gaining entry to the castle. They threw hooks and ropes over the walls as dozens tried to scale over. They were instantly met by the fierce men of the castle who severed their ropes with one swift axe blade, and those who managed to climb over the wall were met by a sword that was swiftly buried within them.

In the safety of courtyard the knights dismounted and several immediately took up a place on the ramparts, beside the men who were preventing the Saxons from climbing the walls. Shouts, screams and the sounds of the onslaught filled the air.

Still in her feline guise, Morgana watched with interest now from the battlements. So the knights were back, she thought, recognising Galahad. Maybe it was time for her to go down and listen to what they had to say. She leapt nimbly from her perch against the wall and ran down the stairs and out across the courtyard as quickly as only a cat could. She arrived in time to see the knights walking away from their horses, so she crouched in the shadows to listen.

"I thank you for your help," said Galahad, finding Gareth dismounting alongside Johnny and Bran. "We would not have made it across the causeway without you all!"

"We would have come sooner if we'd known!" said Gareth, clasping his arm in their usual gesture. "What the hell happened? Did the Saxons attack your camp first? Were many hurt?"

"No, we were lucky that Rachel came to warn us. We were ready for them, we have lost only a few," replied Galahad, looking puzzled. "Did she not tell you?"

"Rachel?" answered Gareth in surprise. "Rachel's not here, she's in Valonia. She went back!"

"Gareth, your sister did not go to Valonia. The Saxons were in the tunnels and she heard their plans. She came to my camp to warn me!" said Galahad, gravely.

"Where is she now then?" asked Gareth.

"She insisted on coming back here to warn you," Galahad answered. "I could not accompany her myself, so I sent her back with Drudwas. Is she not here?"

"No, she isn't! We haven't seen her or Drudwas!" answered Gareth, a feeling of dread gripping him.

There was a silence for a moment, as they all took in the enormity of Galahad's words and a worried look passed between Johnny and Bran.

"I can't believe you let her ride back here, when you knew that the Saxons were around!" shouted Gareth angrily. "If she's dead... it's... it's your fault!" he said, giving Galahad a push.

"At least I sent her with an escort, which was more than you did," replied Galahad furiously. "If you had ensured her safety to Valonia she wouldn't be here at all! When she arrived at my camp she was on foot and soaked to the skin! I looked after her and sent her back with my most trusted aid. Drudwas would have defended her with his life!" retorted Galahad. "If I had known the Saxons were by the castle, I would never have allowed her to leave. I would have protected her myself!"

"Rachel might be dead because of you - you let her go!" insisted Gareth, drawing his sword. "I can't believe you did that!"

"Gareth, she might be in hiding somewhere," said Johnny, ready to step in between them.

"If 'tis anyone's fault, 'tis yours," replied Galahad angrily, raising his own sword. "We have made sure that every woman here is safe, even in the villages. You did not think of your sister's safety when you left her in the tunnel to go back alone!"

"What on earth is going on here?" asked Merlin, rushing towards them as he noticed the two angry young men with their swords drawn. "Gareth! Galahad! Lower your swords!" he commanded.

"Gareth, do as he says," said Bran gently, putting a hand on his arm.

Gareth looked angrily at Galahad and then dropped his sword. He pushed Bran aside roughly and walked away.

"Try not to worry, she might be safe somewhere!" said Johnny, as he and Bran made to follow Gareth, to console him.

"My sister is out there with hundreds of Saxons and you're telling me not to worry?" Gareth shouted back, as Merlin put a hand on Johnny's arm to stop them.

"Leave him; let him be alone for a while. He will be grateful of your company later, when he has had time to calm down," Merlin said wisely.

Gareth walked blindly towards the tower doorway. He had vented his anger against Galahad and felt quite ashamed of himself. He knew that Galahad would never have willingly allowed Rachel to ride into danger and he shouldn't have blamed him. Inside he knew that the fault was his. He knew that he should have gone back with her to Valonia, or at the very least to the pass! Where was she, he thought miserably. Was she still alive? Did the Saxons have her? The thoughts of what might have happened to her were unbearable. Tears sprang to his eyes and he felt more dreadful than he had ever felt in his life.

Chapter Eight
The Sorcerer's Apprentice

Johnny and Bran watched a tormented Gareth enter the tower. Bran told Merlin what had happened and the wizard looked understandingly at Galahad.

"You must not blame yourself," Merlin said sympathetically.

"I am as guilty as Gareth," Galahad answered curtly. "I should not have let her go!" he finished, walking away from them.

"Oh hell, this is awful!" said Johnny, "I feel partly responsible as well!"

"It is no one's fault," said Merlin, patting him on the shoulder reassuringly. "Let us just hope that she is safe."

"Oh, I do hope so!" Johnny answered miserably.

Before Merlin could say any more, a man rushed towards them. "Theodorus is at the South wall with his men. They have climbed up the cliff. Do we let them in?" he asked.

"Do nothing until we have spoken to him!" said Galahad, turning back sharply. "Get some men, it could be a trap. He may be leading half the Saxon army up there!"

Unnoticed in her cat form, Morgana followed Merlin and

Galahad as they went with the guard to the South wall. Bran and Johnny rounded up the young knights and rushed after them. They made their way to the room where the secret entrance to the castle was. As they approached they could hear Theodorus shouting at the guards through the grill.

"Open it up now I say! Do you hear me?" his shrill, pompous voice screamed. "Quickly, before we are all killed!"

"I do not think you are in any position to give orders, Theodorus," said Galahad sternly, as he knelt down by the grill. "Why should we let you in?"

"The Saxons have turned against us; they have killed half of my men and taken my castle. You have to let us in!" he declared.

"No we do not! How do I know that this is not a trick?" asked Galahad. "How do we know that the Saxons are not with you?"

"If you leave us here much longer they will be. They are looking for us!" Theodorus shouted back.

"Then I am quite happy for them to finish you off!" replied Galahad, getting up. "Leave them where they are, let the Saxons kill them!" he instructed the guards.

"Open the grill," said Merlin, from behind him. "Galahad you are still upset; you are not thinking clearly, we cannot risk the Saxons finding this way in."

"Very well, if you insist," answered Galahad resignedly. "Let them up one at a time and take them prisoner," he said to the guards.

Theodorus came first and protested loudly when he was grabbed roughly and bound by a burly man. His men followed one by one, the grill was secured again, and they were all held captive by the knights and the guards.

"Take them down to the dungeons. We will deal with them later!" said Galahad.

"How dare you! You cannot put me in a dungeon!" shouted Theodorus indignantly. "Do you know who I am?"

"I most certainly do, and I will do with you as I damn well please!" Galahad returned. "Be thankful that I have not killed you!"

"You will not take them to the dungeons!" A woman's voice came from behind them and they all turned quickly to see the small, black cat that had been lurking behind them, stretching back into its human form.

"Morgana?" Galahad and Johnny cried in unison, shocked to see the dark sorceress appearing in front of them.

"Aunt!" said Theodorus with satisfaction. "Tell them to let me go. I demand it!"

"Be quiet," she hissed at him. "Snivelling fool, I've half a mind to kill you myself!"

"What part do you play in all of this, Morgana?" asked Merlin suspiciously.

"You will let them go," she said, ignoring Merlin's question. "They will fight with you against the Saxons and when they are defeated, you will take back Theodorus's castle and reinstate him there."

"What?" exclaimed Galahad. "How can you even dare to suggest it? Why would we do anything to help you or Theodorus?"

"Because I have the girl!" Morgana answered defiantly, with a toss of her long black hair.

"The girl?" questioned Galahad sharply. "You mean Rachel? You have Rachel?"

Bran and Johnny looked at each other delightedly, Rachel was alive and safe somewhere!

"Where is she? What have you done with her?" shouted Galahad, grabbing Morgana roughly by the shoulders and shaking her. "Tell me where she is!"

Morgana laughed and touched Galahad's neck. "Such a bad scar, tooth marks from an animal maybe? I'm sure you would not want to have another one inflicted on you."

"You are a nasty piece of work Morgana," he said, pushing her away.

"That's better," she said calmly. "Go along with my plan and the girl shall be returned."

"How do we know that we can trust you, Morgana?" asked Merlin. "How do we know that you even have Rachel?"

"I can show the boy, her brother. He is the only one here that may be capable of receiving a vision," she replied haughtily.

"You could show me, Morgana," said Merlin. "I can assure you that I am more than capable."

"Show a wizard? That would indeed be foolish," she laughed. "Do not take me for an imbecile like Theodorus! Get me the boy and I will show him."

"Can we at least go somewhere comfortable while we await all of this?" said Theodorus petulantly. "I am growing tired of all this nonsense."

"Silence!" Morgana shouted, and with a flick of a pointed finger, delivered a spell with a flash of light that threw her nephew across the room. He hit the wall with a hard bang and slithered down it, landing unceremoniously on the floor. "It is your fault that we are in this mess!" she finished.

With a yelp, Theadorus pulled himself up into a sitting position and leant against the wall in a daze, rubbing a large bump on the back of his head. Satisfied that Morgana's attention had turned back to Merlin, he started to shuffle on his bottom around the edge of the room towards the door, where he was apprehended by a large guard, who yanked him back up and held on to him with a vice-like grip.

"Go and get Gareth," said Merlin to Bran. "He will want to know that Rachel is alive and safe."

Bran left quickly and eventually returned with Gareth, who, in his anger had to be restrained from launching himself at the sorceress. Once Merlin had sufficiently calmed him down, Gareth followed Morgana into a small, dark stone room next door. She stood in the middle of the square chamber and waved her arm in a circle. A picture began to form on the rough surface of the wall. It was very dark and Gareth had to look very hard at it to see anything. Then he realised he was looking at another small, badly-lit room and he could just make out Rachel's figure, sitting on a chair in the middle of it, not moving.

"You may speak," Morgana said to Rachel in the picture, and Gareth saw Rachel look around her, startled by the voice that obviously reached her through Morgana's vision.

"Morgana? Where are you?" Rachel asked, looking puzzled.

"I am with your brother. He wants proof that you are unharmed, you may tell him who captured you, nothing more," the sorceress told her.

"Gareth? Morgana's put a spell on me and I can't move off this chair. I'm in a room under the..."

"Enough!" said Morgana, and the picture disappeared. "Now you will go and tell the others what you have seen," she instructed Gareth.

They went back into the room where Theodorus and his men were still held by the guards and Gareth nodded to Merlin. "I think Morgana is holding Rachel somewhere, she let her speak to me through a vision she conjured up," he said to the wizard, and then turning towards the dark sorceress added angrily, "I'm warning you Morgana, if you hurt my sister I'll kill you!"

"And if he doesn't, we will!" said Johnny resolutely.

"So, are you satisfied?" asked Morgana, ignoring their threats. "Do we have a bargain?"

"It would seem that we don't have much choice," answered Merlin. "Untie them."

"At last!" said Theodorus ungratefully, rubbing his wrists. "Now, I would like to be shown to a room. I am quite exhausted by all of this!"

"You will take your place at the wall with your men," hissed Morgana, before anyone else had a chance to say anything. "You will take your orders from the knights and you will help to defeat the Saxons that you brought here." Theodorus opened his mouth to protest, but she continued furiously. "Before you say any more, remember that I am still tempted to kill you myself, for the trouble and embarrassment that you have caused me!"

Johnny and Bran struggled hard to stop themselves from laughing as Theodorus snorted bad-temperedly.

"Take them down to Bors on the front wall, and tell him to keep a close eye on them," said Merlin.

The young knights nodded, and the men followed meekly. They looked almost relieved to be taking orders from the knights, instead of their insufferable master Theodorus, who complained all the way as to the great injustice of it all, for a person of his great standing. His wining voice grated on every single one of them.

"Now, we have kept our side of the bargain," said Merlin to Morgana. "You will bring us Rachel!"

"I am not that stupid, Merlin," replied Morgana. "The girl is quite safe. I will return her when Theodorus gets his castle back!"

"No, we will bargain again over this, once we have defeated the Saxons," retorted Merlin angrily, as he swept out.

As they followed him into the corridor, Gareth sheepishly

caught Galahad's arm, "I'm sorry, I had no right to blame you," he said. "I shouldn't have spoken to you like that earlier."

"It is not easy to admit to being wrong," Galahad replied after a moment. "We were both worried about Rachel. I will accept your apology, though I was hurt that you would think that I would ever willingly put your sister in danger."

"I know you wouldn't. I was just angry, mainly with myself, and I took it out on you," said Gareth.

"We have all done that," said Galahad, slightly more sympathetically. "The main thing is that Rachel is safe for the moment."

"Thank goodness!" chipped in Johnny. "I just wish we knew where she was."

"I think I know," Gareth whispered to him as Galahad strode off. "She was just about to tell me where she was, when Morgana stopped her. She said she was 'in a room under the...' and I'm sure she was going to say under the castle. There are rooms and corridors deep underneath us here and I wouldn't mind betting that's where she is!"

"So what are we waiting for? Let's go and find her," Johnny whispered back.

"We'll have to wait until everyone's busy outside, we can slip back then. They'll think we're still out there fighting," Gareth said.

Johnny nodded and they followed the others out into the courtyard towards the noise.

Deep under the castle in her dingy room, Rachel was still struggling to free herself from Morgana's spell. She at least had a voice now, as Morgana's attempt to silence her again hadn't worked. She hoped that Gareth had heard her tell him where she was, although it had gone very quiet after Morgana had shouted 'enough'. She tried again and again to unleash the Power, as she had before when she had magically become a seagull. Realising that she couldn't just wait to be rescued, in case Gareth hadn't heard her, she tried to will herself free, to no avail.

She looked down at her unresponsive hand and noticed the large ring that Argante had given her. She willed it to help her and suddenly she realised that she could move her fingers. She stared hard at the ring, silently asking it to break the spell and gradually the feeling came back into her arm, slowly travelling up towards her shoulder. She concentrated intently until she could feel the ability of movement spreading through her body eventually reaching her legs. She tentatively stood up. She was free! Now all she had to do was find her way back.

She went over to the door, but it wouldn't open. Undeterred and confident now, she stood back and imagined it opening, willing the Power to help her. The door burst open, the force almost taking it off its hinges and Rachel fled through it, delightedly, into the corridor. She ran to the right, trying hard to remember the way she had come. She found another corridor and ran on, but this one appeared to be going downwards and she was sure that was wrong. Surely she ought to be going up, not down! The corridors were so dark that she had trouble seeing her way and she was sure that a rat had just brushed her foot. She shuddered and carried on; it had to lead somewhere after all.

Rachel found that it led to a large room, well lit and well furnished, but a dead end nonetheless. She felt like crying now, the former exuberance of escaping had left her and was replaced by the fear that she had no idea where she was.

"Come in, my dear," said a voice, and Rachel drew back, ready to take flight again. "Oh, so pretty!" crooned an elderly female voice. "Do not be frightened, come in, come into the light where

I can see you."

Rachel stepped inside rather nervously and saw an old woman in a long black dress and white pinafore.

"Oh, so pretty," the old woman said again, distractedly. "What brings such a lovely maid down here?"

"I'm lost, I have no idea how to get back up to the castle again," said Rachel, honestly.

"Oh, don't you worry about that, my dear, I will get Alfrick to show you the way back, but come sit awhile with me. We do not get many visitors, and there is a dreadful battle against the Saxons going on up there," she said, leaning forward confidingly. "You are much safer here with us. I would wait awhile before you go back!"

"Thank you," said Rachel politely, realising that this could be Gwelliant, whom her brother had met before and had so much trouble with.

"Tell me, my dear, you are not from the castle, what brings you here?" Gwelliant asked.

"I was with Galahad in his camp. He sent me here for safety, because of the Saxons," she answered, deciding not to mention Gareth. Well, that part was true anyway and she had a feeling that she was going to have to be careful what she said to the old woman.

"And he was right to do so," Gwelliant nodded in approval. "Ah, Galahad, such a lovely young man, and nothing like his philandering father! Oh no, take it from me, he is nothing like him at all. He is an honourable knight and you are so pretty!" she repeated.

"Thank you," said Rachel, awkwardly.

"You will fare well with Galahad, he is a good man," concluded Gwelliant, knowledgably. Rachel nodded politely, realising that the old woman had jumped to conclusions about her relationship with Galahad. She decided to go along with it and humour her, in the hope that they would show her the way back.

After what seemed like an eternity of polite, awkward conversation, Rachel ventured, "I really must go, they will be wondering where I am."

"If you are sure, I will call Alfrick," said the old woman, disappearing through a small doorway, and Rachel breathed a sigh of relief. Gwelliant returned with the strange, lopsided Alfrick, whose toothless smile unnerved Rachel even more, and she shuddered at the thought of travelling back down the dim corridors with him.

He loped along in front and Gwelliant accompanied them to the end of the long corridor as though she was enjoying having a visitor. She held a gnarled hand out and Rachel hesitantly took it.

"It was so nice to meet you, my dear, and if the battle is too much for you, come back down to us, we will look after you," she said, her eyes glazing slightly at her last words.

"Thank you so much," said Rachel politely and the old woman smiled, but as she looked at Rachel's hand, her face changed.

"Where did you get that ring?" she said, gripping Rachel's hand tightly. "Who gave it to you?"

"I... er ... I can't say," Rachel stammered, remembering their promise to Argante.

"It was him, wasn't it?" said the old woman, her eyes gleaming. "You can tell me. I must know."

"I don't know who you're talking about," said Rachel, starting to panic.

Still clutching Rachel's hand tightly, Gwelliant looked up and down the corridor fearfully before answering her. "The young prince of course," she whispered.

"I... I... can't say, I made a promise never to tell anyone," said Rachel, trying hard to pull her hand away from the old woman.

"Of course you did, my dear, but you can tell me, I am the only person that you can tell. I must know where he is," she demanded and Alfrick moved closer, protectively, as he saw his mistress's distress.

Suddenly footsteps echoed noisily in the stone corridor as though someone was running, and they all turned sharply.

"Rachel!" shouted Gareth as he ran towards them, closely followed by Johnny. "Leave her alone, get your hands off her or I swear I'll kill both of you!" Gareth yelled, his sword pointed towards them.

Alfrick shuffled back several paces nervously, and Gwelliant let go of Rachel's hand, but the old woman didn't retreat. Instead, she stood and stared at Gareth, looking confused.

"Who are you?" Gwelliant asked, her eyes glinting suspiciously. "Is it...? No it can't be, you look different, older, and you are dressed as a knight."

"I'm Gareth, I'm Rachel's brother," he answered, pointing his sword defensively, "and she's coming with me."

"It's all right, Gareth," said Rachel, putting her hand on his arm. "Gwelliant wasn't going to hurt me, they were going to show me the way back, weren't you?" she added, feeling sorry for the old woman, who was clearly becoming quite befuddled. "Come on, let's go. Thank you for looking after me, Gwelliant," she finished sympathetically.

The old woman still didn't move. She looked at Gareth, in bewilderment, her head on one side, squinting up at him as though she was trying to work out who he was. She stared at them until they were out of sight.

On the way back through the corridors up to the main castle, Rachel told Gareth and Johnny about everything that had happened to her and Gareth shook his head guiltily. "I'm so sorry. I shouldn't have left you in the tunnel. I'm so relieved you're all right... I can't tell you! From now on you're staying right where I can see you!" he said, and for a moment Rachel thought she saw tears glistening in his eyes.

"Yeah, we were really worried about you," agreed Johnny. "And that old woman was scary enough without everything else that's been happening to you!"

"Tell me about it! It has been a bit eventful to say the least. I'm glad to be back!" Rachel replied.

They reached the end of the corridors, coming out next to an entrance by the stairs. Johnny left them and Gareth carried on with Rachel, through the bustling castle, to take her to the safety of Merlin's rooms.

Rachel filled Gareth in on everything that had happened to her and he was amazed at her story. She told him about Morgause and the undead Mordred and his face paled.

"I knew it was him in Warwick, but it just seemed so unbelievable that I told myself it couldn't possibly be Mordred. Maybe Merlin can do something about it," he said. "Anyway, what happened with Gwelliant, how did you end up with her?"

"I got lost in the corridors and ended up by her rooms," replied Rachel. "Gwelliant was lovely to me until she saw Argante's ring - in fact they were just about to show me the way back up to the castle. She suddenly went really strange, questioning me about it. She seemed to think a prince had given it to me."

"That might tie in with the stuff she was saying before, when I met up with her. She was convinced that I was someone else, so maybe that's Arthurs ring," Gareth answered as they reached the steps to Merlin's tower.

"I don't think so, Argante said the ring was hers, but that there was another one far away with its owner. Gwelliant definitely recognised it though; she looked quite shocked when she saw it!"

"More mysteries no doubt; the place is full of them. Nothing is ever straightforward here," Gareth commented, as they reached Merlin's door.

The old wizard hugged Rachel quite forcibly when he saw her and after a while Gareth left them to join the others against the Saxon attack.

Morgana had gone to watch the battle from the safety of the battlements on the seaward side and eventually grew bored with it. One battle was the same as any other and the Saxon attack was not making much of an impression on the castle defences, so she decided to check on her charge. She slipped back into cat guise again, and made her way through the castle and down the dark corridors before she changed back to herself again. She arrived back at the small room to find the door open and Rachel gone. She shrieked with fury and ran back the way she had come without even bothering with her disguise.

In the small bedchamber Rachel changed out of the rough trousers and tunic that Galahad had supplied. She washed her face and brushed her long hair feeling much better now that she was back in the safety of Merlin's quarters. When she went down the narrow staircase she found he had some simple food waiting for her and she sat and ate with the old wizard, suddenly realising that she hadn't eaten for a long time and was really hungry. Their peace was disturbed by a knock at the door. Merlin unlocked it and Galahad came into the room.

"Rachel, I am so pleased that you are safe!" he said sincerely. "I am sorry that I allowed you to go when 'twas not safe for you to do so. I would never…"

"It's okay, it wasn't you fault. I would have gone anyway, whether you 'allowed it' or not!" Rachel interrupted. "I just feel awful about Drudwas. The arrow looked as though it had gone straight through his chest. I wish I could have helped him, but I had to ride on before they hit me as well. I feel so dreadful that he may have died because he came back with me!"

"Drudwas lost his life following my orders to protect a lady," said Galahad. "He followed that order willingly, as any of my men would have done. He may not have been a knight, but he followed the same code. He has honour in his death and I will make sure that his family are well looked after."

"Oh no, I feel even worse now," she exclaimed. "Please don't tell me he had a wife and children, I couldn't stand it!"

"I will not torment you with any more details. It was not your fault," Galahad replied, and he turned to Merlin. "Morgana has discovered that Rachel has escaped and she is demanding a meeting with you, Merlin. She has guessed that Rachel is with you."

"Well, that was to be expected," Merlin answered. "Give me some time to prepare and then bring her up here. I would like Gareth and yourself to be present at this meeting."

"I will attend to it," answered Galahad. "How long do you need?"

"Half an hour will be ample," Merlin replied confidently.

Galahad left and Merlin locked the door behind him, looking serious as he turned to Rachel.

"Now, we haven't much time and I need to prepare you for this. I will try to disarm Morgana of her magic in this room, but she is clever, she will expect this and she will direct her powers towards any weakness that she can. That weakness will be you, so you must learn quickly," he said. "She will do anything to get you back in her power again."

"What? Oh great! I don't know how to stop her," Rachel returned, not wanting to take on the dark sorceress again.

"I will teach you, do not worry, but first the room," he answered, silencing her with a wave of his hand.

Merlin stood in the middle of the room and drew in a deep breath. He concentrated and then slowly raised his right arm and spread out his fingers. He drew an invisible circle in the air with his hand around the whole room, muttering something that Rachel either couldn't hear properly, or couldn't understand. When he had finished there was a brief, strange sound like electricity crackling.

"There, now, that is done," he said, with a satisfied chuckle. "And now you, my dear, we need to teach you magic!" He rubbed his hands together gleefully, and busied himself by carefully setting up several scrolls of parchment, upending them on his desk in a line. Rachel watched, slightly bemused as he picked up more items and set them along his cabinets.

"What on earth are you doing, Merlin?" she asked eventually.

"Target practice, my dear, target practice," he chortled "We do not have much time, and you must learn very quickly. You must learn how to defend yourself against Morgana's spells!"

He positioned himself and pointed towards the first parchment, which immediately burst into flames and disintegrated. "Like that," he said, clearly enjoying his demonstration, until it threatened to set fire to all of the others. He hastily ran over and removed the last burning pieces, patting a few stray papers that had already caught light, whilst Rachel watched, astounded at his bizarre behaviour.

"A sorceress has spells, set in her mind, that she can tap into straight away and deliver in a second. You have been using the Power, it will protect you from her and deliver your own retaliation," Merlin continued, rubbing his burnt fingers. "It's all quite simple really."

"I'm glad you think so!" Rachel answered dubiously. "But I can't do that, I have no idea how to use the Power."

"You don't have to use it, it is already within you," Merlin answered, undeterred. "Imagine you are Gareth holding Excalibur. He trusts the sword and delivers his blow, knowing that it will meet its target. Your powers are in your mind; direct your thoughts, point at the scroll and believe that it will fall. Now do have a go, my dear," he said, standing back. "It really is quite easy."

"Well, all right then," said Rachel, doubtfully. She fixed her eyes on a scroll tied with a piece of red ribbon at the end of the desk, pointing at it and willing it to fall. Nothing happened, so she tried again, and again, all to no avail. It wasn't until her ninth go that one of the scrolls she wasn't aiming at wobbled slightly, but even then it didn't fall over.

"I don't think this is working," she said dismally.

"Well it's a start," said Merlin, trying to sound encouraging. "Do keep trying, I'm sure you will get the hang of it eventually. Maybe I should have asked Galahad for an hour," he finished rather lamely. They were interrupted by a loud knock at the door and Merlin quickly piled the scrolls into a cabinet, before answering it.

Morgana swept in, followed by Galahad, Gareth and Bran, all three with their swords drawn, looking decidedly mistrustful of the dark sorceress. Her face was cold with fury and when her black eyes met Rachel's, she instantly knew that Merlin was right, it would only be a matter of time before Morgana attempted another spell on her.

Morgana stopped, looked around her and laughed. She waved her hand, and an orange ball of light suddenly appeared. It circled around the room, whizzing over their heads. They all ducked quickly as it passed them, before it exploded with a loud popping noise and a shower of sparks.

"Really, Merlin," Morgana purred. "I am very disappointed that you think I am not capable of detecting a disarming spell in your room."

"One that you seem to have disintegrated quite effectively, Morgana," answered Merlin, dryly.

"Indeed," she replied, with a smug look. "So, what are we to do now that you have the girl? What are your intentions?" the sorceress asked. "I want Theodorus reinstated in his father's estate."

"Sir," interrupted Bran. "I am greatly concerned for my family. They belong to the village next to Theodorus's fortress."

"Quite so, quite so," replied Merlin. "We must take into account the fate of all concerned."

"Are you intending to renege on our arrangement?" asked Morgana angrily. "I will let you keep the girl, but the agreement was that my nephew has his father's fortress."

"Hang on a minute here," joined in Gareth. "You were holding my sister prisoner when we agreed to your terms. You don't have her anymore, so the deal's off!"

"Gareth, please leave this to me," interjected Merlin, knowing that Morgana would instantly turn against Rachel, if Gareth wasn't silenced.

In the same split second Morgana did precisely that, and vented her fury with a spell directed in the form of a green, sizzling bolt of magic towards Rachel. This was exactly the moment that Rachel had been nervously expecting and her reaction was instant. She held up her hand instinctively and shouted, "No!" with a sudden new-found confidence. The magic hit the palm of her hand and bounced back, accompanied by a silver light that hit Morgana firmly on the chest and threw her backwards. She landed on one of Merlin's chairs, which shot back with a jolt, hitting the wall forcibly behind her.

Shaken, and even angrier, Morgana quickly stood up and delivered a second green flash, which was immediately blocked and counteracted by Rachel in the same way as before. The two bolts hit Morgana simultaneously and she fell backwards again into the chair. Rachel stepped forwards, her palm still facing her as the sorceress struggled to get up, only to be thrown back by an unknown force coming from Rachel.

Merlin rubbed his hands together in exuberance, quite delighted that his pupil had obviously learnt so quickly. The others simply stared at Rachel in sheer amazement at her new-found powers.

"You will not get up until I allow you to," Rachel told Morgana firmly. "You will listen to Merlin until we have sorted this out."

Morgana struggled, enraged and mortified to find herself bound by the very person she had held captive in the very same way not that long ago. Her struggles proved useless and she found herself forced to sit and listen to Merlin as he pondered wisely on the situation.

"Hmm," he said, stroking his beard thoughtfully. "Firstly, we still need to defeat the Saxons. Secondly, we will have to remove them from Mordred's fortress, as I am sure you will all agree that we do not want them as our neighbours and Bran certainly doesn't want them as his family's overlords. So it would seem that our original agreement still stands, Morgana. We will take back Mordred's fortress, but its ownership will depend largely on the behaviour of yourself and your nephew."

"Have you lost the plot?" asked Gareth. "Are you seriously saying that you would give the castle back to either of them? It's their fault that the Saxons are here in the first place!"

"Mordred's castle will be taken back from the Saxons," said Merlin. "It will be taken by the knights and its ownership will be given to the rightful person. That person will have to demonstrate that they will treat its servants well and they will also have to agree to join us in our continuing pursuit of Arthur's cause. If there is no one willing to do this, we will not reinstate anyone, and it will become part of the Tyntagyle heritage held by us."

"I think that Merlin is giving Morgana or Theodorus the chance to mend their ways and become a good leader of their people," said Rachel quietly.

"I am indeed, my dear," agreed Merlin. "There are those who know the difference between right and wrong, but will always choose the wrong path. There are also those, however, who have been surrounded by darkness all of their lives and know no other way. They cannot be blamed for this and should be given the chance to see the error of their ways and redeem themselves."

There was a brief silence as they all guessed he was referring to Morgana, who had stopped struggling against Rachel's magical force and was now sitting quietly, digesting Merlin's proposal.

"Are you saying that if I join forces with you, you would give Mordred's inheritance to me?" she asked suspiciously, "instead of Theodorus?"

"I have said that our former agreement still stands," said Merlin firmly. "But once we have secured Mordred's fortress, its fate will depend entirely on you."

Morgana stood up, entirely oblivious to the fact that Rachel had released her from the power that had been holding her. "It would seem that your offer is an honourable one," she said, with a certain amount of surprise in her voice. "I am prepared to make a pact with you; we will fight on the same side and you will return my brother's heritage to me."

"Only if you can prove that you are deserving of it," Merlin reminded her. "These are our conditions, and they are life long.

The minute that the inheritor reverts back to their former ways we will take back the fortress and they will be banished from Cornwall."

"I will accept your proposal, we will continue with our pact," said Morgana, drawing herself up haughtily, as though she had been in control of the whole situation.

"Think long and hard about its implications, Morgana," warned Merlin. "We have made an agreement but if the conditions are not met, we will retract it!"

"I understand that," Morgana said, as she opened the door. "I see no reason to tell Theodorus about this just yet. Leave him with your men," she finished grandly, as she swept out, leaving an astounded party behind her.

"Woah, how did she manage to just make it sound as though she was doing us a favour?" Gareth asked scornfully. "I can't believe that you would even think of trusting her."

"There are many things that you don't know about Morgana. I see no reason not to give her a chance," Merlin replied.

"Well I can think of plenty – Galahad's neck for example," insisted Gareth crossly, "and the fact that you never know what disguise she's in."

"Maybe we should concentrate our efforts on keeping this castle from the Saxons," said Merlin curtly. "None of this will even be relevant if we loose it!"

"Come, let us join the men," interacted Galahad and Gareth nodded, following them out, albeit rather moodily.

Chapter Nine
Chariots of Fire

The battle raged on throughout the rest of the day. As darkness came the Saxons retreated and the castle became eerily quiet. The men made their preparations for the next day and the wounded went inside to be attended to. Despite a day's fighting, the casualties in the castle were superficial and low and the Saxons had not made any headway at all in penetrating its defences.

It was late when Gareth and Rachel met up with Bran and Johnny in the room next to the kitchens, where they sat round the large, rough wooden table to eat. Their mood was sombre and they were all exhausted. It had been a long day fending off the Saxons and they ate almost in silence. Gareth knew that Bran and Sarah were worried about their families since the Saxons had probably returned to Mordred's fortress to regroup. Even if they were to give up their attack on Tintagel, they would most certainly want to keep the fortress.

"Don't worry," Gareth said to Bran. "The women from your village are all in hiding. Your mother and sisters are safe for now, and if the Saxons stay, then we'll bring them here. I promise you that."

"I would ask you to make a further promise," said Bran, looking troubled.

"Anything, ask away," answered Gareth immediately.

"I would ask that if anything should happen to me, you would make sure that my family and Sarah are looked after?" Bran asked earnestly. "It troubles me that since my father and brother's deaths, I am the only man left to take care of them."

"Of course we would, you don't even need to ask that," said Gareth adamantly.

"Bran, that's a dreadful thing to even think about," joined in Rachel, "nothing's going to happen to you!" She turned to Sarah and said quietly, "you know that we would always make sure that you were all right."

"Thank you, miss," Sarah instantly replied. Her subservient attitude and round-eyed look of fear were not entirely what Rachel had wanted to see. She realised then that Sarah would never be a friend; she would always see her as a sorceress, and always be afraid of her.

As soon as their meal was finished, they all decided to retire for the night and went their separate ways, each wondering, what the next day would bring.

The morning proved quiet, the onslaught on the castle, expected at daybreak, didn't happen, but an air of apprehension still remained as Rachel and Merlin had breakfast in his room, joined by Gareth and Johnny.

"We've been down on the front wall for an hour or more and there's no sign of the Saxons," said Gareth. "Do you think they've given up?"

"I doubt that they will give up anything, since they have come so far for it," said Merlin, dampening their hopes instantly.

"Well, it's very quiet out there," answered Gareth, still sounding hopeful.

A knock at the door revealed Galahad with news, and they all listened attentively, expecting the worst.

"The Saxons are back. They line the causeway and are surrounding the approach, but they are not attacking. Instead their leaders approach the gate," he said. "Kay and Bors are on their way down to talk to them, and I thought that you would want to be present, Merlin."

"Most certainly!" Merlin replied, hastily wiping his beard with a napkin. "Lead on, dear boy, I would be glad to hear what they have to say."

He jumped up and went with Galahad down the stairs. They all followed, anxious to hear for themselves, but were all stopped by Percivale as they rushed to join the wizard at the outer courtyard.

"Leave it to Merlin and the knights. If we were all to go, their leaders may feel threatened and order another attack. They will bargain with them," Percivale advised.

Disappointed, the twins and Johnny made their way back to the turret and on to the battlements to watch from afar. Bran joined them and from their high vantage point they could see the Saxon leaders talking to Galahad, Kay, Bors and Merlin and wished that they could hear the conversation. The air was still and quiet and the whole castle was tense. Every rampart was lined with archers poised to fire if the Saxons made so much as a move against their leaders. They watched apprehensively as discussions were obviously underway below them.

"There's something not right here," said Rachel. "I don't even think it's the Saxons, there's something else coming!"

Johnny, Bran and Gareth looked at her strangely, but before they could answer, a voice came from behind them.

"You feel it too?" said Morgana, as she swept onto the battlements.

"What is it, Morgana? It feels... it feels like something evil approaching."

"I do not know, but I feel it strongly. It calls out to me," the sorceress replied.

"Well, it must be something bad then, if it's calling you," replied Gareth rudely.

"Aunt," came Theodorus's shrill voice as he stepped out of the turret doorway and approached them. "They are bargaining over my castle down there, and that awful Percivale would not allow me through. I demand that you do something about it!"

"Shut up, Theodorus!" the whole group replied in unison, the eerie stillness making all of them nervous.

"Have you noticed there are no seagulls," said Johnny. "I've never stood up here and not heard them calling to each other. The place is normally swarming with them!"

"Yes, you're right, it's too quiet," agreed Rachel. "There's something else here!"

"What the hell is that?" asked Gareth suddenly, pointing to the hills on the horizon. "There's a glow coming towards us. It looks as though there's a fire starting over there behind the trees, look!"

"Surely the Saxons wouldn't be starting a fire while their leaders are talking to ours?" asked Johnny.

They stared at the glow in the distance, wondering what could be causing it. Gradually it drew nearer to the edge of the causeway and they found that source of light was coming from a golden chariot surrounded by flames.

"What on earth is it?" asked Gareth again.

"It will be Morgause," said Theodorus delightedly. "She has come to make sure that I have my castle back!"

"You stupid, stupid fool," shouted Morgana, shooting one of her livid green spells at Theodorus in her anger, bowling him straight over into a heap. "You asked her for help while she was with Rathyen? Do you realise what you have done?"

"Of course!" Theodorus replied, picking himself up off the floor and brushing his long embroidered gown fastidiously with his hand. "And it is a good job I did, as you were of no use when the Saxons turned against me! You even allowed these peasants to order me to fight on a wall with the serfs," he continued, with an over-exaggerated shudder. "Before we came up the cliff, I sent a rider to my grandmother for help. She will make sure that my inheritance is returned to me!"

"You brainless simpleton!" Morgana screamed at him. Her second green spell lifted her nephew into the air and threatened to throw him off the parapet. He hovered on the edge, his feet just about touching the stone blocks, shrieking with terror, with his arms thrashing wildly as he struggled for balance. "Rathyen will not return anything to you," she spat at him venomously. "She will only be here for what she can take for herself!"

She dropped her hand, releasing him, and he leapt off the high stone ledge that he had been precariously balancing on, whimpering for a moment until his usual arrogance returned once he realised he was safe.

"How dare you! You will regret this. I will have grandmother destroy you!" he shouted, and disappeared down the turret stairs.

"What the hell is going on here, Morgana?" asked Gareth. "Is that Morgause coming? What's that fire around them? What is going on?" he finished angrily.

"Yes it's Morgause and Rathyen is with her," Morgana answered in a subdued voice. "The fire will be from Rathyen's dragons. She keeps them in chains, but has obviously decided to unshackle them for once, to pull her chariot."

"Dragons?" answered Rachel in surprise. "I had no idea that they even existed."

"Well, you'll be all right then, Morgana," Gareth said scornfully. "They won't hurt you or Theodorus. It'll be the rest of us that they're after."

"You have no idea how wrong you are," Morgana replied, drawing herself back to her usual haughtiness. "Oh yes, since you humiliated Rathyen with the Chalice, she will be out to destroy every one of you. Rathyen had never been defeated before that event and she will not have forgotten it!"

"Why did you say Gareth was wrong?" asked Rachel. "Why would it affect you? You were on their side last time!"

"There is bad blood between Rathyen and myself," she answered.

"And?" prompted Gareth, when Morgana didn't appear to want to elaborate on her statement.

"When I was six years of age, Morgause sent me to Rathyen, to be her apprentice, to learn the dark magic that was much more powerful than her own," she said with a sigh. "I was bound to Rathyen for seven years, guarded by creatures that you could not even imagine in your worst nightmares. I learnt that magic and used it against Rathyen to escape. She has not forgotten that either!"

"But you fought with Rathyen last time," stated Gareth, unconvinced.

"No I did not," Morgana replied. "Mordred asked for my help and I was curious. I had heard of the Chalice and its powers and I was drawn in by him and my mother. I had no contact with Rathyen and I did not know that Morgause had enlisted her help."

"To be fair, Rathyen arrived after Morgana had died, as wolf, in the cave," said Rachel. "I think the two witches were Morgause's contingency plan."

"I have not seen Rathyen since the age of thirteen when I struck her with one of her own spells to escape," answered Morgana. "Rathyen will not kill me, she would do much worse than that. She would bind me for life, as she has done with others. You have no idea how powerful or evil she is."

"Great!" said Gareth, looking towards the chariot approaching across the hills, "and she's descending upon us as we speak!"

As Rathyen and Morgause drew nearer the causeway, Gareth and Rachel could see the dragons quite clearly. They were imposing creatures: huge, with thick green scales, long necks, small heads and wide nostrils. They dwarfed the golden, open-backed chariot that they were harnessed to and they snorted, pulling against the reigns held tightly by Rathyen - who was standing up at the front of the chariot. Her long grey hair straggled down over her shoulders and she was dressed in black. Morgause stood beside her, looking as evil as ever, the wind catching her tatty, black clothing and blowing it out like streaming ribbons all around her.

The talks below between the Saxon leaders, Merlin and the knights ceased instantly as they all turned in astonishment at sight of the new arrivals. The chariot mowed its way through the Saxon men at the edge of the causeway, and they were so shocked to see the dragons that they fell back without even a protest. For a moment the small party of leaders all stared in disbelief, until the dragons snorted loudly and threw back their heads, launching a pillar of flames across the narrow strip of land.

Sudden mayhem began. The Saxon men ran in any direction they could to get away from the dragons' fiery onslaught, whilst the knights and Merlin ran back towards the gate. They dashed inside the stone entrance just in time as the edges of Merlin's gown started to smoke from a lick of flames that singed them. The heavy gate was closed firmly behind them, leaving the Saxon leaders to their fate. The bushes and trees surrounding the causeway caught fire in the blast and the Saxon leaders ran after their already fleeing men. A second roar from the dragons caught most of them on the causeway and those who were not already on fire, jumped into the drop on either side of it to escape the fiery channels that the dragons delivered again.

The third roar contained a blast of fire from both of the dragons that blew the enormous castle gate off its hinges. The entire army of people in the outer courtyard ran towards the inner walls that protected the castle, while the archers on the parapets rained arrow upon arrow at the large, fire-breathing, scaly beasts. The arrows had no effect at all and bounced off them like rubber balls. Instead the dragons looked up at them and the archers were treated to an attack of fire that sent them falling from the battlements into the inner courtyard or onto the rocks below. The wooden roofs on the simple buildings surrounding the courtyard caught fire and everyone ran towards the castle, fleeing for the safety of the great stone building. When the last person was in, the doors were barricaded as the golden chariot was drawn in through the outer courtyard by the equivalent of two giant, fire-breathing, bulldozers.

"This is unbelievable!" said Gareth, breaking the silence between them as they watched the utter chaos below, where everyone was running for their lives. The chariot stopped, but the harnessed dragons' tails swished from side to side, demolishing anything in their way, as they reared up and breathed fire in every direction.

Merlin and Galahad joined them all on the battlements, out of breath from their sprint from the dragons, as another blast of fire in their direction sent everyone ducking down behind the stone battlements for protection.

"The castle will not last long against these dragons, we must use magic to defeat them," puffed Merlin, clutching his side. "We have two Keepers of the Power, and with my help we might just manage to hold them back!"

"Do not forget that you also have a great sorceress," said Morgana, coming forward.

"You would fight with us against them?" asked Merlin in surprise.

"I would indeed, and even better than that," she answered. "I can tell you how to defeat them."

"I am listening," answered Merlin cautiously. "But can we trust you?"

"I think that Morgana has her own reasons to stand against Rathyen," interrupted Rachel. "I think you can trust her."

Morgana looked at Rachel curiously for a moment before answering. "Dragons are particularly unstable animals," she said, as another blast of fire made them all duck again, the dragons indirectly reinforcing her point. "They are not tame. Rathyen is cruel; she dominates them with her powers. If she forces them into a situation they do not like, they are just as likely to turn against her."

"What do you suggest?" asked Merlin.

"Rachel and I will take on Morgause and Rathyen. You, Merlin, will take on the dragons," Morgana said. "Dragons hate salt water and you have the sea all around the castle. Could you summon up waves big enough to swamp the courtyard and the dragons as they are about to breath their fire?" she asked him.

"Ingenious," replied Merlin, ecstatically. "I most certainly can!"

"It is easy to see when they are about to breath their flames. If you watch them, they bring back their heads and breathe in deeply before exhaling their fires. Time the waves to drench them as they exhale, their flames will be extinguished and they will choke on the water."

"Ingenious!" repeated Merlin again, rubbing his hands together delightedly. "We shall do exactly that! Rachel, Morgana, take your places. I shall prepare myself and summon waves large enough to finish off the biggest dragon!" he said enthusiastically. "Now, where shall I stand? Oh yes, I have exactly the right place," he said, looking up at the ledge around the tower. "Come along now, Rachel, make haste! Get in place with Morgana!"

He turned away before Rachel could even protest, and he began climbing up to the highest point he could find. His gowns flapped around him and the wind blew his long white hair into complete disarray as he climbed up onto the narrow ledge. He was so excited and intent on his task that he seemed oblivious to the blast of fire from the dragons that hit the middle of the tower, threatening to catch his long gowns and turn him into a flaming beacon that would be seen for miles.

"He's going to be burnt alive if he isn't careful," remarked Johnny as they ducked again.

"Morgana, I can't take on Rathyen, I'm not as powerful as you," said Rachel honestly.

"Oh yes you are," Morgana replied, pushing her forward to the front of the tower. "I have watched you. I don't know how your power works, but when you are threatened you can release a force equal to Morgause or Rathyen."

"I'm sure I can't!" Rachel answered, as they stood against the battlements, facing their enemy below.

"Well, even if you cannot, and the legend is true, the ring that you are wearing will certainly help you," said Morgana, looking at the large ring on Rachel's finger.

Before Rachel could ask what Morgana meant, she heard Rathyen yelling at the dragons, who drew back their heads, preparing for their next blast. Merlin conjured up two waves that hit the castle, one from each side. A deluge of water hit the parapets and showered over the great scaly beasts. The dragons spluttered and coughed, their tails whipped to and fro angrily, turning the chariot around in a circle.

Rathyen screamed at them again, and pulled hard on the reigns. The metal-studded leather and chains around their small heads bit into them cruelly as Rathen fought to bring them under control. The dragons started to panic, thrashing wildly as Rathyen yanked hard at the reigns again, pulling their heads from side to side. Merlin quickly sent another gigantic swell that rushed towards the castle, spraying everyone on the battlements as it crashed against the rocks and high walls. Then, like a large waterfall, it cascaded into the lower courtyards, swamping the dragons. They reared up, frantically gulping and gasping for air, pulling the reigns out of Rathyen's hands and the chariot spun as the dragons shook their heads furiously. Their strong tails thrashed from left to right, creating even more waves in the water that had filled the courtyard. The water churned and splashed up against them, agitating them even further. Black smoke billowed around them as their flames were extinguished and Rathyen and Morgause clung to the sides of the chariot to stop themselves from being thrown out.

Another large wave from Merlin soaked them all completely. The dragons went wild, the fire they tried to breathe in every direction came out as more smouldering clouds of choking smoke and they coughed and spluttered again, shaking themselves in their determination to get away. They rocked from side to side until the front of the chariot broke up, and they were free. The dragons turned, one to the left and one to the right of the disintegrated conveyance and stampeded back towards the gateway, taking two broken front halves of the chariot with them. Their great swishing tails demolished a section of the castle wall on either side as they rushed past. By the time they reached the stone archway, only the remains of the harness was still trailing behind them, and as they charged through it, the huge stones tumbled down behind them.

Morause and Rathyen lay in a wet, bedraggled heap of dishevelled black gowns, on the chariot floor. They struggled dizzily, to pull themselves back up, but as the dragons wrenched away the front half of the chariot, it tipped forwards with a crash. The two witches fell again, and gripped the chariot sides, to stop themselves from being pitched out into the several feet of water that had turned the courtyard into a pool. Rathyen's once ornate chariot now resembled a smashed cart and they struggled to untangle themselves. The two witches stood up in what was left of it, their eyes sweeping the battlements for the cause of their latest humiliation.

Rathyen saw Merlin first, still perched on his ledge on the tower and in fury she sent a sizzling green laser of magic that flew towards him.

"Now! We need to counteract her spells!" shouted Morgana, quickly pointing at Rathyen's streak of green magic that was heading towards the tower. Morgana sent a green bolt of her own, which hurtled towards Rathyen's spell. The two zig-zags of magic, akin to lightening, fused together in mid air, exploding with a bang and enough sparks to put any firework to shame.

Rathyen and Morgause's attention immediately turned to the two young women facing them on the battlements.

"Who are their sorceresses?" Rathyen asked Morgause.

"'Tis that cursed girl again!" said Morgause. "The one that took the Chalice!"

"And the other?" asked Rathyen. "Is that not your daughter, Morgana?"

"She is no daughter of mine!" answered Morgause firmly, sending her own crackling spell up to the battlements.

This time it was Rachel who intercepted it, she held up her hand and the spell bounced back towards the old witches with an accompanying silver streak. It hit the cart with enough force to tip it backwards again and the two women tumbled back, sliding down almost into the water. They struggled up and whispered to each other in a huddle of wet, black garments.

"We need a much stronger magic to defeat this white witch," said Rathyen. "I will deal with her!"

Rathyen muttered and mumbled, then threw her arms up to the sky with a terrible blood-curdling scream. The appalling screech seemed to amplify, ringing around the tower, and everyone there automatically put their hands over their ears to shut it out. Although her dreadful shriek ended, Rathyen laughed at their discomfort as it continued ringing round and round in their heads. "A spell to drive them insane and destroy their minds," she said proudly to Morgause, with a cackle. "They will still be listening to it when they throw themselves into the sea to escape it!"

Morgause congratulated her druid friend gleefully; impressed by the dark magic that Rathyen could perform.

On the battlements they all held their heads in pain apart from Rachel and Morgana. Merlin almost fell in his haste to get down from his perch and clung to the tower for dear life. Morgana stood transfixed as though the spell had captured her and Rachel found that she seemed to be the only one able to resist whatever force Rathyen was torturing everyone with. Rachel faced Rathyen defiantly; she looked at Argante's ring and summoned the Power with all the strength that she could muster.

"No!" Rachel shouted, directing her resistance at the old, evil sorceress. Rachel held her hands up and it was as though the dreadful noise swept from everyone on the battlements. Rathyen's spell whistled through the air again like a banshee, rushing towards Rachel. She stood firmly and as it came towards her it diminished into a squeaking whine as though Rachel had somehow absorbed it. It rushed around her in a high-pitched resonant and then suddenly it was silent again. Morgana staggered sideways as though released from something, but before she could regain her thoughts, a bright green streak of magic flew from Morgause like a dart towards her. It hit her daughter like a forceful punch and Morgana fell straight over the top of the stone battlements.

Johnny sprang into action and grabbed a handful of Morgana's clothing as she disappeared over the edge. He hung on to her and slowly dragged her upwards, grabbing her arms to pull her up. Gareth joined him and together they roughly dragged Morgana back over the parapet, where she fell in a heap on the stone floor.

Oblivious to the rescue behind her, Rachel was left to deal with Rathyen, who was insanely muttering incantations below. She knew the spell the old woman was conjuring would be directed solely at her now and she dared not take her eyes away in case she should lose control of the Power. Rachel could feel the evil sorceress's eyes burning into hers and she met the stare, refusing to let Rathyen's spell affect her. She tried desperately to visualise the words in the old black book. The spell, *'vanquish thine enemies'* came to mind, but she couldn't remember the words. She tried again and again to remember it, but in the end she just asked silently for the Power to help her.

Rathyen found her efforts to send her strongest destroying spell to Rachel, were not working. She felt a strange resistance to it, as though it were being sent back, and she muttered frantically to protect herself. Realising that Rathyen was having difficulties, Morgause sent one of her green magic sparks flying through the air, intent on it hitting Rachel. To her horror it bounced against an invisible shield in front of the battlements and shot back at her, releasing Rathyen's destroyer spell along with it. The two spells came back like a grenade, landing in-between them. The remains of the golden chariot blew up and the two old sorceresses were thrown into the air like rag dolls, landing in the water with two large splashes.

In the meantime, Merlin had scrambled back onto his high ledge and before the two old women could get up, he sent another large wave over the walls, knocking Rathyen and Morgause back into the water again. They splashed and floundered, choking on the water. Another wave sent them under again and washed them along with chunks of wood from the chariot over to the castle walls. The two defeated witches heaved themselves up, hanging on to the stone masonry. Up to their thighs in water, they scrabbled their way around it, tripping over the debris left by the dragon's departure. They dragged themselves into the outer courtyard, where they found two horses and mounted them, wet and bedraggled.

From the high battlements by the tower, the party watched with great relief, as Morgause and Rathyen rode away, across the causeway. Merlin climbed down, aided by Gareth, and they all surveyed the scene of destruction below them.

"Those two women have managed to do more damage than any army that has ever attacked us," said Merlin wryly, as he looked at the collapsed wall, the spirals of smoke coming from the burnt roofs and the large pool in the courtyard which was now draining away down the sides of the rocks in small waterfalls. "It is unheard of! Dreadful!" he said shaking his head.

"Well, it could have been worse," remarked Gareth. "They could have won!"

"Indeed, you are right, dear boy," Merlin answered. "We must be thankful for that, and the dragons did at least finish off most of the Saxons for us!"

Still stunned and extremely relieved that it was over, everyone made their way towards the turret door. Johnny stood back to allow Morgana to go in front of him.

"You stopped me from falling to my death," she said to him, as she entered the turret. "Why did you do that?"

"What? Well, it sort of seemed the right thing to do really, since you were fighting with us," Johnny answered, looking embarrassed.

"No one has ever done anything like that for me before," Morgana said, looking at Johnny intently. "I must thank you for that," she added, in a tone that was almost humble.

"Oh, right, well, don't worry about it," Johnny mumbled awkwardly, aware of Morgana's searching gaze.

"We will have celebrations in my rooms tonight, I think. A celebration of our victory and our combined magic," said Merlin, from behind them.

"Sounds good to me, Merlin, I'll go down with Johnny to see how the rest of the castle has fared. We'll see you later," replied Gareth, as Merlin unlocked his door. Rachel went in to Merlin's room as he stopped to speak to Morgana.

"You are welcome to join us tonight, Morgana," said Merlin. "Your help was greatly appreciated."

"Thank you," she replied, looking surprised at the invitation.

"I do know what it may have cost you to join us in that battle," Merlin said quietly. "Sometimes we have to face our own demons, and that is not easy."

Morgana said nothing. She merely nodded and carried on down the stairs.

Chapter Ten
Bats across the battlements

Later that night they all met in Merlin's rooms, the food was piled high on large platters and they all recounted their dreadful battle against the Saxons and the sorceresses. Galahad joined them and Bran came without Sarah, who he said had seen the dragons earlier and could not be persuaded to leave her room.

"I will not stay long," Bran said. "I will have to get back to Sarah as she gets very frightened by magic of any sort."

"Oh dear," replied Rachel, guiltily, since it was her appearance originally that had probably started off Sarah's fears. "It's a shame she wouldn't come."

The evening passed pleasantly and everyone was in good spirits. Gareth decided to stay on a few more days until they knew that the Saxons had left. He assured Bran that they would make sure his mother and sisters in the village were all right before they left and Rachel agreed to stay with him so that they could go back together.

Even though Rachel knew that most of the Saxons must have been killed, she still had an uneasy feeling that this wasn't the end of it. Galahad joined her and she mentioned it to him. He looked at her strangely and there was an awkward silence for a moment.

"Sorry, maybe I shouldn't have said anything," she said, rather glumly. "I know you're not very comfortable with magic and visions!"

"Yours is not a sorcery that I am uncomfortable with," Galahad replied, good-humouredly. "In fact, I have grown used to it. I am merely hoping that you are wrong this time. I don't think the castle would stand another assault until we have repaired the damage the dragons have done."

"I'm probably just imagining it," Rachel returned. "In fact, listening to all this talk of today's events is probably making me worse. I think I might go for a walk to get away from it."

"I will accompany you, if I may," said Galahad, courteously.

Morgana had decided not to join their celebrations; instead she stood on the battlements looking out to sea, hurt that her mother had tried to kill her. She knew that the spell Morgause had sent was a strong one and that her mother had intended it to cause her to fall to her death. She was used to her mother's dark ways and she shrugged, wondering why she should have expected anything any different. Morgause had never cared about her, even when she was a child. She heard voices and she walked further round the battlements so that she was out of sight. She waited a few minutes and looked back round the edge of the wall to see Rachel and Galahad talking. She watched them and felt a strong pang of jealousy.

Eventually, Galahad left and Rachel stood on her own, leaning against the parapet and, for a moment, Morgana thought how easy it would be to creep up behind her and just push her over. She resisted the thought and instead walked over to her. Rachel jumped when she realised it was Morgana and looked nervous.

"I have not come to do you any harm," Morgana said, "although the thought of pushing you over did occur to me."

"So what stopped you then?" asked Rachel.

"I have some questions," Morgana replied. "Why did Johnny save me? And why did Merlin ask me to join in your celebrations?"

"Johnny is a really good person, he would do that automatically, as you were fighting on our side at the time," Rachel answered. "Merlin invited you because you helped us; he thought you should be included."

Morgana looked thoughtful before asking, "Why does Galahad court you, when you are a sorceress? He hates sorcery, and I am far more beautiful than you, yet he despises me."

"Yes you are, Morgana," Rachel replied with a laugh, "and he isn't 'courting' me!"

"I saw you together just now and 'tis fairly obvious that he is smitten with you," she insisted. "He has always liked you; I have seen it in his eyes before."

"He's a friend, that's all," Rachel answered, slightly puzzled by Morgana's comments.

"You are seemingly a sorceress with a lot of 'friends.' How is this?" Morgana asked.

"I'm not quite sure what you mean. What is it that you really want to know, and why are you asking me all these questions?" replied Rachel.

"A sorceress is one who is different. They walk a path on their own because of this, despised by most. Yet you are not, I do not understand why everyone falls at your feet and not at mine."

Suddenly Rachel realised what was behind her questions. Morgana was beautiful and powerful, but very much alone. She didn't understand why Johnny would help her or why Merlin would invite her to join them, as she was not used to it. Rachel suddenly felt an unusual amount of sympathy for her.

"It must have be difficult for you, to fight against your mother, I'm sorry that happened," Rachel said quietly. "I'm sure Morgause didn't realise that the spell would hit you!"

"Oh, she knew! She aimed it deliberately to kill me. Morgause has never really cared whether I lived or died, since I brought shame on her by breaking loose from Rathyen's bonds," the beautiful sorceress said, bitterly.

"I'm sure she does care, although it must be hard having a sorceress for a mother," said Rachel.

"Your mother was no better! I heard she abandoned you both as children, she is as bad as Morgause," Morgana answered defensively.

"That's not entirely true," Rachel retaliated quickly. "Bronwyn left us with our father to protect us from your brother Mordred, and all of this. She loved us so much, that she left us, even though she didn't want to. That's not the same at all! Why did Morgause send you to Rathyen anyway?"

"She wanted me to learn Rathyen's magic, which is much more powerful than her own. Morgause wanted me to return with this magic to make her stronger. She was not interested in how I was treated, or what I had to bare to learn it."

"Morgana, if you change your ways, Merlin will let you have Mordred's fortress. You have immense powers. If you used them for the people there, you could do so much good!" said Rachel. "They would love and respect you; you would be like their Queen!"

Morgana didn't answer, but it was clear that she was thinking about it. The concept of using her dark magic to actually help anyone other than herself was not one that had occurred to her before. In fact, the whole idea seemed quite strange.

"There you are, Rachel," said Johnny, as he came through the doorway. "Gareth was looking for you, and Merlin was asking where you were, Morgana, as you didn't join us. I was concerned that you may have been hurt. I'm sorry if we were a bit rough pulling you up, but it was a case of doing what we had to do to get you back!"

"No, I am not hurt, and I thank you for your concern," answered Morgana with a smile; one which, Rachel noticed, looked entirely genuine. "I am indebted to you."

They had turned their backs to the land and walked round to the seaward side with Johnny, and none of them noticed two enormous black bats descending on them from behind, until it was too late.

The bats swooped down on them, Morgana and Johnny instinctively ducked as their wings flapped at them but their claws reached into Rachel's shoulders, lifting her up into the air. Rachel screamed and struggled and Johnny tried to hang on to her legs. He pulled with all his might until a huge wing beat him back and he was forced to let go.

As the bats began to lift Rachel higher Morgana quickly delivered one of her spells at them. One of the bats let go of Rachel, stunned by the green sparks that hit it, and for a moment, Rachel's weight was held only by the other bat. She swung precariously as it struggled to hold onto her by one shoulder. It lost height with her weight and Rachel's legs hit the parapet. She leant forwards to clutch at the big stones, struggling to hold on in an attempt to prevent the bat from lifting her again. The other bat swooped back towards Morgana and Johnny and suddenly delivered a vicious spark of magic, so strong that it threw both of them right across the battlement until they hit the tower. By the time they had recovered, the bat had flown back and reclaimed Rachel's shoulder again and the creatures soared upwards, carrying Rachel in-between them. They cleared the castle battlements easily, and flew out across the sea.

"Do something!" said Johnny in despair, as they became distant.

"I cannot," said Morgana. "If I were to hit them now, they would surely drop her into the ocean."

"Oh no, this is dreadful, what am I going to tell Gareth? Where did they come from? They weren't really bats, were they?"

"No, that was Rathyen and Morgause in the guise of bats," she answered, pushing him towards the turret stairs to Merlin's rooms. "I will come with you, we must tell the others immediately, I know where they are going."

They burst in through the door, and Johnny babbled a slightly incoherent version of the events to the few that were left. They looked at him, astounded, as the reality of his words set in.

"Bats? What are you talking about? Who's got Rachel? Where have they taken her?" shouted Gareth. "I don't believe this, she was with Galahad. She was out of my sight for half an hour and something else has happened to her!"

"Now calm down, let us make some sense of all this," said Merlin.

"This was your doing, wasn't it?" said Gareth, turning angrily to Morgana. "I told you she wasn't to be trusted, Merlin!"

"No, Morgana tried to stop them," interrupted Johnny. "I was there, she tried, but they hit us with one of those spells, she couldn't do anything else! It wasn't her fault!"

"No, but I bet she arranged it!" Gareth returned, nastily. "It's strange that she was with Rachel when it happened!"

"Get Galahad," said Merlin to Bran, who rushed off immediately as Merlin turned back to the sorceress. "Morgana, can you shed some light as to who has taken Rachel and where they may have gone?"

"Morgause and Rathyen have her," she answered. "They will take her to Rathyen's caverns in the black mountains."

"Thank you, Morgana," Merlin answered, "but why have they done this?"

"Because you defeated and humiliated Rathyen again, she would not take that lightly!" she answered. "Although, I suspect that their interest may also be in the ring that Rachel was wearing."

"And how do they know about it? Who told them, Morgana? You no doubt!" interjected Gareth.

"I have not spoken to either of them!" she answered coldly. "Theodorus could just as easily have told them."

"Maybe much more easily. Has anyone seen him since the battle?" questioned Merlin, and they both shook their heads. "I suspect that we may have found our culprit then," he deduced.

A white-faced Galahad and Bran returned, and Galahad immediately began to apologise for leaving Rachel, expecting Gareth to blame him again. Still incensed with Morgana, Gareth held his hand up to silence him.

"It's not your fault, it's hers," he said adamantly, pointing accusingly at Morgana. "Anyway, Rachel ought to be able to stand in the safety of the castle without two damn great bats dragging her away!"

"I will follow them, I will take my men, and I will get her back!" Galahad said instantly.

"We'll all go!" said Johnny, and Bran nodded in agreement.

"Rathyen's caverns are in Wales, you will not be able to follow her easily," said Merlin. "They will have flown across the water with Rachel. It will take many days to get there by land and Bors will not let you take men away from the castle while there is still damage to be repaired and the threat of the Saxons."

"Then we'll go on our own," decared Johnny, "the four of us!"

"You will never find a way into Rathyen's domain," interrupted Morgana. "She has it protected by magic. Nothing you will see there will be as it is, you could search the mountains for months and never find an entrance."

"Will someone get her out of here, or I won't be responsible for my actions!" shouted Gareth.

"I was about to offer you my help," said Morgana. "But if you do not want it, I shall leave," she finished, before sweeping off through the door.

Galahad followed her and caught up with her on the stairway. "Morgana, wait," he said. "You cannot blame Gareth for being mistrustful."

"And what of you, Galahad?" she asked. "Are you still mistrustful of me too?"

"'Tis hard for me to see why you would wish to help them. It is unlike you," he answered cautiously. "But I would ask for your help, as I know that we may not find her without it."

"You would not," Morgana answered. "I was held in Rathyen's caverns, and it took me many a year to find a way out! The entire place is bewitched, so that you will only see what she wants you to. The entrance has two high pillars and is surrounded by dark, jagged rocks of slate, but you will not see that. You will see a landscape of trees and bushes, but as you walk straight past it, her guards will appear from nowhere and you will all be killed."

"Then I shall be grateful for any help that you can give us," Galahad answered.

"You have always been courteous to me," she answered. "I shall extend my offer again."

After a brief conversation with Morgana, Galahad returned to the room, where Gareth was distinctly unhappy that he had colluded with her.

"We have no choice if you want to find Rachel," Galahad answered. "Morgana is to come back later when she has drawn us a map and she will bring us something to help us see through Rathyen's enchantments."

"Yeah, and send us straight into a trap, more like!" returned Gareth scornfully.

"Let us wait and see what she has to offer," said Merlin firmly. "Galahad is right, you will need help against Rathyen's magic and no one knows it better than Morgana."

They waited impatiently in Merlin's room for several hours, and just when it seemed that Gareth's prediction of her not returning was correct, there was a knock at the door.

Merlin let Morgana in and she handed him a neatly drawn map on a piece of parchment.

He laid it on his desk and they studied it carefully.

"I have marked the landmarks that you will see. If you look for them and follow them, they will lead you to a small passage way that goes in through the back of the mountain," she explained. "No one knows of this passageway, save a few, and they do not bother to guard it as it is half way up the mountain under a waterfall. I have some potions for you. When you come to the end of the long mountain track you will see Rathyen's black mountain in front of you and a stream to your right, where a tree leans completely across it. You must drink the potions before going any further; they will enable you to see through her enchantments and the entrance with the guards."

"What?" exclaimed Gareth. "Drink something you've concocted? I don't think so! We'll probably all drop dead as soon as we've tasted it!"

"If you do not use them, you will not see anything inside the cavern as it really is. The cavern is full of deep ravines. You will see only a stone floor and walk straight into them."

"Well, I still don't trust you," mumbled Gareth. "How do we know they won't harm us?"

"I shall prove it to you," Morgana said, and pulled the stopper of each bottle in turn and took a sip from each. "If I am still alive in the morning before you leave, then you will know that they are not poison!"

She replaced the stoppers firmly and handed one to each of them. The fifth bottle she gave to Galahad.

"You must remember that this one is different, I have marked it with a blue stopper. You must give this to Rachel, she will not be able to fight Rathyen's holding spell that will have been put on her. If she did manage to leave the cavern with the spell still on her, she would be dead before you get back."

"Rachel's got the Power, it's helped her before," insisted Gareth.

"Your Power comes from a very different place to Rathyen's. It could not penetrate a place as evil and dark as her domain. Rathyen's caverns are connected with Hades itself and her power comes directly from the dark being that rules it."

Gareth said nothing, silenced by the terrible realisation of exactly how bad the place was where his sister was to be held captive.

"You must take a long rope with you," Morgana said to Galahad, "for it will be you that will attempt to rescue her. I wish you luck, as you will need it!"

"Thank you, Morgana, you have been most helpful, we are indebted to you," said Merlin, gratefully.

"I shall see you by the gate at first light," she said, with a stern look at Gareth, as she left. "So that you may see that I am still alive!"

The door closed behind her and the group was subdued. Merlin suggested they all retire, so that they could get an early start, and they all agreed, going off to their separate rooms.

In the morning, their horses were saddled and waiting for them in the courtyard. They mounted them and Merlin handed Excalibur to Gareth. He took it solemnly: the mood of dread that had captured them all the night before had still not left any of them and they nodded silently as Merlin wished them well.

"Do not worry, you will find her," the wise old wizard said to Gareth, "and remember, that it is not only Rachel who holds the Power. Draw on it yourself; let it lead you to her."

"I hope you're right!" answered Gareth.

They rode towards the gate where a slight figure in black was waiting for them.

"As you can see, I have kept my promise," said Morgana.

"Thanks for helping us," said Johnny, sincerely, as Gareth urged his horse past her, saying nothing. Morgana smiled at Johnny in return, looking even more pleased when Galahad echoed his words before they rode out over the causeway.

She watched them for a moment, before turning back towards the castle. 'Maybe there was something in what the girl had said after all,' she thought as she walked across the courtyard, and recalled her conversation with Rachel. It was quite pleasing to have people thank her. In fact, she was surprised to find that she felt an immense degree of satisfaction knowing that she had helped them, even though she had no reason to. She paused again and looked back as they disappeared from sight on a mission that none of them had to do, save for their own desire to rescue someone they loved.

The dark sorceress felt an emptiness inside her again, as she remembered that Morgause, her own mother, had wanted to do her harm, and for a moment she wondered if Rachel's mother would ever do the same to her.

"Morgana," said Merlin as he caught up with her, disturbing her painful thoughts. "I would applaud you for your actions."

"The potions I gave them were fairly basic, Merlin," Morgana replied stiffly. "They were nothing that you could not have given them yourself; your magic is equal to mine."

"Indeed I could have," he answered, "and I had them ready, but I wanted them to come from you."

"Why?" she asked, looking puzzled.

"Because, my dear," Merlin said wisely. "You have learnt a magic of evil from an evil teacher and your actions will turn that magic against them. There are no potions that I could prepare that could offer that. Dark magic turned against dark magic is the strongest potion they could carry. Its strength comes from the hand that made it, and the reason it was given."

For a moment Morgana looked confused; she had never had so much praise in one day, and had no idea how she should reply to it. "The boy still hates me, even though I have helped them," she answered curtly, instead.

"Gareth does not hate you, he simply does not trust you," Merlin answered. "If your potions work, he will thank you on their return."

Morgana nodded thoughtfully and did not reply.

"Morgana, you have done well, you have done the right thing," said Merlin. "I know it cannot have been easy for you to take a stand against Morgause, she is your mother."

Morgana nodded again, unused to anyone being concerned about how she felt.

"My door is open to you, if you wish to talk," he added,

sympathetically.

"Thank you," she answered, quite humbly for her, as he paused at the turret doorway. "I will think about your words," she concluded.

"Do that, my dear, think about them, and remember that we are only ever as good or bad as the lessons that we have been taught. It is up to ourselves to distinguish whether those teachings are the ones that we should follow!"

He left her with a swish of his gown, which rustled against the door to the stairway as he went through it, leaving her alone again with her thoughts.

Chapter Eleven
The Precipice Prison

Rachel stopped struggling the minute the bats flew out across the sea, terrified that they would drop her. She hung precariously between them, their wings flapping in a steady rhythm, and it seemed an eternity before they reached the shore on the other side. The bats landed heavily on a gravelly beach, as though they were tired. They withdrew their talons from Rachel's shoulders and instantly transformed back into the figures of the dark sorceress's Rathyen and Morgause.

Still breathing heavily from their exertions, Rathyen turned towards Rachel and immediately struck her with a bolt of orange magic, which left her feeling tingly and weak. She then led them to a rough shack not far from the water's edge, where she ordered out a frightened looking elderly couple. They left quickly, obviously terrified of Rathyen, promising to come back in the morning with food and horses for them.

The three of them entered the crude building and Rathyen went straight to the fire where the couple's supper was cooking in a huge pot. She ladled out a grey liquid, swimming with vegetables,

152

into a small bowl and sat down on a rough wooden chair.

"Hmm, peasant's fodder," Rathyen said, sniffing it in disgust. "Put the girl over there and make sure she is still under my spell," she finished, indicating a heap of rough blankets in the corner.

Morgause pushed her, and Rachel fell onto the blankets, the old witch stood over her and prodded her to see if she would respond. Rachel dearly wanted to, but found that she couldn't. Her limbs wouldn't move for her and she recognised the same feeling as before from Morgana's spell.

"She is safe for the moment," Morgause told Rathyen, as she joined her by the fire, ladling out some food for herself.

"Good, make sure she stays that way," answered Rathyen with a mouthful of food.

Watching them eat made Rachel feel quite sick. Peasant's fodder or not, they shovelled in mouthful after mouthful, the liquid dribbling down their chins as they hardly paused for breath. As Rachel watched them with disgust, she really hoped that their undisguised greed would give them both a bad case of indigestion!

Finished, Rathyen threw the bowl onto the floor and searched for more. She found a lump of bread, some cured meat and a jug of mead, which she brought back triumphantly. They both devoured the bread and meat, with Rathyen sucking noisily on the bone, and they both swigged from the jug until it was empty.

"Tie her up," said Rathyen, as she staggered towards a rough bed, the rapid consummation of the mead obviously taking its effect. She yanked the blankets roughly from underneath Rachel.

"But she is held by your magic," slurred Morgause. "Surely that is enough?"

"Just do as I say, the girl has flouted our magic before and I have no mind to pursue her in the dark. Tie her up and tie her tightly," Rathyen said, before lying down on a low straw pallet, wrapping the blankets around her.

Morgause found some rope and bound Rachel's hands and feet as tightly as she could. She spotted a piece of rag by the fire and went to pick it up, returning to stuff it viciously into Rachel's mouth. She joined Rathyen on the rough bed, pulling a blanket away from her, and it wasn't long before loud snores came from both of them.

Rachel lay uncomfortably on the floor. A strong draught came from under the door and as the fire died down she became colder and colder. The ropes binding her bit into her wrists and the fabric in her mouth made her gag. Eventually it became light and Rachel was still awake. She had spent the whole night trying hard to summon the Power or the ring on her finger to help her, but it had proved useless. Her mind wouldn't function properly and she found it hard to concentrate on either, and during the night the snores coming from the bed reached such an unbearable crescendo, it had become impossible to think at all!

The door opened and the elderly man came in, his wife behind him bearing a look of sheer terror.

"I have the horses that you asked for, Your Highness," he said.

"Good, but where is the food?" asked Rathyen, struggling up on the straw bed. "And bow to me when you address me," she said, her voice rising. She aimed a flash of light which exploded on the floor by the old man's feet and sent him dancing from foot to foot.

Rachel watched in horror as Morgause and Rathyen sat up and laughed at his discomfort.

"Please, we do not have any more food," said his wife humbly, looking at the floor.

"Then go and get me some from your neighbours!" screamed

Rathyen. "Tell them that I will curse every one of them if they do not give it! Be quick, because your husband will be jumping until you come back!"

"Yes, yes of course," the old woman said, with a curtsy and a bow for good measure as she backed out of the door. Her poor husband continued to hop from foot to foot as the flashes of magic fired around his feet like fireworks. She gave him a last worried glance before rushing off to beg her friends for food.

Rathyen and Morgause got up, ignoring the old man, who was panting heavily as he tried to avoid the sparks still shooting around his feet. His face was red and he was now looking as though he could have a heart attack at any minute from his exertions. The two witches were unconcerned by this and greedily awaited the woman's return with more food.

When his wife came back, they grabbed the small basket from her and pushed her against her husband. The elderly couple fell backwards, landing next to Rachel, whose eyes were now filling up with tears at the dreadful mistreatment of the old man and his wife.

Rathyen and Morgause sat down and stuffed the bread and cheese into their mouths with the same gusto that they had the night before, chewing loudly, washing it down with a jug of water.

Still on the floor, the old man looked at Rachel and after making sure that the sorceresses couldn't see him, he reached over and pulled the gag from her mouth. Rachel smiled at him and nodded her thanks.

"I'm so sorry," she whispered. "Are you both all right?"

The elderly couple nodded, but stayed where they were, frightened that if they moved Rathyen would inflict another unwarranted punishment.

Their appetite finally satisfied, Rathyen belched loudly and the two sorceresses got up. Morgause dragged Rachel to her feet and pushed her outside where she instructed her to mount the horse. Rachel's body automatically obeyed the command even though she inwardly tried to fight it.

They rode off with Rachel still tormented by Rathyen's dreadful treatment of the poor man and woman they had left. She was now in no doubt that she was held by a despicable, evil woman who was capable of anything.

They rode on and on until the landscape began to change to hills and green valleys, deeply wooded and lush with vegetation, with mountains rising majestically in the distance. They travelled until they reached the mountains where they eventually slowed up their horses, who were exhausted by their fast pace. The landscape had been beautiful until they reached the far side of the mountain where it became barren with dark, loose rocks. They reached an entrance of dark slate pillars that rose untidily against the landscape, guarded by the strangest, half-human looking beings that stepped forward to greet their mistress. They didn't speak, but ushered her past with a bow, grovelling as they beheld her.

Rachel glanced at them and shivered as they rode past. She couldn't even decide if they were animals or humans, or maybe they were even both, as they passed a guard with a distorted face. His skin stretched loosely, covered in facial hair that fell down over his shoulders in a tangled mass. His eyes stared expressionlessly out of sunken, dark sockets, surrounded by yellowed folds of skin that were exposed between the matt of hair.

All of the guard's bodies were encased in black armour, and they stood stiffly to attention as they passed, their faces unflinching and unmoving. Their black, fathomless eyes, set in half-human faces, stared in front of them as though they were unseeing. Each face was as terrible as the last and Rachel shuddered as she passed them, wondering where these dreadful creatures could have come from.

They rode in through the entrance of shiny, black slate rocks that were stacked into uneven columns on either side; onto a steep, wide pathway that sloped steeply downwards into the depths of the mountain. The horses took them into the darkness of the rocky passage, lit by torches that illuminated the dampness glistening on the black walls. At the bottom it levelled out and they dismounted. Rachel was pushed firmly down a long passage by Morgause, until they reached a vast underground cavern blazing with torches emitting a red glow against the damp cave walls.

Rathyen strode towards an ornately carved, black stone seat on a high platform, where she arranged her tattered black gowns around her as she sat down. Like a queen of her dark domain, she was immediately surrounded by creatures more dreadful than the guards. They seemed to appear from all directions, thin, bony, half-dead looking beings who knelt at her feet, slobbering and grovelling, their grey clothing hanging in shreds, barely covering them. They scrabbled at each other with long, blackened nails, scratching and clawing to get a place on the floor as near to her throne as they could.

Morgause viciously shoved Rachel and she fell in-between the creatures, sprawling on the stone floor, unable to move. Rathyen laughed, her evil, cracked guffaw filled the cavern and echoed all around them. The vile, slavering creatures on the floor immediately joined in, imitating Rathyen's cackling loudly in an insane frenzy of slobbering noise.

"Silence!" their mistress shouted, and the cavern became instantly quiet as they obeyed her in a second.

"Get up, girl," Rathyen ordered Rachel, whose mind desperately tried to stop her body from promptly recognising her command. It didn't work and she found herself meekly rising to her feet, obeying Rathyen as quickly as her half-human subjects had done.

Rachel stood in front of her and Rathyen spoke again, "The ring you wear, who gave it to you? Speak!" she snapped, clicking her gnarled fingers.

Rachel's obedient mind wanted to tell Rathyen immediately that she had received the ring from Argante, but a look at the ring brought back the memories that she should tell no-one of their meetings, and stopped the words coming out.

"A friend gave it to me," Rachel said instead.

"We know that, but who is this friend and where are they?" questioned Rathyen, in a futile attempt to sound patient.

"They're at Tintagel," answered Rachel truthfully.

"You lie!" shouted Rathyen, her old, yellowed face distorting in anger. "I will ask you again, where is the owner of the ring that you wear?"

"I have already told you, the person who gave me the ring is at Tintagel," Rachel answered, obstinately.

"You would dare to lie to me twice?" screeched Rathyen again. She drew herself up and directed another orange zip of magic at Rachel that forced her back to the floor. "I will not have this, do you hear me? I will have the truth. Where is the person who gave you the ring?"

"At Tintagel," Rachel shouted back at Rathyen from her submissive, flattened position on the hard floor.

Rathyen's scream almost split everyone's eardrums, as she shrieked in fury at Rachel's answer. The creatures around her muttered and twitched in fear of her, covering their faces with their skeletal hands. Rathyen raised her hand and sent a livid spell that flashed into a blue explosion around Rachel. The spell sent Rachel's muscles into spasms and she writhed in agony, twitching uncontrollably amongst the beasts that surrounded her until Rathyen had vented her fury.

"Take her to the cell by the ravine. Let her sit there for a few days until she will answer me with the truth!" Rathyen said angrily, suddenly releasing Rachel from her agonising thrashing. "Erichanon, take her away from my sight, before I reduce her to dust!"

A large creature, encased in the same black armour as the guards, came forward and gripped Rachel's arm. He dragged her onto her feet and propelled her firmly away from his mistress. Rachel glanced briefly at him, to see a pointed face almost like that of a wolf, with small black eyes that didn't even look at her as he obeyed Rathyen's command. He lurched away, dragging Rachel unwillingly down one dark passageway after another until they reached a heavy door, which he opened and pushed her through. His last forceful push sent her across the rocky shelf, where she stopped just in time to see the floor dropping below her into a deep ravine that disappeared into the very core of the earth.

She heard the door shut behind her and cowered back against the rocks, sliding, in terror, into a sitting position. She closed her eyes for a while until she felt brave enough to survey her surroundings. She appeared to be on a shelf, jutting out into a deep ravine, which went further down than she cared to look. The ravine from left to right was endless. It was part of a jagged split in the rocks that separated her from the other side. It fell downwards like a great canyon, leaving her in a prison with no walls or bars and no escape.

After several long hours, the door creaked open and Rachel tried to pull herself back up, but she couldn't. The spell she was still under forced her to remain in a heap next to the cavern wall with no strength to do anything.

A young girl crept in, she wore a dress almost in rags and her face was pale, with dark shadows around her eyes. Her long fair hair looked as though it hadn't seen a hairbrush in a very long time and hung limply around her shoulders.

"Miss, I have brought you some food and water," the girl said, looking around her fearfully. She put a chunk of dry bread on a metal plate along with a pitcher of water on the floor in front of Rachel. Then, anxiously, the girl looked over her shoulder to make sure no-one was watching, before pulling a lump of hard cheese out of her pocket.

"'Tis not much, Miss, but I stole it for you. Eat it quickly because if Rathyen finds out, I will be in trouble!"

"Thank you," said Rachel, finding it hard to get her words out. "Who are you?"

"I am Bethany, Miss," the girl answered, looking cautiously at the door again. "I have heard that you are from Tintagel, and that you are a sorceress," she said, lowering her voice nervously. "I am also from Tintagel. Rathyen brought me here with my sister a long time ago to be her servants."

"Against your will?" asked Rachel.

"Of course, no one would come here unless forced to do so!" Bethany answered. "I must go, Miss; Erychanon is waiting outside the door to take me back. I cannot risk him telling Rathyen that I have spoken to you, but I will do what I can for you," she whispered as she left.

The door banged behind her and Rachel was left alone again in her unusual prison.

She forced herself to eat the cheese and dry bread as she knew the girl would suffer if she didn't. Even though she hadn't eaten all day it stuck in her throat and she had to drink several mouthfuls of water to swallow it. She curled up afterwards on the hard floor and slept until she heard the door open again. This time Bethany crept in with a thick, rough blanket for her.

"I told them that you looked unwell and were shivering when I saw you," she said. "I told the mistress that you would be dead by morning if I did not bring you some cover. They do not want that, they want you alive. I will come back again tomorrow," Bethany finished hurriedly, before leaving again.

Rachel wrapped the blanket around her, taking comfort in its roughness and the fact that Bethany had gone to so much trouble to get it to her. The night was long and uncomfortable, she slept on and off, exhausted by the journey and the lack of food and sleep from the day before. She had no idea how she was going to escape from Rathyen or even if she had the strength to do so.

She woke from her fitful sleep with no idea of what time it was. Her mind was still foggy and, however hard she tried to release whatever connections with the Power or Argante's ring that were supposed to help her, she found that she couldn't. Aching all over, she was unable to concentrate long enough or hard enough on either. She was still reduced to the powerless state of finding it difficult to even lever herself up into a sitting position against the stony wall.

Finally she managed it and leant against the hard rocks with her blanket wrapped around her, until the door finally opened again to let Bethany in with more dry bread and water. Once she was sure it was safe, the young, frightened girl produced a burnt chicken leg from her pocket and put it on the plate next to the bread.

"Are you all right, Miss?" she asked in a hushed tone.

Rachel nodded in reply, and the girl looked back at the door again.

"Do you know what they intend to do with me?" asked Rachel, still finding it difficult to speak.

"'Tis not you they are interested in," said Bethany in a whisper. "I was waiting on them last night and I heard them talking. Rathyen thinks that someone is coming to save you. This is the person that they want. They think that you will draw them here."

"What?" said Rachel, stunned by her answer. "Well, I've no idea who they're expecting. No one even knows where I am!"

"They were talking about a ring you wear," the girl answered. "They think that the owner of the ring will come for you."

"Well, they'll be very disappointed then, because that won't happen!" Rachel said.

"They say it will. They are sure of it," answered Bethany confidently. "Miss, if this person comes to take you back, could you please take us with you?" she asked, with a pleading look in her eyes. "My sister has not spoken a word since she has been here; she is young and terrified of the creatures. I would give anything to get her away from them!"

"How old is she?" asked Rachel, immediately feeling sorry for them.

"She had just had her eighth birthday when we came here," Bethany answered, tears welling up in her eyes. "But she is not the same child; she has been ill ever since we got here. I try to do her chores for her, but Rathyen has noticed. She will kill her before long, I know she will!"

"I wish I could help you, but at the moment I don't know how I can," answered Rachel.

"When the person comes, if you could...?" Bethany was cut short by the creaking of the door as it opened, to reveal the large figure of Erychanon. He looked suspiciously at her and she mumbled in fear. "I was making sure she was all right, the Mistress said I was to do so. I thought she looked unwell."

He stepped forward and inspected them both. "You come now,

the girl is alive, that will suffice," he said, in a low growling voice.

Bethany scrambled back to her feet and fled past him. The door banged again and Rachel was left alone wondering who it was that they thought was going to save her. Argante never left her cave, so why would they suppose that she would? Or did they expect someone else? If so, who? There seemed to be some confusion over Argante's ring from everyone she had met so far and she had no idea why!

Meanwhile Gareth, Bran, Galahad and Johnny had set out on the long ride to the mountains in Wales. Gareth was becoming more and more frustrated that it was taking so long. They rode all day and made camp at night to rest the horses, leaving again at first light to continue their journey. After two days in their saddles the mountains seemed no nearer. They made camp again and settled down to another long, uncomfortable night.

He voiced his concerns to Galahad. "Are we ever going to get there? She's been with them for days now!"

"We have to stop, the horses are tired. 'Tis these cursed waters, they reach so far inland that we have to travel far to get to the other side," Galahad replied. "We have crossed the borders now though, and tomorrow we will find Rathyen's domain."

"We passed a place I thought I recognised," said Gareth. "We fought a battle there, when I was here before. I'm sure it's not far from Meinir's settlement, on the borders of England and Wales."

"It was, we passed it several hours ago," said Galahad.

"Meinir would have helped us, if I'd known," Gareth answered, piling some branches up to make a fire.

"She would no doubt, but 'tis best not to involve others unless we have to," Galahad answered. "You admire Meinir, I saw it at the battle."

"Yes, well it's hard not to really, she's had it really tough!"

Gareth said, honestly. "She's led her people since the death of her father and mother and she's fought off anyone who has dared to encroach on their territory. What's not to admire?" he asked. "She's one ferocious lady!"

"It would appear that strength in a woman is something that you are drawn to," answered Galahad as he helped him with the fire. "Your sister is strong, maybe this is why you are drawn to this strength."

"Rachel? You're joking aren't you! Rachel's frightened by everything. She can get herself into a state about anything at all!" Gareth said.

"I think you are belittling your sister," returned Galahad, immediately. "I have seen Rachel overcome things that she has been terrified of, and that takes an equal strength."

"And you admire her too," said Gareth with a laugh. "That's fairly obvious."

"If 'tis so obvious, then I will not deny it," replied Galahad, looking slightly uncomfortable.

"Can we just get some food cooking," interrupted Johnny, sensing a tenseness emerging between his two friends. "I'm famished and so is Bran!"

"I have done my part, and Johnny is right, I am starving!" joined in Bran, holding up two dead rabbits that he had caught for dinner.

The meal was finally cooked and they ate heartily, wrapping their cloaks around them to sleep, grateful of the warmth from the fire. Gareth and Johnny went to sleep quite quickly but Galahad could not settle. He got up and inspected the bushes around them as though he had heard something.

"So you feel it too," said Bran quietly. "I thought for a while earlier on, that we were being followed."

"Aye, so did I, but we would have lost them hours ago," he answered.

"I have not heard anything since we crossed the river. We should be safe enough for tonight," replied Bran, "but I will take turns to watch if you want."

"'Twould be best if we did, though who would follow us I cannot imagine," agreed Galahad. "I will take the first watch, you can take second and we will wake the others for their turn."

Bran settled down to sleep and took over from Galahad several hours later. Gareth was last to be woken and was surprised when Johnny told him why.

"Who on earth would follow us?" he asked.

"I don't know, it all seems very quiet. Maybe Galahad and Bran are wrong," Johnny shrugged.

Gareth put some more wood on the fire before he started his vigil. He had no trouble keeping awake as he had already managed several hours sleep and his thoughts turned to worrying about Rachel.

Johnny had been right, there were no sounds at all, he thought, as he leant against a tree trunk. It was all very quiet, almost too quiet. There was an unnatural stillness and Gareth began to feel uneasy. He kept his hand on his sword and his eyes peeled, glancing around him continually into the darkness, listening for the snap of a twig, or a rustle in the bushes.

As soon as the first threads of light appeared he woke the others and suggested they leave. They sensed his uneasiness and agreed to break camp early. By the time they rode out Gareth had the distinct feeling that they were not alone.

Chapter Twelve
The Canyon of Despair

Rachel stayed on the shelf that had become her prison for another day and night, visited only by Bethany with food and water. Her limbs ached from sitting on the hard floor and she felt weaker than ever. A dreadful fear of never getting out of there was beginning to take over her thoughts and she was too tired and listless to even try to summon the Power. She had even given up wondering where the strange light in the ravine was coming from. It flickered and glowed brighter at times but never dimmed, making it difficult to distinguish between day and night. There were also strange sounds that appeared to come from far below her, unearthly murmurings that echoed eerily, as though there were people moaning and groaning in the distance.

If she had known how close her brother and the others were, her spirits would have lifted, but unfortunately she didn't, thinking that she was alone in her desperate situation with only Bethany's brief, frightened visits to look forward to.

Gareth's party stopped to eat for a short while, before travelling on through the green mountains until they reached a winding pathway. Soon the landscape around them began to change. The lush, green vegetation was replaced by a barren, stony pathway. The trees looked withered and the air became void of the varied birdsong that they had listened to on their journey.

"I think we are almost there," said Galahad. "Morgana said we would 'come to a place where naught can grow, where Rathyen's evil, stunts or kills any living thing!'"

"Great!" answered Johnny, sarcastically. "Can Rathyen really be that powerful?"

"Morgana seems to think so," Galahad replied. "I have no reason to doubt her word on that."

"If that is so, we must be on our guard," said Bran, looking over his shoulder nervously.

"I don't care how bad Rathyen is, I'm not leaving here without Rachel!" declared Gareth, determinedly, and they all nodded silently in support, albeit rather apprehensively.

Soon the end of their rocky path came into sight. It sloped downwards, revealing a stretch of land that led towards the base of a stretch of dark, craggy mountains. They were desolate and foreboding and rose up so high against the skyline that they blocked out the sunlight.

"If Morgana is correct, we are very near," said Galahad, dismounting. "Stay here, I will go and see if there is any sight of Rathyen's guards."

"I'm coming with you," insisted Gareth immediately.

They walked stealthily to the end of the passage and looked out over the empty barren plain to the foot of the mountain.

"I can't see anything," whispered Gareth. "Are you sure we're in the right place?"

"Morgana said that we would not see anything. It is protected and altered by Rathyen's magic. We must drink the potions she has given us," Galahad replied.

"Are you mad?" exclaimed Gareth. "I'm not drinking anything that witch has given us!"

"Galahad's right," said Johnny, coming up behind them. "Morgana didn't have to help us; she didn't have to offer us anything! I'm willing to drink it first, to see if it works!" he finished, pulling out the small bottle she had given him.

"Are you sure? I really don't think you ought to. I don't trust her!" replied Gareth, but by the time he had uttered the words, Johnny had already swallowed the liquid and they all looked at him expectantly.

"Well, it tastes a lot better than the ones that Merlin's given us in the past," Johnny said, wryly. "I don't feel any different either."

They all sighed with relief and Gareth murmured his thanks. Johnny volunteered to go forward to the end of the path to see if it looked any different to him, having taken Morgana's potion.

His response was immediate. "Get back!" he whispered urgently, ducking down behind a rock. He crept back towards them, his face pale. "There's an entrance to the left of the mountain and the whole place is crawling with her guards - ferocious looking things in black armour!" he said.

"The potion must have worked then," said Galahad. "We did not see anything like that. Morgana said that we would be exposed to them if we rode out towards the mountain."

"We can't do that, we'd be caught within seconds!" said Johnny. "There are men all around the entrance and they look pretty powerful to me!"

Galahad pulled out the map that Morgana had given them and scrutinised it carefully. "Morgana said that at the end of this path there is some undergrowth on the right that would shield us from them. Look, she has drawn it here," said Galahad, pointing it out on the map. "It should lead us towards a stream, did you see that, Johnny?"

"I did, but the bushes are fairly sparse. We'd have to go one at a time once we leave the shelter of the rocks. It's a risk!" Johnny said. "This path is in full view of her guards!"

"'Tis a risk we must take if we are to enter the mountain without being seen," answered Galahad. "And we must all drink the potion to see things as Johnny does."

"Okay, Morgana, I take back everything that I've said!" said Gareth, pulling out his own bottle. "Maybe you aren't as bad as I thought you were!"

He lifted the bottle to his lips and drank from it. They took the horses back to a small clearing just off the pathway, sheltered by rocks and a small clump of trees. They led them behind the trees and tethered them there, out of sight.

"I hope they are still there when we get back," remarked Bran, as they cautiously continued back down to the end of the pathway. Gareth and Galahad were amazed by the difference in the view that they could now see. The burly - looking guards surrounded the entrance on the left of the mountain and Johnny had been entirely correct when he had said that the foliage meant to camouflage them was sparse. It was! It consisted of withered trees and prickly gorse, with a small, narrow track against the rocks.

One by one they quickly ducked into the overgrown track, after checking that the black armoured soldiers weren't looking, until they were all safe behind the spiky bushes. The trees had just enough leaves to shield them from sight as they crept down the narrow gap between the rocks and bushes.

"Morgana said to follow this path until we reach the end. We will be out of sight there and we can cross the stream on foot," whispered Galahad over his shoulder.

The bushes caught on their clothes and they emerged, covered in scratches, into a small clearing shielded from the guards by the mountain. The stream rushed past them in a silvery torrent, splashing against black stone boulders in its midst.

They sank waist high as they struggled against the streams fast flowing current, holding their swords above the water level. They scrambled up the bank on the other side one by one, wet and bedraggled. There was just enough foliage on the bank to shield them as they moved stealthily on all fours, passing the wide, open space across the plain on the other side of the water. Peeping through the long grasses they could see right across to the entrance, where the guards stood to attention all around it.

"Rathyen must have a formidable force here, by the look of it. I don't think I fancy taking that lot on!" remarked Johnny, unintentionally voicing everyone's thoughts.

"Yes, I was just thinking the same myself!" said Gareth. "There's an awful lot of them and only four of us!"

"We cannot take them on. 'Twould be foolish to even attempt it," said Bran. "We have to get in and out of there unnoticed."

"Your speciality, as I remember: blending in!" replied Gareth with a laugh, as he remembered his friend's resourcefulness at Mordred's encampment, where they had played the part of woodcutters for the soldiers' fire. No one had questioned their presence, assuming that someone else had told them to do it!

"I would welcome your thoughts as to how we are to do that," said Galahad, looking unconvinced.

"Don't worry - Bran will come up with something!" replied Gareth. "He is as wily as a cat burglar when he has to be!" His modern day reference to a burglar produced a quizzical look from everyone and he decided not to even try to explain. "Look, just trust him; he's an expert at going unnoticed!"

Eventually they found that they had crawled far enough along the stream bank to be able to stand up unnoticed. The guards were out of view and they had reached the tree that bent right over the stream, which Morgana had sketched on her map. They waded up to their waist in the gurgling waters, following its path until they could see it pouring out of the blackness of the barren mountain in a silvery waterfall. They found they had to swim across to the other side as the water was much deeper here. They climbed out and followed the rough, stony bank that narrowed into a mere rocky ledge. Eventually they reached the waterfall, cascading down through a small opening in the mountain face high above them. They were presented with a rushing torrent and high, slippery, black rocks up to the small opening in the mountain where the water gushed from.

"We haven't a hope of getting up there!" said Gareth in dismay. "Even if we try climbing it, the water's going to force us back down again! There must be another way in!"

"There is, the entrance you have just seen with the guards!" said Galahad, flatly. "This is the only other option; we have to go this way!"

"Look, I know you don't do the magic side of things, but you are a Keeper after all!" said Johnny, quietly, pulling Gareth to one side. "Maybe now is the time that you ought to try it! You might be able to get the Power to help us. Merlin told you to draw on it!"

"Well, I can have a go, but I'm really not very good at it," Gareth said, uncertainly.

"Might be an idea to try, because we aren't going to be able to do this without some help from somewhere," said Johnny.

"Yeah, you're right, I'll have a go," Gareth answered, slightly more determinedly. "Just give me a minute, while I work out how to do it!"

He left the others and sat on a rock on his own, desperately trying to remember anything out of the old black book that had previously given them their instructions.

"*We invoke the Power,*" he muttered to himself. "*We invoke the Power against our enemies!*"

"*We invoke the Power against the dark ones that...*" He couldn't remember any more and tried again. "*We ask the ancient ones that have gone before us to invoke the Power against the dark ones that... We invoke the Power against... We invoke the Power against our enemies!*"

This was so frustrating, as hard as he tried, he couldn't remember any of the incantations from the old black book. He gave up and, in desperation, he sent up a plea instead.

"Look, I don't remember the words, I know I probably should, but I don't. Please help us rescue Rachel! We really need some help with the water; otherwise we can't get into the cave! Do whatever you can, please?" he finished, rather feebly.

"Wow, that's brilliant," said Johnny after a moment, interrupting his sombre thoughts. "Look the water's subsided; it's reduced to a trickle! We can climb up there easily now. I don't know what you did, but it's certainly done the trick!"

"It's worked?" asked Gareth in surprise. He rushed back to look at the waterfall and saw that Galahad and Bran had already taken advantage of the situation by starting to scale the slippery incline. "Good heavens, so it has!" he finished in amazement.

"I would suggest that you carry on with whatever magic you have," said Galahad, dourly over his shoulder, "as our swords will hold no might against Rathyen's army. We will be vastly outnumbered when we get into this mountain. I hate to say this, but we may be reliant on whatever you can produce to get us through this!"

"Oh no," replied Gareth glumly, as he started to climb the sharp - edged rocks. "I'm sure that was just a fluke, I'm really not that good at magic!"

"You'll manage, just keep doing whatever it was that you did just then, it's worked so far," said Johnny, encouragingly.

They climbed up the rocks beside the waterfall, that had conveniently subsided to a negotiable trickle, and once they reached the top they hid behind some large boulders just inside. To their dismay, they found themselves watching the black-armoured creatures going about their business in abundance. The area was completely full of them. The waterfall opening had led into a large cave revealing a network of dark recesses and tunnels leading off it. The stream trickled past them, in a deep-worn groove in the rocks, gushing down from the right out of a small, dark opening, before making its way out towards the sunlight where they had come in. Rathyen's strange men seemed to be coming and going in and out of the passageways, mostly as though they were on their way somewhere else.

"What now?" whispered Gareth. "There's no way we can get past them here!"

"No, we need to take time to watch them, look at what they do and study how they move and walk," said Bran. "Listen, they grunt and growl at each other. It might be some sort of language, but we can get away with that. It's still a growl," he finished, confidently.

"That's all very well, but we don't look anything like them," answered Johnny. "We're going to stick out like sore thumbs!"

"Not necessarily," answered Bran. "We have to make ourselves look like them, to pass unnoticed."

"And how do we do that?" asked Gareth.

"First of all, we are too clean," Bran answered. "We need to go back and cover our hair and faces in the muddy silt from the waterfall. The rocks are covered in its slime, so it will not be difficult. Secondly, we have to steal some of their armour so that we look like them."

"Brilliant, but how do we get the armour?" questioned Johnny.

"We pick them off one by one, kill them and steal their armour. We only need four and if we drag their bodies back to the waterfall and push them over, Gareth might arrange for it to revert to its former force and the bodies will soon disappear unnoticed downstream."

"This is all sounding too easy," stated Gareth.

"'Twill not be easy, we have to kill four of them first!" replied Bran. "But it could be done."

"Your suggestion is a good one, but we have no way of singling them out to kill them," interjected Galahad, sensibly.

"Oh yes we have, you have not been watching closely enough," replied Bran, rather smugly. "If you look, every now and again one of them disappears into an entrance on the left, on our side of the stream. They come out again not long afterwards. 'Tis my guess that as there is water here, the room they go into may well be somewhere that they eat. I will go first, stay here until I come back," he said, and before any of them could stop him he ducked off, half crouched, towards the entrance.

"Oh no, I hope he'll be all right!" exclaimed Johnny.

"So do I, because if he is found, he will expose us all!" replied Galahad, his voice expressing a note of annoyance.

They waited with baited breath, for what seemed like an eternity, before a black-clad figure lurched towards them. They all drew their swords as the dark, armour-clad figure growled and stopped short of their hiding place. They froze and waited to see what he would do next.

"Pull back your swords, 'tis me!" whispered a familiar voice.

"Bran, we didn't even recognise you!" said Gareth in disbelief, as Bran slipped down behind the boulders again.

"Well, my disguise has obviously worked then!" Bran replied with a laugh, pushing up a black leather helmet with a nose and ear-flaps, to reveal a brown and green slime-covered face and matted hair.

"Yes it has! Did you have to growl like that though? You've just scared the hell out of all of us!" said Johnny, feeling annoyed and relieved at the same time. "So come on then, what do we have to do?"

"First you need to go back to the entrance and cover your faces like mine," said Bran. Galahad declined but Gareth and Bran slipped back to do the same as Bran, covering themselves with the slime off the rocks.

"Now what?" said Johnny, on returning to their hiding place.

"When 'tis clear we will go to the room where they feed. I warn you though, 'twill not be pleasant, these creatures are barbarians!" replied Bran. "There is another small room off the first one, where they store their food. We can hide in there to pick them off one-by-one as they enter."

"Let's go for it then," said Gareth, drawing Excalibur.

They crept forwards as far as they could under the cover of the rocks, until Bran signalled for them to go. They crept stealthily into the dark room, where the stench of rotting meat hit them immediately. Dead carcasses lay on the large stone tables in front of them, torn savagely into half-eaten pieces, and they put their hands to their mouths to stop themselves from being sick.

"This is disgusting!" said Johnny.

"I did try to warn you," said Bran. "The creatures here feed off the dead animals laid out in this room!"

"Oh no, the smell in here is unbelievable!" said Gareth heaving, and he quickly held his nose again.

They followed Bran into a small room, which was obviously their pantry, shelved from floor to ceiling and stacked with more dead animals.

"This is even more gross!" said Gareth, still holding his nose. "I can't believe that anyone would eat this; they must have been here for days. They stink to high heaven!"

"Shh!" warned Galahad, with a finger to his lips. "Someone is coming!"

They peeped through the gaps between the wooden timbers in the door and saw that a large, unsavoury-looking guard had entered the room. He attacked the carcasses on the table like an animal. He ripped pieces off with his teeth and devoured them, swallowing lumps whole before going back for more. Gareth retched again and began to feel ill just watching him.

"Now!" whispered Bran. "While he is still alone!"

Gareth and Bran rushed through the door and grabbed the guard before he could reach his sword. Gareth held his hand over his mouth to silence him as they overpowered him and Bran slit his throat, quickly and deftly. They dragged his body back with them into the small room. Bran quickly stripped him of his armour and handed it to Gareth, who put it on over his own clothing. He pulled a face as he lifted a heavy, leathery tunic, with metal bands fixed to it, over his head.

"The smell from this is really awful!" he said, strapping it in place. "I don't think the person who's worn this has ever washed in his life!"

"You will not complain if it saves your life," answered Bran, as Gareth struggled to tie on some leg shields. "We have two more to go."

"One more," said Galahad. "I do not, and will not, wear the attire of my enemy. I have always fought as a knight under my own banner. I will not alter this now!"

"Galahad, you have to! You can't go with us looking like a knight," answered Gareth immediately. "You'll blow our cover completely!"

"Do you not think the trail of blood that leads to this room from your victim is enough to cause notice?" said Galahad.

"If Galahad wishes to remain as himself, it may even give us a way in," said Bran, thoughtfully. "You would have to pretend to be our prisoner though," he told Galahad.

"I do not mind that," Galahad answered. "I am in favour of duping an enemy, but I will not wear their clothing."

"Ok, so that's one more to go then," said Johnny.

"Right on cue, except there's two of them," whispered Gareth, as two more guards entered the room. Their attention went immediately to the uncooked meat, and they tore into the remains of the dead animal on the table. They ate savagely, growling at each other over the morsels that they tore off, like two lions over a kill. Their appetite almost satisfied, they noticed the trail of blood leading towards the larder door and motioned to each other, silently drawing their swords.

"Here we go, and this time, their coming to us!" said Gareth, as they all moved back from the door with their swords ready to take them on.

Suddenly there were noises, screams and shouts from beyond the rooms, and the two large, burly characters halted for a moment and looked at each other in confusion. The commotion outside became louder, so instead of opening the door to their stinking sanctuary, the guards ran away from it, back towards the outer door. They rushed outside and the door banged behind them.

The hubbub beyond the doors continued and it sounded as though there was a fight going on outside. Gareth's party all held their breath, with swords drawn in anticipation of an attack on them as well. It didn't come. Instead it went quiet again.

"What on earth is going on out there?" whispered Gareth.

"I do not know, but it sounded as though there was a skirmish of some sort outside," answered Bran.

"We will wait," instructed Galahad. "If it remains quiet, then we can break our cover to investigate."

They all nodded and waited in silence for what seemed like an eternity until, eventually, Bran went to the door and peered through the gaps in the rough wood again.

"I do not understand this," he said. "The outer door is now wedged open by two dead bodies! They look like the guards that were about to come for us. I am certain they are dead!"

"But who would have killed them?" asked Johnny.

"There's someone else here," said Gareth, nervously. "I can feel them. I had the same sensation last night in the wood, when I was on lookout. It felt as though we were being watched!"

"We had a similar hunch," replied Galahad. "Bran and I thought we were being followed several times. Have you any idea who it could be?"

"Nope, I haven't a clue!" answered Gareth. "To be honest, Rachel normally does the insight side of things. I just do what you do - use a sword!"

"I will go to the outer door, to see if 'tis safe now," said Bran. "I will get their armour for you, Johnny. Do you still wish to remain as you are?" he asked Galahad, politely. "There are two sets of disguise there for the taking, if you want one."

"I do not, I have not changed my mind," Galahad replied

firmly.

They opened the door and Bran went out cautiously to find out what had happened. He stepped over the bodies and disappeared through the outer door for a moment. He returned quickly with a black set of armour, which he handed to Johnny.

"This is all very strange," he told Galahad, on returning. "There has been an attack, an onslaught of some sort by the stream outside. There must be at least twenty of her guards all lying dead outside!"

"Looks like someone else has done our job for us then," Gareth said, delightedly.

"Yes, but who?" questioned Johnny. "One person couldn't take down that many; there must be several of them."

"We must leave quickly, as the rest of Rathyen's army may converge upon us. She will send more to defend the entrance here, since it has been infiltrated," said Galahad. "We could be blamed for the attack on her guards if we are found. 'Tis not safe here now, we must move on!"

They all agreed and crept out of their hiding place, stepping over the newly deceased creatures as they left. Out by the stream again, they could not believe their eyes, as they beheld a scene of carnage. The entire area was littered with corpses encased in black armour, most with their heads severed. As they stepped over more and more, dead guards, Bran's first guess of twenty was now appearing to be a very conservative estimate, and they followed the stream deeper into the mountain without a living person in sight to apprehend them.

Galahad took a blazing torch from the wall to light their way as they left the tunnel with the stream, and ventured into another that sloped downwards. It twisted and turned sharply, leading them deeper into the dark depths of the mountain. Further along, the narrow passageway forked into two and Johnny and Bran looked at Gareth for some sort of intuition.

"This way," Gareth stated, confidently. He pointed to a steep pathway to the right and immediately started down it. They all followed behind him, in single file, as the rocky walls and the airless passageway closed around them.

Suddenly they heard footsteps and growls echoing behind them and they stopped to see three black guards, with dark, wolf-like faces and small eyes, running towards them.

"Do what I do," Bran whispered to Gareth and Johnny. "Galahad, you are now our prisoner!"

Gareth quickly took the torch from Galahad as Bran grabbed the knight's arms. He held them behind his back and told Johnny to point his sword at him. Gareth did the same and as the guards got nearer, Bran emitted a long, low growl that sounded distinctly like the ones they had heard from the creatures earlier.

"Errrough!" he snarled menacingly. "Errough, errough. Rathyen, grrough!" he shook Galahad firmly, and Gareth brandished his sword, to add to the illusion that they had captured the knight and were taking him to Rathyen. The guards seemed to recognise Bran's bizarre growls and nodded their approval, grunting back at him.

Bran pushed Galahad forwards and Johnny joined in by holding his axe firmly in front of him. As they walked forwards the guards fell in behind them, growling their strange language to each other as though they intended to join them in presenting the captive knight to Rathyen.

"Now what? They're coming with us," whispered Johnny, alarmed that they might actually be walking towards Rathyen.

"Get them further down this passage and when I growl again, we jump them," Bran whispered back. "Have your swords ready, we cannot risk any of them running back!"

They all nodded silently and carried on walking down the tunnel's many twists and turns.

They approached a bend and Johnny nodded to them, alerting them to attack. As they rounded the corner he growled and they all drew their swords. They waited for the guards who were following at a slight distance to turn the corner and then they jumped on them swiftly. A couple of blows from their swords made two of them collapse instantly, before they could even draw their weapons. The other one turned and ran back up the tunnel, but was quickly brought down by one mighty blow from Johnny's axe. All three guards lay dead at their feet and they moved on down the passageway, intent on their quest to find Rachel.

They reached another fork to the left of them, where they could hear noises, so they veered away from it and continued down the passage. At the end of the tunnel they saw an entrance, illuminated by a strange, soft glow. As they ventured towards it and stepped through, they found themselves high up on a narrow shelf with a terrible drop below them. The sheer cliff reached down into the vastness of a canyon that split the inside of the mountain in half.

They stood on the shelf, realising that this was not only a dead end, but a chasm so deep that it couldn't be crossed. One by one they looked down intrepidly and stepped quickly back against the safety of the rocky walls. The huge, jagged fissure in the mountain floor, where it had been ripped from the other side, reached so far down that it appeared to extend into the very bowels of the earth itself and they looked at each other in despair.

Chapter Thirteen
Perilous Descents

Rachel woke out of her weakened stupor to find Bethany next to her with her usual jug of water, dry bread and an extra something that she pulled out of her pocket. She seemed excited and her cheeks were red.

"Erichanon is not with me, Miss," Bethany said, in a whisper. "He is busy; there has been an attack on the other side of the mountain. 'Tis the only other way in by the waterfall!" she announced. "Oh, Miss, could it be him? The one you are waiting for, to save you? The one that Rathyen has talked about?" she finished, eagerly.

Rachel tried to answer, but her voice just wouldn't come. Instead, she shook her head, but Bethany was undeterred in her fanciful notions.

"No one has ever attacked Rathyen's guards here!" she stated. "None can see her domain; she has it protected by her magic! Someone has killed most of her guards by the waterfall and she is furious!"

'Great!' Rachel thought. 'That's all I need, an angry Rathyen thinking that someone coming to save me has attacked her guards!'

"Miss, are you not pleased? 'Tis him, he has come for you!"

The energy to reply was beyond Rachel's capabilities. In her weakened state Rathyen's spell was proving even more difficult for Rachel to fight against. She dearly wanted to explain to the delighted girl that the attack on the soldiers was nothing to do with anyone that Rathyen was expecting to come and save her. Although, as Rachel looked at Bethany's flushed face, she decided that it would almost be a shame to destroy her romantic notions of someone swooping in and saving them all!

"Look, Miss, look," shouted Bethany, her fears vanishing in her enthusiasm. "Look up to yonder ledge!" She pointed to the other side of the ravine, to a shelf high above them, where four figures looked down towards them. There were three black-clad guards and a knight that, even from a distance, Rachel instantly recognised as Galahad.

"Galahad!" whispered Rachel.

"Is it him? Is he the one, is it Galahad?"

Rachel felt a surge of relief in her recognition of the knight, followed quickly by a fear for his safety. He was with Rathyen's guards, had they captured him as well?

On the narrow ridge on the other side of the ravine Gareth looked over the edge and noticed the figures on the parapet jutting out below.

"Look, there's someone down there on the other side of the canyon. It looks like two girls. It is! Look, it's Rachel, she's over by the wall!" shouted Gareth in relief. "We've found her!"

"Thank the Lord that she is unharmed!" agreed Galahad profoundly.

"I hate to put a damper on things, but how on earth are we

going to get across to her?" asked Johnny. "There's a damn great ravine in-between us and her!"

"I will get to her," said Galahad, uncoiling the rope that Morgana had told him to take with him. "Tie the other end to that rock, I will swing across to her," he finished resolutely, as he firmly knotted it around his waist.

"You can't, this is complete madness," answered Johnny, clutching his arm. "Even if you got to Rachel without falling to your death, you couldn't get her back up here!"

"I know, but at least she will not be on her own and I will do everything I can to get her out of the caverns!" Galahad answered.

"No, I'll go, if anyone should risk their lives it should me, she's my sister!" insisted Gareth.

"Have you ever swung over a chasm before?" asked Galahad. "Have you ever used a rope?"

"No, but she's my sister!" repeated Gareth.

"Well, I have used a rope many times before, and I will pledge my life to save her! Let me go, I am far more experienced. She will stand a better chance with me."

"Galahad's right, you've never done anything like this before," said Johnny, gently. "Let him go, you know that he will do anything he can to get Rachel out of here. Sometimes we must look to the best man for the job," Johnny insisted. "In this instance, it's Galahad!"

Eventually, Gareth accepted his friend's advice and helped to tie the rope around the rock in a firm knot that would support Galahad's weight as he swung over the abyss.

Intent on his new pursuit, Gareth didn't hear Bran's words as he spoke quietly to Galahad.

"That rope is not long enough for you to reach her, or the shelf below," Bran warned him.

"I know that, I will use it to swing across from the wall and drop down when I have enough leverage," Galahad answered.

"Galahad that's impossible, if the rope isn't long enough, even if you swing out, you still won't reach it with the rope tied to you," Johnny joined in, overhearing their conversation.

"That is why I will be asking for your help," replied Galahad, pulling at the rope to make sure it was secure. "I will use it to pivot outwards and when I have enough leverage to be propelled right out into the canyon, I will shout to you, and you will sever the rope with your axe!"

"No way, I can't do that, you'll just drop down into God knows where!" Johnny answered, shocked. "This is all far too risky."

"You will do what I ask, as this is the only way I can get to her," Galahad answered, holding the rope firmly, stepping towards the edge. "Just do your part when I tell you to and I will reach her!"

Sombrely, they all watched him step out over the edge towards the huge void. Johnny took the strain of the rope and Gareth helped him. Galahad leant back, using the rope for support as he found footholds to make his way slowly down. They both hung grimly onto the rope to support him, lowering him down a bit at a time. They were so engrossed in Galahad's perilous descent that no one noticed the dark figure come through the entrance onto the narrow ridge.

Dark fathomless eyes stared at Gareth out of a ghoulish face, framed by a black beard and black hair. He ignored the others totally, focusing only on Gareth, and raised his sword, intent on bringing it down on him. Bran turned and saw him and for a second he was rooted to the spot in shock, as he recognised instantly the grey-faced, dead form of Mordred.

"Gareth, get out of the way!" Bran shouted, as he saw Mordred's sword lifted ready to strike his friend, and he immediately brought up his own sword with all his strength to block Mordred's attack.

On seeing Mordred Gareth turned and fell back in shock, landing heavily against Johnny. "It's Mordred!" he exclaimed, as Johnny regained his balance and tried hard to take Galahad's weight on the rope alone.

Gareth jumped up as he saw Mordred's sword strike Bran's. But instead of Bran's sword stopping it with a clash of steel, Mordred's sword went straight through Bran's as though it wasn't even there. Bran was thrown off balance as his heavy strike made no difference, his sword hit the floor with a crash instead and Mordred lurched towards him. As Bran teetered on the edge of the ledge, trying to stop from going over, Mordred gave him one final push and Bran fell backwards over the edge of the ravine, disappearing into the chasm below.

"Bran!" shouted Gareth.

"Oh, God, no!" exclaimed Johnny in horror.

Shocked to the core, both Gareth and Johnny temporarily released their grip on the rope and Galahad plunged downwards quickly. He hit the sides of the rocks on his way down, slamming hard against them until he was left dangling at the end of the rope in the ravine. The rope spun him round and he hung on to it grimly, unaware of what was happening on the ledge above him. For a moment he thought something large passed him and he thought he heard a cry, but as the rope continued to spin him round he couldn't be sure what it was.

The horror and realisation that their friend had just fallen to his death sent a surge of anger through Gareth and he drew Excalibur. He stepped forward and faced Mordred squarely.

"You murderer!" Gareth exclaimed. "I thought we'd got rid of you years ago!"

Mordred's eyes stared blankly in front of him, the only focus in his bloodshot vision was Gareth, and he hacked at the air towards him with his sword, the familiar sneer forming in his cracked black lips. Gareth quickly brought Excalibur up and as Mordred's blade struck it the steel clashed. Instantly Mordred howled, a dreadful blood curdling sound, and he disappeared completely.

Gareth's sword struck the floor as his opponent vanished. He looked around the entrance to the tunnel suspiciously, holding his sword at arm's length but Mordred was no-where to be seen. He ran back into the passage but Mordred was not there either, so he rushed back to Johnny.

In the meantime, Johnny had dashed back to the rock holding Galahad's rope, where he found it was now sawing against the sharp edge of the cliff. He leant over, praying that Galahad was all right and hoping that maybe Bran was clinging on somewhere. There was no sign of Bran at all, but he saw that Galahad had started pushing himself out from the rocks with his feet, using the rope like a swing. He hit the rocks with his feet several times, pushing himself further out with each thrust against the rocks. Eventually he was swinging out, right into the middle of the ravine. He gave one final push with his feet and shouted, "Johnny, now!"

Suddenly remembering his promise, Johnny brought his axe down hard on the rope, which severed as soon as its razor sharp blade made contact.

"Oh, no!" Johnny shouted in despair at the action he had just taken. "Oh please let him be all right!"

Gareth looked fearfully over the edge with Johnny, their hearts thumping in their chests, and saw Galahad's final flight across the ravine with no rope to impede him. He flew outwards and dropped down, throwing himself towards the ledge that jutted out below him as he plummeted downwards.

Watching from the other side, Rachel saw Galahad launch himself towards the platform she was on, and her voice returned instantly in the form of a scream.

"Galahad, No!" she shouted as she saw him drop down like a stone.

She screamed again in terror, thinking he had fallen to his death in the ravine. Then she realised that he had caught hold of the platform they were on, but was hanging on by his fingertips, desperately trying to pull himself up.

"Quickly, we have to help him up!" directed Rachel, her new-found voice commanding, as she dragged herself up and crawled towards the edge, unable to stand. "Help me, I said!" she screamed at Bethany.

Together, bit by bit, the two girls managed to pull him up by tugging at his clothing: one on each side until he was far enough over the ledge to scramble up himself.

He lay panting on the shelf for a moment and when he managed to pull himself into a kneeling position Rachel threw her arms round him, clinging to him in relief.

"I thought you'd fallen into the ravine," she sobbed. "You shouldn't have done that, it was too dangerous!"

He put his arms round her. "'Twas the only way to get to you," he answered with a smile.

"Well you still shouldn't have done it," she replied. "What about the guards you were with? I saw one of them fall over the edge!" she asked. "I don't understand, were you escaping from them?"

"One went over?" questioned Galahad, the smile leaving his face. "Rachel - they were not guards, I was with Gareth, Johnny and Bran, and they were disguised as guards to help you escape," he answered softly, realising with horror that one of them might have fallen.

"Oh, no, one of them went into the ravine. I saw it. Oh no, who was it?" Rachel asked in panic, her eyes scanning the cliff above, where she could only see two figures standing watching from their high shelf.

"I do not know what happened up there," Galahad said gently, "but I do know that it was not Johnny that fell, 'twas his axe that just severed my rope."

"No, no, oh no," she sobbed against him, realising that it could have been Gareth that had fallen, not wishing on the other hand, for it to be Bran either.

"Rachel," Galahad said, shaking her slightly. "We must leave. Whoever it was that fell to their death, whether 'twas your brother or Bran, they have given up their life to save you, let that not be in vain. Come we must go," he finished, trying to pull her up to her feet.

"I can't, I don't have any strength, I can't even stand," she answered, the tears pouring down her cheeks.

"You must drink this," said Galahad, pulling the small potion bottle out of his pocket. "Morgana has given us all a potion to see through Rathyen's magic. This one will rid you of her spell, you must take it."

"Morgana's helped you?" Rachel said, slightly incredulously.

"She has, she gave us a map and the potions we have all taken, 'tis safe to drink it!"

Rachel nodded and drank the potion. The effect was immediate, her head began to clear and her mind began to function again, as the heavy, foggy cloud lifted from her brain. The strength flowed back into her body and for the first time since she had left Tintagel her limbs felt as though they belonged to her again.

Galahad shouted across the ravine. "Go back; we will meet you at the wood where the horses are. Wait for us, we will find a way out!"

Gareth and Johnny acknowledged his message by waving their arms back at him.

"Galahad you're ace, please look after Rachel!" shouted Gareth gratefully.

"That was Gareth's voice! He's not dead!" said Rachel with a sob of relief. "Oh thank goodness!"

"Indeed it was," agreed Galahad sombrely.

"That means it was Bran that fell! Oh no, poor Bran, he's been so good!" cried Rachel, the tears running down her face again. "How are we going to tell poor Sarah? She'll be devastated, she loves him so much!"

"We will deal with that on our return, but now we must leave!" he said, urgently.

"Please Miss, please take us with you!" came a nervous, pleading voice from behind them.

Rachel turned, feeling guilty again that she had forgotten all about the young girl who had helped her so much. "Galahad, this is Bethany, she's been really good to me, we must take her with us!" answered Rachel immediately.

"Very well," Galahad replied. "But we must go now!"

They left the shelf that had been Rachel's prison, and passed through the door into a long tunnel. They walked quietly through it until Bethany tugged at Rachel's sleeve.

"Please Miss, I have to take my sister, I cannot leave her! I have to get her back to Tintagel, please help me get her back, she is not well."

Rachel looked helplessly at Galahad, knowing that he would not ignore the girl's request.

"Where is your sister, how can we reach her?" he asked.

"I can help you leave, I know the tunnels and there is another that will take us up above the waterfall, 'tis our only hope of leaving here. I will take you to it; we will pass the passage that leads to our rooms. We can get my sister on the way," Bethany said, fervently.

"So be it," answered Galahad, and Bethany murmured her thanks over and over again as she led them through the maze of tunnels leading upwards.

They came to a long-dark passage and she halted. "This way, my sister is down here," she said.

They crept silently down the passage until they reached a small door, which Bethany opened to reveal a small, dismal room where a young girl lay on a stone shelf with a ragged blanket over her. She looked thin and pale. Her eyes were dark and framed by long, black lashes and she bore a terrified expression as she saw Galahad and Rachel enter the room.

"Odele, this is Rachel that I have told you of, and the one that has come to save her! He will save us all, we must go with them, do not be afraid," Bethany told her. "We are to go back to Tintagel. You remember Tintagel don't you?"

Odele struggled to sit up, clutching her blanket around her for protection. She gazed from one to another, still looking terrified, and nodded. "The castle," she said, her voice a mere whisper. "I remember the castle."

"That's where we're going, think about the castle," said Rachel, feeling for the poor sickly-looking girl. "We'll take you there."

Odele got up and her knees buckled from under her. Galahad quickly held on to her as Odele looked at Bethany in despair. "I want to go Bethany; I want to go back to the castle. I don't like it here, it frightens me!"

"And you shall," said Galahad, resolutely, scooping her up into his arms. "We will go now; your sister will lead the way."

The tunnels narrowed and climbed steeply, they held the

candle that had been in Odele's room as their only source of light. Eventually they saw a small opening in the rocks and a shaft of light poured in. The opening was just big enough for them to climb through, but it led on to a narrow ledge overlooking the stream. They were above the waterfall and it poured out below them.

"Now what?" asked Rachel. "How are we going to get down from here?"

"If we follow this ledge as far as we can, the water further down will be deep enough for us to jump," said Bethany.

"Jump!" exclaimed Rachel in horror. "If we hit a rock the fall could kill us!"

"'Tis the only way out with no guards," replied Bethany. "And I would rather die on the rocks than at Rathyen's hand. If Odele and I die here, we will go to a good place. If Rathyen kills us she will bind us to a life of the undead as her servants!"

"Can you swim?" asked Galahad, practically.

"I can, but my sister cannot," Bethany answered.

"And you still want her to jump? She could drown!" said Rachel, still horrified by the idea.

"I have to get her away from Rathyen. I have told you what will happen to her if we stay here!" Bethany replied, sadly.

"I don't mind jumping, if we can leave here!" declared Odele, bravely.

"You shall jump with me, we will go together!" said Bethany. "I will look after you!"

Rachel looked at Galahad, still amazed at how calm they both were at leaping from such a height. He shook his head worriedly. It was obvious to both of them that the girls were more frightened of Rathyen than jumping off the cliff!

"What of you Rachel, do you swim?" he asked.

"Yes, but I've never done anything like this before!"

"I am not happy about it either," he answered quietly. "I am sorry I cannot offer you an easier way of escape."

"It's not your fault," Rachel answered. "You risked your life to be here!"

"We must hurry, before we are missed!" urged Bethany.

Galahad and Rachel nodded resignedly, and slowly they all edged their way along the jagged ledge, inching their way downwards as they went. Soon the ledge ended and the drop below seemed just as daunting, even though there were no sharp rocks below them. The stream looked fast-flowing and deep at this point and Rachel felt sick just looking down on it.

"We will all jump together," said Galahad. "We can help each other in the water."

They stood on the ledge facing the water, Bethany clung on to Odele in preparation for the jump and Galahad took Rachel's hand.

On the count of three they all jumped out and fell like four stones towards the water. They hit the surface and went down and down, until Rachel thought they would surely hit the bottom. She began to kick hard with her legs and found herself heading upwards towards the surface. She bobbed up and found the water splashing round her as she gulped for air. The current was sweeping them away fast out of the deep pool they had jumped into and she could only see Bethany struggling to keep herself and Odele up in the rushing water. She fought hard to swim and keep herself up, but the current was strong as it rushed towards a narrow stretch and as fast as she could fill her lungs with air, she was pulled under again.

Each time she bobbed up she tried to look for Galahad, but she couldn't see him or even the girls now, only a torrent of water around her as she was dragged downstream towards the rocks.

Chapter Fourteen
A Recipe for Dark Magic

As the rocks drew nearer Rachel came to the surface again, coughing and spluttering, and a strong hand gripped her arm. She was so relieved to see Galahad that she could have cried.

"Swim towards the middle," he shouted. "'Tis not much further, once we are past the rocks it widens out and becomes shallower. There is a tree right over the stream, hold on to it and pull yourself to the bank!"

"Are the others all right?" she managed.

"Yes, they have just passed the rocks," he shouted back.

They swam together and managed to avoid the rocks. There was a small drop, which the current carried them over, and soon Rachel could feel her feet scraping the bottom. It was a struggle to try and stand up, as the water was still moving quite quickly.

She reached the tree that hung down low over the water and grabbed it firmly. She managed to pull herself onto her feet and wade through the water to the bank, where she collapsed exhausted next to Bethany and Odele.

"Oh, Miss, we are free!" said Bethany. "We are free! We have escaped Rathyen!"

Rachel looked at her bedraggled, wet state and then at the exhausted Odele next to her who looked as though she would never manage a long journey anywhere, and smiled back. She didn't want to dampen Bethany's enthusiasm by telling her that this was only the first hurdle and they had a long way to go. Galahad climbed up the bank and obviously thought the same, as he glanced with concern at Odele.

"We must carry on to keep ourselves warm, we will be travelling wet until we can find a place safe enough to dry out," he said. "Is your sister well enough to travel?"

"I will help her," said Bethany, determined that they were going to get away.

They crawled on all fours, the same as Galahad had done with the others to avoid being seen by the guards. It was slow going, the girls were all hampered by their long, wet dresses and Odele was struggling to keep up, even with Bethany's help. To save time, Galahad pulled Odele over his back and crawled with her weight on him.

Once they reached the cover of the other hills they had to wade back across the stream, the water rushing past them, hitting the rocks intermittently and sending up a spray. It was still difficult for the girls as the current caught their dresses, almost dragging them over. Odele looked weak and pale now, her teeth chattered and she leant heavily against her sister. By the time they reached the safety of the rocks and the sparse leafy cover they were almost too tired to walk. They were starting to feel the cold as the breeze chilled their wet clothes that clung so heavily to them.

They struggled against the thorns that pulled at their clothes in the shelter of the prickly gorse and trees, until they reached the pass in-between the rocks.

"We must be careful here, the guards could see us as we break cover," said Galahad. "We must go quickly, one by one, and hope that they are not already looking for us!"

There were not as many guards as before around the entrance and it would appear that they had not yet been missed as they were able to slip through unnoticed.

They walked back along the path between the mountains and as they turned the next bend they saw Johnny and Gareth waiting for them with the horses.

"Rachel!" shouted Gareth, running to hug her. "Oh thank God you're safe!"

"Bran's not with us," Johnny told Galahad, sadly. "He fell to his death in the ravine!"

"We suspected as much, but how did it happen? Why did he fall?" asked the knight.

"Mordred, that's how!" said Gareth bitterly. "Bran took a strike from him that was meant for me. Mordred pushed him over the edge before we could do anything!"

"Mordred?" answered Galahad, looking astounded. "But he is dead!"

"That's what I thought," answered Johnny. "But Gareth says that Morgause has brought him back to kill Gareth. Bran's sword went right through his, it made no impact, but when Gareth struck it with Excalibur he disappeared!"

"Disappeared?" questioned Galahad, unable to understand what Johnny was implying.

"Yep, just like that. He was gone!" answered Gareth. "He vanished into thin air!"

"I will not even pretend to understand any of this," answered Galahad. "We need to ride quickly before Rachel is missed. We need to ride long and hard until we can reach a place to dry out!

We must leave now!"

"This is so dreadful, I still can't believe what happened to Bran," said Rachel, tearfully.

"'Tis sad, and his loss will be hard for you all to bear, you were his friends!" answered Galahad. "There will be a time for grief, but now we must leave!"

Odele's teeth were chattering loudly and her sister put the blanket around her that Johnny offered.

"This is Bethany and her sister Odele, they are coming with us to Tintagel," explained Rachel.

"No problem, they can ride with us," said Gareth as they all tried to pull themselves out of their deep despondency, realising the urgency of starting their journey. Odele shrank back against Bethany, hiding her face against her sister's shoulder.

"She means no disrespect," said Bethany. "She is frightened by your uniforms, you look like the guards."

"Oh yes, so we do!" said Gareth, untying the leather tunic. "I had forgotten that! Odele, I promise you we are not guards, we stole their armour to get into the cavern. We are here to take you back."

"Give them Bran's horse, she can ride with Bethany," said Galahad. "Rachel will ride with me."

They all mounted quickly and struck up a fast pace through the mountain pass, until they found the green plains that rolled gently ahead of them. The horses, well rested, were happy to gallop on and on relentlessly over green hill and pastures, their riders clinging to them wet, cold and exhausted. Gareth and Johnny took the lead with the others following, the sun went down and they still rode on. Their mood was sombre, as Bran's death weighed heavily on all of them. For once Rachel was quite happy to lean back against Galahad and let him take charge, feeling comforted by his strength as the horses pounded on. Eventually, after riding in the dark for as long as they could, they rode into a deep wood and Galahad called a halt. "We cannot carry on, the ladies are too cold," he said. "We will build a fire to warm them for a few hours before we continue our journey."

They dismounted and Gareth and Johnny quickly collected branches to make a fire. Bethany and Odele huddled together, still wet and shivering. Rachel and Galahad helped to light the fire before sitting next to it to get warm.

"We cannot stay long here," Galahad said. "We need a place of safety to rest in. Rathyen's men will come for us when they find Rachel missing."

"If we can get to the border, Meinir will help us," said Gareth. "I know that if I ask her, she would ensure that her men protected us while we rest."

"Her fortress is at least a day's ride away, maybe more," answered Johnny. "We can make it if we don't stay here too long but I don't like the look of that young girl. She won't make another ride, she's too weak."

They all looked at Odele who rested against Bethany, her eyes closed, her breathing shallow and the dark circles under her eyes looking worse than ever. She looked pale and fragile as she shivered violently, even though they were close to the fire.

"I'm sure she's too ill to make the journey without any rest," repeated Johnny.

"Can you do anything to help her?" Gareth asked Rachel, and she knew that he meant magically.

"Maybe I can," she answered. "I'll try." She went over to the two girls and sat down beside them. She took off Argante's ring and slipped it on to Odele's finger.

"Miss, is that not the ring of your saviour?" asked Bethany.

"You cannot do this," she added, reverently.

"Yes I can, it's just a ring and I don't even know if it will work, but it might just help Odele get through this. You can give it back to me it when we get to Tintagel," Rachel answered.

Odele appeared to be sleeping, but as soon as the ring was on her finger, her breathing evened out and Rachel was sure that some of the colour was coming back into her cheeks.

"Let her sleep for a while, I'm sure the ring will help her," said Rachel.

"We can never repay you for this, Miss," breathed Bethany, with tears in her eyes. "No one has ever done anything like this for us before."

"Just look after your sister. If we can get her back to the castle, Merlin will be able to help her. Besides I haven't forgotten your kindness; I wouldn't have survived there without it!" replied Rachel.

Bethany hugged her briefly before clutching her sister again; wrapping the blanket that Johnny had given her tightly round them to keep her warm.

Rachel returned to sit beside Galahad in front of the fire.

"You must rest," he said, and wrapped a dry blanket around her shoulders.

"So must you," she said. "I don't think I've even thanked you for what you did."

"I do not need gratitude, I would do the same again if I had to," he replied, putting his arms around her, wrapping his own blanket tightly round both of them to keep her warm.

"Galahad, do you have any rings?" asked Rachel, the thought suddenly crossing her mind that maybe he was the person that Rathyen had said would come for her after all.

"I have one, 'twas my fathers but I do not wear it," he answered, looking puzzled. "Why do you ask?"

"Is it the same as the one I have just given to Odele?" she asked, curiously.

"No," he laughed. "It bears no resemblance to it at all! I noticed the ring when you were wearing it though. It has the crest of Arthur's mother's house."

"So could it be Arthur's ring?" she asked.

"I do not believe that I have ever seen Arthur wearing a ring like that. He wore three: one from Guinevere, one made for him as the King and one from his father. He was buried with all of them."

"Maybe he just didn't wear it, maybe he kept it somewhere," she answered, hoping to resolve the mystery of the ownership of the rings.

"No," Galahad answered. "If his mother had given him a family ring he would have worn it. I knew Arthur well; he would have displayed it proudly, he was fond of his mother."

"But you don't wear your father's ring!" she said.

"That is different, you know my history with my father," he replied, curtly. "I am not proud to wear his ring!"

"I'm sorry, I shouldn't have said that," she said, feeling guilty.

"No matter, what is done in the past is done," he answered. "I do not dwell on it as you know. We have so much ahead of us to endure, why so worried about a ring?"

"Oh take no notice; it's just that Rathyen and Morgause seemed to think that the ring belongs to someone very special, they kept questioning me about it. I have no idea who they think it could be, but it definitely isn't the person who gave it to me," she answered. "Although I was told that there is another ring exactly the same somewhere, so it's all a bit of a mystery. Everyone who has seen it thinks it belongs to someone else, but no one will tell me who that is!"

"They are all probably mistaken," Galahad answered. "There are a great many legends about swords, rings, magical sceptres, stones. There are so many of them that none can tell which are true and which are not."

"You're probably right," she answered with a yawn. "I still can't believe what happened to Bran either, he only came to help rescue me!" she finished, sadly.

"Aye, 'tis a tragedy, but you must sleep now, Rachel," Galahad said, wrapping the blanket tighter. "We have a long, punishing journey ahead of us!"

She leant her head against him, feeling safe for the first time in days. All thoughts of the day's terrible events disappeared as she closed her eyes and fell asleep against the comfort of his shoulder.

Johnny and Gareth stayed awake, on guard, by the fire while the others slept. They kept it going by adding branch after branch to keep them warm. Gareth's hand was never far from the heavy sword Excalibur that rested at his side, for he was uneasy that Mordred was still out there, biding his time before attacking again.

"I can't stop thinking about Mordred, he's out there waiting. I know he is," Gareth said quietly to Johnny. "He killed Bran instead of me, and I feel so awful about it. If only I'd been standing where Bran was, I would have seen him first and Bran may still be alive!"

"It's just the way it happened; none of us could have predicted that one! It wasn't your fault, and any of us would have done the same as Bran," said Johnny. "I'll tell you what I think though, Excalibur protected you. Bran's sword had no effect, but when you struck Mordred's sword, he disappeared. I don't think he can touch you as long as you hold that sword!" he finished.

"Do you know what? I think you're right!" exclaimed Gareth.

"But none of us are safe while he's out there. Bran died because of him!"

"Just make sure you keep hold of that sword then," said Johnny. "I think that's the only thing that's keeping him away."

They continued banking up the fire for several hours until Galahad woke the girls. It was still dark but he insisted they continue. Wearily they all mounted and followed Galahad as he cantered off across more plains and valleys towards the borders. Daylight came and they rode on unhindered through the day. There was no sign of Rathyen's men but they carried on anyway, only stopping occasionally for a short break by a stream to drink. At one point there was a sound of snapping twigs in the undergrowth and Gareth jumped nervously, convinced that he caught a glimpse of the grey, dead Mordred.

As the light began to fade again they were fit to drop, hungry and tired. Gareth led them to Meinir's fortress, a small brown stockade, heavily guarded, where her sentries refused to let them in.

"Tell Meinir that Gareth and Galahad from Tintagel are here, she will remember us!" he shouted up at the men on the high wooden stockade walls, their arrows pointing at them ready to fire.

They waited by the gates, the girls shivering from the cold that had penetrated their still damp clothing, until they saw the big wooden gates swing open.

"Garrrethth," came a lilting female voice with a hint of welsh dialect. "What brings you to my encampment?"

"Meinir, I have to ask you for help," said Gareth. "We need food and shelter."

A young, sinewy woman stepped forward; her brown hair was long and fell almost down to her waist. The top part was braided and she wore a long, simple tunic, belted at the waist over trousers and boots, like the soldiers. A simple armour over the top of the tunic indicated that she was as much a warrior as her men. She was attractive, but in a strong way; her face was slightly tanned, with a long, straight nose and high cheekbones. Her bracelet-clad arms revealed muscles almost as big as those of the men watching them and she carried a heavy sword at her belt.

"Come, dismount, you are welcome. But what trouble follows you, that you would need to ask my help?" she asked with a laugh, clicking her fingers towards her men who immediately led their horses away to be looked after.

"Plenty, believe me!" answered Gareth. "Look, I'll be honest with you; we have just rescued my sister and these two girls from Rathyen. She may be following us and I don't want to bring any trouble to your village. If we could just eat and rest for a while we will leave you. I don't want you to get involved with our problems!"

"It has been quiet of late," Meinir laughed. "My men could do with a fight! Take shelter with us for the night, I will double the guards so that you may rest easy," she replied.

"Look, I'm talking about Rathyen here, are you sure?" Gareth asked.

"The black witch, from the black mountains," Meinir answered. "We have held her off, one way or another, more than once before and for you, my friend, we would do it again. Besides, my archers could do with the practice!"

"We are indebted to you, Meinir, for your kindness," said Galahad, with a bow.

"No, sir, we are indebted to you. Were it not for the knights of Tintagel that helped us once before, we would not have maintained our position here," the strong, young woman returned with a smile. "I am merely honouring a dept to you. 'Tis the least that we can do! 'Tis my honour to offer you protection in your plight! My men will guard you well, have no fear of that."

The heavy gates were barricaded again behind them and Meinir shouted orders that were instantly obeyed. They were taken to a small dwelling that was warm and comfortable. Meinir brought them a change of clothes and blankets and they all felt much better once they were in dry garments. Food was brought to them and they ate hungrily.

Bethany and Odele fell asleep on the settle by the warm fire that crackled comfortingly in a heavy metal grate. Odele looked better even though she was obviously still weak, but now they noticed that Bethany was growing pale and had lost her previous excitement about their escape.

"I don't think Bethany looks very well now," whispered Johnny.

"I've been thinking the same; she's been very quiet for several hours. Maybe she's caught a chill," said Rachel.

"There is a healer in the village, I'll ask Meinir if she could get her to take a look at both of them," said Gareth, and went off to find her.

He arrived back with Meinir and an old woman with a toothless smile; she smelt of lavender and herbs and looked at the two girls in concern. She leant over them and felt their brows, holding their wrists in turn to feel for their pulse. They all watched her expectantly, and were relieved when they heard her say, "The youngest girl is not ill, she is just exhausted. She is weak. With rest and good food, she will recover. I have a potion that will help her."

"And what about Bethany?" asked Rachel, hopefully. "She was all right when we left."

"Sadly, I have no potions that can help her," answered the old woman, shaking her head. "I fear 'tis not an illness that ails her, 'tis a powerful magic. Every step she takes away from her mistress will weaken her until she dies. I cannot help her with this. You have come from Rathyen's domain and this girl is her servant. She has been bound by magic to keep her there. I have seen this before with others that have escaped from her."

"I don't understand - Odele was her servant as well and yet she's all right," said Rachel.

"The young miss bears the mark of servitude to Rathyen," the old lady answered. "But you have given her something that is interrupting Rathyen's spell, have you not?"

"I gave her a ring to wear," said Rachel, cautiously.

"Whatever you have given her will work until she takes it off," the old woman told them. "When she does so, death will come quickly!"

"Do you not have anything that can help Bethany?" asked Galahad.

"I have many herbs and many cures," she answered. "But I do not have any magic, nor do I understand it. I will take the girls to my home and do what I can for them tonight."

"Morgana said there was a binding spell that would affect Rachel, that's why she gave us the potion for her. She said she couldn't leave without it. That must be what's happening to Bethany," exclaimed Johnny.

"That's the potion that you gave me from Morgana isn't it?" Rachel asked Galahad. "That's why I'm all right."

"Do you have any of this potion left?" enquired the old woman.

"I've got the bottle," said Rachel, going over to her pile of damp clothes. She pulled it out of the pocket in her dress and gave it to her.

The old woman took off the stopper and waved it under her nose. A strong smell emitted from the bottle even though there could be no more than a few drops left in it.

"Belladonna," she said as she sniffed it. "Root of Elm, arrowroot, primrose and what is that?" she sniffed again. "Oh yes, I have it, root of wild carnation. Seeds from the wild blue Poppy, buds of the wild dog rose, bark of ash and oak, and the hips from the rose of the hedges, purple and yellow... I can smell their fragrances in the bottle. I know this cure!" she said, triumphantly. "It was given to me by a beautiful, dark-haired child that escaped Rathyen's powers years ago. Our men found her dying in the woods and brought her to me. She whispered this secret recipe to me and I made it for her."

"Did it work? Could you make it again?" asked Rachel.

"I have made it for others, but it has never worked. The child was a sorceress, she delivered her own incantation before drinking it," she answered. "She was the most beautiful child that I have ever seen, but her white skin bore the marks of manacles around her wrists, throat and feet. I have never seen marks like that upon a child so lovely!"

"Do you remember her name?" asked Gareth.

"She would not give it, but she said she had been sent by her mother to Rathyen to learn from her. She was to be her apprentice."

"That sounds like Morgana. It must be!" declared Johnny. "We know that Morgause sent her there, and she had a dreadful time before escaping!"

"I can brew this potion, but it will only work with a sorceress to deliver it," said the healer.

"You are a sorceress are you not?" Meinir asked Rachel.

"Well, sort of," answered Rachel, hesitantly.

"Then if you have magic, why can you not save the girl yourself?" Meinir asked.

"Rachel is not the right kind sorceress to activate the potion, Meinir," explained the old woman. "She does not have the dark magic."

"If you could make it again, we'll try to figure out how to make it work," interjected Gareth.

"A good idea," agreed Meinir, growing impatient with all the talk of magic. "Ymyiswyre will take the girls and look after them tonight. She will make this potion for you," she said firmly. "Maybe you would care to join me, Gareth, we have much to catch up on."

Gareth nodded and followed her out. Shortly afterwards, two men came into the hut and lifted up the two sleeping girls to take them to Ymyiswyre's hut.

"I don't know about you two, but I am so tired I could fall asleep standing up!" said Johnny after they had gone. "That big bed is looking very inviting, believe me!"

"Go for it!" laughed Rachel. "You deserve it!"

Johnny climbed in and pulled the blankets over him. "Oh, yes," he said delightedly. "This is so comfortable after nights on the forest floor! Oh, this is pure luxury, goodnight you two!"

"Goodnight," said Rachel, taking off her shoes. "If it's as comfortable as he says it is, I'm in there too! I'm exhausted."

"'Tis not seemly that you should stay with us," said Galahad. "Maybe you should go and sleep with the women."

"I can't, Galahad," said Rachel, climbing into the big bed beside Johnny. "In case you hadn't noticed I wasn't invited and I'm sure the old lady's hut won't have room for another one. Anyway, Gareth will be back soon!" she said, pulling the rough pillow under her head.

"Very well, if that is what you wish," said Galahad, stiffly, before joining them. "Though I would have preferred it if your brother was here as well." He lay down next to Rachel and they all fell asleep almost instantly.

When Gareth eventually came back, there was little room left in the bed for him. He had to push his way in next to Johnny, who was snoring gently. For a moment it irritated him until tiredness took over and he drifted off to sleep, feeling safe in the knowledge that they were protected for the night.

As they slept, Mordred lumbered out of the bushes outside the encampment walls, his blank, crazed eyes searching for a way in. He waited and watched until the guards changed and only two stood on duty. He saw them standing talking, on top of the high stockade fencing and made his way towards it. He scaled it easily and his sword immediately silenced one of the sentries. Terrified by Mordred's dreadful appearance, the remaining archer fired arrow after arrow at him. To his horror, they went straight through Mordred's chest as though he were not even there, bouncing off the wall behind him. Frightened out of his wits, the sentry backed away from him, withdrawing his bow.

Mordred's triumphant leer widened, showing the still gleaming white teeth in his decaying face, and with one swift movement he thrust his sword into the archer and pushed him over the stockade.

Chapter Fifteen
Formidable Feats and Feline Forms

The sentry landed in the courtyard and as soon as his body was found, the alarm went up. A furious Meinir joined her men, only to see them try to apprehend their sole infiltrator to no avail. Their swords went through Mordred as easily as the sentry's arrows had done. They couldn't stop Mordred as he lumbered towards the small hut that sheltered the sleeping party; his sword slashing and killing anyone in his way.

Meinir's duty to her men surpassed her intentions to keep her visitors safe, and after several more were wounded in a futile attempt to stop Mordred, she held up her hand for them to fall back. "God save them," she said, "for we cannot help them!"

The door to the sleeping party's hut crashed open, waking them all in an instant. Mordred's red eyes searched only for Gareth, who was still half hidden under the blankets. Mordred raised his sword and moved towards the bed.

"No!" screamed Rachel, sitting up quickly. Instinctively, in her panic, a flash of white light flew from the finger that she pointed towards Mordred. The bolt of white magic hit him, stopping him for a moment as though dazed. It wasn't long, however, before he recovered and raised his sword. Rachel shouted at him again, kneeling up on the bed, as Gareth scrabbled on the floor to reach for Excalibur.

Her second white beam of magic hit Mordred, and he moaned with pain. It was a deep, unearthly sound that made everyone shiver. His temporary halt gave Gareth just enough time to grab Excalibur and jump out of the bed. Galahad and Johnny joined him with their swords ready to help against the gruesome figure.

"No, stand back, get Rachel out of here," Gareth shouted, determinedly. Mordred sneered and started to move forward. "Quickly, he isn't interested in any of you, he wants me! Just get out now!"

They all fled past Mordred who didn't even notice them; his crazed eyes burned into Gareth's as his sword came up again. Gareth drew the great sword Excalibur back and swiped it at Mordred. It went straight through him, as all the sentries' swords had done. Gareth wielded Excalibur again, and the big man seemed to lose all of his strength. Another blow from Gareth plunged through Mordred's torso and he howled an unearthly cry of defeat. He disappeared, leaving behind the smell of rotting flesh as the only evidence that he had ever been there.

Gareth breathed an enormous sigh of relief, and called to the others that Mordred had gone. Johnny and Galahad rushed back into the hut, followed by Meinir and Rachel. Meinir's men quickly surrounded the building, swords and axes at the ready.

"I fear that we have let you down. I am ashamed to say that we could not stop him," Meinir said. "I have lost the men that tried! I had to call a halt, or he would have killed them all!"

"It's not your fault, you couldn't protect us from Mordred," answered Gareth. "No one could, and I am just sorry that your men have died trying to stop him. We won't stay any longer."

"You will go back to sleep," Meinir told him, determinedly. "I have every man in the camp in position, and we can at least alert you if he comes again. We can match Rathyen's soldiers, but if 'tis her undead army that follow you, then we can only pray for you!"

"Undead army?" questioned Johnny. "Mordred wasn't anything to do with Rathyen! He was sent by someone else."

"He looked like one of Rathyen's undead," Meinir answered. "He must belong to her army from the underworld!"

"What army?" asked Gareth, worriedly. "Johnny's right, Mordred wasn't sent by Rathyen. What do you mean her army from the underworld?"

"There is a story, that Rathyen was exiled from Wales because she terrorised the people there. Instead of leaving, she took over the black mountains as her home. Not satisfied with the size of the caverns there, she enslaved any man she could capture to quarry downwards. It is said that the tunnels went so deep that she opened up a pathway into Hades itself," explained Meinir. "It is also said, that the creatures from Hades escaped and she bound them to her with her magic, as her servants. The Master of Hades was displeased and he came up out of the underworld into the mountain. She made a pact with him and it was decided, due to her black nature, that they could live in harmony. He allowed her to keep the creatures that she had enslaved in return for the souls of all those she brought to her caverns."

"What? That can't be true, surely?" said Gareth in horror.

"I am only telling you what I have heard," continued Meinir. "Until now I did not believe it, but the story says that a servant of the underworld cannot be destroyed by a living mortal. I saw the person you call Mordred with my own eyes and I saw my men's swords and arrows go straight through him. We may not be able to do much to help you, Gareth, but at least we can stand watch whilst you rest tonight. Go back into the hut and sleep, at least until first light, and then you may eat before you continue your journey."

"Thanks, Meinir," said Gareth, "We owe you for this!"

They all went back inside. Galahad, Johnny and Rachel lay down again, still exhausted, in an attempt to get whatever sleep they could before they had to leave. Gareth stayed on the settle, wide-awake, holding Excalibur tightly against him in case Mordred should return.

In the morning, Meinir brought them food and they were joined by Ymyiswyre who was supporting Bethany. Although the girl was at least conscious, it was obvious that she was still very ill. Her sister Odele however, looked much stronger than when they had last seen her and her cheeks even had a faint tinge of colour in them.

"Oh no, Bethany looks dreadful," exclaimed Rachel, in concern.

"I have made the potion. There are two bottles, if you administer one to her now, the other one might just keep her alive until you reach Tintagyle," said Ymyiswyre. "I am sorry that I have been unable to do more for her!"

"No, you've been brilliant," returned Gareth, taking the bottles from her. "We'll do what we can for her now, and thanks for these!" He gave them to Rachel, who looked at him uncertainly.

"Gareth, I really don't know how to make these work," Rachel said, hesitantly. "I don't know any incantations like Morgana."

"Maybe you don't need to," Gareth answered quietly, pulling her aside. "I had to do some magic to get us up the rocks where the waterfall was. I couldn't remember any of the words from the black book and I just asked the Power for help. It reduced the flow of the water straight away. I think you just have to ask it, and I can't imagine that it would ignore someone who's been treated so badly!"

"That's all very well, but you heard what the healer said! Morgana used a dark magic to make it work. I can't do that."

"You can tell me to mind my own business," interrupted Johnny, "but in all the books I've ever read, the power of good works over evil every time, and isn't that exactly what the Power is? Maybe Morgana did use the dark powers that she had been taught, but it doesn't mean that yours won't work!"

"Rachel, Johnny's right, just do what I did and ask!" said Gareth. "After all, you managed to stop Mordred in his tracks without even thinking about it while I searched for Excalibur. In fact, you seem to be able to produce magic quite easily!"

"Well, I'm glad you think it's so easy!" Rachel replied, crossly. "Anyway, I didn't say I wouldn't try! Just leave me alone for a minute while I think about it!"

Gareth and Johnny backed off and in desperation Rachel sent up a silent request to the Power, not knowing if it would be heard or not. She tried to concentrate, but her attention kept straying to Argante's ring, which was still on Odele's finger. 'Was that the key?' she thought. 'Was it a message, or did she just feel more confident when she was wearing it herself?' Rachel couldn't decide. In fact it proved so much of a distraction that she came to a decision.

"Odele has to give Bethany the potion with me," Rachel said. "I don't know why, but I just feel that it will work better if we do it together."

Gareth handed Rachel the bottle and she removed the stopper. "Please, please help her!" she asked silently. Pale and round-eyed, Odele obediently placed her hand over Rachel's and together they raised the bottle to Bethany's lips.

Bethany coughed and spluttered as the liquid poured into her mouth. She had only swallowed half of it, when Ymyiswyre intervened.

"Let her lie down while you prepare to leave," she said. She put a hand on Bethany's brow, looking closely at her. She leant forwards, put her ear to the girl's chest and smiled. "Her heart is beating much stronger. This may have worked just enough for you to get her back to Tintagyle," she finished with satisfaction, pleased that her potion was working.

"Do you think that she will recover?" asked Rachel.

"No," Ymyiswyre answered, deflating them all immediately. "If you keep administering the potion to her while you travel, it may get her to your destination, but she will not recover until you find a sorceress that can remove this spell from her."

"We know just the person to do that," said Rachel. "I believe that the child you saved was Morgana, the sorceress who gave us the potions."

"She is alive and well?" asked Ymyiswyre, in surprise, and Rachel nodded.

"Please remember me to her. I worried about her for a long time after she left us. She was lost and so consumed by hatred of everyone that had let her down. Rathyen had treated her very badly," said Ymyiswyre.

"I will, and thank you for everything you've done!" said Rachel. The old woman hugged her briefly before leaving them.

They made their preparations to leave and by the time the horses were brought to them, Bethany looked slightly better. She rode with Johnny, who supported her in front of him in the saddle, and Odele rode with Rachel as she was still uncomfortable about riding with any of the men.

They thanked Meinir and rode on again, breaking only to camp at night, until they finally reached Tintagel. The journey was long and arduous and despite Rachel and Odele administered the potion several times to her, Bethany, was on the verge of collapsing by the time they saw the welcome sight of the great castle on its rocky perch. Even the ride across the causeway seemed to take longer than ever. Johnny hung on tightly to Bethany, who was now unconscious, and they were all relieved when they passed through the gates into the safety of the castle. Merlin rushed to meet them and hugged Rachel so tightly she could hardly breathe!

Johnny stayed on his horse, still holding on to a limp Bethany. They explained quickly to Merlin about Rathyen's spell that was affecting both of the girls. "We need to find Morgana," said Rachel. "She's the only one who can help Bethany!"

"Morgana is still here," Merlin reassured her. "She said that you would have need of her if you returned, so I allowed her to stay."

At that moment, Morgana swept towards them. Galahad told her their story and she nodded curtly. "Carry the girl to my room, I will rid both of them of Rathyen's evil," she said. Her pale face showed no emotion and she turned sharply, walking off towards the castle.

Galahad and Gareth lifted Bethany down and Johnny dismounted. They carried her into the castle followed by a frightened Odele.

"Do you think Morgana will help them?" Rachel asked Merlin.

"I am sure she will. Morgana suffered in the same way as them," Merlin replied confidently. "She will be sympathetic and do what she can for the girls."

Once again Merlin's rooms became their sanctuary and his ancient wisdom took charge, allowing them to rest and recover from their ordeal. Relieved to hand over their responsibilities, they ate, drank and finally went to bed, sleeping comfortably knowing they were back in the safety of the castle.

Daybreak came and, one by one, they all surfaced, rested and feeling much better as they congregated in Merlin's room. They breakfasted in the knowledge that for them their ordeal was over, apart from the lingering sadness that Bran wasn't sharing this with them.

Galahad and Gareth had felt it their duty to deliver the news of Bran's death to Sarah upon their arrival, and she had been as devastated as they had all expected. There had been no easy way to tell her that the person she loved most was dead, and they both felt awful for having to be the bearers of such dreadful tidings.

Gareth was still subdued as he joined them in Merlin's room that morning, and Johnny clasped his arm in silent support. Tears sprang to Rachel's eyes as they told her about Sarah's reaction.

"I'm going for a walk," she said, as Galahad joined them looking equally distressed.

"I will accompany you, if I may," he returned solemnly.

They walked up onto the battlements and stood looking out over the sea. Wave upon wave crashed endlessly against the rocks, in a timeless certainty. For centuries, whatever the events that had shaped the lives of those within the castle walls, it had no effect on the constancy of the sea or the elements that surrounded it.

Rachel breathed deeply, leaning over the battlements taking strength from the view that had always remained the same. Galahad didn't speak, he simply put his arm around her shoulder in support and they each reflected on the last few terrible days.

Unknown to Galahad and Rachel, Morgana stood looking out to sea on the other side of the battlements. She was congratulating herself on her effective removal of Rathyen's spells from the two young girls. Strangely enough, her satisfaction had become outweighed by the great sympathy that she felt for Odele and Bethany. She alone understood their sufferings and it brought back her own painful recollections of Rathyen's caverns. She shuddered for a moment as dreadful memories flooded back to her, memories that she had firmly pushed to the back of her mind, intent on never thinking about them again.

Her distressing thoughts were disturbed by Johnny, who joined her, leaning against the parapet. "Morgana, I'm glad you're here, we haven't thanked you for everything you've done to help us," he said sincerely. "We wouldn't have got Rachel back without your potions, and Bethany and Odele wouldn't have made it without you either."

Normally she would have puffed out her chest and asked, disdainfully, why he would have expected any less from her powers. Instead, she looked at Johnny, saw warmth in his eyes and didn't answer.

"I've just seen the girls and whatever you did has worked, Bethany looks so much better!" he continued. "You've been really good to us," he finished.

His words astounded her even further - no one had ever thanked her for being good before and she wasn't used to it at all. She looked at him curiously, seeing for the first time, a handsome, strong, young knight.

"My brother Mordred all but destroyed your life, and yet you have no hate in you. How is this?" Morgana asked, looking puzzled.

"I haven't thought about it lately, but I suppose he did really!" Johnny answered, thoughtfully. "Mordred destroyed the life that I would have had, but I've been given a second chance here. I may not be able to visit my family who I love, but I have good friends here and a new life," Johnny continued. "I'm happy with what I have and I'm grateful for it!"

"You have seen the worst of me," Morgana responded. "You saw me as a shape-shifter, a wolf that attacked and maimed Galahad, and yet now I see admiration in your eyes. I do not understand why you do not hate me."

"I probably did for a while, but now I know you, I can understand that you've suffered even more than me," he told her. "I've also seen you turn over a new leaf, Morgana; you've used the dark sorcery that you were taught, for good. You've helped all of us and I admire you for that!"

"Do you?" she asked in surprise.

"Yes I do," he answered honestly. "And since you've stopped being a wolf, or a really bad sorceress, you're probably the most beautiful woman that I have ever met!"

As soon as Johnny had uttered the words that he had never intended to say out loud, he immediately turned bright red and mumbled that he had to go. Morgana was completely lost for words, having just received a compliment from a man that she hadn't even cast a spell over!

Their moment of following awkwardness was relieved by Gareth, who joined them followed by Galahad and Rachel. They all thanked Morgana with the same warmth that Johnny had. Totally overwhelmed by praise that she was completely unused to, and speechless again, the sorceress gave a short nod.

"I must give you this back Rachel," she said instead, reaching into a deep pocket in her dress and pulling out the large ring that Rachel had given Odele to help her. "The girls asked me to return it to you, they have no need of it now." She briefly turned the ring over in the palm of her hand and looked at it closely before handing it back to Rachel, who immediately slipped it on to her middle finger again. She looked strangely at Rachel. "This is a powerful ring, where did you get it?" she asked.

They were all interrupted by the arrival of Sarah, her eyes puffed and swollen from crying. "Gareth, please, you have to help us," she said, tearfully. "I sent word last night to Bran's family in the village, and the rider came back saying that he could not deliver my message as the village is surrounded by Saxons led by Theodorus!"

"What?" Gareth exclaimed.

"Theodorus has taken back Medraut's castle with the help of the remaining Saxons. They have taken over the village and sent every man to the fortress. I do not know what has befallen the women!" she finished with a sob.

"That damned Theodorus! I am not having this!" said Gareth. "I'm going to get Bran's mother and sisters out of there if it's the last thing I do. We owe it to him!"

"I'm with you!" said Johnny instantly, and Galahad nodded his support.

They were joined on the battlements by four of the young knights; Edwin, Cedric, Robert and Ivan.

"We have just heard the news," said Edwin. "We will all ride with you; Bran was our friend as well!"

"You can saddle my horse too," said Morgana, angrily. "I will not stand by and see that imbecile nephew of mine take up with the Saxons again. Does he never learn from his mistakes?"

"It will not be necessary for the women to go," said Galahad. "There will be enough support from the castle."

"I am not a mere woman, I am a sorceress!" replied Morgana, indignantly. "I will be coming with you! Besides, Merlin said that my brother's estate would go to the person who proved themselves worthy of it. Theodorus has taken it by force and he will not care what happens to any of the villagers. As long as he thinks he will get what he wants, he will be stupid enough to let the Saxons do just as they please!"

"I don't think it's necessary for you to get involved..." started Gareth.

"Together, Rachel and I can give you a very powerful sorcery," interrupted Morgana. "Your swords and arrows can only do so much and the Saxons have no magic. The Power of light that Rachel has, combined with the force of darkness that I hold is probably undefeatable. Think hard before you reject it!"

"Me?" said Rachel, in surprise. Apprehensive of wading straight into more problems, she looked nervously at Gareth.

"You don't need to come, Rachel," her brother said immediately.

"Yes I do," Rachel answered, resignedly. "Bran died because he came with you to rescue me! I have to help!'"

"I will summon as many as I can," said Galahad. "We will ride within the hour!"

"Shouldn't one of us tell Merlin?" asked Johnny.

"No need, dear boy, no need!" announced an out of breath, elderly voice behind them. "I would have been here sooner if my old bones were able move faster! Our quest has always been to fight injustice. The Saxons have to be stopped. They will take their lead from Theodorus until they have his castle and then I dread to think what will happen to him and Bran's village. I agree with Morgana, joining the forces of dark and light will give you immeasurable strength!" he finished confidently.

They went back into the castle and changed quickly, before meeting up by the gate where Cedric and Robert held the reigns of their saddled horses. They were surprised to see that all of the new, young knights and many of the older ones with their men had turned out to help.

The small army, led by Galahad and Gareth, galloped out across the causeway and out across the plains and valleys towards the village. They rode for several hours until they came to the wood where they had all hidden with Bronwyn after they had rescued her from Mordred's castle. Edwin and Cedric had volunteered to go ahead as scouts and they all dismounted to wait for them, camouflaged by the trees and bushes.

Eventually they came back and crept stealthily into the shrubbery.

"What news?" asked Galahad.

"The Saxons have the men from the village in the castle; they expect them to help defend it. Most of the women are still in the village and held prisoner by a few Saxons, the others are all at the castle," explained Cedric.

"This is going to make it very difficult," said Galahad. "We will have to attack the castle to gain access, and in doing so we could end up killing the very people we have come to liberate."

"'Twill not be easy to do even that, with our small numbers," added one of the older knights. "That stockade is stronger than it looks and 'tis heavily guarded."

"Oh, if only Bran was here, he knew ways into the castle," said Gareth, wistfully. "He would have got us in without being noticed."

"Well, you were with him when you both rescued Bronwyn," said Johnny. "Can't you remember how he did it?"

"We entered through the gate in the wall, but Sarah got us in," Gareth answered. "We left by a tunnel under the castle; but again, it was opened from the outside by Sarah."

"Well hang on, we're on the outside now," Johnny reminded him. "Can you remember where it was?"

"Yes I can, but we still have to get through the stockade fencing to get to it," replied Gareth.

"There are several gates," stated Morgana. "If you know which one is the easiest to gain entrance into the castle compound, we will open it for you."

"We?" questioned Rachel. "I take it you mean me as well?"

"Of course," Morgana replied.

"With magic?" asked Cedric, his eyes round, with astonishment.

"Do you see me carrying a sword?" Morgana asked him sharply.

"Well no but..." he spluttered, as her disdainful gaze fell upon him.

"No, you do not," she answered, "because I have no need of one!"

"That does not solve our original problem," interrupted Galahad. "If you blow open the gates with one of those flashes of magic, there will be sentries and archers everywhere. They will swarm upon us as we enter and we will have no way of knowing whether they are Theodorus's men or villagers!"

"Do you think I am as stupid as my nephew?" Morgana asked him, indignantly. "I had intended our approach to much more subtle than that!"

"Cedric and I are from the village," interjected Ivan, "If you can get us in, and give us enough time, we can get the villagers to pass on the message that, when we attack, they join us and turn on the Saxons."

"A good plan," said Galahad, "They will know not to stop us, and we will have extra help within the castle. Can you do this?"

"If we can get Ivan and Cedric through the gates unnoticed, we can create some sort of diversion, to make sure that they can cross the courtyard into the castle without being seen. The washing baskets are stored in the room next to the kitchen," said Gareth. "You will need to disguise yourselves as villagers to blend in and deliver your message to them. That's how Bran would have done it," he finished, and there was silence for a moment.

"And he was so good at it," said Johnny, reflectively.

"This could work," agreed Galahad. "But we still have the problem of the guards at the gate. We cannot risk them sounding an alarm."

"Rachel and I will take care of the guards," stated Morgana. "We will open the gate for you, and by the time I have finished with them, they will not even know who their masters are!"

"I have your assurance on that?" asked Galahad, dubiously.

"You most certainly do," Morgana answered emphatically, with a toss of her long, black hair.

"Then half of us will make a small attack on the wall at the other side of the compound. It will create a diversion big enough to ensure that every man runs to the other side of the castle while Cedric and Ivan get in. We will then withdraw, and wait until they have had enough time to alert the village men before we infiltrate the castle through the gate," said Galahad.

"Sounds good to me," agreed Gareth.

"Let's do it then," said Johnny.

There were resounding 'aye's' from all of the men, and a small party started off through the woods to get to the other side of the castle in preparation for their diversion. The others waited, hidden by the trees, as Rachel and Morgana went to the edge of the wood to do their part.

"How are we going to get across the stream without being seen?" Rachel asked. "And how are we going to open the gate?"

"We aren't, the sentries will open it," Morgana replied, calmly.

"And we will be seen."

"I don't like the sound of this at all," said Rachel.

"You are as much a shape-shifter as I am," laughed Morgana. "We will change form."

"No I'm not!" Rachel said in horror. "I've only ever done it once!"

"Well, this shall be your second chance then. We will be black cats," the sorceress replied, as she changed adeptly into the smooth, black feline form that she had used before. "Meow, what are you waiting for," she purred.

"Ok, I'm trying," Rachel answered, and frantically said out-loud. "I have to be a cat! I have to be a black cat. I need to be a cat. I need to change into a cat," she repeated to herself over and over. "Change me into a cat! Please!"

"You really aren't very good at this are you," said Morgana, changing back into herself with a sigh.

"I'm doing my best!" said Rachel. "Ooh!" she exclaimed, as a flick of Morgana's hand sent her shrinking rapidly into cat form. "OOHHH! Meaaaaow!"

"It would have been much less distressing if you had done it yourself," said the sorceress, "but 'tis no matter."

With that, Morgana's sleek cat form padded out of the wood, ran down the slope and picked her way daintily across the stones in the small stream. She ran up the slope, springing easily on all four, black paws and sat down against the gate, waiting for Rachel to join her.

Chapter Sixteen
The Forces of Dark and Light

Struggling to get used to her new cat form, Rachel eventually joined Morgana at the gate. Unlike the sorceress, her new fur was slightly soggy as she had missed her footing on the stones across the stream, unused to walking on four paws. Her long tail felt strange and it had been the first part of her to get wet, as she had forgotten to hold it up.

"At last," meowed Morgana. "You really are not very good at this at all, are you?"

"Never mind that," returned Rachel, crossly, in her new mewing cat voice. "What next?"

"Just do what I do," Morgana answered, clearly enjoying herself, "Meowowowowow!" she screeched loudly, clawing at the gate, and jumping up at the latch. "Meowowowow!"

"Meowowowow!" joined in Rachel.

The sentries all looked down at them in disgust from the top of the stockade, and one threw a stone at them, making Morgana screech even louder. "Meowowowowow!"

"'Tis only a couple of cats," remarked one of the sentries.

"If they keep up that din, I will fetch a bucket of water. A good dousing will soon stop them."

The sentries laughed and turned away, and for a second Morgana transformed back to normal, sending two sizzling green bolts of magic upwards towards the men. Her magic hit two of the guards and they instantly disappeared from view.

"Where did they go?" mewed Rachel, in surprise.

"They have just become two large rats," Morgana meowed back, now in her cat form again.

The two unfortunate guards, who now found themselves a fraction of their normal size, with no voice and an entirely different form, tried desperately to alert their companions. But as rats, all they could do was claw at the other men's legs and gnaw at their boots.

"Filthy beasts!" exclaimed the sentry, in an unfamiliar Saxon dialect. He booted the rat over the side, not realising that it was actually his friend he was kicking. "Go down and let those two damned, caterwauling cats in! They will soon get rid of the rats!"

"The place is riddled with them, how these peasants can live in a place crawling with vermin, 'tis not to my taste at all," replied his large, bearded companion, as he walked down the steps and removed the heavy piece of wood that barred the gate. He lifted the latch and the heavy gate swung open.

Morgana and Rachel padded in softly and, as the guard turned his back to close it, Morgana became herself again. She mumbled something incomprehensible and another bolt of magic hit the man on the back of the head. In a second she was back as a cat again and the man forgot to bar the gate; instead he sat down on a stump of wood by the side of it and began to sharpen his knife, oblivious to anything that was going on around him.

The two sentries still patrolling the wooden parapet eventually missed him and looked over the edge, calling his name. When they received no answer, they walked down the steps suspiciously, holding their swords out in front of them.

Morgana transformed back and hit them with a bolt of her magic, mumbling strange words that Rachel still didn't recognise. She then flicked her hand towards Rachel again, and Rachel suddenly found herself stretching out of her cat form, and began growing at an alarming rate.

"OHHH," Rachel groaned, in a deep gruff voice, as her body distorted. She looked down to see that her fur was gone and had been replaced by strange, rough clothing. She realised to her horror that she was now dressed as a Saxon guard. "Arrahgen, Yorgen!" she exclaimed, even more perturbed to find that could now speak their language, even though she had no idea what she was saying.

Morgana's new disguise was now the same as Rachel's and they both looked like the other guards. The two sentries under the influence of the sorceress's spell, walked straight past both of them, talking together as though nothing had happened and headed towards the castle.

Rachel followed Morgana up the steps to the wooden stockade battlements where the sorceress, looking rather unnerving in her new Saxon body, turned to her excitedly.

"This mission is giving me great pleasure!" Morgana announced, in a deep male voice. "I am finding that helping people is so satisfying. I think I may even do more of it!"

"I'm so glad you're having a good time, Morgana!" said Rachel, sarcastically, as she scratched at the numerous flea bites her new body seemed to be riddled with. "How long have we got to stay like this?"

"Enjoying myself? Oh, I am, indeed!" Morgana replied, enthusiastically, missing Rachel's sarcasm entirely. "We will not stay long in these forms. I do not think I could bear to be one of these Saxon heathens for any length of time. The smell is quite unbearable! Do you think they ever wash?"

"I doubt it, they also have flees!" replied Rachel, scratching her arm. "Why did those two guards just walk off like that, completely ignoring us?"

"Oh, I put it into their minds that we were here to relieve them. They have gone off to bed thinking that their shift is over!" replied Morgana, with a laugh.

"What about the other one down there, sharpening his knife?" Rachel asked, rubbing a particularly itchy bite on her leg.

"Oh, he will do that for hours, he has no idea what is happening around him," Morgana declared. "Stay where you are and act like a sentry, while I go to the gate and let Cedric in. Oh, just a minute, we seem to be a few guards short," she finished, and another wave of her hand promptly recreated three identical Saxon guards standing next to Rachel.

"Do not worry, they will not do anything," Morgana laughed, as she saw Rachel's look of alarm. "They are not real," she added, as she ran down the stone steps towards the gate. "They are an illusion to fool the Saxons into thinking they have a full patrol!"

"Thank goodness for that," said Rachel, looking nervously at the new, life-like Saxon guards standing next to her.

Morgana opened the heavy gate and Cedric and Ivan crept in. They ran swiftly across the courtyard towards the kitchens. Suddenly, the sounds of an attack rang out on the other side of the fortress and they knew that this was Galahad and his men with their diversion. A Saxon leader yelled an order and every able-bodied man ran towards the courtyard. They rushed out of every doorway in substantial numbers, all clutching swords or bows and arrows. A large, scruffy Saxon man shouted up to Rachel and

Morgana, telling them to watch their wall carefully, as he ran after the rest of the men, still hurriedly pulling his armour on.

On the sentry point at the top of the stockade, Morgana and Rachel stood next to the two unmoving Saxon figures that Morgana had created, and the sorceress chuckled again. "He thinks he has four sentries guarding this side, when in fact he has none," she laughed. "When he has gone, we will let the knights in!"

As soon as they saw that the coast was clear, they went down to the gate to open it again. Morgana suddenly realised that they were still disguised as Saxons and wouldn't be recognised by the knights. She flicked her hand again and they both immediately started to transform out of their Saxon disguise into themselves again.

"Ohhhh...! Not again!" groaned Rachel, as her body twisted and reshaped uncomfortably. "You could at least warn me when you're going to do that!"

"You are more than capable of doing it yourself," Morgana replied, "but you take far too long and we do not have time for that!"

The knights and their men filtered stealthily through the open gate, all with their swords drawn. When the last one had entered Morgana closed the gate behind them, but removed the wood that should have barricaded it. She waved her hand again and it disappeared.

"What do we do now?" Rachel asked her. "We've done our part, should we go back to the wood?"

"Indeed not," exclaimed Morgana. "The fun is only just beginning!"

The attack on the other side of the castle, which was only ever intended as a diversion to allow enough time for the others to gain entry to the castle, stopped just as quickly as it had begun. The fortress went quiet as the Saxons lined the walls on the other side, wondering what was happening, and Rachel repeated her question.

"The men will sort themselves out, I am more concerned with their leaders," said Morgana, her previous good spirits replaced by a serious look. "Theodorus needs to be taught a lesson, one that I hope he will never forget! He will be hiding in the castle somewhere in comfort. We must find him!"

Rachel followed Morgana towards the main buildings of the fortress and a man rushed past them, almost knocking them over in his haste to get into the castle. He ran ahead of them up the winding stairs of the turret and along a corridor. They followed him and heard voices coming from a room. The soft, flickering glow of candlelight spread out through the open door and they stood back and listened.

"I tell you that the knights attack us," they heard the man say. "Your men need you, Theodorus, you must go down to them!"

"Phoof," admonished the unmistakable voice of Theodorus. "The Saxons will take care of them."

"But your men need a leader, they need your direction!" insisted the man.

"I shall not go down there," replied Theodorus, going to the window to look out. "I cannot see any battle. No, I shall remain here. After all, I invited the Saxons here to take the castle and protect it. There is no need for me to go down and fight like a common soldier! Do not disturb me again!" he finished, lifting a wine goblet to his lips. "Go I say, leave me in peace!"

"Your father would at least have been with his men," remarked the man, as he headed for the door in disgust. Morgana and Rachel ducked quickly into another room as the man passed by them, muttering to himself angrily.

"You allow yourself to be spoken to like that, by a servant?"

they heard a male voice, with a heavy accent, say to Theodorus. Morgana and Rachel crept forwards to look through the crack in the open door and it was obvious that this was one of the Saxon leaders that Theodorus had persuaded to help him.

"No, I do not," Theodorus answered the thick set, bearded man, indignantly. "Once your men have apprehended the peasants who dare to attack my castle, I will have him killed!"

They both laughed quite unpleasantly and Morgana suddenly swept through the doorway.

"You, my nephew are a disgrace!" she declared, and the smile left Theodorus's face instantly.

"Aunt Morgana, what are you doing here? I have no need of you! I have my inheritance back - no thanks to you or my grandmother with all your great magic!" Theodorus wined, sarcastically.

"So this is the famous aunt of yours? A sorceress I believe?" said the Saxon leader, as he looked Morgana up and down with a leer. "Mmm… quite a beauty! And who is the pretty damsel that accompanies her?" he asked, turning his attentions towards Rachel with the same lecherous smirk. "Quite lovely!" he exclaimed. "Theodorus, I am bored with your castle wenches. These fillies are much more to my taste!"

His hand reached out to touch Rachel's hair and a surge of anger boiled up inside her. As his hand made contact with her hair, he felt a sharp pain as though he had been burnt and he withdrew it quickly. He rubbed his fingers and looked at her suspiciously for a moment. He turned back to Morgana and the same lecherous smile crept back again. "Maybe the dark-haired beauty after all!" he said, as he moved towards her.

"Do not dare to touch me, you Saxon filth!" Morgana hissed at him. One wave of her hand produced a spell in a second and the Saxon's legs suddenly went from under him. He shot across the room until he made contact, very heavily, with the wall.

"How dare you treat him like this, Aunt!" said Theodorus. "Do you know who he is?"

"I most certainly do," answered Morgana, and another swift flick of her hand sent the Saxon rising quickly into the air. His head hit the ceiling and he was suspended there with his legs and arms flailing around him uselessly.

"Aunt Morgana, put him down immediately!" Theodorus commanded, in his nasal, high-pitched voice.

"Oh, but of course, Theodorus," Morgana returned, pleasantly. "If that is what you wish."

Rachel smiled, as she knew exactly what was coming next. Morgana stopped the magic that held him up there and the Saxon fell like a stone. He landed hard on the floor with his arms and legs in a tangle.

"Oh dear, how impolite of us! Maybe we should offer him a seat!" Morgana continued, with a glint of malicious merriment in her eyes, and the man was lifted up in the air again. He spun round and was dropped unceremoniously into a heavy wooden chair, which flew across to the other side of the room and hit the wall again.

The Saxon growled and rushed to get up, only to find he was unable to move.

"Sit comfortably. Do rest yourself a while," Morgana continued, her voice deliberately soothing. "Perhaps you would like a drink?" she said, as her gaze rested on a large pitcher of wine on the table.

"Aunt, no!" shouted Theodorus, as the pitcher lifted upwards, and made its way across the room towards the Saxon. It forced itself to his lips, with half of its contents tipping down his front, as he coughed and spluttered over the rest that gushed into his mouth.

"Aunt, stop it now, I say!" insisted Theodorus, shrilly, whilst Rachel couldn't help but stand and laugh.

"I am merely being courteous to your guest, Theodorus, even though he has shown no respect or manners towards us so far!" his aunt replied, firmly.

The now empty pitcher rose again in the air and then came down quickly, banging the Saxon leader firmly on the head.

"Perhaps you will think twice before crossing me again," she said to the Saxon haughtily, as the metal jug hit him again and again. At this moment there was a knock at the door. Distracted, Morgana allowed the pitcher to fall to the floor with a clang.

"What? Who is it?" shouted Theodorus, irritably.

"'Tis, I sire," said a voice. As the man entered the room, they recognised him as the person that Theodurus had previously dismissed. He looked nervously at the Saxon sitting covered in wine, before saying, "I am sorry to bother you again, Sire, but the villagers have all turned on your men. The castle has been infiltrated by the knights; you must go and help them!"

"Oh, what a nuisance!" complained Theodorus, with a distinct lack of interest. "Where are the guards? Can they not deal with this?"

"No, Sire, they cannot!" replied the man, annoyed by Theodurus's indifference.

The Saxon leader's reaction was completely the opposite. He roared and shouted something in his native tongue that sounded remarkably as though he was swearing, while he struggled angrily against his invisible bonds. "Go down and tell my men to take every village woman out of the castle and kill them in the courtyard in front of the peasants!" he shouted in English. "They will soon realise who their masters are, and stop this nonsense!"

"Do you not want to tell them yourself?" asked the man,

scornfully.

"Do you not think I would, if I were not bound by this witch?" the Saxon exclaimed, angrily. "Your master may be a coward, but I am not. Give the men my instructions immediately!"

"Yes, Sire, right away," the man said, bowing hastily, as he made his way towards the door.

"Not so fast," said Morgana, as he pulled at the handle, and the door instantly refused to open for him. "I have a much quicker route for you. After all, you do not want to keep the Saxon men from executing their leader's orders."

The man was lifted off his feet and propelled through the air by Morgana's magic, towards the open window. It took several attempts to ram his heavily-armoured, portly figure through the narrow frame. Morgana's more forceful fourth attempt proved successful and he shot out of the window, where she immediately released him from her magic and his cry was heard as he went down.

"Oh dear, I am so sorry," Morgana said politely, turning to the Saxon. "It would seem that he will not be able to deliver your orders after all. But then, you did say that you would have preferred to deliver them yourself! We are detaining you, do let me help you!" she finished with a mischievous smile, as the Saxon rose up into the air again.

"Now wait a minute, I do not want to... agghhh..." he bellowed, as the chair tilted and she launched him head first, still sitting on it, towards the same window. "Aggghhh! Theodorus, call off your damned witch, I demand it... agghhh..." he yelled, as his torso went through the window, but the chair got stuck.

"Demand it?" reprimanded Morgana, "Demand it, indeed! Why, my nephew cannot help you!" she laughed. "Oh dear, you appear to be stuck, but have no fear, I will make sure that you join your men!"

She waved her hand to-and-fro, and the chair moved back and forth with it, her magic ramming the chair forcibly against the stone window again and again. Gradually the chair began to break up, a leg or an arm dropping off one at a time until only the back and the seat still remained firmly fixed to the Saxon leader. "Aggghhh," he yelled again and swore a long string of Saxon abuse at Morgana.

"Aunt, do stop it, please!" protested Theodorus weakly, as the chair hit the window frame again. A final bang sent the remains of the chair through the stone window, shaving an inch off each side as it went, with the Saxon leader still sitting on the rest of it.

For a moment she suspended him in mid air above the courtyard, before shooting him upwards and releasing him.

"Oh Aunt, well done, bravo!" simpered Theodorus immediately, in an attempt to appease her. "I always knew that you would help me. You shall take my castle back with your magic!"

"Your castle?" spat Morgana, angrily. "If you want this castle, you will have to fight for it like a man! Do not expect any help from me!"

"But Aunt Morgana, this is so tiresome when you can do it so easily with your magic. Why do I need to fight?"

"Because I am not going to help you, you weak, snivelling idiot," she replied, angrily. She pointed at her nephew and he rose up from the floor, his legs adopting a fast, walking motion in the air as he headed, with a shriek, towards the same stone ledge that the Saxon had disappeared over.

"You will go and help your men. Do you want to take the stairs or the window?" Morgana asked. She clicked her fingers and his sword flew at him from the other side of the room, its handle landing neatly in his unwilling hand.

"The stairs, the stairs!" Theodorus shouted in panic. "Let me down, I'll go! I promise I'll go!"

The door opened on its own and Theodorus picked up speed, flying through the air towards it. Terrified, he accelerated straight through the door, towards the stairs. They could just see the beginning of his rapid descent before the door banged shut again.

Rachel was laughing so much at this, that she could hardly speak. "That was brilliant Morgana!" she finally managed, "but I'm surprised that you let him go."

"Theodorus will not last long out there, he has never used a sword in his life," answered Morgana. "Besides he is my brother's son, I cannot kill him!"

"No, he is part of your family, I suppose," Rachel replied, sympathetically. "I shouldn't have laughed either, but I just couldn't help it. That was so excellent seeing that awful Saxon flying around on his chair! You were amazing!"

"I am not as clever as you think," sighed Morgana, looking out of the window. "The Saxon appears to have survived his fall and, although he is lying on the ground, he is shouting orders at everyone."

"Good heavens, so he is!" said Rachel, looking down on the courtyard with her. "Oh no, look, the Saxon's men are dragging out all the women!" The terrified women's screams below could be heard quite plainly. "They'll kill them!" she finished in horror.

"We must stop them!" declared Morgana, striding towards the door. Rachel followed with the same determination and they ran quickly down the stairs into the courtyard.

In the midst of all the fighting that was going on, twenty frightened girls and women were held by the Saxons in the middle of the courtyard.

"Kill them!" came the order from the Saxon leader, still lying on the hard floor, angry and in pain. "Kill them all!"

Immediately the fighting stopped. The village men looked on worriedly and the knights started to move forwards, their swords drawn ready to protect the women if they could. Even the Saxons stopped to observe this new spectacle, one that promised bloodshed.

The Saxons holding the women lifted their swords and, before Morgana needed to do anything, Rachel screamed at them. The Saxons looked at her in surprise and saw bolts of light coming towards them from each of Rachel's fingers. She swept her hands left and right, and the light streamed at them. As it passed over their swords it turned them to molten metal in their hands. They dropped them quickly as the pain seared through their palms. The light hit them again and they let go of the women to shield their eyes against it with their burnt hands. The women ran for their lives.

"Fools!" screamed the Saxon leader. "Get them back, and kill them!"

The Saxon men looked uneasily at the group of women who were now huddled together by the wall and then looked back again at the two sorceresses.

For good measure, Rachel sent another sweeping bolt of light at the men, which sent them cowering on the other side by their leader.

"Kill them, kill the witches! Can you not see what they do? They will destroy all of you. You must kill them! They must be burnt at the stake!" bellowed the Saxon leader.

The Saxons started to move towards Rachel and Morgana and they knew that Galahad, Gareth and the knights, would instantly spring into action to prevent them from being hurt. Their protection from the Saxons, by the knights, was obviously going to cause a blood bath. Rachel could see it coming, and felt an extreme anger towards the Saxon leader, who was still shouting orders. Without even realising what she was doing, she sent a bolt of magic so fierce, that she almost fell backwards as it left her. It exploded on the ground next to the Saxon leader like a cannon ball. The force threw him upwards and he hit the furthest tower, slamming against the stone masonry. His fall back down to the ground was one that even he, could not survive this time!

In a second, mayhem started around them. The Saxons turned on the village men and the knights joined in to stop them.

Rachel saw Gareth clash swords with men on either side of him and without even thinking about it she delivered another magical strike that threw both of the Saxons across the courtyard. Morgana joined her and soon a sizzle of green from the sorceress picked off a Saxon that clashed with Johnny and another that threatened to jump Galahad from behind.

Morgana and Rachel stood together, firing lasers of magic at every Saxon they saw, as the men converged on their friends and the villagers. The knights and the men from the village all fought together until eventually, with no leader, the remaining Saxons were rounded up and bound by their wrists.

"Take them to your dungeons," instructed Galahad. "I need a head-count of every man, woman and child that is here from the village, and another of their dead."

"It shall be done," said a tall, lanky youth with long hair. "We failed you, I am so sorry, you entrusted the fortress to us, and we failed! The Saxons outnumbered us; they threatened our mothers and sisters if we did not obey them. We did what we had to do, to save those that we could!"

"What is your name?" asked Galahad.

"'Tis Marcus, Sire," the youth said, bowing humbly.

"There is no shame in protecting your own, Marcus!" said Galahad. "The fault was not yours but ours, as we greatly underestimated the amount of Saxons that were still here. 'Tis plain to see that you have all done your best!"

"Thank you, Sire," said Marcus, with another bow. "I will get you your count and we will not fail you again!"

Rachel, Gareth and Johnny followed Morgana into the main hall. They sat down wearily on the heavy, wooden, carved seats that served as the only luxury in the austere surroundings of the fortress. There were no comfortable cushions or rich tapestries lining the walls, the room was devoid of any decorations at all. The furniture was heavy and functional and apart from the long, wooden tables and rough, wooden chairs, the only slightly ornate objects were two high-backed, carved chairs set on a platform, which were obviously reserved for the Master and Mistress of Mordred's estate.

They were brought pitchers of water and goblets to drink from while they waited.

"You were amazing!" said Gareth to Rachel, in rare admiration.

"You were pretty good yourself," she answered. "I had no idea how good you are with a sword. I saw you take on two Saxons at once, and you got both of them easily! You were absolutely brilliant!"

"Yeah, but you took your fair share of them out! I saw those white bolts of lightning coming from your fingers! I've no idea how you managed to do that!"

"Nor me!" laughed Rachel. "Morgana was helping though and if it hadn't been for her we wouldn't have even got in here. Even Bran would have approved of her magic! She had us disguised as cats one minute, and then as dreadful smelling Saxons the next!

I've still got the flea bites to prove it!" she finished, showing him the red lumps on her arm. "Believe me, that's only a few! I'm covered in them!"

"Bran would have loved the disguises! Well done, sis!" said Gareth, and turned to Morgana. "I believe I need to thank you as well!"

"I may have done the first part," Morgana replied, unusually modestly. "But your sister took over against the Saxons. It would appear that she cannot manage the most basic of spells, but her magic works extremely effectively when she is angry!"

They all laughed, in an easy, although previously unlikely, comradeship as they waited anxiously for news of Bran's family.

Galahad returned with Cedric and Ivan, their expressions immediately alerting them that the news was not going to be good.

"We have no word of Bran's mother or sisters; they may still be held in the village but they are not here," said Cedric. "We have the village count, and we have lost a few men. Two of the Elders have been killed and we do not know what has happened to the other one. Most of the men from the village were brought here to be soldiers along with half of the women as servants."

"What about the others left in the village? Do you think that they are all right?" asked Gareth.

"I do not know what has befallen those who were left behind," said Owen. "But I have heard that they were mainly women and they were all set to work in the fields, to look after the crops."

"Well, that doesn't sound too bad," said Rachel, in an attempt to sound positive. "Bran's mother and sisters might be doing that!" A worried look passed between Galahad and Johnny. They knew that the Saxons would have the women working from dawn till dusk and would probably have beaten them if they flagged, but neither of them were going to tell Rachel this!

"There is more, I have heard tell that the Saxons have a creature there to guard them!" continued Owen, dourly.

"What sort of creature?" asked Gareth.

"I do not know, but I have heard said that it is ten feet tall and they have it shackled. It bellows night and day and the women are terrified of it!"

They all looked at each other, mystified, until Morgana spoke up. "I do hope that they have not captured one of Rathyen's dragons!" she said. "Does the creature breathe fire?"

"I do not know, my lady," he replied. "All I know is that they have the creature tethered with iron links."

"If they have one of the dragons, they will not have looked after it and it could be very dangerous!" said Morgana.

"Surely it wouldn't be one of Rathyen's dragons! Anyway, there were two of them and they would have gone back to Wales long ago!" reasoned Rachel.

"Well, whatever creature they have there, we're going to have to fight it as well, if need be," interjected Gareth, firmly. "I'm not leaving Bran's mother and Imogene to the mercy of the Saxons. I owe him that much!"

"We are with you on that," replied Galahad, putting his hand on Gareth's shoulder. "We will only have a small party though, as some of the men will have to stay behind to defend the castle. We cannot risk any Saxons fleeing here from the village, or we will have the same situation again.

"We will come with you," answered Morgana. "Our magic will make up for the shortage of swords."

"I don't think the women should come," said Johnny, immediately. "You've both been put in enough danger already."

"Women?" questioned Morgana, for once with a friendly

laugh. "We are not mere women, we are sorceresses! We have a new combined magic, one of dark and one of light. I don't think we have even tested its measure yet!"

Galahad and Gareth looked at Rachel, to see if she was in agreement with this, and were surprised to see that she looked as enthusiastic as Morgana.

"Morgana's right, we can help, and we will! Besides I think I'm just getting the hang of this magic now," Rachel said, determinedly.

They all laughed. Gareth slapped her on the back and they all went out into the courtyard to retrieve their horses and begin the next part of their mission, to rescue the village!

Chapter Seventeen
Gethin and Boranin

They rode out across the stream towards the wood, and when the foliage became too thick to ride through, they dismounted and walked. As they neared the edge of the forest, they could hear the creature's roars before they even saw the village.

"'Tis Gethin," announced Morgana. "I remember his call. He is distressed!"

"Who's Gethin?" asked Rachel, as they all stopped to listen to Morgana's answer.

"He is one of the dragons that pulled Rathyen's chariot, I remember him from my time there. Gethin was young when she captured him. His mother had been killed and Rathyen starved and beat him into subservience, as she does all of her captors!" she said, bitterly.

"How can you sound so sympathetic about the creature that set fire and almost destroyed Tintagel castle?" Gareth asked in surprise.

"You do not understand dragons," Morgana answered. "They are shy, gentle creatures that keep to the hills and forests. They only become dangerous when they are threatened. 'Tis only then that they breathe fire and wreak havoc in their attempts to get away."

"Well, at least this one is tethered," said Johnny. "Hopefully it'll stay that way while we sort out the Saxons."

"I would not rely too heavily on that," warned Morgana. "Gethin is calling for Boranin."

"I take it that Boranin is the other one then," said Johnny.

"He is, and he will come for Gethin, if he hears his cry," she answered. "They have been in Morgana's captivity together, they are inseparable!"

"Great, that's all we need! Two dragon friends helping each other! As if we haven't got enough problems with the damned Saxons!" replied Gareth.

"The dragon is secure at present, he cannot harm us," interjected Galahad, sensibly. "Let us move now on those who can!"

"Yeah, let's just get in and out of here as fast as we can," agreed Johnny, slightly apprehensive about tackling the dragons that had almost wrecked the castle.

They all agreed, creeping out of the cover of the bushes and into the village. It was quiet and the first two sentries were silenced immediately by Johnny and Galahad's swords. They moved on through the village, the only noise around them being the consistent roars of the dragon and the clanking of its chains as it tried to escape.

The cottage doors were closed and there was no one around. They walked on past the huts and no one challenged them. There were plumes of smoke that drifted upwards from each home that showed that their inhabitants were there, but apparently there were no guards and no Saxons to challenge them.

"I do not like this!" stated Galahad, looking around cautiously.

"It is too quiet: we may be walking into a trap if they are expecting us!"

"How could they be? Who would have told them?" said Gareth, his sword held out in front of him, expecting to have to use it at any moment.

As they reached the middle of the silent village, there was suddenly, a clink of armour and Saxon shields. The Saxons closed in on them, forming a circle, surrounding them with an impenetrable wall of tightly locked shields. Hidden behind their wall of metal, the Saxons drew their swords. Galahad, and their small party, all looked in dismay at the battery of swords all around them, and their hearts sank as they realised they were vastly outnumbered and very effectively cornered.

"We have been expecting you!" said the simpering, voice of Theodorus. He swept pompously, down the steps of the large hut that Gareth remembered as the Elders' Council building. For a moment his voice was drowned by the distressed calls of the dragon at the other end of the village.

"I can't believe Theodorus has managed to do this," whispered Gareth to Galahad. "He must have brought some of the Saxons with him from the castle."

"He has indeed, there must be twenty or more that have followed him," Galahad answered, looking around him. "Add that to the ones that were already here and we are in trouble!"

"Kill them!" Theodorus said, with a squeaky voice of conceited authority. "These are the ones that killed your leader. Kill them now, I say!"

"Theodorus, I lose patience with you!" shouted Morgana, furiously. "I have given you chance upon chance as my brother's son, but you have denied them all!"

Her angry reprimand was accompanied by a fierce, red, magical spell that caused the Saxons to duck in fear as it passed over their heads to strike Theodurus's throat. Theodorus clutched his neck and tried to gurgle his apologies in terror, but Morgana didn't relinquish her magic. Instead she held the red bolt firmly until her nephew fell to his knees, fighting for breath, and eventually sank to the ground. For a moment there was a stunned silence, only broken by the relentless bellowing of the dragon.

"Eeeeerooooh," it screeched mournfully, "Eeeeeeerooooh! Eeeeroooooooooh!"

There was a resounding sound of metal shields linking together again as the Saxons, undeterred, took up their battle stance around them again.

"Earoooopph! Earoooopph!" came another, deeper bellowing from further away. It was unmistakably the answering call from Gethin's friend Boranin, the dragon that they had all been hoping wouldn't turn up.

The Saxons moved in towards them, their shields locked firmly together again.

"We have to break their circle," said Galahad. "We cannot fight them whilst they are behind their shields."

Before anyone could answer, the ground began to shake. Thundering footsteps could be heard, as the dragon drew nearer.

"Eeeeerooooh," cried Gethin, forlornly.

"Eaaaaroooooophhhhhh!" came the reply, and the ground trembled beneath all of them as Boranin thundered into the village.

As the angry dragon came up behind the wall of Saxons that surrounded their party, it called again, and the Saxons turned. They threw their lances at Boranin and jabbed at him with their swords, but they made no impact on his leathery scales and he reared up angrily. Suddenly he threw his weight forwards, stretched out his long neck and blew an angry pillar of fire at them.

The Saxons, who had conveniently shielded Gareth and their small party from the blast, now ran screaming as they tried to put out the flames that had caught their clothing. The nearby roofs all caught fire and flames quickly ran along from one building to another.

"Now!" shouted Galahad, and they all turned towards the remaining few Saxons. The clashing swords and the following fight served only to anger the dragon even further and he lashed out with blast after blast of fire in every direction.

By now, all of the main sections of the buildings in the village were alight. The cottage doors opened and women and children began running out into the mayhem of battle and fire. Once they saw the dragon, people ran in all directions and the fight against the remaining Saxons continued. Morgana and Rachel joined in and fired magical flashes of green and white against them, while the dragon became so frantic that he sent a channel of fire that blasted its way right to the very end of the village. They all ran quickly between the blazing cottages to escape it.

This was enough for the Saxons! They abandoned the fight and disappeared as fast they could, just as the dragon began to stamp its way through them. Its tail swished from side to side, demolishing each blazing building it came into contact with.

The plumes of smoke choked everyone, as flames lit up the remains of the village.

"We need to get the women and children out," instructed Galahad. "Take them out of the village to a safe clearing!"

The knights nodded, and moved into action. They covered their faces against the smoke, picked up the smaller children and quickly led the remaining women away.

"I can't see Imogene or Bran's little sister or mother!" said

Gareth, worriedly. "The door's still closed on their cottage!"

He ran towards it and Johnny followed him. The roof was on fire and parts of the simple structure were beginning to fall. The door was jammed and they kicked it open. Gareth ran in, just as the building became engulfed by flames. Johnny fell backwards, choking, as part of the roof fell down over the doorway in a thatch of flames.

Horrified Rachel screamed, "No, Gareth, no!"

"We need water, we need rain," said Morgana, grabbing her arm. "We can put these flames out, but I cannot do it alone. My magic is not strong enough to control the elements!"

"But I don't know how to do it!" cried Rachel in alarm.

"You do it your way and I will do it mine. We have to try!" said Morgana, lifting her arms towards the sky, and chanting something incomprehensible.

After a few seconds, Gareth had still not reappeared and Rachel watched in dread, rooted to the spot.

"Rachel, you have to help me!" Morgana insisted, grabbing her arm again. "Now!"

Rachel looked at the sky and imagined a heavy downfall. "Please, please help Gareth, help him to bring Bran's family out!" she begged, aloud. To her delight, she was rewarded by several drops of fine rain on her face. "More," she shouted. "Please, we need more! We need rain, heavy rain. We need a deluge! Please save Gareth!"

There was a crack of thunder and it poured. It pelted down so hard that the flames ravaging the village began to subside, but everyone's attention was still drawn to the open doorway of what was left of Bran's home. The rain soaked them and they didn't even notice the channel of water that ran down the village street in a flash flood. It doused the flames and washed its way down like a small stream. Morgana still chanted and Rachel continued to offer up her pleas to the Power.

Suddenly, Gareth appeared in the doorway, coughing. He helped out a woman holding a young girl. Johnny ran forwards and took the girl from her and Ivan led Bran's mother to safety.

"Imogene!" sobbed Bran's mother, trying to pull away from Johnny. "She is still in there! I fear she may be dead!"

Before anyone realised what he was doing, Gareth soaked his cloak in the rainwater that was running past them and then threw it over himself, before dashing back into the smouldering cottage.

Rachel shrieked in horror again, as she watched her brother disappear again, and she pleaded frantically for more rain.

It seemed like an eternity before Gareth reappeared again, carrying Imogene out through the blackened doorway. He lay her down, unconscious, on the ground. "Imogene, Imogene, wake up!" he shouted at her. "You will not die! Do you hear me?" He knelt next to her and began to push on her chest and breathe into her mouth to resuscitate her.

"What is he doing?" asked Morgana, curiously.

"He's using a life-saving technique to help her!" Rachel answered.

"He is using his own breath to breathe life into her?" she marvelled. "This is very clever, does it work?"

"I really do hope so!" answered Rachel, as they all watched him in anticipation.

Eventually Imogene coughed and took a great gasp of air before she spluttered and coughed again and again. They all clapped and cheered as Gareth held her in his arms, still struggling himself from the smoke that he had inhaled in rescuing her. Bran's mother rushed forwards and fell to her knees crying, holding her daughter in relief.

"Well done, Gareth, but that was very foolhardy," said Galahad. "You could have died!"

"Gareth, I was so worried," shouted Rachel, as she ran over to him. "Don't you ever do anything like that again!" she finished, crossly.

"Oh, stop panicking," Gareth answered, modestly. "I'm all right aren't I?"

"All right?" echoed Johnny. "You're a blooming hero, that's what you are!" he enthused with a large slap on the back, which set Gareth off coughing again.

The rain still fell, softly now, and the village was full of dense smoke and smouldering ashes. The Saxons were gone, and when they grouped again in the clearing to recover and make preparations to leave, it was decided that the villagers would go to Mordred's fortress with some of the knights and Bran's family would go to Tyntagyle with the rest of them.

At the end of the village, the noise from the dragons grew louder. Gethin clanked his chains and moaned, accompanied by frantic bellows from Boranin.

Ivan came over to them, leading their horses. "That dragon has pulled on its chains so hard, that they cut right through its legs!" he remarked, as he handed them the reigns.

"Oh, that's awful, poor thing!" said Rachel.

"Poor thing?" questioned Johnny, "have you seen the damage its friend has done here?"

"I know, but he must be in pain!" Rachel answered.

"Come, mount your horses, and be thankful that the dragons are occupied," interrupted Galahad. "We still have Bran's family to get out of here."

Morgana walked off in the direction of the bellowing and Gareth and Rachel hesitated.

"We can't go without her!" declared Rachel.

"What's she doing?" asked Johnny, holding Imogene in the saddle in front of him. "Where's she going?"

"You go, Galahad," said Gareth. "Take them to Tintagel, we'll follow after you."

Galahad looked down from his horse at Rachel and she knew that he didn't want to leave her there.

"Go!" Rachel insisted. "We'll be alright!"

Galahad's expression still indicated that he wasn't happy about her decision, but the safety of the remaining people was now his responsibility. He nodded gravely and turned his horse with a sigh and a backwards glance as they left the village.

"That must have nearly killed him to do that!" remarked Gareth, as they walked through the smouldering village towards the deafening noise of the dragons. "He worries more about your safety than anyone else's."

"I'm sure that's not true," replied Rachel, stiffly. "Galahad does everything he can to help everyone!"

"Oh, for goodness sake, Rachel," exclaimed Gareth. "Everyone knows he's nuts about you! Why would he risk his life to swing over a ravine, and then ask Johnny to axe his rope! No-one in their right mind would do that, but he was prepared to do anything to save you!"

Rachel didn't answer and the noises from the dragons grew more alarming as they approached.

"Just be careful, Rach," said Gareth. "Look, I'm just saying that I don't want you to make the same mistake that I did, by giving yourself an excuse to keep coming back here! We aren't supposed to do that. I've found that out to my cost! I've now got a dead Mordred trailing me everywhere!"

She nodded briefly as they joined Morgana, who was speaking

softly in welsh to the two dragons. They snorted suspiciously, but they seemed much calmer. Gethin had stopped pulling at his chains and Boranin looked at Morgana, as though her soothing words were registering somewhere in his small dragon's brain.

"They remember me," Morgana whispered, confidently. "I used to go down into their cavern and feed them. Get some leaves and some water, Gethin is half starved."

"What do they eat?" asked Rachel. "What about apples, do they like them?" she asked, seeing an enormous basket filled with them, by the remains of a burnt-out cottage.

"Probably," said Morgana. "He is so hungry he would eat anything. Get leaves, or anything green and they will eat them as well."

Gareth dragged over some branches with the leaves still attached and Rachel nervously offered Gethin an apple in the palm of her hand. The dragon sniffed at it, and then at her, before gently taking it out of her hand. He munched on it hungrily and Boranin bellowed protectively. He stamped his feet and Gareth put the branches on the floor in front of him.

"Easy boy, easy now," he crooned, soothingly, in the same way he spoke to difficult horses. "Come on now, there's a good boy."

Boranin sniffed at the leaves and Gareth continued his soothing words until the dragon finally bent his head and tore a mouthful of leaves off the branches. He chewed them slowly, still looking at Gareth cautiously.

"Try to keep them occupied," instructed Morgana, as she inspected the heavy chains that were biting into Gethin's legs. "Oh, this is dreadful; we cannot sever these with a sword or an axe. They are too heavy, we must burn through them and melt them as a blacksmith does with fire!"

"Can you do that?" asked Rachel, doubtfully, as Gethin took

another apple from the palm of her hand, chomping noisily and dribbling long streams of saliva.

"We must do it quickly, you can help me," Morgana answered, kneeling next to one of Gethin's legs. She muttered and pointed at the heavy metal around it. The metal began to glow and a red molten split began to form. "When I tell you to, pull the metal apart," she said.

Boranin stopped chewing and began to come forwards, looking anxiously at them.

"Easy now boy, it's alright," said Gareth again. Boranin turned to look at him and backed away, drawing himself up menacingly. "Come on now, here, have some more leaves," said Gareth, trying to distract him "We're not going to hurt you," he continued, soothingly. "There's a good dragon! Good boy!"

Behind him, the metal links were suddenly pulled apart by Rachel and Gethin groaned loudly as his leg was freed. He tried to move forwards, but was still held by the chain around his other leg. He screamed again as he pulled against it and the metal links bit even deeper into his leg. Boranin reared up and Gareth moved out of the way quickly, retreating to a safe distance, along with Morgana.

"Oh, you poor thing!" said Rachel in sympathy, as the large scaly Gethin pulled and pulled to get away.

"Eeeeerooooooh," he groaned, woefully. He bent his long neck down, shaking his small head.

"We'll get you out, I promise," she said, and the dragon looked down at her sorrowfully. She gently put her hand up and stroked his nose. He put his head on one side and nestled into her shoulder, as though he knew that she was trying to help him. He snorted gently and a stream of green slime dribbled down her shoulder.

"Ohh," she groaned in disgust, looking at the gooey substance that slid down her dress. "I could have done without that!"

"I think he likes you," said Morgana. "He seems to trust you! Keep him happy while we get rid of the other chain."

Rachel gently stroked Gethin's nose and looked into his big sad eyes, tempting him with more apples, whilst Morgana worked her magic on the second chain. Gareth stooped next to her, ready to pull it apart.

Boranin looked on protectively, but even he was calmer now that he saw Gethin nuzzling up to Rachel. More globs of green mucus slithered down her dress again, as the big dragon snuffled into her shoulder.

Gareth pulled the metal link apart and the dragon was free. They expected him to run off immediately, but he didn't. He stepped forwards to Boranin, who bellowed loudly. This time it wasn't menacing, it was as though he was greeting his friend. The dragons ignored Gareth, Rachel and Morgana as they shook their heads at each other. Boranin extended his long neck down to sniff at the wounds on Gethin's legs.

"Come on, let's leave them to it," said Gareth. "Let's get back to the castle."

They made their way back through what was left of the deserted village and mounted their horses. They rode down the remains of the main street and were about to leave when Gareth looked over his shoulder, only to see the two dragons trailing behind them.

"I think they're following us!" he remarked. "Surely not, why would they do that?"

"They have been in captivity; they are used to serving Rathyen. They do not know any other way," answered Morgana. "I think they may follow us because they do not know what else to do."

"Oh, great!" said Gareth. "Does that mean that we're now going back with two pet dragons? They can't go to the castle; everyone will freak out when they see them!"

"Oh come on, let's just go, we'll worry about them when we get there. It's a long ride and I'm tired already," said Rachel.

They rode on, leaving the smouldering village far behind them as the horses sped over the plains until they reached a small hill bordered by a wood, where Morgana pulled her horse up next to Gareth.

"Your sister is exhausted, we need to stop," she said. Gareth turned and saw a white-faced Rachel hanging on grimly to the saddle, and agreed. They rode up to the edge of the small wood and dismounted, with Rachel protesting.

"I can get there, I'm all right really," she said, indignantly.

"I'll make a fire, it won't hurt any of to sit next to it and dry out," answered Gareth, adamantly. "Besides that, we don't want you dropping off to sleep and falling off your horse!"

Morgana sat next to Rachel as Gareth gathered some dead wood, and bent down to light it.

"Do not feel ashamed," said Morgana, sympathetically, to Rachel. "Your magic is different to mine, it comes from within you. It drains you."

Gareth sat down next to them as the fire sprang to life. He threw more wood on it until it crackled and blazed, warming them all.

"How do you mean?" asked Rachel.

"You are not a sorceress," said Morgana. "Rathyen, my mother and myself, we are sorceresses. We cast spells and the power that is released does not come from us, it comes from somewhere else."

"I don't understand," said Rachel. "I've stood next to you and done the same. I sent magic that killed the Saxons. How does that make me any different?"

"You are very different," said Morgana, looking into the flames of the fire. "I learnt my trade as a dark witch from a very early age. My mother taught me and Rathyen gave me a knowledge that surpassed hers. Magic comes from one of two places. It comes from the darkness, or it comes from the power of light. Yours comes from the power of good, but you hold it within you. To deliver it takes part of yourself and your own energy."

"I must admit, I always feel dreadfully tired after I've had to do any magic," answered Rachel.

"That is why," said Morgana. "It is not a craft that you have learnt, or are even used to."

Gareth looked at Rachel, and saw that her eyes were closing and shifted uncomfortably, staring at the fire. Half an hour, he thought, and he would wake her, he could just about manage the sorceress's company for that length of time. The flames crackled and eventually it was Morgana who spoke.

"You still do not entirely trust me do you?" she said, quietly.

"I'm sorry, Morgana, I know how much you have helped us but I just find it really hard to believe that someone who was as bad as you were can suddenly change so much," he said, meeting her cool gaze.

"Everyone else seems to have accepted it," she answered. "What would I have to do to convince you, I wonder?"

"You don't have to convince me of anything," Gareth replied. "I really do hope that you have changed, but I still have this feeling that you have some sort of hidden agenda here. Mordred's estate maybe?"

"You are no fool," laughed Morgana, "and you are not afraid of speaking your mind, even when you know that if I took exception to your words I could destroy you in a second."

Reminded sharply of how dangerous she had been in the past, Gareth shifted again even more uncomfortably. He was regretting that he had been quite so frank. There was an awkward pause until Gareth decided that he had most probably offended her anyway, and might as well just continue saying what he thought, albeit a little more carefully in future.

"So I am right then, you're doing whatever you can to make sure that you get Mordred's castle," he answered. "Not that I blame you, it's a fair fight I suppose," he added, quickly.

"Yes, you are right," confessed Morgana, quite good-humouredly. "That was my original intention, and still is, but in fighting along-side you all, I have experienced things that I am not familiar with. Johnny saved me from falling to my death; no one has ever done anything like that for me. No one has ever cared before whether I died or not!"

"Surely not," answered Gareth, quickly. "You've got family; they must have cared about you!"

"No, my family have never cared about me. My mother sent me to Rathyen to gain her more power. When I escaped and came back to her, she banished me as I had disgraced her and she wanted to appease Rathyen. I went to my brother, Mordred, where I stayed for a while until he decided to pretend to be a knight and joined Arthur. He then did not want to be associated with a sorceress and I was turned away again. It was easier for me then to use the magic I had learnt and make people so afraid of me, that they would not dare to turn me away."

"I'm sorry; you've obviously had a bad time, but I still don't see what would suddenly make you change," Gareth replied, obstinately.

"I have helped you, and I have been appreciated. I have been thanked and invited to join in with celebrations," Morgana answered quietly. "Your sister is but half the sorceress that I am, and yet I admire her. If someone were to attack her, I would defend her, because in the short time that I have known her, she has been almost like... a friend," she continued. "I have never had a friend before," she finished, as though it were painful to admit this, leaving Gareth speechless and in no doubt as to the sincerity of her words.

"I'm really sorry, Morgana, if I've been..." he didn't have a chance to finish his words as they were disturbed by the cracking of twigs and the rustling of the bushes on the far side of the fire. Suddenly out of the undergrowth, appeared the unearthly form of Mordred.

He raised his sword, and his white teeth gleamed in his grey face as he made straight towards Gareth, who immediately realised that for the first time in days he didn't have Excalibur by his side. He had unwittingly left it strapped to his horse in order to see to the fire and his sister.

Before he could do anything, Morgana got up and stood between him and her dead brother.

"Mordred, stop now! Save your soul. I can rid you of our mother's spell if you would just let me," she told him.

Mordred turned towards her and sneered. His cracked, black lips formed the words 'Traitor,' and he brought his sword down on her, slicing straight into her shoulder. She fell heavily, and Gareth rushed towards his horse to get his sword. Mordred moved surprisingly quickly for someone who had stumbled so blindly before. He cut off Gareth's path to the horse and stood facing him. He smiled again, a dreadful, evil leer, as he raised his sword towards Gareth.

Rachel woke with a start and struggled up out of her exhausted sleep. She saw Mordred and immediately pointed at him, expecting a bolt of magic to appear. Nothing happened and she tried and tried again.

Still unarmed, Gareth still looked helplessly at her and back again at Mordred as he advanced towards him. Morgana lay by the fire, unconscious and bleeding from the deep wound in her shoulder, and at that moment there didn't appear to be anything that either of them could do to stop him.

Chapter Eighteen
The Presence of Darkness

Mordred raised his sword to attack Gareth, but suddenly the trees parted with a crash and Boranin's head appeared angrily between them, quickly followed by his large, scaly frame. He stamped through the trees, pushing them apart and snorting furiously.

Mordred seemed oblivious to the dragon's presence and was completely undeterred by it. Just as he was about to bring his sword down, Boranin breathed a snort of fire that ripped towards Mordred. His already soulless body caught fire, and he screamed an unearthly scream.

Gareth took advantage of the flames that were creeping up Mordred's already decaying body and made a dash for his horse, where he grabbed Excalibur and turned to face him. Mordred stood with his arms out, watching the flames that were engulfing him as though he were totally bemused by it and had no idea what to do. Only temporarily distracted, he soon focused again on Gareth as he came towards him. He raised his sword again, but Gareth was too quick for him. He delivered a fatal strike that went straight underneath his sword, and disappeared into Mordred's flame ridden body as though it wasn't even there.

At the touch of Excalibur Mordred screamed again, an unearthly, desperate sound as he disappeared. The stench of charred, rotten flesh lingered in the smoke that was left in his place.

"Gareth!" said Rachel, struggling to get up. "I'm so sorry; I just couldn't do anything to help you!"

"Don't worry about it! I had a flame-throwing dragon! Who needs magic?" he answered. They both rushed over to Morgana, who was lying on the floor, to find that her wounded shoulder was bleeding heavily. Rachel quickly tore off strips of her dress to make a large pad to put over Morgana's injury, tying it firmly in the hope that it might stop the bleeding.

"We need to get her back to Merlin as fast as we can, she looks in a really bad way," Rachel said, as the two dragons came out of the trees with their heads on one side, as though they knew what had happened.

"Good boy," said Gareth, as Boranin's head came down to sniff at Morgana. He stroked the dragon's nose and Boranin responded by lifting his head, gently blowing a stream of green slime at him. It hit the front of his tunic and slid downwards.

"Don't say anything," said Rachel. "I think they do that when they like you. I've still got two big, disgusting, slimy patches on my dress."

"Great! Dragon snot, on top of everything else! Good boys!" he added, stroking both of their noses as they sniffed at Morgana in concern. "Come on, Rachel, help me get Morgana onto the horse, we've got to get her back quickly."

Between the two of them they managed to get the helpless sorceress onto Gareth's horse. He climbed up behind her and supported her while they rode. They went round the wood instead of through it and eventually they saw the castle on the skyline and breathed a sigh of relief.

Boranin and Gethin followed close behind, never leaving them.

"We can't take the dragons into the castle," said Gareth. "I've no idea what on earth we're going to do with them!"

"You worry about getting Morgana to Merlin. I'll see if I can persuade the dragons to stay in the wood," Rachel answered.

Gareth carried on across the causeway and Rachel dismounted by the wood. The dragons plodded up quite amiably and looked at her inquiringly. She stroked their noses and pointed towards the wood.

"Go on, off you go," she said. "In there!" They looked at her, their small heads to one side as though they were trying to understand, but they didn't move.

Rachel sighed and walked into the wood in the hope of leading them in there. They followed her quite happily into the undergrowth. She pulled down some branches and fed them some leaves. Eventually they started to venture further into the thicket and she took the opportunity to leave them. She started to walk away and Boranin looked at her for a moment, as though he was wondering whether to follow her again. She pointed again and said, 'No' quite firmly. He paused for a second and then, as if he understood, he turned towards the dense foliage and his great body lumbered away after Gethin.

Rachel made her way towards the causeway and saw a rider coming towards her. As he drew nearer she recognised Galahad. As they met he turned his horse around and rode beside her.

"I was concerned when Gareth told me what you were doing. I came to escort you back," he said. "You must be tired."

"You really didn't need to," smiled Rachel. "I'm fine and

besides, I would have thought that you would all have been in bed by now!"

"The men have retired, but all of the knights are awaiting your return," he said. "None of us would have been able to rest, knowing that you and Gareth were still out there."

They crossed the causeway, and found the outer gate already open for them. They rode into the main courtyard, where Galahad helped Rachel to dismount. Ivan appeared and led the horses away, saying that Merlin and Gareth were with Morgana.

"I will walk you to your room, Rachel," said Galahad.

"I'm all right, honestly," laughed Rachel. "You really don't have to escort me everywhere, I'm quite safe here!"

"I know you are," Galahad replied, seriously. "I do it because I want to."

Her hand reached to open the door of Merlin's room at the same time as his. She looked at Galahad and for a brief moment she thought he was going to kiss her.

"Oh, there you are!" came Gareth's voice from behind them, as he came up the stairs two at a time. "I was worried that you hadn't got back, until Ivan told me you were with Galahad!"

"How's Morgana?" asked Rachel immediately, the moment broken.

"She's not good, Merlin's with her, but he's not holding out much hope!" Gareth informed her.

"Oh no, that's dreadful! I thought Merlin would be able to help her!" cried Rachel in anguish. "I must go and see her!"

"No, you will not! You will eat and rest, at least for a while!" insisted Galahad, in concern. "You have done enough for one day."

"Galahad's right, you were exhausted earlier on," agreed Gareth. "Anyway, Johnny has taken up a bedside vigil and is refusing to leave Morgana's side!"

They all entered Merlin's usual cluttered room and sat down. There were plates of cold meats and vegetables on the table waiting for them, along with pitchers of mead. Galahad poured some into the goblets and handed one to Rachel.

"I do hope Morgana will recover," she said, taking the goblet. "I'm glad Johnny's with her, but have we missed something here? Is there something going on between Johnny and Morgana?" she asked.

"Judging by the way Johnny has acted since we brought her back, I think there must be. He was completely distraught, to say the least, and he hasn't left her side since!" answered Gareth. "Although I'm not sure that she's very suitable for Johnny! There are loads of girls in the castle that are interested in him, and he doesn't give them a second glance."

"'Tis not up to ourselves, who we feel for," stated Galahad. "Sometimes a bond may be forged even though it may be entirely impossible, or even unlikely."

No one replied - they helped themselves to the food and ate in silence. Gareth was in no doubt that Galahad's sentiments referred more to his sister than to Morgana, and for a moment he wished that everything wasn't so complicated.

Below them, in a small room, Morgana lay pale and weak, drifting in and out of consciousness. Johnny sat quietly by her bedside. "Morgana, you've got magic - use it," he implored. "Can't you use it to make yourself better?"

"I cannot," whispered Morgana, "If you want to help, bring Merlin to me."

"Of course," he said, jumping up. He left the room and found Merlin sitting outside in the outer chamber.

"Morgana's asking for you," Johnny said. "Surely you can do

something to save her?"

"I will attend to her," said Merlin, rising immediately. "But you must prepare yourself for the worst, Johnny. I have already done everything that I can for her!"

Gareth and Rachel arrived just as Merlin entered the room, and he motioned for Johnny to wait with them outside. The wizard closed the door behind him and looked down at Morgana, his old, lined face bore a kindly expression. "How are you, my dear?" he asked.

"You and I both know that I will not last the night," said Morgana, her voice almost a whisper.

"You should sleep, it would do you good, my dear!" he answered, soothingly.

"I cannot, I feel the pull of Hades. The creatures of the dark are on their way and it won't be long before they take me. When I close my eyes I can see them!"

"Morgana, you do not know that it is Hades you are destined for if you die," Merlin answered, sitting down on the edge of the bed.

"Oh, I do Merlin! That is a certainty," she replied, with a deep sigh. "I was one of Rathyen's captives. She made her pact with the Master himself and all of our souls belong to him. There is no escaping that!"

"I wish I could do something to help you," the old wizard said, putting his hand on hers sympathetically.

"You can," she whispered. "You can do two things for me."

"Of course, what are they?" he asked.

"You promised that my brother's estate would be mine if I changed my ways."

"I did indeed and you have more than proved that you are deserving of it," Merlin answered.

"I want you to get a parchment and write it down, so that it is legally mine," Morgana said. "When you have done that I have another request."

Merlin went to the door and called out to Gareth to bring him a pen, ink and a parchment.

"Why is this so important to you?" Merlin asked Morgana, while they waited. "Do you not think that I would still give you Mordred's fortress if you recovered?"

"No 'tis not that, I do not want it falling into Theodorus's hands," she replied.

"But I thought Theodorus was dead?" said Merlin. "Gareth said that you..."

"I did not kill him Merlin; I merely cut off his air supply for long enough to render him unconscious. He will have recovered and crawled away somewhere to avoid the fighting. Theodorus will have survived."

There was a knock at the door and Merlin went to it. He came back with the quill, ink and a roll of parchment that Gareth had brought him. He sat down and started to write, in a beautiful, spidery handwriting.

"Write quickly, Merlin," sighed Morgana, "I have another when you have finished that one, and I do not know that I have the strength to stay awake much longer."

Merlin quickened his pace and once the document was written he signed it and handed her the pen to do the same.

"What is your second request?" he asked, as she put her signature on it.

"Now the estate is mine, I want you to draw up a second parchment. I want to sign it over to Johnny."

"Are you sure, Morgana?" Merlin asked, stunned by her reply. "Think carefully, if you should live, the estate will not be yours if you have given it away!"

"If I should ever be lucky enough to escape the dark creatures that are coming for me, I know that Johnny would never turn me away like my family did. He is a good person! I insist that you write it! Write it quickly!"

"As you wish," sighed Merlin, and quickly resumed his spidery writing. He handed her the pen for the second time and she weakly put her name on the parchment.

"Thank you, Merlin," she said, in a faint voice. "At least now, I may have done something to put right the wrong that my brother did him. I want you to go now and make sure that none of them stay."

"Rachel and Gareth are outside with Johnny, they will want to see you," he replied.

"I do not want anyone to see me," Morgana said. "I want you to lock the door. I have seen people taken by the Dark Master's henchmen and it is a dreadful sight. I do not want any of them to be here when that happens, especially Rachel!"

"As you wish, my dear," Merlin said, as she closed her eyes. "Why Rachel?" he asked, with his hand on the doorknob.

"Because Rachel was also captured by Rathyen; her soul will belong to the master, as much as mine does," she said, her eyes still closed. "You must not tell her, Merlin, and you must help her. You must find a way to save her from the same fate!"

The old man nodded, but his heart chilled, and he followed Morgana's instructions to lock the door behind him. They all jumped up expectantly in the corridor, and Merlin saw that Galahad was with them now.

"How is she?" asked Johnny immediately. "Why are you locking the door? I want to stay with her."

"Morgana has asked that you all go, she doesn't want any of

you here," Merlin answered, with another heavy sigh.

"But we can't leave her on her own, she might d..." As she saw Johnny face drop, Rachel stopped herself from saying the word that was on everyone's mind – the word that was so final!

"Let me in there, Merlin!" Johnny demanded. "I can't leave her on her own!"

"No!" said the old wizard, firmly. "You will respect Morgana's wishes and do what she has asked! Come, we will go to my rooms," he concluded, pushing Johnny forwards. "I will return in a while and stay outside her chamber."

"But I..." protested Johnny.

"Come on, mate, do as Merlin says," prompted Gareth, putting an arm round his friend's shoulder. "If it's what Morgana wants, then you have to do it!"

Johnny reluctantly went with him. A tear trickled down Rachel's cheek and Galahad immediately put his arm around her. She leant against him and they all made their way towards Merlin's rooms, where they all sat down sombrely. Johnny was clearly distraught although he was trying to cover it up, and Rachel, feeling exhausted now, still clung to Galahad, despite the concerned glances from her brother.

"This is all just getting too bad!" stated Gareth, as he poured out some mead into several goblets. He handed them out to everyone and they all took them gratefully.

"I will go back to Morgana. She does not want me there either, but I will sit outside and when she is asleep I will look in on her," said Merlin, reassuringly, as he sipped his mead.

"Why did she want the parchment and ink?" asked Gareth.

"I'm sure Morgana wouldn't mind me telling you, as long as you all respect her wishes and stay away," Merlin answered. "She asked me to give her Mordred's estate and I drew up a parchment to make it legally hers."

"Oh, why doesn't that surprise me?" interrupted Gareth, as the others looked at him, quite shocked. "You don't get it do you?" he continued. "Tomorrow she will make a miraculous recovery and swan back to her new castle!"

"You misjudge her completely, Gareth," said Merlin, as he got up to leave. "In fact, Morgana has made a completely unselfish decision. If she wakes up tomorrow, she will not be mistress of anywhere, because we drew up a second document that makes Johnny master of Mordred's estate!"

"What?" said Johnny, in surprise. "Me? Why did she do that? I don't want Mordred's castle!"

Merlin briefly explained Morgana's final request, before draining his goblet and leaving to take up his vigil outside the locked room where Morgana slept. They all sat in silence for a moment, digesting his news.

"Okay. I'm really sorry. I feel quite bad now, but I just didn't trust her," admitted Gareth, guiltily, as they all looked accusingly at him.

"You were looking out for your friend," said Galahad. "No one should criticise you for that! Sometimes others can see things that their friends cannot. There is no shame in being wary on their behalf!"

"Yeah, except that I may have got it all wrong here," Gareth answered, humbly. "I'm really sorry, Johnny!"

"I know you meant well," said Johnny.

"I think we all ought to go to bed," said Galahad. "Everyone is tired and we can do nothing more."

"I can't sleep," Johnny replied, adamantly. "I'll stay here and wait for news from Merlin."

"I'll stay with you," answered Gareth.

"Rachel you are tired, you need to sleep," said Galahad, and wasn't in the least bit surprised when she insisted on staying with Johnny as well. "Then I suggest that we all try to get whatever sleep we can here, until Merlin returns," he concluded, sensibly.

No one disagreed with him and they settled back against Merlin's soft cushions to wait. It wasn't long before Rachel fell asleep against Galahad's shoulder, and he closed his eyes, holding her protectively against him. Only Gareth and Johnny stayed awake.

"Why have you got such a problem with Galahad?" asked Johnny, noticing Gareth's glances at his sister.

"I haven't got a problem with him," Gareth answered.

"Well, it looks as though you have to me," said Johnny, adamantly. "I just can't understand why. He's perfect for Rachel!"

"I know he is," Gareth agreed. "If I could pick anyone for Rachel, it would be him! But it's all wrong, Johnny, we aren't meant to be here!"

"Well, it's worked for me. I have a good life here, and you could say that I shouldn't be here either!" he answered.

"I know, but you deserve that, Johnny," Gareth answered. "It's different for us because we come from somewhere so much further away than Valonia. The time thing is just messing everything up completely and I'm really worried that Rachel might want to stay!"

"And would that be so bad?" Johnny asked.

"Yes, it would!" Gareth answered, profoundly.

For a moment there was a silence between them, suddenly broken by a strange unearthly noise. At first it appeared to be in the air around the castle, as though it whistled around it, but then it grew louder as though it had entered the building, and a dark, low vibration filled the air. The candles flickered and the room felt suddenly chilled. The unearthly noise continued, an oppressive, sinister growling sound, and the hair prickled on Gareth's neck. Galahad and Rachel woke up immediately and Rachel covered her ears with her hands, seemingly more affected by it than the others.

For a few moments it was as though something unseen, dark and malevolent passed through the room and they all felt its presence. The sinister noise gradually diminished as though it had left the room and travelled away to another part of the castle. They could still hear it, but it was much fainter now.

"What the hell was that?" asked Gareth, with a shudder.

"I do not know," replied Galahad, "and I have never heard anything like it before!"

"Me neither," agreed Johnny. "Are you all right, Rachel?" he asked, noticing her white face. She looked visibly shocked and was trembling.

"That was so awful, did you see them?" she asked, and they all shook their heads.

"There were five figures in long, black robes, their faces were so dreadful, I couldn't even describe them," she said, with a shiver. "They weren't real; it was as though they were part of a black cloud that came through the room. They started to reach out towards me and then all of a sudden they went!"

There was a silence as they all looked at each other nervously; none of them quite knew what to say. Before they could answer, the castle was suddenly filled with a low, dark rumbling noise that built up into a dreadful, deep, unearthly screaming. Doors banged in the castle, the windows shook and several objects crashed to the floor. It was as though something angry and evil was ripping its way back through the building.

Chapter Nineteen
The Moaning Mass

Eventually the bloodcurdling noise could be heard disappearing on the wind after it had blasted its way through the castle. The four of them, extremely shaken, looked at each other for a second.

"What was that?" asked Gareth, on regaining his thoughts. "You don't think that it was something to do with Morgana, do you? Do you think that was why she didn't want us there?"

"I think we ought to go and see if Merlin's all right!" said Galahad, sombrely. They all dashed for the door, headed by Johnny, and ran back through the long corridors where they had to push their way past groups of people talking nervously about the strange happenings.

When they reached the passage to Morgana's room, they found the door open and Merlin on the floor outside. They rushed over and found the old wizard just coming to. They helped him sit up against the wall, where he shook his head. "Oh, such an evil, such a dreadful evil! I tried to stop them but they came for her!"

"Oh, no, Morgana! What's it done to you?" shouted Johnny, and pushed past them into her room, where she was lying pale and still. "Oh, no, no! I think... I think she's dead!" he said in anguish, looking to Merlin for help.

Merlin struggled up and joined him at Morgana's bedside. He lifted her arm and felt for a pulse on her wrist. He bent his head and listened for a heartbeat whilst Johnny anxiously held his breath.

"No, Morgana is not dead!" declared Merlin. "Miraculously, she is still breathing; she is still very much alive! She just appears to be in a very deep sleep!"

They all breathed a sigh of relief and Merlin ushered them out, carefully closing the door behind them, so as not to disturb her. They went back to his rooms again and Gareth handed Merlin a goblet of mead as the old man still looked shaken.

"You said you tried to stop them, who were they?" asked Rachel.

"Soul Snatchers," answered Merlin, taking a hasty sip of mead, his hands still trembling. "Evil, dark servants of death, sent by the Dark Master of Hades!"

"But Morgana's not dead though," said Johnny. "Why would they have come?"

"No she isn't," said Merlin, "but I think she may have been close to it. They would want to take her minutes before she died, to enslave her as one of their undead. The door was locked but they passed straight through it, and it sounded as though there was a struggle in there. Suddenly the door flew open and the dark force flew past, knocking me to the ground."

"We heard it rip through the castle," said Gareth. "It sounded very angry, even the walls seemed to shake!"

"They came with the intention of taking Morgana and there must have been a reason why they could not lay claim to her. That would anger them greatly as her soul was supposed to belong to them!" Merlin answered, gravely. "She was destined to be one of their undead. She would have been a great prize to them as a dark sorceress."

"So have they taken her soul?" asked Johnny, worriedly. "What have they done to her?"

"I do not believe that they were able to do anything! No, I suspect that they tried and for some reason they couldn't," answered Merlin. "They would have taken her body as well, not just her soul. I think that maybe her last unselfish act may have saved her, as she had just given away everything that she had always wanted!"

"That is so awful! Will she recover?" asked Rachel.

"She has a long way to go," Merlin replied. "But I think she may."

Realising they could do no more, they gradually drifted off, exhausted, to bed, as the sun was just about to rise and they all slept late into the next day.

When Gareth arrived back in Merlin's room, Rachel was already up and they all went down to the kitchens in search of, what was now, lunch. They joined the young knights who had helped them in the small room next to the kitchen, and they discussed the events of the last few days, as they ate.

Bethany and Odele arrived, looking shyly round the door.

"Come in and join us," said Rachel, pointing to two vacant chairs. "Gosh, I can't believe the difference in you two! You look so much better, Odele, I hardly recognised you!"

Both girls now wore simple dresses, Bethany's hair looked thick and shiny and her pinched, frightened face that Rachel had seen every day in the cavern, was replaced by a healthy glow and a tentative smile. Odele, wearing a pale blue dress was unrecognisable as the sickly girl they had rescued. Her face was still pale but her cheeks were tinged with pink and her blue eyes looked bright and sparkly.

"'Tis not seemly, Miss," said Bethany, respectfully. "'Tis not for the likes of us, to sit with the knights or the masters to eat. We are servants."

"Don't mind them," replied Gareth, indicating the young knights. "I'm sure they will be more than happy for you to join us," he laughed, looking at Cedric's face as he quickly jumped up and pulled the chair back for Bethany. "Anyway, you're a friend that helped Rachel, don't put yourself down!"

"Thank you," said Bethany, her pretty face turning red at Cedric's attentions.

"You're not a servant to us, you were my friend when I needed one," insisted Rachel, firmly. "Anyway, I want to hear what's been happening to you, you both look so much better."

"The Lady Morgana has looked after us, she has been so kind," Bethany told them. "She has said that we are to be her personal maidservants, but she is ill now, and I pray that she will recover."

"We all do," agreed Cedric quickly, obviously intent on making a good impression on her.

"I am worried," said Bethany, quietly to Rachel, "The Soul Snatchers were here, we saw them, they came to us first, as though seeking out their prey. Odele has not left my side since, she was terrified that they would claim us, but they left."

"I saw them as well," whispered Rachel. "What does it mean?"

"They came looking for the souls that are marked, those that belong to them as Rathyen's captives. We were not the ones they searched for though, it was Morgana that was close to death, it was her they came to claim," Bethany answered. "This is something that we must live with, knowing that in death we belong to them!"

Rachel didn't answer as the enormity of Bethany's words sank in, and for a moment her blood ran cold.

"I am frightened for the Lady Morgana. Did they take her?" Bethany asked, nervously.

"No, they didn't, I think she's recovering. Merlin's looking after her," said Rachel.

"Oh, I am so pleased, the Lady Morgana is so good and I wanted so much to be her maidservant, to repay her. She has never had a maidservant - can you believe that?" continued Bethany in relief. "That someone of her standing has never had a maid? 'Twould be such an honour for us. She understands us, and she knows what we have been through with Rathyen. She has looked after us so well."

"I'm really pleased, Bethany," managed Rachel, still shocked by the earlier conversation about the Soul Snatchers.

"Did I hear the last bit right?" whispered Gareth to Rachel, catching the last bit of their conversation. "Is she referring to Morgana?"

"Shh, yes she is," hissed Rachel. "Don't be so nasty, she's been really good to them!"

"Morgana's maid? Sounds like out of the frying pan into the fire to me!" he answered.

"Well, just shut up and keep your opinions to yourself for once," snapped Rachel, her curtness surprising him.

Gareth did as he was told, slightly surprised by his sister's resolute support of Morgana, and realised he had no one to turn to, who might agree with his opinions. As though to compound this, Johnny arrived and told them that Morgana was still asleep and that Merlin was pleased with her progress. Everyone seemed so pleased to hear his news that Gareth decided to keep quiet. Instead he changed the subject, saying, "I'm surprised that we haven't heard anything more from Rathyen. She must have been seriously hacked off when she found Rachel and the girls missing!"

"Let's hope that she's given up then," said Johnny. "Although hasn't she got some sort of pact with this Master of Hades? Maybe that was something to do with those things coming."

"Dunno, but it's all very worrying," Gareth responded, taking a large bite from a chunk of bread. "I just hope that this is the end of it all! Anyway, talking about 'masters', when are you going to go and visit your new estate?"

"I can't take Mordred's estate," Johnny answered, modestly. "What would I do with an estate?"

"You'd run it properly and look after the village - well, what's left of it that is!" answered Gareth. "Don't forget that it's Bran's village and his people! Don't you think it's time someone good was in charge there?"

"I suppose so, but it still doesn't seem right," Johnny agreed, dubiously. "I'll wait until Morgana's better and discuss it with her."

They all parted and the rest of the day passed quite pleasantly. In the evening they all met up again in the busy room next to the kitchens and were joined by Merlin and Galahad. They ate a substantial meal and as they were all still tired, it wasn't long before they went their separate ways to retire.

Rachel walked back along the vaulted corridors with Merlin.

"I saw them you know," she said, once they were on their own. "The Soul Snatchers, they came to me briefly, but fortunately they left."

"What?" said Merlin, stopping in shock. "You saw them?" he asked in disbelief.

"Yes, five black figures in a black cloud. I was terrified!" she said. "Why did I see them?"

"No idea," mumbled Merlin, into his beard. "No idea at all! It must be because you are a seer."

"So it wouldn't have anything to do with the fact that I was one of Rathyen's captives would it?" she asked suspiciously, noticing his guarded look. "Because I wasn't the only one they visited. Bethany and Odele saw them as well and they were also held by Rathyen against their will!"

Merlin sighed; he had promised Morgana not to tell Rachel, but he knew that he couldn't lie to her. She trusted him and her questions deserved an honest answer.

"It is, isn't it?" said Rachel, in alarm, before he could answer. "What does it mean, Merlin? Does my soul belong to them as well? Is this going to happen to me? Are they going to follow me?"

"I don't fully know, my dear," he answered, worriedly. "I fear that I don't have an answer for you. I plan to visit Argante and ask her wisdom on this subject. I really cannot tell you much more at this stage."

His answer did nothing to console her and after they parted she spent a restless night dreaming of dark, menacing figures, waking with a start the next day. The sunlight was pouring in through the window and she got up, deciding that however bad things seemed at night, at least they always seemed much less daunting in the daylight.

She dressed and went down from her small bedchamber to find Merlin's room empty. He had left platters of food and she helped herself to a chunk of bread and meat and sat by the window to eat it. She looked down and saw Merlin striding out towards the causeway purposefully; she guessed that he must be on his way to see Argante.

She stared out of the window absentmindedly, watching the castle inhabitants going about their usual business. Her heart felt heavy, as she reflected on everything that had happened and thought gloomily, that they had more problems now, than when they had arrived. The scene in the courtyard seemed almost surreal as she watched it in a detached fashion, remembering her own life at university that now seemed so uncomplicated and so far away.

Eventually, Gareth broke her thoughts as he came into the room. "Morning, sis, on your own then?" he asked, as he headed for the food.

"Yes, I think Merlin's gone to see Argante," she replied, joining him.

"Ah, yes," mumbled Gareth, with a mouthful of food. "He did say he might, he wants to talk to her about this problem I've got with Mordred."

"He's going to talk to her about a problem I seem to have as well," Rachel answered with a sigh. Gareth looked at her quizzically and she elaborated on the dark beings that had appeared to her.

"No way!" he exploded angrily. "This is just going from bad to worse! This is exactly what I was talking about before. We shouldn't be here; we're just giving ourselves more and more problems every time we return!"

"Well, you're a good one to talk," she retorted, hotly. "You're the one who's been coming here regularly, not me!"

"Yes, and don't I regret that now," he answered. "Merlin thinks that this is how Mordred has latched on to me. If I hadn't kept on coming back here, he would have never found me and wouldn't have been able to follow me into the future. I have slept with this sword in my hands ever since, but I can't take Excalibur back to Warwick, into our time, and walk around the university campus every day with it. Mordred could still come again for me there, and next time I might not be able to defend myself. This is all because we've been here again, and all of this rubbish will come with us, back to our own time and lives! And now it's affecting you as well, this is even worse!"

"I don't know what to say," Rachel answered, deflated. "Does this mean that when we go back, this dark, soul-catching Hades thing is going to come after me as well?"

"I don't know," Gareth replied, "but I'm really worried that it might. We've messed things up completely! I really think that we need to leave as soon as possible before anything else happens."

"Well, we need to speak to Merlin first," suggested Rachel. "Maybe Argante will come up with a solution for both of us."

"Yes, I can go along with that, we'll wait to hear what Merlin has to say, but then we're leaving!" he finished adamantly. "As soon as possible!"

Their dismal conversation was broken by Johnny's arrival as he bounded through the door looking flushed and excited.

"Morgana has regained consciousness," he announced, delightedly. "I've spent some time with her and I want you two to be the first to know that I have asked her to marry me!"

"What?" exclaimed Gareth.

"Oh Johnny, I'm so pleased for you," said Rachel, immediately throwing her arms round him. "Oh, but hang on a minute, did she accept?" she asked, drawing back.

"She did!" Johnny answered, and Rachel smothered him again in her excitement. He looked over her shoulder at his friend as she hugged him fiercely.

"Yes, good luck, mate," said Gareth, slapping him on the back. "If that's what you want then go for it, you deserve to be happy!"

"Is that it?" enquired Johnny, unwrapping himself from Rachel's hug. "I was expecting a lecture from you!"

"No, who am I to say who you should marry?" said Gareth. "So far I've managed to get everything wrong here anyway!"

"You'll both come to our wedding won't you?" Johnny asked, and Gareth glanced at Rachel.

"Yes, sure, mate," Gareth answered, reluctantly, remembering his earlier vow to leave as quickly as possible. "So, will it be quite soon?" he asked hopefully, having already decided that they shouldn't return to Tintagel again.

"Give me a chance, I only asked her half an hour ago!" Johnny replied, with a laugh. "Anyway, Morgana will want to be fully recovered and there will be a lot for us to do on the estate before we can even think about a date. We will have to rebuild the village for a start! I just came to tell you the good news. I'll go back to her now."

"We're really pleased, Johnny," Rachel called after him as he disappeared through the door.

"That's going to be difficult," said Gareth, sitting down on the settle looking worried. "Once we leave here, I really don't think we should come back again and I still think he could have done a lot better than Morgana! Black witch, wolf, sorceress... personally I think he's lost the plot."

"Well, at least you didn't say so! He would have been really upset. Look, we'll worry about his wedding when it happens," answered Rachel, as the door opened again to reveal Merlin this time, looking subdued.

"I do declare, that cliff gets higher every time I climb it," he puffed, settling himself into his chair, ignoring their expectant looks. "And I think I'm getting far too old for all these stairs!"

"Did you see Argante?" asked Rachel, handing him a drink.

"I did, I did indeed and she is most concerned," Merlin replied, sipping from his goblet, thoughtfully.

"Well, did she come up with anything then?" asked Gareth, impatiently.

"Not exactly," Merlin replied. "She is going to talk to the Guardians. She is hopeful that they might be able to find a way to resolve your problems."

"How long is all this going to take, Merlin?" asked Gareth. "I really think we ought to leave as soon as possible."

"You cannot leave, dear boy, until a solution is found for you," answered the old wizard. "You must understand that these problems you have are not going to be easy to solve. You must have patience!"

Gareth was just about to explode when there was a knock at the door. He strode over angrily and flung it open. Galahad and Ivan looked surprised as Gareth curtly indicated for them to come in. They side stepped him and bowed to Merlin and Rachel.

"We have news that I think you should hear," said Galahad, politely, to Merlin. "I will let Ivan tell you his story, as I cannot make head nor tale of it."

"Go ahead, my boy," prompted Merlin, as Ivan shifted uncomfortably in his presence.

"'Twas a strange sight, Sire. I know not what it was, but 'twas moving quickly and we rode back as fast as we could to the castle!"

"Ivan, what are you on about?" interrupted Gareth. "Who's *we?* What did you see and where? And what was moving quickly?"

"I am sorry, I did not explain myself properly," replied Ivan, still in awe of Merlin. "Owen, Cedric, Edwin and I were to ride to the village by Mordred's castle. We were halfway there when the horses grew nervous, they refused to continue and reared up. We tried to calm them, but they were terrified. Then we noticed a strange sound in the air, like none I have ever heard before, and then we saw it! The hills in the distance darkened as though a black tide were trickling over them. It covered the hills and crept on into the valley. We knew not what it was and we were frightened, so we turned the horses and came back!"

"How far away was this?" asked Merlin.

"Almost three parts of an hour, Sire," Ivan answered, lowering his head respectfully.

"Thank you, Ivan, you have done well," said Merlin. "You had best summon the other knights, put the castle on alert and make sure the women stay inside, until we know what this is."

"'Tis already done, Merlin," stated Galahad. "Join the others, Ivan, and take up your position with them."

Ivan bowed again respectfully and departed quickly, to be met by Johnny on his way in.

"What's going on?" he asked. "I have just heard the strangest story from Cedric!"

"No idea, mate!" replied Gareth, with an exasperated sigh, hoping that that this was not another epic about to start that would prevent Rachel and him from leaving.

"I think we should all go up to the battlements to see if there is any sight of this strange phenomenon," said Merlin, rising.

"I take it that the bit about the women staying inside doesn't apply to me then?" said Rachel, sarcastically, as Merlin stood back to allow her through the doorway.

"Of course not, my dear, you are a sorceress, that is entirely different," he replied matter-of-factly. "We may very well need your help!"

"Silly me, how could I forget that one!" she muttered to Gareth, as they started to climb up the winding stairs. "Now what? Can anything else possibly happen here?"

"I have heard tell of plagues of insects that have turned the horizons black, from the knights who returned from crusades," came Galahad's voice from behind them as they made their way up the stairs. "Maybe this is all it is."

"Yeah, in Egypt maybe plagues of locusts would look like that, but not here!" answered Gareth. "We don't have plagues of insects in Cornwall surely?"

"Stranger things have happened," said Merlin, as Johnny pushed open the heavy door to the battlements.

"Tell me about it!" said Gareth. "Strange isn't the word for most of it!"

Normally they would have been hit by a strong sea breeze as they stepped out onto the great height of the battlements, but there was none, the air was quiet and still. As they walked toward the highest point overlooking the front of the castle they could see the archers lined all around the battlements ready to fire on an enemy. The castle was still with anticipation of a possible unknown challenge. The only noise came from the animals below them in the courtyard as the young boys struggled to lead them into their shelters at the side. From afar they could hear a bellow from the dragons in the wood that mingled with the frightened whinnies of the horses below.

"The animals are really jittery down there!" stated Gareth as he leant forwards to watch the boys struggle with them. "Even the dragons are sounding distressed again."

"Yes, and there are no seagulls again! Listen to how quiet it is," said Johnny. They listened and all they could hear were the waves crashing below them on the rocks. They all stood in silence, listening carefully. None of them spoke but they could all feel the tension in the air, a tension that was almost too quiet and foreboding.

"Listen," said Rachel, eventually, "can you hear that?"

They all strained to hear anything unusual and shook their heads in turn.

"I've heard that sound before," said Rachel, listening hard to the discord that only she appeared to be able to hear on the light breeze that drifted towards the castle.

"You would have heard it in Rathyen's caverns," came a voice, from behind them all. "I hear that sound in my nightmares every time I shut my eyes to sleep!"

"Morgana?" said Johnny. "You shouldn't be up here; you're not well enough yet!"

"Are you all right, Morgana?" asked Rachel, turning quickly to see the sorceress in the doorway. Framed by her long black hair, Morgana's face was white, and her beautiful, dark eyes were circled by black shadows, forming a stark contrast to her pallor. She leant heavily against the doorframe, as though it were supporting her.

"What is that sound, Morgana? I've heard it before," asked Rachel, softly. "I know I heard it in the caverns. I heard it at night, and it was always there in the distance."

"If you had gone deeper into the caverns, as I did, you would have heard it even louder. It is the sound of the enslaved dead!" the sorceress replied.

"What?" exploded Gareth.

"Listen, it draws nearer," Morgana said, as she stepped out onto the battlements, her knees almost giving way underneath her. Concerned, Johnny rushed over to help her, reiterating his words that she shouldn't be there.

"Leave me be," she insisted, straightening up. "If this is what I think it is, I would rather die facing it up here than alone in my bed! Besides I may be the only one that can help you!"

"What the hell is that? Look!" shouted Gareth. "Look at the hills in the distance!"

Everyone's attention turned to look in the direction that Gareth was pointing at, and it was exactly as Ivan had said: the green hills in the distance were gradually being covered in black. It was exactly as though someone had tipped a tin of treacle over them, as it crept downwards, covering everything in its wake. The noise became louder until everyone could hear it; a strange, moaning, gibbering sound crept up with the blackness that was slowly enveloping the countryside.

"Morgana, what on earth does this mean?" asked Rachel.

"Rathyen is here," Morgana answered, her knees giving way completely. Johnny helped her to the wall, where she sat down heavily on the ledge. "The Master of Hades must be really angry, if he has given her an entire army of the Underworld! Because that is what you see before you, and it will destroy every living thing in its path!"

"What?" said Gareth again. "How do you know it's Rathyen? And what is all this nonsense about an army? Rathyen hasn't got an army, we saw her men, she didn't have that many!"

"These are not Rathyen's men, these are the dead, unleashed from Hades!" Morgana answered. "They will come for all of us, because we have slighted him!"

"Morgana, there must be something we can do," said Merlin, his face almost as white as hers. "Between us we can defeat this with our magic, surely?"

Morgana laughed: a brittle sound against the rising moaning that was spreading towards the castle. "Merlin, there is no magic that can defeat this," she said. "There are no arrows that can kill something that is already dead. Your castle is doomed and its inhabitants are all doomed along with it. We cannot fight this, it will destroy us all! What you see approaching is the whole of the dark Underworld, sent by its master!"

They all stood in horror, digesting her words while the black, moaning mass edged over the hills and onto the land in front. The air became chilled and Rachel shivered, partly with fear and partly with the sudden drop in temperature. The whole of the grassy plain between the causeway and the woods gradually became a black, moving sea, as the army of the Underworld edged nearer.

Chapter Twenty
The Battle of the Underworld

"What are we to do?" Merlin asked Morgana. "We must be able to stop them with combined magic! I shall put a protective spell around the castle!"

"Do whatever you can, Merlin," answered Morgana, in a tired voice. "At best you may delay them, but you will not stop them."

"Merlin stood up on the highest point waving his hand in a semi-circle from left to right and a thin blue light like an electric field passed around the castle. It crackled fiercely at first and then gradually faded away so that it would be undetectable to the enemy.

"There!" said Merlin, proudly. "They will not see the spell, but it will stop anything from reaching the castle walls. I guarantee it!"

Still the creeping mass edged closer and the horrendous sounds of moans and groans grew louder along with it. The castle prepared itself again for battle. Under Kays command the archers stood firm along the battlements and below them, Bors hurriedly assembled the soldiers to guard the outer courtyards. The castle men balanced on the apparatus that stood by the castle walls, ready to pour oil, and set fire to anyone who dared attempt to breach the castle's defences. All were nervous, as none of them were entirely sure who their enemy was. This was no ordinary army that approached, and every man there knew it. The archers' hands quivered slightly as they held their bows and the men that lined the ramparts crossed themselves hastily, before drawing their swords.

The slithering, clawing multitude of decaying beings converged onto the causeway, and the desperate moaning grew so loud, that Gareth, Rachel and everyone with them, wanted to hold their ears and silence it in any way they could. The sound of the dead, enslaved to their master, was so terrible that every man, woman and child shivered as it drew closer.

"They will not penetrate my spell," said Merlin, confidently, as they grew nearer.

"I hope you're right," answered Gareth, dubiously, as they all watched the groaning mass of decaying bodies draw nearer.

On both sides of the castle two strange black clouds were moving quickly across the sea. As the cloudy, billowing darkness drew nearer to the castle, it hovered menacingly. Rachel, Gareth, Merlin and everyone on the battlements looked up at them, and saw to their dismay that they were not clouds at all. Instead they could now see dark, ethereal cloaked figures that floated through the air together, under the disguise of a storm cloud.

"It's the Soul Snatchers!" cried Rachel, in horror. "Those are the ones I saw before!"

This time she was not alone in her vision; everyone else could see them and gasped.

"What do they want Merlin?" asked Gareth. "There are loads of them, and no one's died!"

"Not yet," interrupted Morgana. "But I suspect that many will and they will take all of them."

"But the soldiers here aren't anything to do with Rathyen, they haven't been her captives! I don't understand, how can they take them?" Rachel asked her.

"It would seem that they have instructions to do just that, or they would not be here!" Morgana answered. "It is worrying that you can all see them, it must indicate that we are all close to death!"

No one answered, as her last statement struck fear into them all. Meanwhile the gibbering bodies crossed the causeway and, as they neared the castle walls, the archers fired. They rained a torrent of arrows into their midst that had no effect. A battery of stones followed, from the men on the wooden scaffolding, followed by hot oil and arrows of fire to ignite it. The mournful wailing reached an unbearable crescendo, but the men's efforts did nothing to halt their advance. The ungodly creatures struggled from under the stones, pushing them away with gnarled, bony hands and continued slithering forwards. The burning oil had no effect on them either. The rags that clung to their skeletal bodies caught fire, but they still came, the flames having no impact on them at all.

In the distance on top of the hill stood two black horses surrounded by an army of twenty to thirty black-armoured guards, instantly recognisable to Johnny and Gareth.

"That's Rathyen, with her black guards!" Gareth said. "Morgana's right, she must be leading these... dreadful creatures."

Rathyen stood firm on the horizon, but did not approach, whilst her Master's army from the Underworld crept on.

"What's she doing?" asked Johnny. "Why aren't they coming forward?"

"She is merely watching this," answered Morgana. "They are

following their instructions from the Master of Hades. Rathyen has no control over them. She may very well be here just to gloat and watch our destruction!"

"My spell will prevent them from penetrating the castle defences!" repeated Merlin, confidently. "Nothing will get through."

They all stood and watched as the black, gibbering mass crept over the causeway until it reached the castle walls, despite the attempts of every man defending the narrow approach. The Underworld beings clawed their way over the rocks and began to climb the walls. They started to scratch and slither their way up the heavy gate, where an avalanche of arrows from every archer on the battlements did nothing to deter them.

"Merlin, your spell isn't working against them, it isn't stopping them at all!" cried Rachel in alarm, as they watched the men on the lower battlements swipe ineffectively at the undead beings with their swords. One clawing hand after another just pushed them away and the guards fell backwards into the courtyard below. The archers rained arrow upon arrow against them, but still the dreadful creatures from Hades kept on coming as though nothing would ever stop them. As they cleared the lower battlements and climbed onto the parapets, they were confronted by the castle men with swords and axes. Their weapons had no more effect than the arrows had done, the swords plunged straight through the rotting creatures, and didn't even injure them. There was no blood, from what should have been wounds, and the undead reached out for the men who had struck them.

They swarmed in their hundreds, creeping up and over, infiltrating the lower compound easily. The scene below was terrible; it was as though everyone died as soon as they were touched by a long claw from a decaying hand. The dark, hovering

Soul Snatchers swept down two at a time and converged on the injured men, sweeping them up and away in-between them. Most were still alive and screaming as the black spectres of death flew them out over the sea with their legs thrashing wildly, as they struggled to break free from the dark, unearthly beings.

Seeing this, the rest of the archers ran down the steps as fast as they could, their battle positions forgotten. Kay hastily shouted for them all to retreat and the men scrambled from the parapets. Some even risked jumping into the courtyard below, to get away from the scrawny, skeletal like beings that were still clawing their way forwards, their burnt rags hanging off their bony bodies. The temperature dropped even further and there was a mass exodus of everyone from the lower courtyards as they ran to the inner gates, to get away from the deathly enemy.

The Soul Snatchers swooped again and again, lifting the injured away with them, only to be replaced by another black cloud of dark ghouls of death, waiting and hovering for their next victim.

"We need to summon the Power," said Merlin, his face was white and his voice contained a note of panic. "The Power of good can defeat this! Rachel, Gareth, summon the Power! "

"I need the black book, I don't remember the spells!" said Rachel, in distress.

"You don't have time for that," snapped Merlin. "You are both Keepers, join hands and ask for the Powers protection! God knows we need it!"

He pushed Rachel and Gareth forwards to the front of the battlements. Gareth's hand reached for his sisters, as he said worriedly, "I have no idea what we are going to do! I hope you can come up with some magic!"

Johnny came forwards, held Rachel's other hand and said quietly, "Maybe it'll help if I join you."

As Rachel looked down in dismay at the people fleeing to the main castle building for sanctuary she noticed a young boy grabbed from behind, by long, grey, skeletal fingers as the army of the Underworld caught up with him. The fear and distress that she was feeling, suddenly turned to anger when she heard him scream in terror as he tried to wrestle the figures off him. The Soul Snatchers swooped down and he screamed again as their long claws reached towards him.

"No!" Rachel shouted at the Soul Snatchers. She pulled her hand free from Gareth's and pointed Argante's ring at them. "No!" she yelled again, and a current of magic shot out in their direction. It made a large crack as it exploded around them.

For a second the dark figures let go of the terrified boy, and the skeletal figures released their hold. He ran stumbling and tripping in his haste to get away to the safety of the castle doors. Rachel felt a cold ripple pass through her as the Soul Snatcher's dark cowled hoods turned towards her, revealing a black, empty space, devoid of any human features.

They began to float upwards towards the battlements, their black garments rippling and flapping around them, and although their hoods may have looked completely empty, Rachel felt unseen eyes boring into her. They reached out, and their pointed sleeves revealed long, black, clawed fingers, which moved in a mesmerising grabbing motion as they came nearer.

Frightened to death, Rachel managed to stand firm and pointed the ring at them again. This time a bolt of white light came from her, intended for the Soul Snatchers. It had no effect on them, but the deathly army below shielded their eyes and shrank back, gibbering and clawing their way back to the exterior walls.

Undeterred, the Soul Snatchers came forward, suspended menacingly above them, over the high battlements as though about to pounce again.

"Rachel cannot hold them all off on her own," said Morgana. "We must help her, Merlin. You and I shall deal with the Soul Snatchers, while Rachel holds back the Underworld."

"How?" asked Merlin, dismally. "My magic has already failed; nothing should have penetrated that spell."

"There isn't a spell that can hold back death itself, Merlin, you should know that!" said Morgana. "But you are a druid, you must remember the old incantations that everything is from the earth and shall return to it?"

"That is very dark magic, are you suggesting that I...?" he started, indignantly.

"Merlin, I know your background," interrupted Morgana, sharply. "Your father was a druid high priest and you were trained to be his successor as a druid warlock, which is how you learnt your magic! You walked the earth for years to try and rid yourself of it, but you couldn't! You are what you are, the same as I am. Our roots both began with evil!"

Merlin's face went even whiter, and he didn't even notice that Rachel had sent another bolt of light at the sinister Soul Snatchers who were now surrounding the battlements.

"How do you know these things about me?" whispered Merlin.

"I feel it in your depths, Merlin," she answered. "I feel the same suppressed evil that I have learnt and used. The sacred teachings of the Druids that you grew up with will always dwell deep within you."

"No... no..." stuttered Merlin.

"Say the words, Merlin!" Morgana commanded. "Say them in the ancient language you learnt from birth!"

"No... No! I cannot! I vowed never to use those ancient dark powers again!"

"Say it, Merlin! Say it in druid! It's our only chance! If we use our combined dark forces against the evil of the Soul Snatchers we might just be able to hold them off!" Morgana cried, pulling him towards the tower wall. Resignedly the old wizard climbed up and balanced on the ledge with her, both of them leaning against the solid stones for support.

Morgana held her arms up to the sky and began her spell in English. Merlin stood still, his face as white as a sheet, looking anguished at even hearing the words again.

"Merlin!" shouted Morgana. "Say it! Say the incantation!"

Eventually in a trembling voice, Merlin joined her.

> *"Ardtiarna, giver of all, hear our words.*
> *From the depths of the earth comes life.*
> *Man was born from the earth, where all life shall return.*
> *As the fruit shall fall from the trees and rot,*
> *So shall man.*
> *He will return to the dust and his flesh will rot in the soil.*
> *All creatures shall die,*
> *Death will not escape any, and the earth shall take back its own.*
> *From the depths of the earth we ask for cumhancht...*
> *Bunchur!*
> *Bring forth nealita and scalach!*
> *Arracht..."*

Gradually their words changed into the ancient language, and together they carried on in Druid, asking their ancient ancestors for help.

Meanwhile, Rachel continued to fire bolt after bolt of white light from Argante's ring at the gibbering Underworld army in the castle courtyard below. Johnny and Gareth glanced nervously over their shoulders on hearing Merlin uttering the same strange language as Morgana.

Below them each flash of light kept the unearthly army quivering by the castle walls, but as soon as the brightness subsided, they started to creep back into the courtyard towards the main castle buildings. Rachel was beginning to find it more and more difficult to deliver the magical lightening. Each flash of light from the ring, sapped her energy and she held onto Gareth and Johnny as though she needed their strength to help her. The bolts of white magic were growing weaker and finishing more quickly. Exhausted, Rachel carried on determinedly.

The Souls Snatchers' attention was taken entirely by the two druids on the ledge now. They whirled towards them angrily and suddenly, as Merlin and Morgana shouted one last exclamation in druid, there was a green flash, which showered everyone with sparks as it went off like an explosion. Everyone ducked in surprise and the Soul Snatchers were flung backwards, separating across the sea.

"Well done!" shouted Johnny. "You've got rid of them!"

"Only temporarily," said Morgana as she stepped down weakly to join them. "They will be back."

"Can't you use the same magic on this lot," suggested Johnny, indicating the advancing army of death as it crept back again. "Rachel's getting really tired, she can't keep this up forever."

"No," replied Merlin. "They are not here of their own free will, it will have no effect."

"What about the Soul Snatchers though?" asked Johnny. "It worked on them, what's the difference?"

"We turned death against death itself," explained Morgana. "It worked on them because they chose to be here and we turned their own magic against them. The Soul Snatchers are not spirits that have been claimed by the Master of Hades. When they were alive, they would have been dark warlocks or wizards who offered themselves to the Dark Master to become one of his elite few. In their world of the living dead, it is a prized position and they enjoy it."

"Never mind them, we've got another problem," said Gareth over his shoulder. "Rathyen and her men are on the causeway and Morgause is with them"

They all looked to see the two witches, flanked by Rathyen's black guards, riding across the narrow strip of land quite quickly. There was no one to stop them, as all of the men were inside the safety of the castle or lining the high ramparts further back. However, when they reached the castle gate their horses reared up nervously and they stopped abruptly.

"Ah," said Merlin, with satisfaction. "At least my spell is preventing them from entering!" he said, just before seeing Rathyen raising her arms to the sky.

Instantly the blue sizzling light of Merlin's spell ceased to be invisible. It could be seen crackling and sparking viciously all around the castle. Rathyen laughed, she weaved her gnarled hands to-and-fro and Merlin's magical defence was drawn towards her. It fizzled and popped like a damp firework before changing into a thin, blue ribbon. The old witch caught it in her hands and crumpled it together, transforming it into a blue ball of light that she balanced between her palms. Suddenly, with a loud howl, she threw it at Merlin.

They all ducked as it shot towards them like a blue cannon ball and exploded into a cloud of blue smoke, like a bomb. Rathyen's cackle of delight rang around the castle walls.

"Merlin, you have to do something!" shouted Gareth.

Merlin did, he instantly unleashed a jagged laser of magic at the encroaching party that sent several of her men over the sides of the causeway and caused the two women's horses to rear up again, almost sending them to join the unfortunate guards in the deep ravine below.

The old hags calmed their horses and dismounted. They stood together chanting for a moment as several other spells from Morgana and Merlin missed them and hit their guards instead.

"Rathyen's put a protective spell around them," said Morgana, in frustration. "Our magic is just bouncing off it!"

In a second the ancient sorceresses retaliated forcefully, each sending a livid green spark, that fused together in the air and flew towards them like a rocket. They all quickly dashed away from the tower as the spell hit the top part and enormous chunks of the castle started to crash around them.

Rachel fell sideways as a large piece of stone narrowly missed her. Galahad, who had just stepped out of the tower to join them, dragged her away from the rest of the falling stones. He put his arms around her protectively, shielding her from the loose stones that were still falling around them, leading her to the battlements behind the tower.

"Where are Gareth and Johnny?" Rachel asked Galahad, frantically.

"Here," answered Gareth, appearing out of a cloud of dust, caused by the falling chunks of stone smashing into fragments. A trickle of blood ran from a wound on his head, where he had been struck by a piece of falling masonry, and he was limping badly from a nasty gash on his leg. "It's all right, I'm okay!" he added, on seeing Rachel's worried look.

Gareth was followed by Merlin, and Johnny supporting Morgana, who had been stunned as the edge of the fierce bolt of magic had caught her. Johnny's other arm hung limply by his side and he winced with pain as they propped Morgana up against the stone wall.

"What's happened to your arm?" asked Rachel in concern, as Gareth draped his neck scarf around Johnny's neck, tying it into the shape of a sling. Johnny gratefully placed his arm in it, grimacing with pain.

"It's not too bad," he said, unconvincingly. "A huge bit of rock just caught my shoulder!"

Their conversation ended abruptly as another bolt from Rathyen and Morgause brought more of the tower down with a crash. The air was filled with dust and they all drew back again, coughing and spluttering.

"We cannot stay here," gasped Merlin, panting from the exertion of his dash from the damaged tower. "This is exactly what Rathyen wants; she is stopping Rachel from holding off the undead from Hades!"

"I don't think I've got the strength to do much more, Merlin," said Rachel.

"You have to, you must," said Merlin, pushing her forwards. "We will all help!"

For a moment, Galahad looked as though he was going to prevent Merlin from leading her any further when Gareth laid a hand on his arm.

"Leave her, she has to do this. At the moment none of us have any choice!"

Reluctantly, Galahad stepped back and allowed them to pass. They all walked forwards, stepping over the debris from the fallen part of the tower, only to find that their temporary retreat had allowed the Underworld army to swarm back across the courtyard, where dozens of them clawed at the heavy castle doors.

While they all concentrated on stopping Rathyen's magic, the Underworld drew closer. To the side of them a long bony hand reached over the side of the battlements, and as the dreadful figure pulled itself over, it was followed by another and another. The dark, cloaked figures of the Soul Snatchers had also regrouped again and floated towards the back of the battlements.

The decaying army of the Underworld was swarming the castle walls from all sides, clawing its way upwards, undeterred. The air chilled and the temperature dropped so dramatically that Rachel shivered and turned to see the dreadful creatures converging on the archers and men behind them. The Soul Snatchers were claiming their victims and more of the dead were scaling the walls.

She quickly turned and screamed as she saw the long, bony, clawed fingers about to reach for Galahad's throat as one of the deathly figures came up behind him. Two Soul Snatchers swooped towards him and terrified, Rachel screamed again. "NO!"

This time the flash of white light that came from her was so bright, it sent every unliving being back over the sides of the walls. The light didn't diminish this time, it shone out like a beacon, blinding almost everyone in its path. It illuminated the whole battlements and there were screams and groans as the undead fell or slithered back over the stone parapet to get away from it.

It shone so brightly that even the Underworld army in the courtyard below shrank back from the main castle doors and huddled in a squirming mass to shield from its brightness. Even Rathyen and Morgause drew back in alarm, returning to the far edge of the causeway.

"Blimey, Rachel!" said Gareth, as they all blinked. "You nearly blinded all of us! Where did that come from?"

"She was protecting Galahad," said Merlin, his eyes watering.

"I'm sorry, I panicked. I thought they were going to kill him!"

Rachel answered, shakily.

"Well he's okay, but could you warn us if you're going to do that again!" said Johnny, rubbing his eyes. "I'm still seeing stars!"

"Well, at least its sent them all back again for the moment," said Gareth.

"Not this time," said Morgana, looking over the edge of the parapet. "They are already starting to climb up again."

"Oh no!" they all groaned in unison, as they prepared to take up their places again.

At the edge of the causeway, Rathyen looked back at the castle in annoyance. "That girl is a damned nuisance," she stated. "If I had known that her powers were so strong, I would have destroyed her when I held her and sent her to the Master!"

"She has been naught but a blight from the beginning!" agreed Morgause. "Still, this is much more than I would ever have expected her to be able to do."

"'Tis no matter, she may be a strong sorceress, but she cannot defeat death, or the Master of Hades - even her powers cannot surpass his. She cannot keep this up, 'tis only a matter of time before her strength runs out. In fact, I doubt that she will have any strength left at all after that!" said Rathyen. "I will ask the Master for the girl after he has finished with her. As an undead slave she will make a formidable servant. The Master will be pleased enough to have the old wizard and your daughter. I will ask for the girl as my prize!"

"The Master will be pleased, you will be held in great esteem for this conquest," answered Morgause.

"I am already held in the greatest esteem by the Master!" crowed Rathyen, disdainfully.

"Of course, of course," Morgause agreed quickly. "What do you intend to do now?"

"I intend to do nothing!" Rathyen informed her. "The Underworld army has a good hold now. 'Twill not be long before the Soul Snatchers have their victims." The two witches cackled delightedly and mounted their horses to watch.

Back on the battlements, the air chilled again, and the Soul Snatchers hovered closely as the Underworld creatures reached the edge of the parapet at the back of the battlements. This time, they had crawled their way across the rocks to gain access on the seaward side. The castle was now surrounded by the converging mass of unearthly beings.

Rachel, Gareth, Merlin and Morgana all tried valiantly with whatever magic they could muster to stop them, but they all that knew they were starting to lose and it would only be a matter of time before the dark beings took over completely and they would all meet their fate with the Soul Snatchers.

Chapter Twenty One
The Silver Knights

"Why hasn't the Power done anything else to help us?" shouted Gareth angrily to Merlin. "There's hundreds of them and they're all coming this way! Is this it? Is this all the Power is going to do for us?"

The old wizard shook his head, as for once he had no words of wisdom and no answers.

"There is only one person that can defeat the Master of Hades," said Morgana, "if the legend is true."

"That is just a legend!" Merlin answered, crossly. "Old wives tales, bah!"

They saw the advancing underworld creatures all around the back of the battlements. They rushed back to what was left of the front of the tower, only to see more skeletal figures climbing upwards, determinedly.

"We're done for," said Gareth, bleakly. "There's no way we can hold off this lot without a miracle!"

"Look, over there on the top of the hill, there's a silvery light," exclaimed Johnny. "Look, it's a knight! The light's catching his armour; I couldn't see him at first. What's he doing? It looks as though he's just watching us!"

As they all turned to look, they saw the knight in gleaming armour raise a long silver sword and, as light caught it, a beam shone across to the castle. He moved it from left to right and the beam moved across the battlements like a laser. As it passed across the creatures from the Underworld, they shrieked and moaned and scrabbled for the walls, disappearing in an instant. Even the Soul Snatchers backed away, hovering uncertainly over the sea.

"Who is he?" asked Gareth. "And what is he doing?"

"Who cares," said Johnny. "Somehow he seems to have bought us some time with the Underworld. They didn't like the light that came off his sword; they've gone again, for the moment at least!"

"Look, Rathyen's seen him, they're mounting their horses, it looks as though she's gathering her men together," cried Rachel, as they watched the sorceress regroup her remaining men and start riding towards the new knight.

"Why isn't he moving, they'll kill him!" said Gareth, as the black horses started up the hill. "She's got all her guards with her; he won't stand a chance against them!"

Suddenly, the light caught the blade of his sword again and they looked away quickly as the beam was so bright. When they looked back there were two more identical knights either side of him. The blade flashed again and there were another two more, and another and another, each flash producing more and more knights until the hills were covered with hundreds of knights in identical, shining, silver metal armour.

Rathyen drew up her horse abruptly as she stared in amazement at the arrival of the silver army. She quickly turned and galloped back down the hill with her black-armoured bodyguards as fast as their horses would carry them, realising they were vastly outnumbered. They turned right as they reached the causeway and galloped along the top of the cliffs out of sight.

The new knights made no move to follow them; in fact, they made no movement at all. They sat silently along the horizon just watching, in a long, shining line of silver armour on black and white dappled horses. Everyone on the battlements stared at the knights in amazement. The Soul Snatchers hovered over the sea again, their black cowled hoods facing the silver knights, indicating that they were watching them uncertainly.

"Who are they, Merlin?" asked Gareth again. "There must be nearly a thousand of them, the hills are covered in knights!"

"I do not know," he answered, shaking his head. "But their arrival is very timely if they can help us. Do you recognise them, Galahad?"

"I do not know of anyone with an army of such numbers and I have never seen armour such as that!" stated Galahad, looking puzzled. "It covers them completely!"

"Of course," interrupted Gareth. "That's medieval armour, like the heavy ones that we wear at Warwick. You don't have armour like that here yet! I can't believe I didn't even notice that!"

His outburst merely confused everyone even more and Galahad and Merlin looked at him, dumbfounded. Rachel gave him a curious glance, but said nothing.

"Do you recognise these knights?" asked Galahad. "Are they from this Warwick?"

"No, no, not from there but... I don't know," Gareth finished, lamely, realising he couldn't explain to Galahad and would have to talk to Merlin on his own.

"They don't seem to be moving, are they going to help us?" asked Johnny. "The creatures are going to be all around us again soon, we'd better prepare for them."

They could hear the scrabbling and moaning getting louder again and saw the first clawed hand clutch the top stones, followed by more and more slithering back over the stone battlements. The Underworld creatures converged at once from every direction. The men rushed forwards with their swords and slashed at them, but nothing happened, they went straight through them and hit the stone. Undeterred by even the mightiest blow, the decaying figures continued to pull themselves over.

On the top of the hill, the silver knight raised his sword, and without so much as an instruction, the other knights did exactly the same in perfect unison. They turned the blades in their hands to form a beam of silver light, which bounced off the shining steel of their swords. It shone out in a silver arc that hit the castle as though someone had faced a mirror the size of the hills to reflect the light. It bathed the whole castle in a bright, dazzling glow and a thousand gibbering screams filled the air. The light was so bright everyone on the battlements had to turn away and cover their eyes.

The unearthly screams and screeches grew so loud from the undead that it was ear-splitting. A dreadful, scrabbling noise joined their wailings as the whole army of the Underworld was on the move. They streamed back down the walls, landing on their fellow creatures, all moving in a frenzied, scratching tide as they fled towards the castle perimeter. They clawed their way over each other in a frantic attempt to escape the beam of light directed at them from the shining swords in the distance. As the Underworld reached the castle gates they almost crushed each other trying to cram through, at the same time.

The light moved down from the ramparts, still bathing the Underworld army in a fierce white glow. Everyone on the battlements now watched, mesmerised, not daring to believe that the Underworld creatures were finally leaving. They found that even the Soul Snatchers had disappeared and they were on their own again.

"Ingenious," said Merlin, in wonder. "They are using the light to destroy them, the creatures cannot stand it. What a pity we did not think of that, to use the sun's rays to create such a light!"

"Have you looked behind you, Merlin?" asked Gareth, dryly. "There is no sun! The whole sky is covered in cloud!"

Merlin turned and looked at the sky. Gareth was right, it certainly wasn't bright enough to cause such a reflection and yet the beam of light from all of their swords still shone as brightly as ever. He tugged his beard thoughtfully but didn't make any comment.

They watched with complete satisfaction as the stream of grey, half decomposed beings clawed their way across the causeway, with the rest still scrambling to get out behind them. The light continued to shine on the Underworld; it was aimed directly at them and they squirmed as though they could not stand its ferocity. They were escaping as quickly as their decaying bodies could carry them.

"This is so brilliant!" exclaimed Johnny, hugging Morgana in his excitement. "Who are these knights?"

"I know not," said Galahad, "but as soon as 'tis safe, I will ride out with the other knights to thank them and invite them to enjoy our hospitality."

"We'll come with you. If anyone deserves a feast it's them!" agreed Johnny.

The light followed the army of the Underworld across the causeway, bathing every last one of their withered bodies. They ran in a moving tide of scrabbling, rotting bodies in the same direction as Rathyen had along the coast and the light stayed with them.

Even when they couldn't see them any more from the battlements, they could still see a bright white light through the treetops. It had become quiet without the unearthly sounds from the creatures of death and the call of the seagulls could be heard again with the crashing waves beneath them.

The silver knights on the hill remained motionless, until suddenly, as they lowered their swords, the light bounced back at them. For a second the flash obscured them and as it faded away they were no longer there. It was as though they had simply disappeared with it, leaving only the original, lone knight on his black and white speckled horse. The knight lifted his heavy visor and they all stared at him in stunned silence. He raised his sword again, as though in a salute, before snapping his visor down. He turned his horse and it carried him slowly towards the horizon, where he disappeared over the top of the hill and was gone.

A chill went up Gareth's spine as he realised that he could just as well have been watching the silver, armoured knight that had saved him from Mordred at Warwick Castle. After his last salute Gareth was convinced that this was the same man.

"They've all gone, I don't understand, why didn't they want to come to the castle? And who were they?" questioned Johnny. "Why did they come to help us and not make themselves known?"

Everyone seemed mystified and, if Merlin knew, he wasn't giving anything away. "Whoever they were, we are indebted to them," the wizard answered, vaguely. "Come; let us see how the others in the castle have fared."

As Merlin dismissed the subject with a wave of his hand and disappeared into the castle, they all picked their way over the rubble towards the tower doorway with no answers to any of their questions. They made their way carefully down the stairs in single file as a lot of the steps had been damaged and parts of the walls were now missing. Galahad held on to Rachel diligently and as they reached Merlin's rooms, which thankfully were still intact, he held her arm for a moment as the others passed them.

"It would seem that yet again you have saved my life," Galahad said, his brown eyes looking intently at her. "Who would save me, if you were not there?"

"You probably wouldn't need saving if we weren't here, it's almost as though trouble follows us and you just seem to get caught up in all of it!" Rachel replied with a laugh, trying to make light of it. "Anyway, we're equal on that one, you rescued me when the tower was coming down and I probably still owe you a very large one for risking your life to save me in Rathyen's caverns."

"And I would do it again if need be," he answered, seriously. "But you are the only sorceress that I would risk my life for though," he added, his usual impudence returning. "I do not do that for most!"

Rachel laughed and he left her to join his men, saying that he would come back later. Gareth gave her a disapproving look as he walked past them, which she chose to ignore as she joined him in Merlin's room.

They were both expecting a post mortem on the events that had just happened from Merlin but there was none, in fact, he seemed reluctant to talk about it, despite their questions. Instead he insisted loudly to everyone that the knights on the hill, had used the reflection from the sun on their blades, to remove the Underworld army. After all, he concluded, the creatures had already demonstrated that they were affected by brightness, when Rachel's bolts of light had previously hit them.

As Rachel and Gareth talked to the others, it became apparent that everyone had completely forgotten about the injuries they had sustained. Even stranger, the wounds had miraculously disappeared. Gareth had no mark on his head where the stones had hit him, his leg injury was completely forgotten and his limp was gone. Johnny's shoulder was back to normal and his arm worked again with no pain as though nothing had ever happened to it. Even Morgana remarked that she felt quite recovered, and yet it was only a short time since she had been at death's door. Rachel's exhaustion seemed to have left her and there wasn't a mark on anyone.

"It is the euphoria," explained Merlin. "The fact that things could have been so much worse has made everyone forget their injuries altogether! Come now, we are all safe, let us be thankful and ah, yes, we have food," he said, looking relieved at the distraction as Isolde and three other young girls, looking rather nervous, arrived with several platters of food. "Come, let us eat and be merry as we are all here to face another day!" he finished.

They were all hungry, but strangely enough, not tired. They followed Merlin's example, helping themselves to a large platefuls of food. Gareth sat down next to Rachel and whispered, "I don't buy any of this! Merlin's fobbing us off here. He doesn't want to talk about those silver knights!"

"Do you think he knows who they were?" asked Rachel.

"If he does he isn't saying anything, and I'll tell you something else," he whispered, looking around to make sure no one was listening, "that knight was the same one that I saw at Warwick Castle. The one that made Mordred disappear as soon as he saw him. He isn't a knight from this time, his armour is from a much later period, it's medieval! None of it makes any sense at all!"

"But all of the knights on the hill looked the same, they all wore the same armour," said Rachel.

"Yes, and they all had exactly the same white horses with black markings, all of them! How unlikely is that?" he replied.

"I don't know, it does sound strange, but I'm not quite sure what you're getting at here," his sister answered, looking puzzled.

"How likely is it, that an army of hundreds would all have exactly the same horses?" Gareth asked her, with an exasperated sigh. "How many horses do the knights ride here that look the same? None! They're black, brown, grey, white, brown with white flashes. They all look different! That strange knight's horse was quite distinctive and yet an army appeared with exactly the same unusual horses! It just isn't possible! And if that weren't enough, all of the knights were identical; they all held the same weapons and moved in total synchronisation. It was like a film scene where they reproduce hundreds of images exactly the same! In real life, it's just not possible!"

"Well, if you put it like that, it was a bit odd, I suppose," Rachel answered, hesitantly.

"Exactly, it was very odd!" Gareth answered, triumphantly. "And another small point, how could they be wearing armour that hasn't even been invented in this time? And worse than that, how could the same person possibly appear to me at Warwick Castle in our time?"

"I don't know, but you keep saying 'the same person', Gareth! There were hundreds of them across the hills," she replied.

"But were there though?" Gareth questioned, "or were they all the same knight that somehow managed to duplicate himself into hundreds?"

"Do you have any idea how impossible that sounds?" she asked.

"No more impossible than the same person appearing to save me at Warwick, in the same armour, on the same horse, disappearing into thin air the same as his entire army did here!" he answered, crossly. "And another thing, whenever we have been here before, Merlin's been congratulating us and giving us two-hour lengthy explanations that go back to the year dot, even if we haven't wanted to hear it. Is he doing that now? No he isn't! It's almost as though he's avoiding talking to us about it, and that's not like him at all!"

"I'm sure he isn't," Rachel answered, in Merlin's defence. "He's busy talking to everyone."

"So has Merlin given you any explanations?" Gareth asked, with a note of irritation in his voice. "Because the ones I've heard so far aren't really saying anything!"

"No he hasn't, but..."

"Exactly!" her brother replied, defiantly, "and if you corner him, he still won't say anything!"

"Have you told Merlin all of this about the knights?" Rachel asked.

"I tried to, but he swept it all aside. I'm telling you, this is just not like him at all!" Gareth replied.

They decided to ask Merlin again, only to receive another vague answer, and another wave of his hand, murmuring that they had all done well. Rachel did finally have to agree with Gareth that the wizard seemed to be avoiding any discussion of the silver knights that had saved them.

"Merlin, I think you know who the silver knight was," insisted Gareth, firmly. "I'm sure that he was the knight that saved me from Mordred in our time at Warwick, but how can that happen?"

"I have no idea, my boy," Merlin answered quickly, "I am sure though, that they were brought to us by the Power to protect us in our hour of need."

"They?" questioned Gareth. "Or him? Because I don't think that there was ever any more than one person there. I think that he duplicated himself into a line of identical knights that gave the illusion of an army."

"Maybe, maybe, my dear boy," answered Merlin, distractedly. "Whether there was one or a thousand it makes no difference. The Power provided either an army or the illusion of one! It defeated a dark presence at whose hand we would have all perished! Ours is not to question the whys and wherefores, the Power saved us all!"

Before Gareth could ask Merlin anything else he swept away in his elaborate, but dusty gowns, saying that he had heard from Argante who thought she may have a solution to their problems. He mumbled over his shoulder that he would meet with her first thing in the morning. Gareth tried to get him to elaborate, but he was already striding across the room towards Kay and Bors.

"There you are! Just as I predicted," exclaimed Gareth, in annoyance. "He has no intention of talking about the knights!"

Before Rachel could answer, Johnny interrupted their conversation by telling them that they were all going down to join the young knights, Cedric, Ivan and Owen, to celebrate their victory. Rachel refused the invitation, and after they left she found herself alone with Morgana.

"I'm going for a walk," said Rachel. "I really need to clear my head."

"I will join you if I may," agreed the sorceress.

The two young women picked their way back up the tower staircase to the battlements, where they were met by the destruction of the day and a strong sea breeze. They leant against the stone structures and looked out to sea. The sky was clear and the stars shone brightly against the dark sky.

"It wasn't that long ago that I would have been terrified to be up here with you," remarked Rachel. "So much has gone on since then!"

"Maybe I owe you an apology for the way I treated you," said

Morgana.

"That seems like another time," reflected Rachel. "You've helped us so much since then, I'd almost forgotten it! You've almost been like a friend."

"I am glad you do not hold it against me. I have enjoyed working magic with you. We have worked well together!" stated Morgana, as she leaned against the stone battlements, the wind blowing her long, dark hair. "I have spent most of my life working against people, even my family! It was a pleasant change to share it with another."

"I have to admit that there were parts that I almost enjoyed as well," agreed Rachel, with a smile. "Except for when you changed me into a cat and then squeezed me in and out of those disgusting Saxon bodies!"

"Oh, and they were so bad!" laughed Morgana. "Do not forget that I was a Saxon as well, and the stench of his unwashed body was quite repugnant!"

They both laughed as they recounted their experiences and it was as though they had forged a strange bond between them.

"There were a couple of things I meant to ask you, Morgana," said Rachel. "You said something about my ring which I didn't understand. In fact, everyone has said odd things about it. I also heard you mention a legend to Merlin; you said that there was only one person who could defeat the Master of Hades. I was wondering if that could be the silver knight who appeared on the hill."

Their brief moment of companionship was broken as Galahad stepped through the turret doorway and Rachel's questions were never answered.

"I will leave you," said Morgana, quickly. "I am sure you have much to discuss with Galahad."

"It really isn't necessary," said Rachel, the importance of her questions forgotten as soon as she saw Galahad.

"Yes it is," answered Morgana, with a smile. "There was a time when I would have been too jealous to leave you alone with Galahad, but not now. I have all that I need and I wish you well!"

"Thanks, Morgana," Rachel answered, as Galahad joined her and Morgana made a discreet exit.

A gentle night sea breeze blew over them, Rachel shivered and Galahad immediately wrapped his cloak courteously around her shoulders.

"You said you wanted to talk to me earlier on?" Rachel inquired.

"I do, I fear that you will be thinking about leaving soon," he answered.

"Yes, we will," she returned. "We have some problems that Merlin is going to sort out for us first, but once he's done that, we'll go home."

"I have something that I must ask you," Galahad mumbled, and Rachel looked at him enquiringly, surprised by his sudden awkwardness.

"I would ask you to stay," he blurted out. "If you stayed, I would hope that one day you would consider marrying me."

Rachel was so surprised at his request that she couldn't say anything at all.

"I am pressed to ask you now, as I have been asked to join a crusade. I have nothing to keep me here if you go," he continued. "I have no family left, and the cause is a good one, but if you were to stay I would not leave!"

"A crusade, but you could be killed!" Rachel answered, in alarm. "You'd be away for years!"

"Not if you were to stay," he returned, quietly.

"Oh, this is so difficult," she said, with a sigh. "When are you supposed to go?"

"In a day or so," he answered. "I know this does not give you much time, but if there was even the slightest possibility that you might consider staying, even if 'twere only for a while, I would not go."

"I don't know what to say," Rachel answered. "If only you could just come back with me, everything would be so much easier!"

"I would be willing to come to Valonia with you, if 'twere possible for me to do so," he answered instantly. "If it is so difficult for you to live in my world, I would be willing to live in yours."

Apart from another heavy sigh, Rachel didn't answer. She tried for a moment to imagine Galahad in her world of cars, mobile phones and televisions and she looked up at him bleakly, knowing that it would never be possible. What would he do, with no battles to fight and no horses to ride?

For a moment, Morgana couldn't help but look back at the couple from the turret doorway and for the first time she felt sorry for Rachel. Her heart had been warmed by her earlier conversation with the girl, whose words had meant more to the lonely sorceress than she could have ever have realised. She watched Rachel with Galahad and instead of feeling envy or jealousy, her intuition told her that this was a doomed relationship. As Morgana left, she thought of Johnny, and realised that for once in her dark life, she felt happy.

After a long talk, Galahad walked Rachel back to Merlin's rooms and, outside the door, he said earnestly, "You have said that it is not possible for me to come with you, but please say that you will at least consider my words!"

"Of course I will," said Rachel. "I'll give you my answer tomorrow."

He leant over and kissed her gently before leaving to join the men downstairs.

When Galahad arrived in the small room, next to the kitchen, he poured a drink from a large pitcher of water and sat down next to Gareth, feeling it his duty to tell him about his conversation with Rachel. He had been hoping that his honesty would be received well, but instead Gareth looked horrified and he hastily drew Galahad into the corridor away from the others.

"You can't ask her stay," Gareth said, flatly. "Rachel can't stay here!"

"I know you disapprove of me as a suitor for your sister," Galahad replied. "But I would look after her like no other. Surely you must know that?"

"It just isn't as simple as that," said Gareth. "If I could pick anyone for my sister, I would pick you!"

"I do not understand," said Galahad. "I thought you disliked the idea of a relationship between us. If 'tis the idea of her staying, I have said I will go with her to Valonia."

"It's not even as simple as that," sighed Gareth. "Rachel hasn't told you everything about us and maybe you deserve to know things that no one else here knows apart from Merlin."

Galahad looked even more confused and Gareth decided that he owed the knight who had been his friend and mentor the true explanation.

"We don't come from Valonia, Galahad! We come from a time much further forward, thousands of years to be precise! We have to travel back in time just to get to Valonia and then we come even further back to reach your time and come here," Gareth told him, and continued to elaborate on why they were there and their extraordinary heritage that continued to draw them back. Galahad listened and said nothing. Instead, deflated, he sat down on a seat in the corridor trying to understand Gareth's story.

"The whole point of all of this is that we aren't supposed to be here!" concluded Gareth. "If Rachel stayed here with you, I dread to think what could happen to her. She has defied the most evil people here and they wouldn't let it rest. They'd come for her again with more magic! These are things that you just couldn't protect her from. You've always hated anything to do with magic and quite honestly you've been right about it all along!"

Galahad nodded slowly in agreement with Gareth's last statement.

"I'm really sorry, Galahad, it's not you," Gareth ploughed on. "If Rachel stays, and she may well do that if she wants to be with you, Rathyen will still come for her and her soul will still belong to Hades. We've messed things up as it is by coming back. If you love her, and I think that you do, you won't ask her to stay!"

There was a heavy silence and Gareth felt dreadful at having delivered his news so brutally. Galahad looked at him for a moment, and Gareth could see that his friend was quite devastated.

The knight stood up and said stiffly, "I thank you for your trust, and none shall ever hear of this conversation. I must consider your words, and you may have no fear that I will do what is best for Rachel."

With that he walked away, leaving Gareth feeling even worse. He probably wasn't even supposed to have told Galahad their story, but he knew that Galahad would keep his confidence. Galahad wouldn't tell anyone, but what would Rachel say when she learnt of their conversation? Gareth knew that he had intervened in something that he probably shouldn't have, as it was Rachel's decision to make. He felt guilty for telling Galahad and very worried about how Rachel would take it when she found out what he had done. He decided not to join the others again and instead

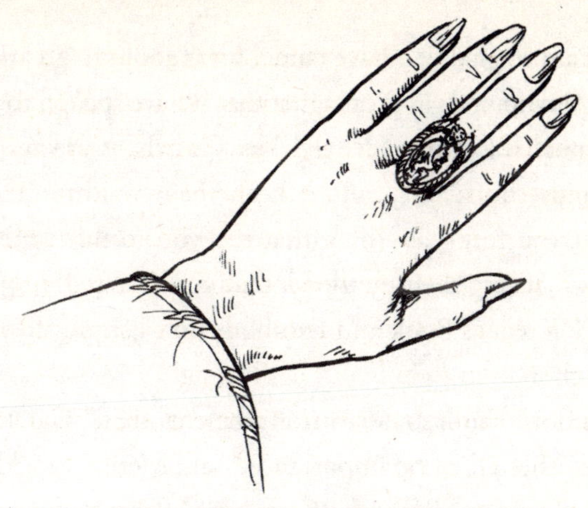

Chapter Twenty Two
Unsolved Mysteries

Sleep was difficult for Galahad, Gareth and Rachel with each one of them tossing and turning in their own rooms for different reasons. The morning came with the patter of rain on the windows and Rachel was up early, sleep having evaded her. She went downstairs expecting to see Merlin but the room was empty. She waited for a long while and eventually Gareth joined her, looking tired. After a restless night, he had finally decided that it was best he didn't mention his conversation with Galahad to Rachel.

The old wizard didn't make an appearance, so they decided to go down to join Johnny and the others for breakfast. The room next to the kitchen was full and everyone was in good spirits. Kay and Bors were leaving as they arrived, but the young knights were all still eating. There was no sign of Galahad, and Gareth noticed that Rachel glanced at the door every time it opened. He felt even guiltier every time one of the other knights entered and her face fell.

They finished eating and made their way back to Merlin's rooms, where they found him waiting for them.

"Ah, I am so glad you have come. I was about to go and search for you," Merlin said, in great agitation. "I have spoken to Argante and we must leave immediately. The Guardians are waiting for us. You must hurry, we cannot keep them waiting! They have asked that you bring anything that ties you to this time or that of Valonia." Seeing their puzzled look, he elaborated, impatiently. "The black Keeper's Book and Excalibur for example, do you have anything else?"

"No. I don't think so, apart from these clothes," said Gareth.

"The clothes are of no importance," said Merlin, quickly. "This is indeed a great privilege; the Guardians appear to no one, even I have never met them. We must go directly to Argante's cave, get your things together quickly, as they intend to send you straight back to your own time."

Excalibur was already at Gareth's side, where it had been constantly in case Mordred should make another unexpected appearance. Rachel dashed upstairs and brought down the old black book.

"Hold on, Merlin," she said, with a worried look. "Did you just say that we are going straight back home? Does this mean that we aren't coming back here again?"

"No, you will not come back to the castle," answered Merlin. "The Guardians have decided that you will relinquish your positions as Keepers. The responsibility of the Power will return to Argante, who will look after it as she did years ago. Everything will return to her safe keeping, in the magical lake."

"I can't just leave," Rachel replied, obstinately. "I have to see Galahad, I promised him that I would speak to him today."

For a moment Merlin looked at her and sighed. "Rachel, Galahad is not here, I saw him ride out at first light, while I was on my way to see Argante."

"He'll be back later," Rachel insisted. "I'm sorry, but I have to see him before I go."

"Rachel, I spoke to Galahad as I passed him this morning," said Merlin, gently. "He told me he was leaving for a crusade. He won't be back for a very long time. I'm so sorry, my dear."

"He can't have, he said he wasn't leaving for a couple of days. He said he would see me this morning," persisted Rachel. "He wouldn't leave without talking to me first!" Her face fell as she saw Merlin's sympathetic expression and knew that he was telling her the truth. She turned angrily to Gareth. "Did you know about this?" she demanded.

"No, no, I had no idea that Galahad was leaving today," Gareth replied, truthfully. He breathed a large sigh of relief, realising that Rachel wouldn't find out about his conversation with Galahad the night before, and he would not incur her wrath after all! Galahad had obviously decided to spare Rachel the difficult task of making a choice and had left early. One look at his sister told him that she was upset by this, even though she said nothing. Gareth's temporary relief was instantly replaced by guilt again as he knew that his good intentions were the cause of the knight's sudden departure.

"We must go," said Merlin, opening the door. Rachel walked out, wrapping her cloak around her and proceeding down the steps. Merlin produced a large bunch of keys and sifted through them until he found the right one to lock his door. He glanced at Gareth as he put the key in the lock and said, "You did the right thing, my boy." Gareth knew immediately that the wise old wizard somehow knew that he had talked to Galahad. "Sometimes we have to do things to protect the ones that we love, and both you and Galahad have done this. There is no need to feel any anguish over your actions."

"I'm sorry, Merlin, I had to tell Galahad everything," whispered

Gareth.

"And in this instance you were correct to do this," answered Merlin, as he turned the key in the heavy, ancient lock.

"You said that Argante will take over the Power," said Gareth, as they walked down the spiral stone steps. "What about Mordred and the Soul Snatchers? Have the Guardians come up with something to stop them coming after us?"

"They have indeed," confirmed Merlin as he strode out across the courtyard. "You are to hand over the Power to Argante and the Guardians intend to close the tunnels of time forever. No one will ever be able to cross from one time to another again. This will stop Mordred, as neither he nor the Soul Snatchers will be able to follow you. This will enable you to go about your daily life in your own time. You will have no connections with Valonia or any way back to this time."

"So we will never be able to come back?" questioned Gareth. "What about Valonia?"

"Valonia will carry on in its own time, but it will be sealed off as well. There will be no more transferring through time by anyone," the old wizard replied. "It has been this hopping back from one time to another that has caused all of these problems and the Guardians are not pleased about it!"

"You mean we will never be able to come back?" asked Rachel, with a look of panic crossing her face.

"That is what I have said," replied Merlin, rushing them towards the exterior wall as though he was expecting them to refuse to go. They didn't, although they followed him very down-heartedly.

"I wish I'd known," grumbled Gareth. "I would have liked to say good-bye to Johnny at least! He's expecting me to be at his wedding."

"I will say your farewells for you - Johnny will understand," said Merlin over his shoulder as he negotiated the steep cliff path to Argante's cave. "Farewells are the least of your problems. If the Guardians are giving you a solution you must take it!"

They followed Merlin until they reached Argante's cave, where the misty vapours greeted them in their usual eerie greenness. This time Merlin didn't have to call Argante, she appeared immediately, rising from the water and mist that shrouded her. For a moment, her beautiful, cold face expressed a fleeting look of displeasure at being kept waiting.

"I am sorry if we have kept you waiting, Great Lady," said Merlin, bowing. "I am old, I cannot scale these cliffs as nimbly as I used to."

Argante smiled at him fondly. "And you should not be expected to. Take your time, my wise friend and get your breath back."

"You are very gracious to an old man, Argante," Merlin replied.

Argante laughed; it tinkled around the rocks and the cavern glowed with her pleasure. She was obviously in much better humour than they had initially thought. She even smiled at Gareth and Rachel and they nodded respectfully at her in relief.

Two elderly male figures rose out of the mist at the far side of the mystical lake. The vapours glowed an emerald green around them as they floated across the water. They didn't come to the edge; instead they hovered behind Argante as though suspended just above the water. The now vivid green mist curled and swirled around their long white robes in an unearthly way. Rachel and Gareth caught only glimpses of their grey, lined faces, pure white hair and straggling white beards that must reach down to their waists. The Guardians' appearance may have been ghostly but their expressions were benevolent, and strangely enough, neither of the twins felt frightened by them. Their extreme importance was obvious by the way Merlin bowed low to them.

"'Tis such a great honour! Oh, such a great an honour indeed!" Merlin mumbled into his beard, as though frightened to look up at the two Guardians.

"You have done well, Merlin. We do not hold you responsible for these problems that have arisen with the safety of the Power or its Keepers. Maybe we should have foreseen it," said a kind, elderly voice.

"Oh thank you, thank you," said Merlin, still with his head down.

"All that remains now is to relieve your charges of their responsibilities so that they may continue their lives in their own world," said the other Guardian. "Come forward, young Keepers and hand your effects to Argante."

To the twins surprise, Merlin stepped up first and drew out the Orb of Resolution from under his cloak. He handed it to Argante and she lowered it into the mist, where it disappeared completely.

Gareth reluctantly gave her Excalibur and she held it out. The vapours swirled around the great sword and it was gone. Gareth stepped back and Rachel took his place in front of Argante. She handed her the old, black Keepers Book and it disappeared in the same manner as the other two items, into a flurry of green haze. Rachel went to take off the ring that Argante had given her and, to her surprise, Argante put her own hand over it as though she were clasping Rachel's as she spoke to her.

"You have done well, Rachel, I am greatly pleased with you," she said.

"But don't you want me to give you..." started Rachel.

"You may go, you have fulfilled your obligations," said Argante, as though deliberately ignoring the question Rachel had started. Instead she looked knowingly at Rachel and let go of her hand.

Argante waved her away dismissively and turned away from her. Rachel went back to join her brother rather puzzled. Argante had made it quite obvious by the way she had covered the ring with her hand and cut her short, that she didn't want the ring mentioned or returned.

The Guardians drifted forwards, still partially obscured by a cloudy, billowing green film that served to make them look even more mystical and ethereal. As it moved gently around them, the ancient men moved closer and their features became clearer. Their faces were pale and creased with deep lines and their faded blue eyes appeared to hold the wisdom of centuries. They both smiled at Rachel and Gareth.

"You have done well," said a low voice that echoed around the cave. It was difficult to tell which one of the Guardians had spoken. It was as though the voice had come out of the air around them.

"From this moment we will take the Power from you and you will return to your own time," the voice reverberated again. "The task you were given is beyond that of mere mortals and we should have realised this. It has caused us to question our own wisdom, in that we did not see the problems it would cause. The tunnels of time shall be sealed forever. Be assured that alive or dead, none shall ever follow you. Your time in the future will now be as it should be. Your duties here are done and your tasks..."

The voice began to sound distant and for a second both Rachel and Gareth felt a sinking feeling as though their knees were giving way underneath them, and the cave began to disappear in a smoky green fog. The fog lapped upwards until they couldn't see anything at all and Rachel reached nervously for Gareth's hand. He gripped it firmly, feeling the same apprehension as his sister when the mist became so dense that it became difficult to breathe.

They blinked as the mist was suddenly replaced by bright

sunlight and they felt the hard coldness of metal against them. With a shock they found that they were leaning against Rachel's car, where they had parked, as though they had never left it! Gareth realised that they were back in their own clothes and put his hand in his pocket and felt the car keys. They stared at each other, dumbfounded, still feeling slightly wobbly as though they had passed out for a moment. They knew exactly where they were and what had happened, but it still took a few moments for them to gather their thoughts again.

Gareth pressed the automatic lock button, and the lights flashed briefly on the car. Wordlessly they opened the doors and got in, sinking into the seats as though still mesmerised.

"We're back," said Gareth, stating the obvious. "Well, I suppose that's it then, we'll never see any of them again."

"No, I suppose not," agreed Rachel, flatly. "That was what Merlin said."

"I can't believe this," said Gareth as he turned the key and started the engine. "After all that, it would have been nice to at least say good-bye before we were whisked back and dumped by the car!"

"Yes it would," said Rachel and Gareth glanced at her briefly before driving off. The sad expression on her face told him instantly that she was referring to Galahad.

"I can't face going back to Warwick just yet. I'll drive us home to Chesterton and stay the night with you. I'll get the train back on Monday morning, I don't think I've got any early lectures, although to be honest, I can't even remember at the moment," he said, and she nodded gratefully.

They were both quiet for a while, each of them immersed in their own thoughts until Gareth broke the silence.

"Strange really," he reflected. "We never did get the answers to all of our questions. I suppose we will never find out now. I hate that - I'll always be wondering who the knight was that saved me from Mordred at Warwick!"

"And the silver knights that saved us from the Underworld," said Rachel. "We'll never know who they were either, but if we're never going back, I suppose it doesn't really matter now."

"No," agreed Gareth, "but I would have liked to know though. I'm still convinced that the knight at Warwick was the same person as the one on the hill at Tintagel. I still think there was only one knight and he duplicated himself somehow."

"There were other things as well," answered Rachel, looking at the large ring on her finger.

"Yeah, there were! What about that weird druid chanting Merlin did with Morgana as well? That was all a bit strange too; she really had to force him to do it."

"So much has happened I'd forgotten about that," said Rachel. "But now you mention it, Morgana said Merlin had learnt his magic from the same evil as her, and that his father was a druid warlock! I can't believe that!"

"Well, that's just something else we'll never find out about," Gareth answered. "In fact, I don't think we ever really got the full picture there."

They lapsed back into thought and eventually they arrived back at Chesterton. Gareth pulled on to the drive, and they were surprised when the front door opened and Bronwyn waved to them.

"Oh, no I'd forgotten they were back," said Rachel. "I was hoping we could have some peace on our own tonight."

Bronwyn was already by the car, sporting a golden tan and smiling delightedly. "Oh, I'm so pleased you're here as well, Gareth," she said, as she opened the car door.

"Nice tan," said Gareth, as he got out of the car. "Good holiday then?"

"Oh, it was lovely, I can't wait to tell you all about it!" she said, as they followed her into the house.

"Great," Gareth said to Rachel under his breath, as Bronwyn rushed off to get their father. "I'm really not in the mood for this."

"No, nor me," whispered Rachel, and as Mr Moore came into the room she added with a false brightness, "Hi Dad, did you have a good time?"

"Yes, lovely, but it's still good to see you two though," her father answered and Rachel couldn't help noticing that, for someone who had just had a fortnight's holiday, he looked rather tired.

They sat down to dinner later and the conversation was all about their parents' holiday.

In the evening, Bronwyn insisted that Mr Moore got their holiday pictures up on the computer and she talked them through every shot. Gareth and Rachel tried hard to sound enthusiastic, but after the enormity of their own trip, it all seemed rather unimportant.

Eventually, Mr Moore switched his laptop off and went for a bath.

"Is Dad all right?" asked Rachel. "He seems a bit quiet and he looks quite done in."

"I was going to talk to you about your Dad later," said Bronwyn, shutting the lounge door in case Mr Moore overheard her. "I'm quite worried about him, he hardly slept at all while we were away and when he did he had the most awful nightmares. He was muttering and tossing and turning every night and then he would wake up. Every time he went back to sleep the same thing happened and then eventually he would just stay up."

"Doesn't sound like Dad," said Gareth. "What was he dreaming about?"

"He has no idea, he doesn't remember any of them," answered Bronwyn. "It even happened by the pool in the afternoon. I went to get us an ice-cream and when I came back there was a crowd round him. He had dropped off to sleep and was groaning so loudly they all thought he was ill!"

"Maybe the heat was affecting him," said Rachel, sensibly.

"I did wonder that myself," replied Bronwyn. "I think I'll see how he is now we're back and if he isn't any better I'll make sure he goes to the doctor."

"I'm glad he's got you to look after him now," said Rachel.

"Yeah, the old fellow looked after us for long enough, it's good he's got someone to make a fuss of him," agreed Gareth.

"Oh, that's so nice of you to say that," said Bronwyn, referring to the fact that Gareth had not accepted her very readily.

"Look, I'm really tired, Bronwyn," Gareth said. "My old, comfy bed is calling me."

"Me too," said Rachel, getting up. "I'm sure Dad will be fine now he's home."

"I'm sure you're right," said Bronwyn. Rachel bent down to kiss her on the cheek, and Bronwyn suddenly noticed Argante's ring on her finger. She caught Rachel's hand and examined the ring closely.

"Where did you get that?" she asked, sharply.

"Someone gave it to me," Rachel replied, cautiously.

"Who?" she asked. "Who gave it to you?"

"A friend, I can't really say any more than that," said Rachel, awkwardly. "Why do you want to know anyway? It's just a ring!"

Bronwyn let go of her hand and it was her turn to look awkward. "I must be mistaken; it's very similar to one I saw a long time ago.

It's quite distinctive and it looks very old, but maybe it isn't the same one after all."

"Where did you see it?" asked Rachel, intrigued now. "Who did it belong to?"

"Just someone here," answered Bronwyn, quickly. "It really doesn't matter."

"Someone here?" Rachel exclaimed in surprise. "Do you mean someone in Chesterton?"

"Well, sort of," said Bronwyn, looking flustered. "Just forget it. It just reminded me of one I'd seen before. I just made a mistake. Do you know, I think I might go up to bed myself now. Gareth, could you check the doors and I'll see you both tomorrow?"

She left quite quickly and Gareth and Rachel looked at each other.

"She was lying," said Gareth, flatly. "I can always tell, she goes red and looks guilty. That's exactly what she was like before, when they were trying to cover everything up in Valonia."

"But why would she lie?" puzzled Rachel. "That was so strange. It sounded as though she thought it belonged to someone in this time."

"I didn't realise you still had that ring, that means you've brought it through time with us," said Gareth. Rachel followed her brother into the kitchen and told him about Argante's strange behaviour when she had tried to return the ring to her in the cave.

"It was as though she wanted me to keep it and she didn't want the Guardians to know," she finished, as he bolted the door.

"So, let's get this straight," said Gareth. "We were told to give everything back to her from that time. The Guardians whisked us away, quicker than the speed of light, our clothes changed back into the ones we were wearing when we arrived and the only thing that has survived it all is that ring! Argante must have wanted you to bring it back with you!" he concluded, as he turned out the kitchen light.

"But why? It doesn't make any sense at all, if we're never going back there," Rachel replied.

"Argante must have had a good reason for doing that, since the Guardians were so specific about us having to leave everything behind. She has deliberately allowed you to come back with something that ties us to Tyntagyl and her time," he returned.

"But what reason could she possibly have for doing that?"

"I think I know why," replied Gareth, as they walked towards the stairs. "It means that this is not the end of it all! Mark my words, it'll come, there will be more and Argante knows it. That's why you are still wearing her ring!"

Katie Paterson

Katie Paterson, of Scottish descent, has lived most of her life in the Midlands.

As a mother of two grown-up children herself, she has an ambition to help keep reading 'alive' for children, and was inspired to write 'The Chronicles of Valonia' by a lifelong fascination with the Arthurian period and legends.